Billionaires Make Bad Lovers

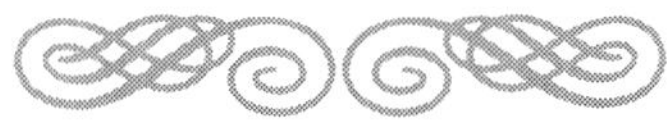

A Novel

by

Andi Bryce

This book is a work of fiction. Places, events, and situations in this story are purely fictional. Any resemblance to actual persons, living or dead, is coincidental.

Published by Literary Delights, an eBook original imprint from
Maiden Lane Press
811 Palmer Rd Suite AA Bronxville, NY 10708

ISBN-10:1940210089
ISBN-13:978-1-940210-08-7

For Ruth and Bryce Booker (Mom and Dad), who taught me kindness and acceptance of all people through example. And who taught me truthfulness and honesty by telling me I was the worst liar they'd ever come across.

Dad, we miss you so much.

Prologue

Grave Robber, Gold Digger, Beggar Woman, Thief. It was finally, blessedly, Martini Thursday. I looked around the living room of my rented house in Aspen and smiled at the nicknames I'd given my crazy friends. Kind of a strange group, the four of us, with personalities and backgrounds as different as Gordon's and Grey Goose. But we're bound by our strange connection to billionaires: landing one, getting over one, or in Mary Beth's case, cashing in on a past billionaire. Make that *passed* billionaire.

Yep, Mary Beth is Grave Robber, the only one of us with any real money these days. Almost married to a billionaire who made his money the old fashioned way – he inherited it. Rolf was a peach, to hear Mary Beth tell it, but apparently, a poor planner. Four days before the wedding, he died of a heart attack while working out with his personal trainer. Rumor spread that it was more coitus than cardio, but Mary Beth never commented. She was more concerned with his estate. Rolf had never changed his will – even though he insisted Mary Beth sign an airtight prenup. Mary Beth is no stranger to money. She grew up rich in Connecticut. You wouldn't think a billionaire would be afraid of a millionaire. Now Mary Beth spends her days fighting his estate – but it's not what you think. Everyone assumes she's fighting for her share of Rolf's money, but I know different. The head lawyer in charge of Rolf's estate is his ex-girlfriend, Mary Beth's arch-nemesis. Let's just say it's not going well.

"I'd like to wring her skinny little neck," said Mary Beth, swirling her martini. "She's evil. And anorexic. Or bulimic. Or maybe on the Colombian diet." She made a motion as if she were snorting a line of cocaine.

I'm not ashamed to admit it - the rest of us are just a little bit afraid of Mary Beth. She's a highly-polished badass, who I know for a fact has a good heart hiding beneath her silk blouse and Guia La Bruna bra. I used to think her heart was like the heart of the Grinch – two sizes too small. But then I got to know her and realized her heart is actually bigger than most.

Here's the thing about Mary Beth – she has a habit of doing really nice things for us and for other people. For the whole world, for all I know. But she doesn't want anyone to know. If you ever accused her of being nice, she would be really pissed and might even punch you.

Cheyenne screwed up her face. "Mary Beth, Rolf had a slew of really good lawyers, right?"

MB barked out a laugh. "Judging by the bills from my own lawyers in this aberration, I'd have to say yes."

Cheyenne frowned and looked to Dallas. "What's an aberration?"

"It was a scary movie," said Dallas. "About a girl and her evil boyfriend."

"Seriously, MB?" I asked. "Aberration? Who talks like that?"

Mary Beth shrugged one shoulder and smiled. At least she had the good sense to laugh at herself. A product of elite private schools, MB tended to be a bit bombastic when she could have just as easily used a word we'd all understand.

Cheyenne fidgeted with her second-hand Chanel chain belt. "How could they forget something as croosh as changing the will before Rolf married you? How can you keep from getting hosed like that again?"

Between Cheyenne's love of slang and Mary Beth's big words, we needed an interpreter every time we got together. Cheyenne's concern about Mary Beth *getting hosed* had nothing to do with Mary Beth, and everything to do with Cheyenne.

Previously married to a cop in Denver, Cheyenne had stumbled onto a taste of the good life during a ski weekend in Snowmass where she'd met Michael, a billionaire with a hedge fund and a collection of Ferraris. She'd left her blue-collar roots and middle class life behind – including her husband – changed her name to Shy, and went after Michael with both barrels. But like the rest of us, Shy's found out life with a billionaire isn't all it's cracked up to be. He's busy making his money, or counting his money, or spending his money, so she hardly ever sees him. But Shy, a former bartender, is determined to trade in her Miller Light past for a Krug Champagne future. Cheyenne is Gold Digger – on the surface. But things aren't always what they seem; there's a lot more to the story.

"Y'all can be sure, I'll never sign a prenup without seeing the will first," said Dallas, gorgeous and gentle and pure of heart, the most beautiful of all of us. The only one who's never been married, Dallas is Beggar Woman – currently in danger of losing her house and looking for a man to save her.

Born and raised in a trailer park in Ft. Worth, she began modeling early on and eventually developed a knack for drawing the attention of rich guys, mostly at high-end car shows. We were roommates in college – both on scholarships. Dallas was volleyball, and I was track. She was the pretty one, and I was the roommate of the pretty one.

About four years ago Dallas found herself with child. Everyone thought she was sleeping with two different men at the same time – but she wasn't. Her well-known Dallas oilman boyfriend had dumped her the week before she took up with the center for a top NBA team – who told her he was separated, nearly divorced. Big lie. Baby Bentley was born, there was a paternity test, and the basketball player was ordered by the court to pay his part – which he somehow keeps forgetting to do. Dallas continues to hook up with guys, looking for that elusive sense of security she's never had. With a slightly mixed up moral compass, Dallas always does the right thing – except when it comes to men.

"Dallas," I said, refilling the funky martini glasses I'd bought on sale at Target. "You went through a lawyer when you made your deal with Baby Daddy, right?" We never called him by his name even though we knew who he was.

Dallas nodded, "Yes, but it was on the QT, you know. We couldn't talk about it. Or I couldn't talk about it, anyway."

Dallas has just enough Texas drawl to be charming but not so much you want to stick a sock in her mouth. "They tried to get me to take a lump sum," she continued. "But I thought it might be a trick. Baby Daddy was starting to get endorsements and other offers, so I made a deal for a percentage of his annual income every year until Bentley's eighteen."

Cheyenne whistled through her teeth. As a former bartender, whistling is just one of her special talents. "Good one, Dallas. Way to go, girl."

MB shook her head and smiled at Cheyenne's wild enthusiasm. Like I said, MB comes from old, moldy money. And Cheyenne comes from almost no money at all. MB is slightly rebellious when it comes to her fancy upbringing and likes to wear jeans – strictly forbidden when she was growing up – but pairs them with designer stilettos and silk blouses. She is class and elegance but with an edge.

Cheyenne is a cross between a cheerleader on crack and a mob wife, trying to wrap her arms around the American Dream. She has the fashion sense of Carmela Soprano and an aggravating perkiness that will not be squelched. I could not love these three kooks more if they were my real sisters.

I know what you're thinking. Grave Robber, Gold Digger, Beggar Woman. Where's the Thief?

Right here. I'm not proud of it, but I'm the Thief.

My billionaire ex-husband dumped me for a tiny young pixie with short blond hair and a penchant for thigh-high boots, and she's getting all the good stuff that should be mine. He just bought her a Mercedes SL65 at around two hundred large, a Patek Philippe watch, and a matching set of Louis Vuitton. I know because I have a horrible habit of going to their huge house on Red Mountain and going through their stuff. I know it's wrong, it's beyond wrong.

But it used to be my huge house until I agreed to give it up in our divorce settlement. And that's just the beginning of what I gave up. Our marriage never was about the money, and neither was the divorce. All I wanted was Rufus.

Thomas and I fought like bare-knuckled cage fighters over the rescue dog we adopted back when we could barely afford to feed ourselves, let alone a dog. Black and white with one ear that flopped over, he always looked sort of confused. Thomas wanted to name him Doofus but had settled for Rufus.

By the time it was all said and done, I came out of the divorce with hardly more than a house in Houston and my precious furball. And what did Rufus do to thank me for my brave act of loyalty? He died in his sleep at the foot of my bed six weeks after the divorce was final. I couldn't even believe it. The vet said it might have been a heart attack. Or a blood clot. But I think it was a broken heart. Our happy little home had turned into a battlefield, and Rufus chose to surrender rather than pick sides. I didn't think I could ever hurt as much as the day Thomas left me, but I was wrong. Losing my sweet Rufus was the crowning blow.

Thomas was so totally preoccupied with his new bride and his new life, he never got around to changing the locks at the house, and I still have a key. Yesterday I stole a rare Baccarat rooster and a black and platinum Montblanc pen. I don't even like either one of them, it's just the principle of the matter. That stuff should be mine.

I know I sound like a pouting snotty teenager, but I'm just so lost. When Thomas dumped me, I somehow lost all my bearings. Like he was my due North, and now my compass is forever spinning, trying to find a direction. Any direction.

My only solace these days comes from my wacky friends and our beloved Martini Thursdays. But it's not like I'm the only screwed up one in the bunch. We all have our little idiosyncrasies, our issues. It wasn't really our fault.

It all started with billionaires.

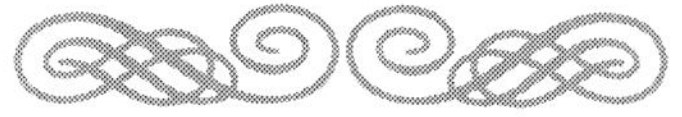

Chapter One

"Really, Dallas? Main Street Bakery? How plebeian."

We were leaving Montagna at the Little Nell, where we'd just devoured a late brunch. Things were going pretty well. There hadn't been any bloodshed or hair pulling or smackdowns of any kind, only a few snarky words. But Mary Beth, God bless her, was about to change all that.

"Come on, Mary Beth," said Dallas. "It'll take ten short minutes. I have to pick up Bentley's birthday cake. You can sit in the car if you want. Or, you can come inside and have another cup of coffee. Maybe that'll put you in a better mood."

"Hey!" said Cheyenne in a tone she might have used at one time to yell *last call.* "Isn't that Jack Nicholson?" She pointed, but Mary Beth didn't even bother to look. I used it as a golden opportunity to change the subject.

"Dallas, is Baby Daddy coming to the birthday party?" I was hoping I could drag him aside and open a little can of whoop ass on him, and try to make him pay up. Mary Beth would probably help me. Cheyenne too.

Dallas shook her head and inched her way through the pedestrians streaming across Main Street. "Nope. He sent a teddy bear and an autographed picture of himself. Can y'all believe that? What kind of man sends an autographed picture of himself to his own daughter? *Dear Bentley, happy birthday and many more.* And then this squiggly signature you can't even read. If I could copy his handwriting, I'd tweak it a little to read *Love, Daddy.*"

Baby Daddy had no idea what he was missing because Bentley was about the cutest kid I'd ever seen in my life. With her mama's blond hair and her daddy's deep blue eyes, she was a three-year-old with the personality of a Vegas lounge singer; she knew how to work a room. Always smiling. Always happy. All you had to do was hold your hands out and she would launch herself into your arms, all wiggly and warm and smelling like sunshine. I couldn't imagine how her daddy could turn his back on her. But then I reminded myself, her daddy was married to someone who didn't know Baby Bentley existed.

We walked through the pink front door and into the homey little café – old hardwood floors, gingham curtains over the windows, and the rich smell of fresh coffee. Dallas pulled a short stack of coupons from her purse and went to the counter to check on her birthday cake while the rest of us picked up a coffee mug from the stack near the coffee machine and poured ourselves a cup of Joe. I was all for going out the side door to the sunny deck until Cheyenne jabbed me in the ribs with her elbow.

"Look at that hottie," she said, loud enough for everyone in the place to hear. Luckily, at this hour – too late for breakfast and slightly too early for lunch – the place was almost empty.

Mary Beth walked to the nearest table and noisily pulled out a chair. Cheyenne and I sat beside her at the scarred oak table, and I checked out the only guy in the room over the top of my steaming mug. Wavy blond hair, cut a little longer in back and looking sort of windblown. Bronzed skin – but not sun ravaged or over-tanned like the local extreme skiers and bikers. He wore faded jeans and a plain white T-shirt, and sat with his long legs out in front of him, reading from a leather bound book. Either he felt my eyes on him, or the constant chatter coming out of Cheyenne drew his attention, because he looked up and met my eyes. And for a split second, my breath nearly caught in my throat.

Which, seriously, is not like me. Men don't have that effect on me these days. Ever since Thomas dumped me, I've been avoiding men like Superman avoids Kryptonite. Lately I liked my men the same way I liked my coffee – ground up and in the freezer.

But the eyes. Something about the startling blue eyes. And the easy half-smile. It was like walking into Barney's in February and spotting a baby-soft pastel cashmere sweater in the new spring line after a long winter of dark and nubby wools. And your hand just naturally wants to reach out and touch it.

Dallas clicked over to our table on her four-inch pointy-toed pumps.

"Ta-da!" she said, placing a white bakery box in the middle of the table. She flipped through the coupons and leaned over to stash them in her purse. "We're all set. Let's roll."

"Not so fast," I said, watching the cute guy watch us. "Get some coffee and take a load off."

Dallas put one manicured hand on her hip, shrugged, and walked over to the coffee bar.

"That girl has a coupon for everything," said Cheyenne.

"I heard that," said Dallas from the coffee bar.

There wasn't a man in Aspen – or any other town for that matter – who could keep his eyes off Dallas. So I wasn't surprised to see the guy watching us. But amazingly, he seemed to be looking at me instead of Dallas.

Being dumped at thirty-five for a younger, curvier woman does a number on your spirit. On your soul. Not to mention your self-esteem. I wasn't feeling especially desirable these days. So when the guy locked eyes with me and gave me another one of those delicious half-smiles, I decided to do something about it. My self-esteem may have taken a major hit, but I still had that *get up and brush yourself off* mentality I'd been raised with.

As a kid, when I skinned my knees or wrecked my bike, my parents always said, "You're okay, get up, brush yourself off, and go on." And so I did. All my life. Which I guess can be a good thing in a way. But if you only brush the outside off, and the inside is still skinned and scraped, then you end up with tough outsides and a train wreck on the inside.

Dallas pulled out the chair next to me, saw me looking at the guy, and whispered, "What you need is a bald one."

Years ago when Dallas was between boyfriends and all the Baldwin boys were constantly on Entertainment Tonight – Alec was fighting with Kim Basinger and Billy was marrying Chynna – I told Dallas what she needed was a Baldwin to get her out of her funk. She'd said, with a perfectly straight face, "What is it with you and bald guys?"

Maybe it was my parents' words ringing in my ears, telling me to shake it off. Or maybe it was Dallas telling me to go for the love. Or maybe it was just being in a bakery surrounded by every kind of sinful dessert. But feeling those stunning blue eyes on me and knowing he was watching me woke some long dormant goddess essence inside of me. It was like suddenly developing a sweet tooth and being drawn to those tiny cheesecakes they serve at fancy parties. I just had to have me some cheesecake.

Leaving my coffee on the table, I walked over. He didn't stand, didn't offer me a chair. Just watched me walk right up to him while I gave him a quick once-over. Muscular arms. Worn out jeans. Casual, unaffected style. Arresting eyes. Disarming smile.

When he didn't say anything at all, I started to question this little, spontaneous act of courage. This impulsive walk across the room to prove I was still attractive and desirable while my friends sat and watched. But like so many times in my life, my second thoughts were arriving a beat too late. There was no graceful way out.

So I gave myself a mental "you go, girl!" and rested my hands on the back of the chair across from him. "How's the breakfast here?"

He smiled a full smile this time. "Not bad. Want some?"

I looked at his plate and the remnants of what looked like huevos rancheros, now cold and dried out.

"No thanks." I pulled out the chair and sat across from him at the table. He moved the blue silky ribbon to mark his place in the battered book and sat up, wrapping his hands around his coffee mug. His hands were huge, and the nail of his left thumb was black and blue as if he'd slammed it in a door or hit it with a hammer. Not the soft hands of an executive.

"You're not from here," he said. Since he knew I wasn't a local, I decided he must be.

I lifted one shoulder. "What's in the book?" I asked

That smile. Those eyes. "The secrets of the universe."

I laughed. "Good to know. I'll keep that in mind next time I need a superhero."

We sat in silence, total strangers looking across a table at one another. I felt the strangest sense of calm sitting there, but at the same time, he stoked this new unexpected craving inside me. Neither one of us tried to fill the silence or fumbled to ask each other the usual trivial questions. We just sat there like old friends. Comfortable. Peaceful.

I could have sat there all afternoon, but the scraping of chairs behind me signaled my posse was leaving. I stood, but my new friend kept his seat. "Maybe we'll run into each other again," I said.

"Maybe," he said. Which should have made me mad. I mean, really, shouldn't a man at least stand and offer his hand? And why was I sitting at his table anyway? Normally drawn to clean cut guys with big brains and glasses, how did I end up sitting with a long-haired local wearing dusty boots and faded Levis, who never even invited me over in the first place?

I didn't know. I only knew there was something about him. I was drawn to him like a four-year-old to a book of matches.

I followed the girls out the front door and turned to look just before the door closed behind me. He was sitting. And smiling.

Had I known then what I know now, I would have been a little afraid.

Chapter Two

The squeal of the alarm system nearly split my eardrum. I closed the heavy front door and hurried over to the panel in the wall, slid the cover, and punched in the five-digit code. If I'd been a burglar, I'm pretty sure it would have scared me away.

But I wasn't a burglar. Technically. I mean, how many burglars use a key and have the code to the burglar alarm?

The house was as quiet as a convent, and sunlight poured into the living room from arched two-story windows. I shook my head, remembering the months of work and the two high-powered interior designers from New York who helped me redecorate the house after we bought it. And when they were through, I'd added a little whimsy and a whole lot of comfort, a coziness the designers despised. But I didn't care. I loved the results. Each room had our personal stamp. Mine and Thomas's. So how was it possible I no longer lived here with him?

I leaned against the arched doorway and felt a little like a beauty queen stripped of my crown, sash, and title. Thomas and I had laughed like little kids on the day we bought this house. And over the course of the next year we made love in every room.

I walked over to one of the deep chairs near the windows and stood for a minute, looking out at the summer day. What a view. There had to be a better word. A bigger word. Mary Beth probably knew a fancy way of describing this awe-inspiring scene spanning the mountains from Independence Pass to Mount Sopris.

I looked around at the treasures from all over the world. Most brought back Technicolor memories of vacations with Thomas. And my stomach lurched at the thought of the pixie living here. How had things deteriorated to the point that he would walk away from me after eleven years of a mostly happy marriage, to take up with a woman who was barely old enough to vote? Okay, she was old enough. But I had a feeling she'd have an easier time naming the Jersey Housewives than the Vice-President and Speaker of the House.

What had become so intolerable about me? So resistible? I sank deeper into the chair and sighed.

Somewhere along the line, Thomas reneged on our wedding vows: To honor each other, even when one was acting dishonorable. To cherish each other, even when one was being less than charming. To love, even when the other was being an ass. There came a point when he gave up. And the worst of it was, he moved on and started a new life before ever telling me he was through with the old.

The old life. The old wife. That's what I was. His life would forever be broken into two distinct realms. There would be *now, my current wife, today.* And there would be *then, my ex, years ago.* I was then. I was the ex. I was years ago. My life wasn't broken into two distinct realms. My life was just broken.

I met Thomas when I was a senior at Stanford and he was living and working in Palo Alto. It was my sorority's second most popular annual charity event – the first being the bikini carwash. But there were no bikinis at this event. Just boxed lunches made by each sorority sister, auctioned off to the highest bidder. It was more about winning a date with the girl than buying the lunch. And that day, Thomas was the highest bidder for my turkey and Swiss on rye. He had a huge crush on Sandra Bullock at the time, and we have the same straight brown hair, the same wide-set brown eyes. He didn't know

I was the roommate of the pretty one. With Thomas, I was able to shine on my own.

These days, Thomas is always perfectly put together. He wears contact lenses and Armani jackets, has his hair cut by Sally Hershberger every two weeks, and never goes anywhere without a clean shave. But back then, he looked like a cross between a hunky athlete and a mad scientist. He still had the great bone structure, the deep-set gray eyes, and the gorgeous, shy smile. But he wore thick glasses and needed a good haircut worse than I need my morning caffeine. The thing that really got me – the thing that still gets me – is that right in the middle of this perfect face, this movie-star handsome face, was a broken nose.

Thomas was a basketball star in high school and during his freshman year in college – before he became obsessed with semiconductors and spent all his time in the lab. During the last practice of his last year, he took an elbow to the nose. And being a man, and not a vain one at that, he never had his nose fixed. He wore it as a badge of honor, a salute to his days as an athlete. I can't imagine him with a perfect nose. He would be too handsome. I think of him as having *almost-leading-man good looks*. If the lead character were a boxer. Or maybe a warrior.

When he outbid all the others and won a date with me, I was impressed, thinking he was gorgeous and might even have deep pockets to boot. I never guessed he'd spent his last two hundred dollars on my silly sandwich.

On our first date, we went to the park and played Frisbee. On our second date, we went to a free concert. On our third date – dollar night at the drive-in movie – he had held my hand and explained that he was not wealthy, poor in fact, because he was pouring every cent into his dream. A company dedicated to designing and implementing semiconductor solutions.

But I didn't care. I loved everything about him. Thomas saved me from a life of serial dating. I dated a lot in college, but nothing ever quite clicked. It was all just fun and games. Until Thomas, a major study in contradictions. So blatantly masculine, but slightly nerdy and bookish. Brilliant in the lab, but naïve when it came to women and what made them tick. Capable and in-charge, but so tender and generous. Indulgent. He'd bring me little gifts. Not expensive, but creative. Even after we made our money and the sky was the limit, he'd always come up with these sweet, funny gifts. In the early years, it might be a handful of flowers he stole out of someone's yard and tied with a piece of string. Or a runner's magazine and a pair of running socks. One year, he paid attention every time I mentioned a song I liked, and had a friend mix a CD of all my favorite songs. That CD means more to me than if he'd given me a Harry Winston diamond necklace. If my house ever goes up in flames, that CD is one of the few things I'll try to save.

By the time I graduated, I was living with Thomas and the obvious next step was to join him in his company. And when I say company, I mean just him and his partner Dave, working from a rundown warehouse. Needing a real job to support his wife and new baby, Dave soon gave up and let Thomas buy him out. And in order to buy Dave out of the business, Thomas had taken out a loan using his 1992 Honda Civic as collateral.

I worked from a card table in the front room of the warehouse, wearing my one halfway decent business suit on days we had meetings with clients, acting as receptionist, secretary, accountant, financial manager, and head coffee maker. Thomas's company was named Moore Silicon Solutions – and I took a lot of calls from women asking about breast implants.

The next year we married in a twenty-minute ceremony at city hall. One year later we sold Moore Silicon Solutions to a publicly traded company in Newport Beach for $600 million dollars. Back then we didn't even know what expensive champagne was. We bought a bottle of our favorite ten-dollar red and made love on the floor of the living room in front of the fire, because we'd never had the money to buy a couch.

We moved to a beach house near Long Beach, and I finished my MBA at CSU, wanting to be part of whatever came next. Thomas had a knack for working hard - and making money. The combination made us billionaires five years later. He also had a knack for risky investments. So by the time we divorced, a big chunk of our money had been lost in a *sure thing* – a company that nearly sucked us dry.

But what good is money anyway without someone to share it with? What good is achieving the dream if it destroys the dreamers?

Sometimes I wondered, what if we'd failed? What if Moore Silicon Solutions had never made it, and we'd had to go to Plan B? Would we still be sitting side by side in a rundown warehouse, tired and poor, but happy? If we hadn't achieved The Dream, would Thomas have walked away?

I could still remember the last time we made love. If I'd known it was the last time, I would have kissed him like a teenager in the backseat of a borrowed Buick. Left all the lights on so I could see his face. Looked in his eyes as he said my name. But I didn't know.

Tears are sort of foreign to me. Or at least they were until the past year. Before Thomas sat me down on our patio in Houston and told me about his pixie, told me he was leaving to start a new life. Until that time, most of my tears were brought on by dicing onions for Thomas's favorite vichyssoise, or watching a Hallmark movie at Christmas, or once in a while, from the stick of a needle attached to a syringe of Botox.

I mopped up this latest, messy round of tears and thought about sending out a distress call to my crazy friends. Over the past excruciating year they'd been beyond loyal, going the extra mile – or martini – to drag me out of my doldrums.

The chime of the doorbell snapped me out of my reverie. My heart skipped a beat and started hammering in my ears. In a panic, I stood stock still at the edge of the living room. Thomas and the pixie were in Europe, right? Besides, they wouldn't ring their own doorbell.

The bell rang again, and I hurried toward the door thinking I shouldn't have left my car in the circle drive out front. I was getting too brash. But when I peeked through the window of the foyer, the familiar sight of the UPS man in his brown suit gave me a rush of relief. Wiping my tears on the backs of my hands, I opened the door to his smiling face.

"Mrs. Moore?"

I nodded. He didn't have to know I was the *other* Mrs. Moore.

"Could you sign here?"

I took the electronic clipboard and scribbled something illegible, then took the two boxes and tried to act normal. Both were addressed to Thomas. Both were from stores in London.

Using the key to our house in Houston – no, wait, *my* house in Houston – I opened the first box, spread the tissue, and ran my hand along the soft calf leather. Black, custom-made wing tips from John Lobb. I'd treated Thomas to his first pair six years ago, and he'd fallen headlong in love.

I tucked the shoes back in their box and slit open the second package. Lots of packing, lots of tissue, and nestled inside, half a dozen cotton bespoke shirts from Turnbull & Asser. Ah, Thomas did love these shirts, made to fit him like a glove.

I could see him now, standing in front of me in our bedroom. I watched myself walk toward him, wearing nothing but a smile. Taking my time, untying the perfect Windsor knot of his tie. Then slowly unbuttoning each of the buttons on the custom shirt until it hung open and I could feel the full length of his bare chest against mine. I sucked in my breath at the thought of his warm skin – smooth, tan, with a hint of spicy Clive Christian cologne. His hands moving over my body, wanting to touch every part of me. I ached for his touch. For his smile. For this other half to my soul that I never dreamed I would have to live without.

I shook my head to make the memory go away. These crippling walks down memory lane were about to put me under. I sniffed and wiped at my wet face, then stood and draped my bag over my shoulder. Standing in the foyer, I looked out over the living area, and the incredible view beyond, feeling small. And forgotten. And left behind. Then I reset the alarm, grabbed my keys, tucked both packages under my arm, and left.

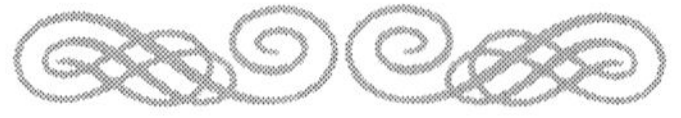

Chapter Three

"What's a Ponzi scheme?" asked Cheyenne.

We were in my used Jeep Grand Cherokee on our way into town. Mary Beth sat in the passenger seat with Cheyenne and Dallas in the back. I glanced at Cheyenne, who had taken to wearing oversized designer knockoff sunglasses.

"Why do you ask?" I said.

"Well, Michael was on the phone just before I left and he was all harshed up and yelling. And he said something like, 'This is not a Ponzi scheme!' And I walked to the door of his office to blow him a kiss, and he wouldn't even look at me."

Michael definitely had his issues. He'd never welcomed our presence at his overpriced, ostentatious crib. And from the bits and pieces Cheyenne fed us, he came across as pretentious, sometimes borderline cruel, and perpetually full of himself.

Mary Beth answered. "It's a scheme to abscond with investor funds."

"What do you mean?" asked Cheyenne.

"You live with a freaking Ananias, Cheyenne. The idea of him running a Ponzi isn't much of a stretch. Promise me you'll watch out for yourself and not get involved."

We were on our third trip around the block trying to find a parking place.

"In English, *por favor*?" said Cheyenne.

"Let me take a shot," I said. "And help me watch for a parking place. A Ponzi scheme basically promises abnormally high returns on an investment. But the returns are paid from the investors' own money or from money of the people who invest after them. So only the first few investors ever make any money. It's highly illegal. Finally!" I pulled into the last parking spot on earth.

We piled out into the warm noon sunshine where crowds of people filled the sidewalk, and a furry menagerie of dogs snoozed in the sun, happily oblivious to the high-end real estate all around them. I reached down to rub the fuzzy head of a Golden Retriever, and my reward was a happy tail thump, making me ache for Rufus. Cheyenne squatted down beside me as Mary Beth and Dallas walked ahead.

Cheyenne was wearing a very *Cheyenne* kind of outfit – black Christian Audigier leggings patterned with wild gold crowns and silver chains. Which *might* have worked with plain black heels and a tunic-style top. But instead Cheyenne had added a gold tank top, vintage Chanel jacket, and crystal encrusted platform flip flops. Something about the getup made me want to hug her.

"Do you really think Michael's involved in something suspicious?" I asked, standing and pulling her up beside me.

Cheyenne shook her mane of teased chestnut hair. "No, he's not like that. He's totally driven, but not like, dishonest, you know? What the heck's an Ananias?"

I changed the subject, putting my arm around her and pointing out a chunky necklace in the window of Christopher Walling. No need for Cheyenne to know MB had just called her boyfriend a big fat liar. We caught up with Mary Beth and Dallas, and got into the swing of shopping – that is, watching Mary Beth shop. Because here's the thing about me that drives Mary Beth the craziest: I'm a bargain shopper. I never pay full price. For anything. Ever.

I learned it as a kid from my grandma. She used to always say, "Don't go to the store with money burning a hole in your pocket. Be choosy. Find a bargain." So between my love of bargains and my love of fashion, it's sometimes a challenge. I shop a lot on eBay and Net-a-porter. I try not to buy anything I couldn't explain to my Grandma without feeling ashamed or stupid. Some people like to brag about how much they paid for something, but I'm constantly saying, "See these? I got these for twenty bucks at Target!" It drives Mary Beth over the edge.

I should mention here, Mary Beth is a bit of a narcissist. She's never wrong, believes only her ideas are good ideas, and could be a little more sensitive to other people's feelings. She's one of the smartest people I know and has an interesting take on this mad world we live in, but seems to be filled with some kind of inner demon most of the time. She can be completely charming when she wants to be. The problem is, she doesn't often want to be.

We sat in the shoe department of Boogie's for a while and watched Dallas try on jeans. Dallas drew a crowd, as usual, because tourists sometimes mistake her for someone famous. One rough looking guy with full sleeve tattoos and a beer gut actually stopped to take photos of her with his phone.

When Dallas had tried on just under a dozen pairs of jeans, Mary Beth rolled her eyes, picked up the two pairs that were Dallas's faves, paid for them while Dallas tried on another pair, and gave me the bag with strict instructions to slip it to Dallas later and never tell her where it had come from. I put the shopping bag into my oversized shoulder bag and wondered why MB couldn't just give it to Dallas. Sheesh.

Walking to a late lunch, we were on the Hyman Avenue Mall when I spotted a familiar form up ahead. I walked between Cheyenne and Dallas with an arm linked through each of theirs and Mary Beth walked just slightly away from us. Like she might be just the tiniest bit embarrassed that we were acting like junior high girls. I broke away from the group and walked toward him, the stranger from the bakery with the deep blue eyes.

He stood across from Wheeler Opera House, near the famous dancing water fountain. With sprays of water shooting up from metal grates in random patterns, the fountain was a favorite playground for kids. He leaned easily against a light pole with his thumbs in his front pockets, watching the squealing kids run and jump around in the water.

Mary Beth called to me, but I couldn't take my eyes off him. He wasn't classically handsome, not like Thomas. He was more outdoorsy. Hunky build, rugged, and muscular. Like maybe he could grab the front of his T-shirt and rip it right down the middle. Which I really wished he would do.

"We meet again," I said, unable to come up with anything less lame. Mary Beth's big words had somehow fried the vocabulary center in my brain for the day.

His smile was easy. "So we do."

"Lucy Moore," I said, reaching my hand toward his, wanting to touch him, wanting to know everything about him

"Glacier Jones," he said. His hand was warm and strong, callused at the knuckles of his palm but smooth where his fingers wrapped around mine. It was like sliding my hand into a favorite gardening glove – rough, but somehow familiar and comforting. I wanted to hold it and never let go, but I was distracted by his odd name.

"Glacier?" I asked, letting go of his hand. "Your real name or is that your Aspen name?"

He laughed, and his face came alive. "It's real."

"Glacier," I said, trying out the name. Like Heaven, or Chardonnay, or Saffron – it was the kind of name movie stars might inflict on their poor, unsuspecting children. Was he the child of movie star parents? Or had he legally changed his name from something common or old fashioned like Ralph or Earl or Bob? It didn't matter. The name fit him.

My gang walked up and I made introductions. Cheyenne grinned at him, Dallas gave him her best wide-eyed fawn look, and Mary Beth looked bored.

"We're about to get lunch," I said. "Come and join us."

"Thanks, but I've eaten." He turned his attention back to the little kids.

"Watch that one there," he said, pointing to a funny little boy wearing an orange balloon animal on his head. He was drenched from head to toe. "Watch him try to time the water."

The happy kid jumped and shrieked when the water below him sprayed up, and Glacier laughed with him. Even Mary Beth turned to watch for a minute. But not a second longer than that.

"I'm starving," she said, turning on her heel and walking away. Dallas and Cheyenne made appropriate good-byes and began to follow Mary Beth, but I couldn't leave. Like iron filings in a third-grade science experiment, I felt drawn to his magnetic field. To the warm circle of calm and happiness that seemed to radiate from his core.

"We like to get together every Thursday night," I said before I could stop myself. "You should join us." I took a card out of my purse and gave it to him.

He glanced at the card, then tucked it in the back pocket of his faded jeans. "Alright. Thursday night."

I smiled. The winds of change were gathering with cyclonic force and blowing straight for me. But I was so busy imagining Glacier Jones naked, I didn't even see them coming.

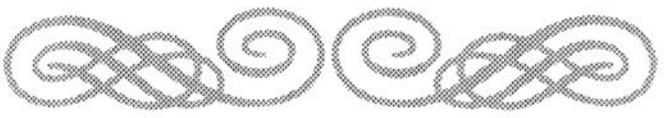

Chapter Four

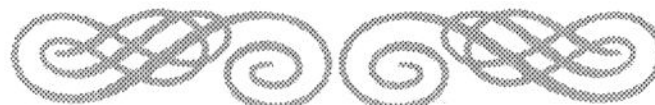

Wednesday, Mary Beth almost got me arrested. Apparently, she'd learned more in boarding school than big words and a slightly snotty attitude. She'd learned to pick locks.

"Mary Beth," I said as we drove toward the mansion of the lawyer for her deceased fiancé's estate. "Just for the sake of argument, say you're able to pick the lock. She's bound to have an alarm system, right? And what if she has a housekeeper? What if someone's there?"

"Don't be such a crybaby. Where's your mettle?"

Well, at the risk of being a crybaby or being told to grow a pair, I wanted to say that it took plenty of mettle just to ride in a car with MB. I'm guessing she spent most of her life being driven rather than driving. Winding Colorado roads were not the best place for her to improve her skills, if she'd had any to start with. Forget that we were in a Maybach, an ultra-luxury high-performance sedan that made me feel like I was in a presidential motorcade en route to the United Nations Security Council. Being in a beautiful car won't save your life - even if it does have hand-polished wood trim and soft leather seats made from cows forced to moisturize and exfoliate regularly. If you run off the road and die in a Maybach, you're still dead. And since Mary Beth was taking the tight corners at sixty-five miles an hour, there was a good chance it could happen. I looked out the window at the magnificent

Roaring Fork River and wondered how cold it would be when we went crashing in.

Not only was Mary Beth a less than ideal driver, but we were drinking and driving. Well, MB was drinking and driving. I was just drinking. We each held a tumbler of scotch on the rocks.

"Have you really thought this through?" I asked, taking a big swig of scotch to improve my mettle.

"I have," she said. Her glass was almost empty. "Once we open the door, if Cruella had the brains to turn on an alarm system, we should have two to five minutes."

"How do you figure?"

"Sixty seconds from the time the alarm's tripped until the alarm company gets the message. Another minute or so for them to call the police. And however long it takes the police to drive to the house."

I took a much bigger sip of my scotch. Okay, call it a gulp. Not terribly ladylike, but if I was about to commit a felony, I wanted to be relaxed. MB clearly had thought this through. But not in a good way.

"If the police happen to show up, we'll be back in our car and on our way out. We'll just say we were driving around, looking at property."

"Right. And if we're still in Cruella's house when the police arrive? We were, what? Feeding her Dalmatians?"

MB waved her hand, dismissing my valid and – in my opinion – well-grounded concerns. I looked at my feet and wondered if the cops would let me keep my favorite black patent sandals with me in jail. Probably not the best look with an orange jumpsuit. But then, it's Aspen, so surely they have something more couture. Maybe white linen? In that case, the shoes would look yowza.

MB pulled into a long, gated drive while she dialed a number on her cell phone. The gates were open, and we drove up to the evil one's palatial estate – a cross between a movie-star's mansion and a Scottish castle, complete with turrets and a fancy weather vane. I looked around for a moat and had a brief vision of killer Dobermans, armed guards, razor wire, or some as yet unknown deterrent that would keep us from this madcap scheme.

We parked directly in front of the massive stone steps leading to the front door, and Mary Beth flipped her phone onto the console.

"No answer," she said. "Game on."

I watched her reach into her Fendi purse for a small black leather case. She opened it, revealing a matched set of something shiny and silver.

"Seriously?" I said. "You have real tools for this kind of thing? Is that even legal? I thought you'd just use your American Express card like they do on TV."

MB rolled her eyes. She reached into her handbag a second time and brought out two pairs of white cotton gloves. "Here. Put these on but not until we're at the door."

I took the gloves, drained my scotch, and opened my car door, wondering how I would explain this to a judge. And my parents.

Mary Beth reached into the backseat for a small bag, then we got out of the car and started walking up the impressive stone steps.

"I forgot to ask," I said. "Once we're inside and have all of two to five minutes, then what?"

"You'll see," said Mary Beth, and I felt my stomach clutch.

At the door, I followed MB's lead and put the cotton gloves on. And in less time than it would take the police to read us our rights, she had the lock picked. "Get ready. Five minutes."

"Make it two," I said. "Just to be safe."

"Three then," said MB. "We're looking for the master bedroom. Probably upstairs. Probably at the end of the hall. Ready, go."

And with that, she opened the door to the piercing shriek of the alarm. Even though I'd known it would go off, even though I was expecting it, my heart nearly jumped out of my chest.

I followed Mary Beth up the beautiful curved staircase, somehow taking the steps three at a time even in three-inch heels. She pointed at the top and we split off. My shoes sank into the thick carpet, and my legs felt heavy - like in those nightmares where you're trying to get away from the crazy killer but your legs will only move in slow-mo. Stark contrast to my runaway pulse and the adrenaline rushing through my body.

Before I got very far down the hall, Mary Beth called out, "In here!"

I turned around and ran back down the hall into a gorgeous master bedroom. There was no time to admire the fancy linens, or draperies, or what looked like a Picasso on the wall by the bed. I followed MB into the huge walk-in closet, and over to the built-in dresser. Quick as a bunny, she reached into the white paper sack and pulled out a circular wooden box with writing on the top. I knew immediately it was her favorite cheese – Époisses. A French cheese so utterly stinky, it's been banned from public transportation in France – a country normally tolerant of stinky cheeses. Mary Beth likes to serve it with a good Burgundy. I waited for her to pull a bottle out of the sack. But instead, she opened the wooden top revealing the orangey-red cheese – cut perfectly into two halves. The pungent smell hit me full in the face and nearly made my eyes water. I held my hand over my nose while she pulled open the top drawer of the dresser, exposing fancy lingerie. MB gently moved the bras and panties aside, then placed one half of the cheese in the bottom of the drawer. She carefully positioned the lingerie back over the top while I stared in disbelief. This was what we were risking our lives for? To soil a drawer of expensive French lingerie? With stinky French cheese?

It seemed so, I don't know, beneath her capabilities. Mary Beth had one of the most brilliant minds I'd ever come across. I expected something more high tech, more white collar. You know, lying, cheating, stealing. Not stinking up the place!

MB opened the next drawer – full of cashmere sweaters – and repeated the process. Then she turned to run out of the closet. I was somehow rooted to the spot, so she came back in, grabbed me roughly by the sleeve and dragged me out.

We ran like girls down the hall, down the stairway, and out the front door. We piled into the Maybach, MB started it up, and we pulled slowly away from the house. I thought we would squeal out and lay rubber, but I realized that might look suspicious.

My heart was beating so loud, I didn't hear anything she was saying. She looked as cool as a tin of beluga on ice, which would go really well with stinky French cheese. We got to the end of the long drive, and MB stopped and looked at her watch.

"Two minutes, forty-five seconds. Not bad." She smiled at me.

"Don't stop! Keep going! *Geez!*"

She gave me a look that seemed to say "wimp," and then pulled onto the main road. It felt like half an hour before we saw a police car go speeding by in the other lane. Mary Beth looked at her watch again.

"Eight and a half minutes," she said. "Damn, we had more time. Next time, we'll know."

I rolled my eyes and looked out the window, wishing for another tumbler of scotch. Because my mind was racing. And my mettle was waning.

"How about the Maroon Creek Club for a drink?" asked Mary Beth in the cheerful, nonchalant voice of a psychopath.

I nodded. Yes. Absolutely. A drink. A toast to our life of crime. I wondered if they served happy hour in the Aspen jail.

Chapter Five

Thursday morning I woke up early, wrapped in my favorite girly peach-colored sheets. Thank God. I wasn't in jail after all. I guess dreaming about something all night long doesn't make it so.

In a single day I'd taken the leap from breaking and entering with a key and alarm code to breaking and entering with a narcissistic maniac carrying a set of lock picks in her Fendi bag. What was next? Putting a pair of pantyhose over my head and bursting into Bvlgari, waving a sharpened nail file?

My life had taken a very strange turn, and I wasn't exactly comfortable with it. Lifting things from Thomas and the pixie was just sport. Just my way of getting back at them. But it was wrong. And yesterday's little caper was way over the top. It had to stop. I had to find another outlet for my boredom, the monotony of my life, my broken heart.

I felt diagonally parked in a parallel universe. There had to be more to life than this, didn't there? More than shopping and drinking and plotting revenge. I needed to think about getting a job. Or a dog. I needed a good reason to get out of bed in the morning.

I sighed and rolled over to look at the clock, then smiled when I remembered it was Martini Thursday. Sometimes known as Thirsty Thursday. And almost always the best night of the week.

It reminded me of college. Dallas used to make me laugh so hard that drinks came out of my nose. We liked to get half-crocked and decide to do something we'd never done before. Like in our senior year, when we both signed up for intermediate jazz dance class. Had either of us ever taken beginning jazz? No. Had either of us ever taken any kind of dance class? No. But we were athletes. We figured how hard could it be?

Well, turns out, it's pretty hard. We were horrible. Beyond horrible. But we worked each other up into such a humongous case of the sillies during each class, it was worth it. The teacher discouraged us from moving on to her advanced class. We still do *jazz hands* to make each other laugh. That never gets old.

And that whole *how hard can it be* thing? That's gotten us into more trouble than I can even say. Like the time we decided to paint Bentley's nursery and put the crib together ourselves, three days before Bentley was born. Or the time we decided to try changing out a ceiling fan in my house. I called Thomas at work.

"Hey Hon, is the black wire the grounding wire?"

"I'll be right there," he said.

Anyway, back to girlfriends. I always thought having Dallas was enough, but when we met Cheyenne and Mary Beth, it just seemed to double the fun.

Dallas met Cheyenne one night at Jimmy's when both were sitting at the bar, and Dallas ordered a Bubblicious. The bartender just looked back at her like she was kidding. Former bartender Cheyenne piped up and explained to him it was a martini made with bubblegum-infused vodka, which Jimmy's didn't have on hand. But it was a great start to a friendship.

MB and I met early last summer over shoes. But that was the second time. The first time had been just after Rufus died.

I was sitting in a corner of the Living Room of the Little Nell, bawling my eyes out. Too lonely to sit home by myself, I embarrassed myself instead in front of a roomful of strangers. Mary Beth had walked up, handed me a Kleenex, and said, "Whoever he is, he's not worth it."

I'd cried even harder. Kindness has a way of doing that to me. "My dog," I said between sobs. "He died."

"Oh. In that case, let me buy you a drink." She sat down and ordered martinis before I could even blow my nose. I mopped at my face with the tissue and swallowed a hiccup, feeling a total mess in front of this cool, graceful woman wearing stilettos, skinny jeans, and a form-fitting red silk blouse.

When her cell phone rang, she glanced at the caller ID and held up a finger. "It's my daughter," she said, holding her hand over the phone. "I can't stay."

The waiter came over with two martinis and set them on the table between us. Mary Beth stood and laid a hand on my shoulder. "Drink up. It might not help, but it sure couldn't hurt. Really sorry about your dog."

She walked away, and I never even got her name. I had no way of contacting her, or thanking her for contributing to my martini addiction while offering support on one of the darkest days of my life. Until a month later.

For some crazy reason I was trying on a pair of four-inch, knife-edged heels in bright red. They weren't on sale, so there's no way I would really have bought them. They were just sort of wild, and I wanted to see what they looked like on. But it was my lucky day because they were the last size seven in the house, and Mary Beth wanted them. A lot. Especially when she thought I wanted them. And like the fancy schmancy red pumps with gold hardware at the heel, MB was not shy.

She sauntered over, sat down beside me, crossed her long legs and quietly said, "I'll give you a hundred dollars for those shoes."

I saw the determination in the sharp lines of her face. She showed no sign of recognizing me as the sobbing mess she'd offered a tissue to a month earlier. But the slight twinkle in her eye, the tiny smile at the corner of her mouth, told me she knew exactly who I was. And feeling sporty, and desperately needing fun in my life, I played along.

"I don't know. They're exactly what I was looking for, and so different. They feel like *butter* on my feet."

"One fifty," she said, looking at me and not at the shoes. I made a face as if I were considering, moving my foot back and forth and admiring the shoe, which didn't feel anything like butter on my foot and was so totally and completely not me.

"Fine," she said, "two hundred. Final offer."

"Sold," I said, smiling. "I'm Lucy." I stuck out my hand.

She took my hand and tucked two crisp hundred-dollar bills into my palm.

"Mary Beth."

"Well, Mary Beth, why don't you buy these shoes from the nice man, and let's go to lunch."

I paid for lunch that day with MB's money. And I liked her immediately. Liked her no-nonsense conversation and her way of getting right to the point. No little niceties. No disingenuous flattery. Nothing fake about that girl. And she could hold her liquor without getting loud or shrill or teary.

Not to mention the fact that she'd been nice to me when my dog died. That's something you never forget. That single act somehow carved her name in the wet cement of my heart. I felt like I sort of owed her.

So later that week I decided I needed a social shot in the arm, if not a full-fledged social physical. My life was pale and lethargic and sickly. It was my first summer in Aspen without Thomas, and I was desperate to fill the void. I invited Dallas and Mary Beth over for cocktails, and Dallas brought along Cheyenne. And voila. Martini Thursday was born.

Having girlfriends was way better than having a boyfriend. That's what I kept telling myself. There's just something so good about being with your girlfriends. But tonight there would be a boy at our all-girl party: Glacier Jones.

He intrigued me, which was strange since I'd basically cut men entirely from my diet for the past year. Much easier than cutting out carbs, by the way. But in my tiresome habit of second-guessing myself, I began to wonder if Glacier would really fit in with our martini crew. Would it be weird? Would Mary Beth snub him and insult him and make me wish I'd never invited him?

And what would I do with him once I got him to my house? I wondered if he knew the effect his smile had on me. I wanted to pour it into my hands and rub it all over my body, like my favorite lotion. He was, at the same time, both unnerving and pacifying to my sex-starved, love-ravaged soul.

At 6:30, I surveyed my living room. The bargain basement martini glasses sat waiting for the first cold splash. Caviar – ordered online and on sale – runny Brie, grapes and kiwi, fat Mediterranean olives and a view to die for. You'd think that would be enough to make a person happy. But maybe not, because I was about the most unhappy camper on the planet.

No time to wallow in it though. I had martinis to mix. At the bar, I reached for vodka, vermouth, and way up on the top shelf almost out of reach – the last shred of my self-esteem. My mind bounced from my loveless, pathetic life to Glacier Jones. And I had to wonder if the two might go together somehow.

The girls and I were halfway into our first martini when Glacier showed up. I reached to give him a quick kiss on each cheek and caught a whiff of his scent – warm, clean, masculine. I felt the tiniest quiver of excitement and wondered what it might be like to kiss him in a not so chaste kind of way. More like a down and dirty, long and slow and deep kind of way.

I showed him into the living room, and everyone said hello. He took a seat near the picture window and rested one boot on his knee.

"Help yourself to snacks," I said.

"Yummy," said Dallas, smiling at him and licking her fingers. The sight of Dallas licking her fingers sent most men into a horny tailspin. But he just smiled and declined the food. I poured a martini and tried to hand it to him. He held up his hand.

"No thank you." His voice was husky, like maybe he needed a lozenge instead of a martini.

I cocked my head at him. "It's Martini Thursday. You have to drink a martini. It's the rule."

"Yeah," said Cheyenne, loading a blini with caviar, "you're the first guy we've ever invited to Martini Thursday. Don't blow it."

"At the risk of blowing it," he said, "do you have coffee? Or maybe tea?"

MB gave me a look that said, "Are you kidding me?" I walked into the kitchen to make a quick pot of coffee. While it perked, I schemed up ways to get rid of the girls so I could have Glacier all to myself. And the very fact that I was willing to trade in my night with my tribe for a night with a boy signaled the start of something new. A metamorphosis I wasn't sure I was even ready for.

Back in the living room, there was a lively discussion going on about gun control. Dallas was for it, being the mother of a three-year-old. Shy was against it, as the ex-wife of a cop who carried a gun to work every day. And Mary Beth – God love her – had the final word.

"Guns don't kill people. Pirates kill people."

Cheyenne laughed and reached for more brie. "Totally."

Mary Beth poured herself another martini and downed it in two swallows. Glacier sat quietly, taking it all in.

I handed him the cup of coffee, then took the chair near him.

"You don't drink?" I asked.

He sipped the hot coffee. "Sure. I drink. See?"

Very funny. I tried again. "It doesn't have to be a martini. I think I might have beer around here somewhere." I didn't think I'd ever met a man who didn't drink. Or at least go for the food.

Dallas picked up the pitcher of martinis and began refilling glasses. Walking up to Glacier, she put a hand under his chin and smiled down at him. I half expected him to melt into a puddle and disappear into his boots.

"Leave him alone," she said, looking down into his eyes. "I think it's sexy when a man is sober. It's more of a challenge."

Glacier looked up at her and smiled, but sort of *politely*. Not eagerly or lasciviously or adoringly, not the way most men smiled at Dallas. He seemed somehow unaffected by her touch, or by her Playmate-of-the-Year looks. She let go of him and filled my glass.

Mary Beth gathered her purse and waved a quick goodbye to everyone, apparently completely finished with this week's Martini Thursday. I walked her to the door, wondering if Dallas would still have all her clothes on when I returned.

"New rule," she said. "From now on, no men invited to Martini Thursday, agreed?"

I shrugged. "Sure. Whatever. Talk to you tomorrow." The evening was not turning out like I'd planned.

Back in the living room, Dallas and Cheyenne each had one of Glacier's hands and were trying to pull him to his feet.

"Come on," said Cheyenne. "It's salsa. You'll love it."

Judging from the pulsing sound of maracas and horns now blaring from the speakers, I was pretty sure she was talking about a dance and not a condiment. But Glacier didn't seem interested either way. And suddenly, it all became just too much for me. The chattering. The flirting. The showing off. I wanted them to leave.

"Can I see you ladies in the other room for just a minute?" I jerked my head toward the door.

They both looked at me like I was the mom and had just given them a time out. I did jazz hands to Dallas in time to the music, and it worked. She laughed.

"You okay?" asked Cheyenne, cha-chaing into the dining room where I stood near the floor to ceiling windows. Dallas was right behind her.

"Look, you guys," I said, lowering my voice, although I don't know why. Latin jazz echoed off the walls in a riotous 4/4 rhythm. I half expected Gloria Estefan to make an appearance. "I'm really sorry to pull the plug on your fun. But here's the thing. This is the first guy I've even looked at since my divorce. He might be my bald one, you know?" I said, looking at Dallas.

"Huh?" said Cheyenne.

"And I'm not really in the mood for craziness. I don't think he is either. How about we call it a night, and tomorrow night I'll treat us all to the Caribou Club?" Continuing the mother versus naughty children scenario, I offered them a treat tomorrow if they would just be good today.

"You got it," said Cheyenne, raising her hands in the air in some kind of victory salute. "Get it on, lady! But what's with the bald thing?"

"I'll tell you in the car," said Dallas, then she gave me a hug. "Be gentle with him."

I laughed, but she had a point. Glacier didn't seem like your average male – full of ego and testosterone and hubris. Well, testosterone for sure. But no hubris. I hugged them goodbye and locked the door behind them.

Back in the living room I stood just inside the door and smiled. Glacier sat, hands wrapped around his coffee cup, looking out the window, unaffected by the silly salsa music. I changed the music to Adele, dialing down the volume by half. Her soulful voice filled the room.

Glacier gave me a little nod. "Better," he said. I sat in the chair next to his and sipped my martini. He watched me but not in a way that made me feel sexy and desirable. More in a way that made me feel like I was doing something I shouldn't.

"More coffee?"

He shook his head. "I'm trying to cut back. Trying to quit, actually."

I laughed because I thought he was kidding, but he looked serious. "I'm pretty sure coffee isn't one of the great evils, is it?"

He shrugged. "Just trading one addiction for another. One more attachment."

Hmm. Interesting.

"I feel like I put a damper on Martini Thursday," he said.

"No, I just wasn't in the mood for all the noise. Sometimes it's fun. Sometimes it's just too much."

He nodded, and I tried to remember if I'd ever seduced a man without plying him with alcohol first. Then I remembered I hadn't been with anyone but Thomas since I was a senior in college. I wasn't even sure I knew *how* to seduce a man. I should have asked Dallas for a tip sheet. I sipped my drink and prepared to put the moves on him.

"I was thinking," he said.

I raised my eyebrows over the top of my martini glass and swallowed. Maybe I wasn't going to have to make the moves. Maybe he was going to make the moves. Goody.

"Have you ever thought of changing Martini Thursday?"

Here we go. Maybe it could be Third Base Thursday. Or Naked Hot Tub Thursday. Or Crazy Sex in Every Room Thursday. "What would you suggest?" I asked, deciding on an innocent look instead of a lascivious grin.

He turned to face me, leaning forward with his arms on his knees. Let the games begin, I thought. Thank God I got rid of the girls. Be gentle, I reminded myself. Not too crazy the first time. Don't scare the poor guy.

"I was thinking, Meditation Thursday."

Oh hell.

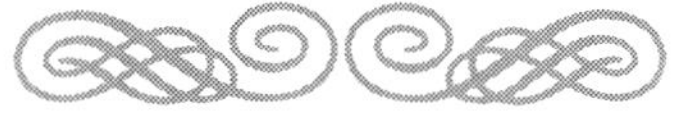

Chapter Six

As promised, I took the girls to the Caribou Club – affectionately known as the Boo. And before we could even make our way to the English pub-style bar, we were surrounded by a bevy of eager beaver suitors.

A few approached me, but my witty repartee was weak, and I wasn't feeling the least bit flirty. Most didn't even try to approach MB since she was wearing an expression of complete boredom. But Dallas was all over the attention like a hobo on a ham sandwich. Within minutes, she was at the bar with one of the fastest skiers in Aspen on her left and a filthy rich movie producer on her right. I watched as she batted her big brown boy-killers and ordered a Bou Bou – champagne, vodka, and pomegranate juice.

"I can't watch the local sycophants fawn over Dallas," said Mary Beth, even though Cheyenne wasn't around to hear the big words. Her billionaire boyfriend hadn't granted her permission to come with us tonight. Someone should have pulled him aside to let him know women had been emancipated years ago.

We picked up our martinis, and I followed MB into the Great Room where a cozy fire burned and just a few people lounged on the comfy couches and overstuffed chairs. Indian blankets, Western art, and warm lamplight gave the room a romantic sort of Western-chic atmosphere. MB and I settled into suede chairs. She seemed preoccupied, looking into the fire while I watched the steady stream of folks walking through the Great Room on their way to the bar or one of the dining rooms. Mostly well-dressed and mostly gorgeous, the parade of partiers made people watching worth the effort. Even the waiters and waitresses were beautiful. Sort of like being in LA, but with mountains.

The martini was perfect. The warm fire relaxed me. Even Mary Beth seemed to melt just a little.

"Fifty bucks says Dallas has sex in the bathroom with the skier before we finish our second drink."

"Make it a hundred," said MB. "I'll take the movie mogul. Third drink."

I smiled and waited to collect my hundred dollars.

We were into our third martini when Dallas led the movie mogul through the Great Room, winked at us, and disappeared into the elegant ladies' room.

I handed over the Benjamin, and Mary Beth tucked it away in her back pocket.

"Maybe you should try your luck in Vegas," I said, swirling my drink.

MB turned up her nose.

"Oh, sorry. I mean, maybe you should try your luck in Monte Carlo," I said. "Let me guess, you learned to gamble at boarding school. In fifth period, right after lock picking."

"Actually, it was almost every night. We'd find a window with a loose screen and hang out over the window sill, smoking cigarettes and betting on how long it would take an instructor to walk by."

It sounded fun to me, but her voice indicated otherwise.

"What was the best part about boarding school?"

Mary Beth looked toward the fireplace. "Being away from my parents, I guess."

"They were strict and mean, and you couldn't wait to get away and stretch your wings?"

"No. They were cold and distant and incapable of love."

I looked up at MB, but she was looking away. It was the most personal, most emotional statement I'd ever heard her make. And it was sad. I never imagined I would have the occasion to feel sorry for Mary Beth. Afraid of her? Sure. Frustrated with her? Most of the time. But until now never sorry for her. Maybe I was starting to see the birth of her prickly side. Maybe it had come from trying to protect herself against rejection by her own parents.

I had to know more. "So, you didn't really relate to your parents? Even when you were little?"

MB shrugged and stared into the fire. "I don't remember ever getting affection from anyone except my nanny. My father was a disciplinarian. My mother was my biggest critic."

"That's horrible," I said. "Where'd they learn to parent? From sea turtles?"

Mary Beth turned and raised one curious eyebrow at me.

"Well, sea turtles bury their eggs in the sand and then leave, and the babies have to fend for themselves," I explained. "Never mind. I'm just curious why your parents were so bad at taking care of a kid."

"Probably passed down from a long line of ancestors who insisted on a sense of decorum and finishing school etiquette. And now I worry about Alissa." Mary Beth's voice went hoarse. "She's so little. God, I just miss her so much. I know she's getting the best education, but still..."

Alissa was Mary Beth's daughter from a previous marriage. All of six years old and away at her first year of boarding school. My heart hurt for her. And for Mary Beth.

"Maybe you're the one who could change the pattern," I suggested, trying to sweep all judgment out of my voice. Trying to approach the touchy subject of child rearing with the same easy tone I might use to say, "Maybe we should check out the music later at Belly Up."

"Maybe," said Mary Beth. "I call her every day. Tell her I love her constantly. I can't stand the idea that she might feel the way I felt when I was her age. For the first ten years of my life, I thought I was bad. Thought I'd done something to deserve the indifference of my parents."

I shook my head. What a load to put on a child. I wanted to slap MB's parents and hug the little girl. Don't worry, I knew better than to hug Mary Beth. You don't hug the coolest girl in school. But the little girl, the ten-year-old, needed a hug.

I learned a lot about Mary Beth that night. I thought I might be seeing the path to her narcissism and imperialism, and maybe even the root of her psychopathic tendencies. The realization made me love her even more. Because now, not only was she interesting and really smart and just a little bit scary, she was also flawed. Like me.

And I learned a little bit about Dallas too. I learned that four Bou Bous and sex in the bathroom with a movie mogul were apparently a toxic combination for her. Because she threw up in my car on the way home.

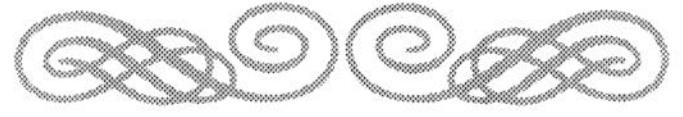

Chapter Seven

Early the next morning I strapped on my Asics trail runners and headed up Smuggler for a run. It was a great way to clear my head and organize my thoughts. Too bad that wasn't what I was doing. Like some hormone-crazed teenage girl in study hall, I had boys on the brain. Not all boys, just one. Glacier.

Martini Thursday had been a total bust. A complete waste of my favorite black silk panties – which I'd worn that night, just in case. Serves me right for trying to be the instigator of sex. Apparently I was stuck in the nineties, when instigating sex was as easy as walking across campus in short shorts. I had no idea how it was supposed to work at this point in my life. Honestly, I liked it a lot better when men were the instigators.

These deep, cerebral thoughts were interrupted by the ringing of my cell phone. Without slowing down, I dug the phone out of the pocket of my jacket.

"Hello?"

"I'm worried about Cheyenne. I think something might be wrong."

It was Dallas, and it was early. Especially for a girl who drank too many Bou Bous the night before. I could hear Baby Bentley chattering in the background with her nanny, a sweet-natured Hispanic woman who worked really cheap in exchange for room and board. In danger of being homeless when Dallas came across her through a friend, it was the perfect solution for everyone. And she was teaching Bentley to speak Spanish. Is there anything cuter than a little blond three-year-old saying "*Eres mi angel*" – you are my angel. Or "*Tu me vuelves loca*!" – you drive me crazy!"

I was just getting into my stride on Smuggler and didn't want to stop and chat. But Dallas really did sound worried, and she'd never been one of those overly dramatic kind of girls. Instead of stopping completely, I slowed to a fast walk. The trail was busy with hikers, runners, and a few mountain bikers. A woman and her three black labs nearly ran over me, all four of them wearing bright pink bandanas. I thought of my sweet Rufus and felt a sharp stab of grief. He'd been way too cool to ever wear a pink bandana. His was black and said *Bad to the Bone.*

I moved to the far right side of the trail and let them pass, but the competitor inside me balked, whining for its place in front. Once I got past the observation deck, most of the hikers and bikers would drop off, and I'd have the trail more to myself. I was probably half a mile from the deck, and then I could open up and run the eight miles of Hunter Creek Loop and come out on Red Mountain Road. My legs were itching to run.

"Lucy, are you there?"

"Yeah, sorry. I'm on Smuggler, and it's busy. Why do you think something's up with Cheyenne?"

"Well, I just called and asked her to go into town with me, and she said no. I even offered to take her to those consignment shops y'all like, you know?"

Did I ever. Cheyenne and I loved to hunt for bargains in the luxury consignment shops – more like fine boutiques than collections of dusty cast-offs. Susie's and The Little Bird on Mill Street had a laundry list of designers on their racks. And since Cheyenne had very little money of her own and wanted to dress nice for her billionaire boyfriend, the consignment shops offered the perfect solution. There was just one problem: Cheyenne had a tendency to wear *all* her jewelry and *all* her designer fashions at once. Sort of like a well-appointed bag lady who wears everything she owns to keep it from being stolen.

Mary Beth must have bought Cheyenne a line of credit in each of those shops because the last time we shopped, the owner had tallied up Shy's purchases and told her she still had over five hundred dollars' credit. Cheyenne just looked at her. The woman said, "Your gift certificate, remember?"

Cheyenne looked at me, I shrugged, and she gave me a high five. She thought her over-possessive boyfriend was behind it, but I'd bet two to one it was MB. It made shopping a hundred times more fun for Cheyenne.

So the news that she didn't want to go to the consignment shops was alarming. I'd never known her to turn down a consignment shopping trip, especially now that she had credit just waiting for her.

"You're right," I said. "There's definitely something wrong."

"What should we do?" asked Dallas.

There was nothing I wanted more than to run the loop and work off my long list of frustrations. At the very top of that list was *Being Dumped by my Ex*. The yard guys who didn't show up were near the bottom. And somewhere in the middle was Glacier Jones and all the wild monkey sex we *weren't* having.

"I'll come pick you up," I said. "We'll go to Michael's and talk to Cheyenne."

"Sorry to mess up your run, but I think we should."

Cheyenne's billionaire boyfriend, Michael, took ostentation to a whole new level. His little crib was twenty thousand square feet on sixty private acres. There was a Vegas-style fountain out front, a tree-lined pond with a fifteen-foot waterfall, a huge outdoor pool and grotto, and a herd of Arabian horses grazing lazily on this warm summer morning. Cheyenne had grown up riding horses and loved the gorgeous creatures. And therein lay part of her secret, as she had explained to me one night when I'd driven her home.

Dallas and I rang the bell and were shown inside by a petite woman wearing a starched gray uniform and white apron. Seriously, who does that? I half-expected Michael's manservant to appear. Like Alfred Pennyworth, butler to Bruce Wayne in Batman, I could imagine an older gentleman in tie and tails who laid out Michael's clothes and ran his bath and served him Glenfiddich on a small silver tray.

We were shown past the formal dining room, through the overly-large great room, and down a long, wide hallway. Just as I was wondering if we should have packed water and food for this trek, we reached the game room where we found Cheyenne curled up watching Good Morning America on a TV that took up most of one wall. The room was dark, the TV was loud, and Cheyenne didn't see us at first.

"Hey, Shy," said Dallas, moving toward the couch and sitting gently on the edge.

Cheyenne looked startled. No. More than that. She looked scared. She sat up, grabbed her oversized sunglasses from the coffee table, and put them on. Kind of strange. But, after all, it was Cheyenne. And she was going through her movie star phase.

"What are you guys doing here?" She didn't sound happy to see us. Which was also strange. Cheyenne loves everyone all the time. She loves people and activity and noise.

"We thought we'd surprise you and take you to lunch," I said, trying to think on my feet and really sucking at it.

"It's not even nine o'clock," said Cheyenne.

Dallas laughed and leaned back on the couch, pulling her legs up under her. "She means brunch," said Dallas.

"Right. Brunch," I said. "We thought we'd go up to Snowmass and sit outside. It's gorgeous out. We could start with a mimosa or a Bloody Mary. Want to?"

The blinding light of a laundry detergent commercial filled the room like a brilliant sun. Cheyenne shook her head. And when she did, Dallas leaned closer and looked at Cheyenne's face, frowning.

"What on earth happened to your cheek?"

Cheyenne's hand came up to her face and she looked away. I took a seat on her other side and gently moved her hand. Then I removed her sunglasses. A big purple and black bruise covered her cheekbone.

"What the hell!" I said.

Cheyenne shrunk back into the couch. "It's nothing. I'm such a klutz. I got up in the night and didn't turn the light on, and *whack*! I ran into the door."

"Uh-huh," I said, leaning forward and peering at the bruise.

She grabbed the glasses out of my hand and put them back on.

Dallas had gone pale. "Let me get you some ice," she said, her voice sounding strained. "Which way to the kitchen?"

Cheyenne shook her head again. "Really, it's fine. You guys go without me. Rachel Ray's on next. She's making a salad with hot dogs. I don't wanna miss that."

I looked away because it was just too hard to look at the sadness in Cheyenne's face. I looked instead at the huge built-in bar with the old fashioned soda fountain. At the billiards table and pinball machine and foosball game. And wondered, with all those toys and all that money, couldn't Michael find something better to do than punch his girlfriend in the face? I wanted to kill him.

"Is Michael here?" I asked, feeling myself getting ready for a fight.

Again, Cheyenne shook her head. "He left for New York this morning."

"When will he be back?" I wanted to make sure Cheyenne was safe.

She shrugged. "Not sure. Probably a few days."

A few days. That would give me time to figure out the best, most painful way to kill him, and then somewhere to hide the body.

Dallas and I did go to Snowmass, but without Cheyenne. And we did sit outside and we did start with a Bloody Mary. Dallas had a coupon – two for one.

I tried to enjoy the view and the perfect mix of Grey Goose, tomato juice, and spices – and the fact that it was half price. But I was too preoccupied with Cheyenne, who seemed locked in a fifty-million-dollar prison.

Dallas stirred her drink then sucked on the end of the celery stalk. And even I, who had not one gay corpuscle in my body, couldn't take my eyes off her.

When the waiter came, we both ordered eggs benedict and eventually another drink. And by the time the meal was through, we were united in our decision to keep close tabs on Cheyenne but not to do anything crazy. Dallas didn't think Cheyenne was quite ready to leave Michael.

I sighed. "Seems like she's sacrificing what she needs for what she wants."

"Exactly," said Dallas. "The harder she tries to fit into Michael's world, the more she feels like cheese whiz on a wheat thin, surrounded by fancy hors d'oeuvres. She's dazzled by all the things he makes available to her, you know? She keeps trying to find the good in that, but I think on some level she realizes she's getting short-changed."

I shook my head. "It's like that old joke. He's handed her a giant, beautifully wrapped box of horse poop, and she keeps digging through the box, thinking there's got to be a pony in there somewhere!"

Dallas laughed, and now seemed like the right time to talk about Cheyenne's secret. "You know about Cheyenne and her thing with horses, right?"

Dallas shrugged. "I know she's crazy about 'em."

"She knows everyone thinks she's after Michael's cash, but it's really more about the horses. Did you know Shy had an abusive childhood?"

"I knew it was pretty rough," said Dallas.

"She told me riding is the only time she really feels like herself. And her ex kept telling her they'd get horses someday, but kept putting her off. Even when she told him how important it was. She finally got sick of it. When she found out Michael had horses, she was all in."

Dallas looked at me. "But Michael won't even let her ride his dumb fancy horses."

"I know, the controlling bastard. He drew her in with the promise of letting her ride. It's so sad, because they're her sanctuary, you know?"

Dallas tipped her head. "How are horses tied to her abusive childhood?

"That's the part that's so hard to hear. She said it has to do with horses being the ultimate prey animal. They have no defenses. They have to be on their toes all the time, ready to run from danger."

Dallas's beautiful face looked pained.

"Their main job is to get through the day without anyone or anything hurting them." I felt my throat tighten and my eyes fill with tears. "She said she knows how that feels."

We drove down the mountain toward Dallas's house, both of us quiet. We knew we couldn't force Cheyenne to leave Michael. And that if we pushed the issue, she was likely to just dig in deeper. We agreed not to rush in and try to rescue her. For now. But that didn't mean I'd put aside my plan to get even with Michael. Or have him whacked. I'd talk it over with Mary Beth. Anyone with a matching set of lock picks and a penchant for gambling should know the best way to do away with a body.

Chapter Eight

I woke up the next morning thinking about Thomas. And Glacier. And wondering what Thomas would think if I ran into him with Glacier on my arm. And that thought made me deliriously happy. Because I was pretty sure Thomas would be crazy-jealous.

Even though Thomas can hold his own beside the most handsome man, he's older than I am by six years, has distinguished graying temples, and a slightly buttoned up countenance. Enter Glacier: A little hard to place age-wise but hunky and sexy and about as far from buttoned up as a guy can get. Thomas would look down his nose at him and be painfully polite, but inside he would be a wreck. Because Glacier would be gracious and warm and completely at ease. And I would be smiling from ear to ear and looking happier than ever. And Thomas would know I'm completely over him.

Which was so not true. But I wanted him to believe that. Even Glacier's unusual name would probably get all over Thomas.

So I got out of bed and stood in my closet, trying to figure out what a girl might wear for seducing or enticing. Or at least finally getting Glacier's attention and seeing where that might take us. But as I stood in the shower, I realized I had no idea how to get in touch with him. He had my phone number. My address. And even knew my brand of coffee and my three crazy friends. I knew almost nothing about him.

And I had to wonder, if I'd spent the past year avoiding anyone with a Y chromosome, why was I suddenly trying to track one down like some over-zealous autograph hunter trying to bag Ashton Kutcher?

I didn't really have the answer; I just knew I was drawn to him. So I decided I would drive into town and start at the bakery where we'd first met. If he wasn't there, maybe someone would know how to find him.

But this carefully contrived scheme fell apart when the doorbell rang. I was about to dry my hair and wearing only a short silk robe. I thought about not answering, but I worried it might be Dallas or Cheyenne. Or even MB, here to implicate me in her next crime.

Sometimes life is funny. And the thing you least expect happens. Because standing on my porch was none other than Glacier Jones.

"Good morning," I said, cracking the door and feeling self-conscious about my wet hair, tiny lavender robe, and no makeup.

He smiled and held up a cloth bag. "I brought breakfast. Let's take a drive."

He could see just the smallest sliver of my face. Otherwise, he would have seen my look of complete surprise. Breakfast? A drive? Maybe my powers of seduction were better than I thought.

"I'm not dressed," I said. "Wet hair. No makeup. Come back in an hour."

"Ten minutes. No makeup. Leave your hair wet. It looks nice like that."

His slow, gravelly, just-woke-up voice was irresistible. "Want to come in?"

He shook his head and turned to look out over the front deck. "I'll stay out here. Ten minutes."

I shrugged and closed the door. Then ran upstairs like a madwoman to put on mascara, lip-gloss, deodorant, white shorts, and a red T-shirt.

I didn't know what Glacier had in mind, and since he always wore boots that bore evidence of many dusty miles, I decided not to chance wearing good shoes. I slipped into a pair of gray and red New Balance running shoes, grabbed my purse, and was out the door in eight minutes.

"How's that for fast?" I asked. Glacier sat with one hip resting on the low stone wall that ran along the deck at the front of my house.

"Fast," he said, and I noticed he wasn't wearing a watch. He reached inside the canvas bag and pulled out a tall plastic glass with a lid. The whole thing disappeared inside his huge hand as he passed the glass to me. "Breakfast," he said, then reached in the bag for another glass for himself.

I looked at the thick, purpley-colored stuff. "Smoothie?"

He nodded. "Full of natural, organic ingredients. I thought you could use some balance to your martini and five-star-food diet."

Aw. Nice to know someone cared. "No coffee this morning?"

Glacier smiled with one side of his mouth and didn't answer, meaning he'd probably already scarfed a cup or two.

He led me down the stone steps to an old blue Ford pickup. The passenger door squeaked tiredly when he opened it for me, and I climbed in smiling to myself. It had been a while – okay, make that never – since I'd been escorted to a rusty, battered pickup.

An Indian blanket in all the colors of a sunrise covered the front seat, and a hawk feather hung from the rearview mirror by a leather cord. I took a tentative sip of the smoothie and was pleasantly surprised. Taking a bigger sip, I could feel it coating my upper lip in a purple mustache. Licking my lips as Glacier climbed in on the driver's side, I held up my glass.

"This is good stuff. You make these yourself?"

He nodded and touched his glass to mine. "Cheers."

He turned the key in the ignition and the truck coughed and wheezed and sounded like it was on its last legs, but it finally started and we rolled away from the house.

"Where to?" I asked.

"You'll see."

I had a split second of panic when I realized not one soul on earth had any idea where I was or who I was with. If Glacier decided to chop me up into little pieces and put me in his freezer – beside the wheat germ and whey and flaxseed, and whatever else was in this smoothie – no one would ever find me, and Glacier would surely get away with murder. But then I looked out the windshield at the brilliant summer day, the big blue sky and aspen trees glittering in the sun, and decided it was time to quit being a crybaby and grow some mettle.

I sipped my very healthy smoothie and imagined it squeezing the vodka out of my liver while adding iron to my blood and a spring to my step. Glacier took a side road I'd never been on, and soon we were driving along the edge of the Elk Range. Even Glacier, who was surely used to the spectacular views of this magnificent valley, seemed awed by the scene before us. He pulled the old truck off the road, cut the engine, and the beautiful summer day filled the space between us. He smiled at me.

"Best seat in the house," he said and got out of the truck.

I followed him a few yards to a large flat rock. He climbed up and offered his hand to me, pulling me effortlessly up beside him. And I had to admit, it was definitely the best seat in the house. Maybe the universe. We sat in silence and sipped our smoothies as birds chattered noisily around us.

Glacier pointed out a fox, running along the ridge. And as he did, I noticed a tattoo on his left biceps.

"What's that?" I asked, sliding his sleeve up enough to see. His skin was golden brown in the morning sun, his arm muscular and tight. I had to stop myself from petting him. My fingers longed to run the length of his arm, skin to skin.

He let me move his T-shirt and then watched my face as I read the tattoo. "*Here.*" I cocked my head to the side. "What's that supposed to mean? Is it a work in progress? Is it going to say more? Like 'Here lies Glacier Jones…'"

He chuckled. "No. That's all. Just *Here.*"

I frowned at him. "So, what does it mean?"

He looked at me, one side of his mouth turned up in a smile. I wanted to reach out and cup my hands around his face, lay him back on the big flat rock...

"What do you think it means?" he asked.

I forced myself to focus. "Here," I said, trying out the word. "Wait a minute, is there anything on the other side?"

He twisted slightly so I could see his right arm, which read *Now.* I screwed up my face at him, because *now* I was really confused. I mean, why not just a heart with his mom's name or a buxom pinup like every other guy?

"*Now*? Now what?"

"What does *now* mean to you?" he asked.

"Now. Just...now. Right now. Right here."

He smiled.

"Here and now," I said. "Right here and right now?"

A bigger smile and a nod. "Yes."

"But so what?" I asked, not impressed. "Right here and right now, and then what?"

"And then, nothing," he said in a quiet voice.

"But what's the big deal? I mean, it has to be a big deal, or why would you put it in ink?"

"It is a big deal," he said. "It's all that matters."

"Here and now? That's all that matters? Are you kidding me?"

He looked at me, clearly not kidding me. But I didn't get it. Maybe this guy was too weird for me after all.

"What about the future?" I asked. "That's all we have."

"But we don't have the future," he said. "We only have right now. This moment."

I shook my head and looked out over the mountains, wondering where this guy came from and why he couldn't just have a funny tattoo with a great story about getting trashed on tequila in a bar in Mexico. And that reminded me of something I wanted to ask him.

"So, Glacier...your parents named you that?"

He turned to look at me, and his eyes cut through me. I imagined a glacier cutting through water. Or more like water moving around the glacier. That was a better analogy, because it seemed like everything moved around Glacier Jones so smoothly, in perfect order.

"They named you for your eyes, right? Because your eyes are icy blue?"

He smiled at me, sort of like you would a five-year-old who'd said something cute. "No. Not for my eyes."

"You have to admit, it's pretty original," I said. "So, did your parents tell you how they came up with the name?"

"When I was twelve years old, they told me there was symbolism behind my name. But that it was up to me to discover what it was."

"How did they know you'd be able to live up to it?"

"My father's always been spiritual, even when he was young. He had a keen sense of intuition by the time I was born."

"Like knowing something will happen before it does? Like a gut feeling?"

He nodded. "Some people think of intuition as knowledge without effort. Without using the senses."

"And where are your very intuitive parents now? Do they know you're calling before the phone rings? When you give them a gift, do they know what it is before they open it?"

Glacier didn't react to my sarcasm. "They travel a lot," he said, probably wanting to push me off the rock into the canyon. "Right now they're in Myanmar, helping victims of Cyclone Nargis."

Well, that wiped the silly grin off my face. At that very moment, my parents were probably downing Bloody Marys at Applebee's.

"And so, did you? Discover the meaning of your name?"

He nodded. "I think I did."

"You've been spiritual all your life? Like your father?"

He looked away from me out over the valley to the range of mountains beyond. His peaceful countenance and deep composure seemed to slip just a bit. He seemed almost upset, although I couldn't explain why I got that feeling from him.

"No," he finally said. Which surprised me.

"So when did you get all *here and now*? Tell me the story behind your name. Come on, please?"

I tried to tease him back to his prior peaceful self, but he wasn't having it. He just sat looking across the valley.

He finally turned to look at me, studying my face as if trying to read something in my eyes. Then he drained his smoothie and set the glass aside. "You're not ready."

"What's that supposed to mean?" I asked, irritated. What did he want from me? How do you make yourself *ready* to hear the meaning behind some hippy-dippy name from parents who were probably smoking a giant doobie and weaving their own ponchos at the time they named him?

He looked at me. "When you understand *here* and *now*. When you appreciate the importance of living in this moment, then you'll be ready."

Screw that, I thought, finishing off my smoothie. Here and now was over. I was ready for whatever came next.

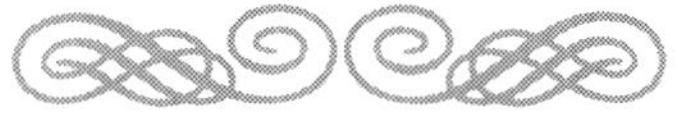

Chapter Nine

In stark contrast to my ethereal morning of word games and a pop quiz on the meaning of life, my evening was more like a reality show with Dallas and Mary Beth as its stars – unscripted and dramatic.

We were at Jimmy's – an upscale but unpretentious bar and restaurant, known for its great American food and its "Jimmy" signatures on the walls. We sat at a table in the bar area, surrounded by a mix of under-dressed locals and over-dressed tourists. It was a high-energy crowd with loud laughter coming from the dining room. We were halfway through our second round of martinis and had just exhausted the topic of Cheyenne and her billionaire butthead when the waitress came to our table with another round of drinks.

"From the gentleman at the bar," she said, smiling and unloading the tray of martinis. I looked to see a somewhat handsome guy, mid-forties, good hair, and wearing an Alexander McQueen sport shirt. I recognized it from my last trip to Barney's, where I'd actually looked to see if they had it in Thomas's size. Old habits die hard.

I watched as Dallas gave the man a little wave. We cashed in on a lot of free drinks when Dallas was with us.

"Okay, Dallas. Do your thing. Go thank him for us." Mary Beth tipped her glass to her lips, ignoring the man completely.

Dallas approached the man at the bar and offered her hand. His eyes lit up, and I'm guessing his penis said howdy. I mean really, how could it not. He stood and offered a barstool to Dallas. Then he ordered her yet another drink because she'd left both of hers on our table. Good. More for us. I was determined to overcome the healthy karmic cleansing of my liver and other organs from Glacier's New Age all natural here-and-now smoothie. That much organic stuff can't be good for you.

"MB, do you know anything about here and now? You know, living in the moment?"

Mary Beth looked at me as if I'd just offered her the leftover half-eaten meatloaf from the plate of the woman behind us. "Have you been watching Oprah again?"

Dallas came over with her man. "Mary Beth, Lucy, this is David. He invited us to dinner at Cache Cache. Doesn't that sound like fun?"

I looked at MB, who looked away – clearly giving me the signal for "I'd rather be boiled in oil."

"Very nice of you to offer," I said, "but Mary Beth has a bit of headache." Make that – Mary Beth *is* a bit of a headache. "Why don't the two of you go on?"

"Are you sure?" asked Dallas. "We could just stay here, and David could join us."

"No, no," said Mary Beth, maybe a bit too emphatically. "You go on...enjoy your dinner. We'll be right here."

I watched as Dallas and the man, who until half an hour ago had been a complete stranger, walked toward the door, he with his hand at the small of her back.

"Do you think she'll be okay?" I asked.

"Well, let's see." MB looked at me and acted as if she was giving real thought to the question. "Every man in this town wants to have sex with Dallas. Just walking into a place nets her free cocktails and a dinner for two. Bartenders fawn over her. Maître'd's give her the best tables. Yep. I think she'll be fine."

I gave her a look. "I mean, do you think she'll be *safe?*"

"Oh. Let's see. She's in a public place, she's just down the street, and if he touches a hair on her head, I'll kill him with my bare hands. Shall we eat?"

Did we ever. Big warm pretzel sticks with mustard, and crab cakes with sautéed mushrooms. But I could hardly enjoy all the calories and cholesterol for worrying about Dallas. It was one thing for her to hook up with a man, treat him to bathroom sex, then ride home with us, regaling us with the titillating details. But it was another to watch her walk off with a stranger and hope he wasn't a psycho or a pervert or a drunk driver. Of course, MB represented two out of three of those, but that was different.

We ordered dessert and coffee, and I was about to suggest we walk over to Cache Cache and kidnap Dallas. I knew MB would look at me like I was the fly in her punchbowl of life, but I didn't care. Maybe Cheyenne wouldn't let us protect her from her abusive boyfriend, but we could at least try to watch out for Dallas.

In the end, I didn't have to risk the wrath of MB because Dallas walked in the door, holding her man by the hand and wearing a big smile.

"Here she is," said David. "I return Dallas to you, none the worse."

Dallas gave him a peck on the cheek and thanked him. Which was a far cry from the way she normally *thanked* a man. Poor David. I guess he wasn't restroom-sex worthy.

"I'll call you," he said, smiling at Dallas, then walked out the door.

Dallas slid in beside me at our table.

"Sorry it didn't go well," I said, moving my key lime pie over so Dallas could take a bite.

"Are you kidding?" she said, putting a tiny bite on her fork. "This could be the one."

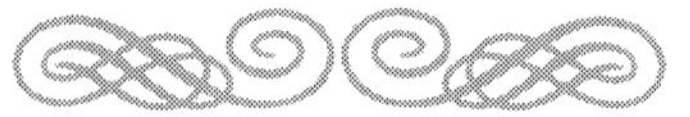

Chapter Ten

It was Dallas's turn to host Martini Thursday at her house. She has a thing for fresh flowers, and there were always sunflowers in her kitchen and usually an orchid or two in her living room. But tonight there was a huge vase sitting front and center on the coffee table – yellow spider mums, calla lilies, tulips, and gladiolas spewing from a crystal vase filled with lemons. It was all sunshiny and happy but also elegant – just like Dallas.

"From your guy?" I asked, taking a seat on one of the two couches in front of the fireplace.

"Aren't they perfect?" Dallas handed Mary Beth and me each a martini. Cheyenne had yet to show up, and each passing minute made me worry more about her. But Dallas assured us Cheyenne was just running a little late. It was my plan to knock some sense into her – check that – to *encourage her* to leave her abusive butthead and come and stay with me for a while. I may not have a stable of Arabian horses, but at least I wouldn't hurt her. Besides, if I *did* have a horse, I would darn sure let her ride it.

I kicked off my sandals and tucked my feet up under me on the comfy couch. I really did love Dallas's style. Unpretentious. Inviting. Warm and friendly. Mary Beth sat in her normal way, sort of regally, with one arm across the back of the couch and her legs crossed, sipping her drink. For some reason I thought of Cleopatra. A little more eyeliner, an ornate headdress, and a gold snake around her upper arm? She caught me looking at her and raised an eyebrow. I turned to Dallas.

"So the guy," I said, taking a small sip. Dallas wasn't the best martini maker in the world. "You really like him?"

Dallas curled up on the opposite couch and hugged a fringed pillow to her impressive chest. "Oh y'all. He makes me about as happy as a bird with a French fry!"

I laughed. I knew that was one of her mom's favorite sayings.

"He's everything I've dreamed of. He looks good, dresses nice, he's super smart. He has a sense of humor. And nice manners."

"And," said Mary Beth, setting her martini on the coffee table, "I guess his cupidity is part of the draw?"

Dallas looked at me and sort of frowned. "Oh. You mean the flowers? I definitely love a man who sends flowers." Her look was so sweet you could spread it on a cupcake, and I couldn't bear for Mary Beth to lessen that in any way.

"Really Mary Beth? Cupidity? God, if you're bound and determined to teach us all a new word, at least make it something we can use without people laughing at us."

Mary Beth shrugged and smiled.

"She means," I said, shooting the stink eye at MB, "David probably has a desire to be successful, you know, wealthy. That always helps."

Dallas nodded. "Oh. Sorry. I thought cupidity, cupid, you know. Who uses that word anyway? But for sure, he's successful. Some kind of land developer. He's only here visiting, but he's looking for something to buy."

The doorbell rang, and as Dallas rose to answer the door I turned to Mary Beth.

"Seriously? Cupidity? Give it a rest because I forgot to bring my Thesaurus."

Cheyenne and Dallas came into the living room, chattering away like chipmunks. Cheyenne was, of course, wearing her new favorite accessory. Tonight's sunglasses sported black ovals with leopard print temples. They fought valiantly for attention with her short, tight giraffe print jersey dress in bright blue. But the dress was winning.

I gave her a big hug, then looked her over. She blushed, but as far as I could tell, there were no new marks of her boyfriend's hostility, and she was either wearing a lot of concealer or the previous bruise was nearly gone.

She sat beside Dallas and listened while Dallas caught her up on the story of her newest Prince Charming. I'd been afraid Cheyenne would come in all depressed and gloomy and feeling like a whipped dog. But she was the opposite – all smiles and enthusiasm and perkiness as usual.

"Look at this," said Cheyenne when Dallas finally took a break from itemizing the super-human qualities of her newest conquest. She held out her right hand, showing us a large, gaudy bauble on her ring finger. It probably cost more than MB's car, but it was so big and showy, it looked like something that might have come in a plastic egg with a ball of gum.

Dallas made the appropriate oohing and ahhing noises while I smiled at Cheyenne and MB looked away as if gazing directly at the ring might damage her eyes.

"Isn't it totally the bomb? Michael took me to dinner last night and this little baby was hidden in my dessert! Isn't that the coolest? And I know what you're all thinking."

God, I really hoped she didn't. Because I was thinking that must have been some bigass dessert.

"But he's super sorry for getting a little peeved the other night. And he promised it'll *never* happen again. And he's taking me to St. Bart's! Can you even believe that? It's in the West Indies – wherever that is – and he's got this fancy yacht all lined up. I can't wait!"

Oh boy. She looked so happy. Completely placated. As if a bauble and a boat could make up for the fact that he'd smacked her right in the face. Or in her words, *got a little peeved.*

"He got me a passport, which usually takes forever, but he somehow got them to fast-forward it."

And as Cheyenne basked in her happiness, all I could think of was talking her out of going. "When do you leave?" I asked.

"Tomorrow! Isn't it great?"

No, I thought. Not so great. "Cheyenne, maybe you should think about this—"

MB put her hand on my leg to shut me up. Dallas was asking Cheyenne what kind of clothes she was planning to pack, and I looked at Mary Beth. She didn't look back at me, but instead of wearing her usual bored look, she looked like she had that day I was crying over my dog.

"I'm really happy for you, Shy," said Dallas, "but you need to be careful."

Cheyenne waved the concern away. "Really, you guys. Everything's super good. Michael and I worked everything out, and things are going totally good for him at work. I think this trip is just the ticket."

But I wasn't so sure. What if things got *super bad*? What if some little thing set him off, and she was halfway around the world in St. Bart's? And while Cheyenne went on about the cute bikini she'd bought and the fun sundress and the cute sandals – which I hoped were a little less busy than the multicolored wedgie flip-flops she wore tonight – I looked to Mary Beth for help. I wanted to stop Cheyenne to keep her from going. I wanted to keep her safe. But all MB gave me was the slightest shake of her head, as if to say, "shut up, there's nothing we can do."

I ignored her and leaned forward. "Cheyenne, maybe you should just give it a little time before you go away with Michael. Make sure he's settled down and isn't going to blow up and hit you again."

Cheyenne looked at me as if *I* were the one who had hit her. Her face crumpled, and she slumped back into the couch. A tear slid down her face, and she angrily wiped it away.

"You guys would never understand," she said in a sad, tired voice. "How could you? All your lives, you probably got everything you wanted."

It is just no fun at all trying to convince someone you love that there is no pony in their beautifully wrapped box of horse poop.

She wiped at another tear, and then the inner fireball of grit and enthusiasm that normally drove her every minute of every day returned. She pushed herself forward on the couch and finally, blessedly, took off her sunglasses and looked at us.

"I'm always the outsider," she said, trying to make us understand. "While everyone parties their asses off, what am I usually doing? Serving cocktails. Cleaning up the mess. Watching from behind the bar while my feet ache and my back feels like I'll bite it if I lift another case of beer. It's finally *my* turn!" She thumped herself on the chest. "With Michael, I'm finally at the party." And before any of us could respond, she grabbed her sunglasses and left.

Suddenly the pieces started to fit together. The cheerful enthusiasm she brought to every situation always seemed a little like she was trying too hard. She wore her *gotta-party* attitude to every gathering – along with her mismatched second-hand designer get-ups – because she just wanted to be part of the crowd. It was heartbreaking. There was a sense of desperation to her light-heartedness, and now I thought maybe I understood. She just wanted what the whole rest of the world wanted. A sense of belonging.

Dallas ran after Cheyenne. MB turned and gave me a look that clearly said "I tried to tell you." And then she said the most profound thing.

"We can't help her until she's ready to be helped. Whenever that is, we'll be here."

Chapter Eleven

After Cheyenne left, we exhausted the topic of how to help her and downed another round of martinis. Then Dallas lightened the mood by going on about how darn happy she was.

"I'm serious, y'all," she said, curling up on the couch in a graceful ball. "I just have a feeling he's the one. There's not anything about him I want to change, and that never happens."

"Dallas, seriously, you've known him all of four days," said MB. "How can you be so sure already?"

I was proud of Mary Beth for leaving her world of superlative vocabulary behind for a nanosecond. The drama with Cheyenne had worn me out, and I didn't think I had it in me to translate for the rest of the night.

"We had a long lunch yesterday," said Dallas, glowing with love or lust or whatever sits between the two. "And I just totally fell for him. I usually let the guy do most of the work. But this one's different. I really want him to like me. It's like being back in high school all over again."

"Oh brother," I said, imagining Dallas in high school. Gorgeous, popular, every poor adolescent guy's dream girl – just like she was in college. "I supposed this is where you tell us you were homely and gangly as a teenager and how you still see yourself as that knock-kneed, buck-toothed, four-eyed nerd."

"No," she said, taking a sip of her drink. "I pretty much looked like this as a teenager."

"Yeah," I said, "that's what I thought."

"But I was really self-conscious. My clothes were mostly hand-me-downs my mom bought at Goodwill. And none of the girls could have sleepovers with me because I lived in such a rotten part of town. I didn't want guys seeing where I lived, so I just started making up stories. Like we were having our house redone by a famous Hollywood decorator – who was painfully slow because he was also decorating Tom Cruise's house and had to fly back and forth. Or that my parents were missionaries and we gave all our nice clothes away to help raise money for people in South America. Or that I couldn't go out for cheerleading because my father was a prince from Iran and they didn't allow women to jump."

I laughed. "Did the other kids actually buy these stories?"

Dallas shrugged. "Sometimes. I used to sit on the front steps of our trailer and daydream that my mother was Naomi Judd – she loved to sing The Judds' songs when I was a kid – and my father was George Straight, who my mom was totally in love with back then. And we lived in Nashville and I had my own wing of the mansion, and I dressed exactly like Madonna. And I was popular at school."

She laughed, and it was all said in a funny way. But there was a look in her eye that didn't quite match her laugh.

"Well, I don't think you'll have to make up any stories to get your new guy to like you," I said. "Because now you *can* dress like Madonna if you want to. And you live in a really nice part of town. And I'm pretty sure they even let women in Iran jump now."

Dallas pushed her hair back over her shoulder. "You never know what goes through a guy's mind. But we can talk about anything, so that's a good sign. We both want kids."

"That's propitious," said Mary Beth, "since you already have one. Where is that little cutie?"

"The nanny took her across the way for a play date." She looked at her watch. "They'll be back any minute since it's almost time for bed. And David *loves* Bentley. Yesterday she crawled up in his lap and started talking a blue streak to him. And he practically had little hearts coming out of his eyes like on cartoons. She definitely has a way with the guys."

An image flashed through my mind, and unfortunately, right out my mouth. "Just think," I said, "in twenty years or so it'll be Bentley, drinking martinis with her girlfriends and having sex in the bathroom of Cache Cache with some industry titan billionaire." I laughed. I thought I was sort of clever. But all the color drained out of Dallas's face.

"Don't even say that!" she said, holding her hand up to her heart.

"What's wrong?" I said, confused.

Dallas shook her head. "Bentley won't drink. Definitely not martinis," she said, setting hers down. "Maybe a glass of wine once in a while with dinner. And she won't have...."

"Sex," I said, laughing. It was the first time I'd ever known Dallas to be shy about using the word.

"She won't be doing that in bathrooms," said Dallas, sounding hurt. "You love Bentley. You're her godmother. How can you say that about her?"

Wow, I felt horrible. I did love Bentley. With all my heart. And I hadn't meant anything by it. I was just goofing around, and Dallas should have known by then that when I drink, my filters get fuzzy. I was just about to apologize when Mary Beth – a girl who has probably never been accused of being subtle – sharpened things to a fine point.

"Well, if it's wrong for Bentley, did you ever think it might be wrong for you?" asked Mary Beth in a surprisingly gentle tone. "Not so much the martinis," she said, holding on to hers protectively, "but maybe the bathroom assignations in the Caribou Club? I'm first in line when it comes to youthful rebellion, but you might want to reconsider now that you're thirty-five and have Bentley to think about."

You could have heard an olive pick drop. There it was. The thing we'd all wanted to say to Dallas. And even though Mary Beth had used a soft, compassionate voice, even though she was trying to help Dallas, and even though she loved and cared about her and Bentley, the words hung in the room like a bad smell.

I got up and sat beside Dallas, putting my arm around her. "Honey, I'm so sorry I started this. You know I get mouthy when I drink. And Mary Beth just means—"

"I know what she's saying," said Dallas in a wooden tone. She looked hurt, pulling away from me and curling tighter into the couch.

It was too late. I couldn't get myself or Mary Beth out of this one. I couldn't translate in a way that would take the sting out of the words or the look of shame off Dallas's face.

"Maybe she's right," she said, then looked down, concentrating on picking at a cuticle.

Mary Beth downed the rest of her drink and looked uncomfortable. Even though she was kind of a badass, she was not a mean, heartless badass.

"Sorry," she said after a pregnant pause during which we just looked at each other. "I just worry about you. I don't want anything to happen to you."

Better, I thought. Much better. Dallas rested her sad eyes on Mary Beth.

"So, more about David," I said in a much-too-cheery voice, leaning in to get Dallas's attention. "Tell us everything. Has he been married before? Does he already have kids? Where does he live when he's not hanging around Aspen?"

She looked up at me, and a tiny smile started at the corners of her mouth. She reached for her martini and sat back on the couch. Dallas wasn't one to pout.

"Well, he wants to get to know my friends. He invited all y'all to the Boo tomorrow night, and you can ask your questions then. We'll all have a Bou-Bou and celebrate me being in love."

Mary Beth made a little noise at the mention of what she considered an offensive drink - something between a gag and coughing up a hairball. But I was relieved to see Dallas smiling again. And if drinking a Bou-Bou would show my support, I planned to choke one down.

I woke in the middle of the night and started worrying. About Cheyenne and what would happen if Michael got violent and there was no one around to help her. And how I needed to remember to get the ice machine in the bar fixed. And about Dallas and Baby Bentley, how I wanted all good things for them and maybe Mary Beth's admonishment would help put an end to Dallas's fetish for bathroom sex. And how I needed to find a deal on a new pair of running shoes. And how in the hell had I ended up sleeping alone at the ripe old age of thirty-five. And what would happen to me now that I'd been dumped by the love of my life. And how would I ever stop feeling so lonely when the only man who might even possibly be my new bald one talks to me in riddles or not at all.

And that got me thinking about Glacier. About how he never seems to worry about anything. Except maybe for that few minutes on the mountain the other day when I asked him about being spiritual all his life. But how most of the time he was so peaceful and calm. And how I really wanted me a whole bunch of that.

So after tossing and flopping around in my bed for another couple of hours, I got up early for a run, then dropped in at Main Street Bakery. And sure enough, there he was sitting at the same table in a patch of warm morning sun that seemed to hover over just him. He was reading that same battered book. And wore that same serene look.

This morning the bakery was humming with activity, every table full. There were shouts from the kitchen and the noisy clatter of dishes, and an overall sense of happy chaos. Waitresses zigged and zagged across the small room, arms loaded with plates of hot breakfast. A line of people was even waiting for a table. But I didn't have to wait in line. I had a reservation.

I walked over to Glacier's small table and sat across from him. He looked up and smiled.

"Still reading the Big Book of Answers?"

He nodded slightly.

"Can I have a look?" I reached out my hand. "I could really use some answers."

Glacier closed the book, set it on the table, and rested his elbow on top. "Maybe someday."

It was said in a cheerful way. But still. "For a guy who's all *here and now and live in the moment*, you sure have a way of putting me off."

He smiled his easy smile, a rock of serenity in the midst of the racket and madness of the breakfast rush. I leaned forward, wanting to be heard over the noise.

"I'm ready," I said, hearing the fervor, the near desperation in my voice. I took a breath and tried to dial down a little.

"Ready for what?" He was so relaxed, so unhurried. It made me feel even more wound up for some reason.

"I'm ready for here and now, living in the moment, whatever it is that makes you so peaceful. I need to know more about it."

I thought I saw compassion in his eyes. Or was it pity? "There's not really anything to know. It's a practice."

"So practice makes perfect?"

He nodded. "Yes."

I was getting frustrated. "So tell me about it. What does it mean exactly?"

"What do you think it means?"

"Come on! Cut the word games. Just tell me!" My voice was loud and rang out through the breakfast crowd, causing a few people to turn and look.

And finally Glacier's smooth persona seemed to crack a little. A line formed between his eyebrows, and he leaned slightly forward. "There's nothing to tell, Lucy!" He sounded more like a regular guy now, when you've pushed him too far.

"Why are you being pissy with me?" I asked before I could stop myself. It hurt my feelings. I thought he would help me. I thought he would understand.

"I'm not being *pissy*!" he said, his face tight and angry. And then all at once, as if he suddenly realized just how pissy he was being, he sat back. He looked away from me and ran a hand over his face. And I was equal parts scared and relieved. Part of me didn't like seeing this human-ness, this regular guy-ness about him. I needed him to be the superhuman teacher with all the answers, the one who would save me. But part of me, maybe slightly less than half of me, was relieved to see he was capable of emotion after all.

Within the space of a minute, the old Glacier started to come back. As if rubbing his hand over his face somehow rubbed away crankypants Glacier, and the slow breath he blew out sent with it all his anger and frustration. He still wasn't looking at me though, and I wished I could hear whatever was going through his head.

When he finally turned back to me, his face had softened. The little line between his eyebrows was almost gone. If possible, his voice became even more soothing. "There's nothing to tell, Lucy. It's the simple act of not regretting the past, and not worrying about the future. It's about enjoying right now. And not letting anything else intrude."

Which was kind of ironic, if you thought about it. Because he had clearly just let me intrude on his moment in a big way. "This moment? Right now?"

He nodded.

"I can do that," I said.

"Okay, let's do that." He smiled at me.

"I need coffee," I said.

"I'll get it for you."

I stared at him and frowned as he stood. This was new, him getting me coffee.

I watched as he wound his way through the crowded tables and walked over to the coffee bar. His movements were slow and deliberate, just like his words. He waited patiently while a woman in a gray sweatshirt and a hairnet added stacks of fresh mugs and refilled the cream pitchers. Then he filled one of the heavy white mugs with steaming coffee and brought it to me. He placed a napkin on the table in front of me and placed the mug on top.

"Thank you," I said, smiling, starting to relax.

He bowed slightly and sat across from me.

"Where's yours?" I asked, wrapping my hands around the mug.

"None for me," he said.

"Really? You're off coffee?"

He didn't answer. Ah-hah. No wonder he was pissy.

I blew on the coffee and looked at him over my mug. "Come here often?"

He smiled and nodded. "Fairly often."

I took a sip. "Good coffee. Good way to start the day. You sure you don't want some?"

He crossed one leg over his knee and rested his hands in his lap.

"So, have you had a good week?"

He nodded.

I sighed and looked away, focusing on the activity buzzing around me. I'd always thought of myself as pretty good at small talk. In my former life with Thomas, I'd been to countless cocktail parties and formal dinners, forced to chat up some of the most unchatty people on earth. But this was ridiculous. With determination on my side, I tried again, raising my voice as a cute red-haired girl bussed the table beside us and a couple waiting in line rushed to claim the table.

"We had some drama this week. Cheyenne – you met her the night you came to my house – anyway, she got into it with her boyfriend. Who is a complete butthead in my opinion. Wealthy. Full of himself. And apparently sometimes violent. We spent the week trying to figure out how to help her."

I told him all of this hoping he might have a wise solution. But when he looked at me and didn't respond, I realized I'd done it again. Moved out of here and now and into last week. So I stopped talking, looked down at my coffee, and regrouped.

It was now an issue. I knew without a doubt I could sure as hell do here and now just as well as the next person. Probably not as well as Glacier but better than the average woman. So instead of talking, I concentrated on staying in the moment. I looked at him, studied his face, his lips, those icy eyes. He seemed relaxed and calm now and completely comfortable with my scrutiny. Before today, I was beginning to think he was not so much calm and centered but a complete freak of nature. Right up until the moment he'd lost patience with me. Maybe he wasn't a freak after all.

I concentrated on his clear blue eyes – fringed with dark brown lashes and so serene – and I had the sudden sensation of falling. Spilling headlong into their peaceful glistening blue, like taking a dive into the ocean. I imagined him in my bed, staring down at me from that ocean of blue. And I realized I was no longer doing here and now because I could certainly not take him to my bed – not here. And not now.

"How did you become so peaceful?" I asked instead.

He stiffened just slightly and took longer than usual to answer. "I had to seek it out. I had to work through a lot of stuff, and look inside."

"I don't really have time to look inside. And if I did, I'd probably be afraid of what I saw."

I was kidding. I thought I was kind of funny. Glacier didn't crack a smile.

"When it gets painful enough. When this life becomes so painful that you want something different, that's when you'll seek something else."

"Is that what happened to you?" I asked. "Your life became so painful, you needed something different?"

It was fascinating to watch. This man who was usually so open, so easy-going, seemed to close up. It wasn't a physical move. It wasn't an angry thing. He didn't cross his arms over his chest or back away. It was all in the eyes. Something dark came over his clear blue eyes.

"Yes," he finally said. "Something really bad happened. Something I wasn't prepared for."

Seeing the sadness in his eyes was like looking in a mirror. And to my great embarrassment, tears sprang to my eyes before I could stop them. I looked away and used my napkin to dab my eyes.

Why couldn't he just wave his magic wand, or give me the secret word, the quick fix to feeling better? Why did he have to expose the bleeding wound inside of me?

"Yeah," I said, sniffing and balling the napkin in my lap. "I'm there. Something really bad happened. And I most definitely wasn't prepared for it. And I *am* seeking. I'm asking you for your help. But I feel like you keep talking in riddles and putting me off. And I can't do this on my own. I can't find my way to the other side of this. I've tried."

I don't know if it was the tears or the honesty or maybe his own memory of what it felt like to be where I was. But suddenly Glacier was approachable again. "Lucy, I'm not putting you off. I know how it feels, I had to fight my demons too. I still do. You have everything you need, inside yourself. You just have to reach for it."

I was so frustrated. "I don't know what that means! I don't know how to look inside. I don't know how to reach for the answers. I only know that my life was perfect. And now I'm alone. And there's no way out."

He shook his head gently back and forth. "You're never alone."

I thought he was going to say something about how he would always be there for me or that I could always count on him. But he didn't.

"Do you ever get out in nature and just be?" His voice was soft and compassionate.

"What do you mean *just be*? I'm in nature all the time. Seriously, we're in Aspen. We're surrounded by nature."

"Do you ever spend any time just being quiet, just being by yourself?"

I frowned at him. "Well, I take a run up Smuggler nearly every morning. It's sort of crowded usually, but most of the time I do the whole loop and not many people do that. It's pretty quiet at the top."

"Find a place that's quiet. Somewhere peaceful where you won't be interrupted. Find a place like that and sit by yourself and just get quiet. Just be."

I nodded. Finally. I mean, it was strange advice. But at least it wasn't a riddle. Or a word game. Or a question I didn't know the answer to. Somewhere peaceful. Get quiet. I could do that.

"Okay." I wiped again at my nose with the napkin, feeling a little better.

He looked at me, and some of the sadness had faded from his eyes. I wanted to know about this horrible thing that had the power to wipe the smile from his face so easily. His demons. I wanted to reach across the table and take his big hands in mine. I wanted to spend time with him somewhere besides a small wooden table in the middle of a crowded bakery.

"You wanna come with us to the Caribou Club tonight? Dallas has a new man. She thinks this guy might be the real deal. We'll have a cocktail, then some dinner. It'll be fun."

He finally smiled and leaned back in his chair. "I don't think so, but thanks."

I wasn't really surprised. "That's just not your thing, is it?"

He shook his head. "No. It's not my thing."

I checked my watch. "I better get going." I reached in my purse for money for the coffee. Glacier held up a hand.

"I've got it."

"Thanks," I said, standing. As usual, he kept his seat. But he looked up at me.

"Look inside."

I looked at him and shrugged. "I'll try."

Chapter Twelve

We walked into the Boo, David and his three angels, and he seemed proud as punch to have Dallas on his arm. Tonight she wore a pink knit dress that showed off her impressive breasts, but not so much that she looked trashy.

The cozy Great Room was full of stuffy old people – couples in their forties – so we sat at the bar even though it was crowded. Mary Beth and I sat on either side of Dallas with David standing just behind her. We looked like salt and pepper shakers beside Dallas who stood out as the fancy main course. MB wore a white silk pantsuit, and I wore all black, the classic good guy/bad guy duo. Although if MB was the good guy, we were all in a heap of trouble.

True to my word, I joined Dallas in ordering a Bou-Bou while Mary Beth rolled her eyes. Dallas and I clinked our Bou-Bous to MB's martini and David's scotch on the rocks.

And while the Pussycat Dolls sang "Happily Never After," we sipped our drinks and got to know David. And I have to say, I really liked him. He seemed to have his act together and was clearly smitten with Dallas. But who wasn't? What made David different was that he seemed to actually care about Dallas and Baby Bentley. And dare I say, he respected her. I wanted that for Dallas. Her gorgeous looks and sex kitten body were sometimes all a man could see. But the way David looked at her, the way he talked to her, made me believe he saw more in her.

"How did you get the name Dallas?" he asked, looking at her as if she were an exotic jewel he'd really like to own but wasn't certain he could afford.

Dallas tossed her hair and swiveled toward him. "My mom named me for a town she believed would be the starting point of her meteoric rise to fame as a country western singer."

David smiled. "And did she rise to meteoric heights?"

I leaned in to listen, even though I already knew the story.

She shook her head. "Unfortunately, no. She made a few demo tapes, and she was really good, but she just never got the break she needed. She had the chance to sing in a band in Fort Worth, but she refused to leave me alone at night."

David took her hand in his. "Sounds like your mom was a good parent."

Dallas smiled. "She was. And she did it all by herself. Once in a while she'd get the lady next door to watch me while she went out, but she was always home early and never brought men to our house. We lived in a dumpy trailer park on the edge of Fort Worth and Mom worked as a waitress at IHOP. But I didn't really know we were poor until I got a little older. I thought everyone lived in a trailer and collected aluminum cans and cut out coupons."

I smiled at her, my little coupon queen.

"She got breast cancer right after Bentley was born, and she just wasn't strong enough to fight it. I guess all that hard work wore her out."

David wrapped her in his arms, and I almost got misty myself. Dallas excused herself to go to the restroom to fix her face, and David watched her walk away.

"What a beautiful spirit," he said. It was the first time I'd ever heard a man talk about Dallas's insides rather than her outsides.

He took a sip of his scotch and seemed to be far away. "I've looked a long time for a woman who has it all. Finding beauty and brains isn't all that hard. But when you add a beautiful spirit to the list, it's almost impossible. I didn't think she existed until now." He seemed to realize what he'd said and made apologies to MB and me, but I wasn't insulted. I had to agree with him. Dallas might be the only woman I knew with all of that.

Dallas returned to our group, perching seductively on the edge of her barstool. And as she did, an older man walked up and put a hand on David's shoulder. The two were soon engrossed in business talk which gave the rest of us a chance to drink another round.

"To David and Dallas," I said, lifting my second Bou-Bou. It actually wasn't bad. Kind of a nice change from martinis.

"I really like him," I said to Dallas.

She smiled big without a trace of her earlier tears and gushed like a teenager. "Isn't he just the best? I really think I'm in love." She said the last in a whisper, then peeked over her shoulder to make sure David was still deep in conversation. "I just love everything about him."

David stood a few feet away talking shop, leaving us alone so long we had yet another round. And by this time, Dallas was getting, well, trashed. She melted against my shoulder.

"Dallas," said Mary Beth. "Why do you always go for rich guys? Why not just a nice regular guy once in a while?"

I thought this was a little odd, coming from a woman who'd done the very same thing, only to lose her own rich guy to an apparent intercourse overdose administered by one seriously buxom personal trainer.

"For Bentley," said Dallas.

And there it was. Dallas's secret. The thing that drove her. Her overwhelming need for security – but not for herself. It was all about Bentley.

"I don't want to end up like my mother," she said.

"What do you mean?" asked MB. "You said she was a great mother."

Dallas nodded. "She really was. I want to be exactly like her when it comes to raising Bentley. But I want the opposite of what she got out of life."

"You mean, money?" asked Mary Beth.

"I mean, everything. My mother worked like a dog her whole life," she said, and the happy gleam left her eyes. "Her feet were always swollen and sore from being on them all day. Her hands were rough and red. She never had a vacation, never had a new dress that I remember until after I was grown. She died at forty-nine after living a life of poverty and broken dreams. And that just breaks my heart," said Dallas, dabbing at her eyes again. "She deserved better than that. But she wouldn't let men into her life. I think she worried something might happen to me if she brought a man to our house. I know she was lonely, but she tried to do it all on her own. And failed. I want better for Bentley. I don't want Bentley to ever have to worry about lunch money or a winter coat…or not feeling good enough."

"Oh, honey." I put my arm around her shoulders. "Don't cry. We get what you're saying."

Mary Beth nodded. "We definitely get it. You're a great mom, by the way. Every kid should be loved like that."

"And David is crazy about you," I said. "He said so while you were in the bathroom. So I don't think you have anything to worry about there. Just be yourself. He seems to love everything about you."

That brightened her up. "Really?" she asked, smiling as she dabbed the corners of her eyes with her cocktail napkin. "He said he was crazy about me?"

I nodded, and Dallas sighed and leaned into me.

"I think it's time for me to seal the deal with him." She giggled.

"Like how?" I asked.

"You know," she said, taking a sip of her drink and somehow not spilling it on either of us. She made wiggly eyebrows, and I laughed. She was just so cute.

MB leaned in so that only Dallas and I could hear her. "Dallas, if you're planning an encounter in the loo, nix it."

Dallas turned to me, "What did she say?"

"She said don't do David in the bathroom. Remember, we talked about this the other night?"

Dallas nodded. "I know, but maybe just this one last time?" She leaned in and whispered, sort of. "Y'all, every guy loves that! Are you kidding me?"

"Honey," I said, "I have to agree with Mary Beth this time. I mean, I know most guys love that. But David is different. I think he looks at you as more than that."

Dallas smiled. "I know. That's why I love him. That's why I want to *reward* him."

"I guess you're the expert," I said. "But you really might want to think about it. Maybe you could reward him some other way. Maybe take him home tonight and give him a little reward, but not a great big reward, you know? Maybe he wants this to go more slowly."

"We'll see," said Dallas, with a naughty glint in her eyes.

"We'll see what?" asked David, walking up and giving Dallas a squeeze.

Dallas swiveled to face him, pulling his head down to hers and whispering something in his ear. He smiled and seemed to almost blush. Dallas slid from her barstool, took him by the hand, and led him away. And I got a bad feeling. But maybe she was right. I mean, honestly. What guy wouldn't want Dallas to drag him into the elegant restroom for quickie sex?

Glacier, I thought. He wouldn't go for that at all. And then I wondered what kind of sex Glacier *would* go for. Or if he ever had sex at all. Surely he did. Because if not, it was the biggest waste of vigor and virility—

"What!" I said.

Mary Beth had kicked me with her bronze, four-inch heel. I rubbed my shin while she made a rude comment about two women sitting at the end of the bar who wore low cut blouses and the look of women on the prowl. They were so tan they looked crispy and sounded slightly hammered as they sang along to the music. Mary Beth was offended by their choice of manmade fabrics and white wine spritzers. And by the time she'd made colorful observations about just about everyone at the bar, Dallas and David had rejoined us.

Dallas was all smiles and satisfaction, sitting gracefully and reaching for her drink. But David looked rather serious, standing stiffly behind us.

"I'm so sorry," he said, leaning in between Dallas and me. "I'm afraid business has intruded on our evening, and I really need to tend to it. But please, have dinner on me. I'll make certain you're all very well taken care of."

"Oh, David. Can't you just have dinner with us and do business after?" asked Dallas, no longer smiling.

He kissed her forehead. "I'm afraid not. I really am sorry." He kissed me on the cheek and sort of smiled at Mary Beth. Good move. No one kisses Mary Beth on the cheek. Then he walked out.

Chapter Thirteen

Early the next morning I decided to punish myself with a run up Smuggler for drinking too many Bou-Bous. After David left, the mood of our group had taken a nosedive. So we drank more and talked louder and laughed when things weren't even really funny just so Dallas wouldn't feel too bad. Mary Beth seemed especially determined to shelter Dallas, and even told funny stories from her boarding school days.

So this morning I was a little fuzzy, a little thick headed, and a lot low on patience for chatty hikers or their cute bandana-wearing dogs. I ran faster than normal to get away from everyone, and in spite of my pickled internal organs, I got into an easy rhythm. Before I knew it, I passed the observation deck and kept going. The cadence of my steps and the steady pattern of my breath helped put me in a state of quiet. And as I was basking in that delicious state of not thinking, not worrying, not really being in my brain, I thought of Glacier. He seemed to almost always be in that frame of mind. Sure, there was that momentary blow-up at the bakery and the sadness that sometimes welled up in his eyes. But most of the time he seemed to live on a runner's high. I could usually get there after an eight-mile run up a mountain. But he seemed to have that same serenity in the middle of the clatter and clang of any given day. How was that possible?

Thinking of Glacier reminded me of his homework assignment for me. I rolled my eyes to myself, wishing he would just give me the quick fix and be done with it. Like maybe a secret chant I could do early each morning. Or maybe a magic herb I could infuse into my daily smoothie. Something simple, but powerful enough to erase my short-term memory, my constant compulsive thoughts of Thomas and his pixie.

I reminded myself that Glacier had apparently suffered through his own trail of tears – which I was dying to know more about – and maybe knew what he was talking about. And since he'd finally given me a straight answer to one of my questions, I decided to give it a shot.

As I climbed higher on the trail, I started looking for a good place to stop. A place to – what was it he said? Sit. Be quiet. Just be. But I had my doubts. Seriously, how could sitting and *being* pull me out of the slump of a lifetime? How could being quiet in nature tidy up the bloody mess of my broken heart? I didn't know. But before I could go back to Glacier and tell him it hadn't worked, then beg him for an alternate cure, I had to give it my best shot.

I slowed to a trot and then grudgingly to a walk, feeling everything slow down. And then I saw it. The perfect place to sit and be. I walked off the trail to the edge of a ridge. The softest breeze blew across my sweaty skin and cooled me down. I found a spot thick with pine needles and sat cross-legged, looking out over the valley to the mountains beyond. My leg muscles jumped and twitched, complaining at being crossed into a pretzel shape. But I was hell-bent to make this work. Anything to achieve the peaceful state that seemed to envelope Glacier like an incense cloud over an ashram.

So I sat still, or as still as possible. My hands weren't sure where to go. I started with them on the ground beside me but moved them to my knees. Then to my lap. Then I crossed my arms. Finally I linked my fingers and settled them in my lap like I'd seen Glacier do before.

Looking out from my mountain perch, I took a minute to just breathe in the beauty around me. There were clouds tinged with sun, blue in the middle and slightly pink around the edges. Graceful, wispy clouds, perfectly backlit by the sun, as if heaven were showing off. It reminded me of the ceiling in the Forum Shops in Las Vegas.

I know what you're thinking. I should compare this radiant sky to a million rays of light, kissed by heaven and tinged with pink from the glory of the universe. But we all have our own reference points. I felt much closer to Vegas than I did to heaven these days.

And then I thought about Glacier, and wondered where he stood on the whole Vegas versus heaven scale. Had he figured out the mysteries of life? Did he understand the idea of Something Bigger? Was it all around him and within him all the time and was that why he was so darn happy? Was it some unconventional, mystical Grandmother Earth? The leader of the flower children? The bohemian bellwether of gypsies and free spirits?

I really hoped not. I really needed whatever it was that Glacier had. The thing that could help me out of the mess of my life. But I couldn't quite commit, knowing it would be my luck to follow his advice to the nth degree, only to discover his peaceful persona came from smoking ganja and dancing naked in the moonlight while chanting to the Goddess of Clarity.

I started thinking of Glacier naked. He seemed like the kind of guy who would like to be naked. Natural. At ease in his own skin. And as I was picturing him naked, I realized this was probably not what he'd meant about getting somewhere beautiful and being quiet. So I abandoned my mental eight by ten of Glacier naked in front of a blazing fire and tried instead to be quiet. Which wasn't easy.

The quieter I tried to be, the more noise filled my brain. I thought about Dallas and David, and the look on his face when he came back from quickie sex in the bathroom of the Boo. Cheyenne and her butthead and being so far away from us in the West Indies. Mary Beth and all the demons she seemed to be fighting. And of course, me. How sad it was to be me. How pathetically, stupidly lonely it felt to be left behind. And I closed my eyes to try to stop the thoughts.

But they kept coming. Grocery list. Reminder to call my parents on Sunday. Something funny Dallas said last night before David left and ruined her mood. The back of my neck where it was itchy and sweaty under my ponytail. The appointment I needed to make for a hair trim. My mind was like an orchestra, but not in a good way. More like when all the instruments are tuning up, all playing different songs. Chaos. Confusion. Noise.

This couldn't be what Glacier had in mind. *Look inside*, he'd said. But that was where all the noise was. Think *here and now*. Stop thinking about then or later. But that didn't really help either. Thoughts and emotions and memories came at me like asteroids. I fidgeted and shifted in the pine needles, stretched my back, smoothed the hair out of my face. And decided to give up. Finish my run. This was getting me exactly nowhere.

But I've never been a quitter. And this had become an issue. I wanted to be able to tell him I'd done exactly what he told me to do. And that it worked. And that I was cured. So I thought about how peaceful my mind had been while I was running and tried to get that back. Deep breaths, long and slow. I breathed rhythmically, same as when I ran, trying to concentrate only on my breath. On drawing the fresh mountain air deep into my lungs and feeling my chest expand, then letting the air out and imagining all the noise in my body going out with the breath.

I don't know how long I sat there, thinking of my breath. I know I started to feel relaxed. And then I started to feel peaceful. And then I forgot about my twitching legs and my itchy neck and my cold bottom. And even my breathing.

And then, just when I thought I was all alone in the world, and that I would live the rest of my life with deep sadness and loss filling every pore, and that I would never be loved again, I felt...peace. All around me. Inside of me. Breathing new life into my lungs. Wrapping me in a blanket of relief.

And then I knew. Glacier might actually know what he was talking about after all.

Chapter Fourteen

I didn't have long to revel in my new state of bliss. Because Mary Beth – bane of my existence and yin to my yang – was waiting for me, ready to drag me back into her life of crime.

She called as I was driving home from Smuggler in heavy traffic. And I almost didn't answer. Partly because I was trapped behind a minivan from Alabama that wouldn't pass a string of bicyclists riding two abreast – going so slow I felt like I was in a parade. And partly because I was reeling from my *incident* on the mountain. Wondering if it really happened or if I just imagined it. Thinking it would be kind of hard to explain even to Glacier. And never to anyone else.

I did finally answer my phone because I knew Mary Beth would keep calling until I did.

"Hey, where are you?"

It was more of a demand than a question, a little bit like an accusation. Every once in a while Mary Beth had a tendency to treat people – including me – as if they worked for her. Like servants. Like her royal cortege.

"I did a run up Smuggler. Where are you?"

"Sitting in front of your house. How soon can you be here?"

"Give me ten minutes," I said. I hung up and wondered if she would just pick the lock before I got there.

I sat on the back deck with Mary Beth, wishing desperately for a long hot shower. I settled for a big glass of water while Mary Beth sipped a Bloody Mary.

"I had to fire one of my attorneys," said MB, apropos of nothing.

"How come?"

"Let's put it this way. A zombie would walk right past him."

"Huh?"

"Zombies eat brains."

"Okay..."

"He doesn't have any."

"Ah. Funny. So how's the lawsuit going anyway?"

Mary Beth sighed and shook her head. "I have to come up with something. Some proof."

"You're still convinced Cruella's taking money from the estate and not sending it on to the children's hospital?"

There it was. MB's big secret. When Rolf was alive, they'd researched the best way to help kids with Rolf's money and came up with the idea to build a children's hospital. Mary Beth never did trust Cruella to handle Rolf's business. But he wouldn't listen to her when she begged him to ditch the evil one. He told Mary Beth she was the best at what she did. I had a feeling it had more to do with a little action on the side. We all knew Rolf was not exactly faithful to Mary Beth.

Mary Beth nodded. "I'm positive. I just have to find proof."

"The attorneys haven't come up with anything in discovery?"

"Not yet." Mary Beth took a sip of her Bloody Mary and looked me right in the eye. "We need to do another break-in."

Oh boy. "No, Mary Beth. No way. That first break-in took five years off my life. Why don't you just give the attorneys a little more time? Let the courts handle it."

"Where's the fun in that?"

"I don't know. Maybe all the energy you're spending fighting Cruella could be used for something better."

"Such as?"

I shrugged. "What do you like to do? What makes you happy?"

I thought it was an insightful question. MB thought otherwise.

"You're missing the point completely. Does running erode your mental capacity?"

"MB...sometimes you're mean."

"I'm not mean. You're just a sissy."

But she smiled when she said it. Most of Mary Beth's bravado and snottiness was a big put-on. Just part of her role. I was still somewhat peaceful from my morning of looking inside, so I let it slide and took a moment to wonder what Mary Beth would find if she looked inside. The thought sent a shiver up my spine.

Chapter Fifteen

The entire day turned out to be full of girlfriend craziness. The morning edition featured Mary Beth trying to coax me into being a repeat offender, and by late that afternoon I had Dallas crying in my arms. It seemed David had given her the big heave-ho.

"I just can't believe it." Dallas sniffed and wiped her nose on the linen napkin meant to rest beneath her martini. Oh well.

"I thought we were so right for each other. I thought we were so much alike."

More tears. I reached over and gently rubbed her back. She wore a chic ivory raffia blouse over a beaded jacquard skirt, but somehow she looked all of sixteen years old, crying over her first boyfriend. Her long silky hair was pulled back in a ponytail and mascara ran down both cheeks. I wanted to hug her and tell her not to worry, prom was still three weeks away and someone else would surely ask her. I mean honestly, she just looked so young and sweet and pitiful. "What exactly did he say?" I asked, keeping my hand on her back.

She took a deep shuddering breath. "That he wanted to be with a woman who was a lady. A woman who conducted herself properly in public." Her face crumpled, and I couldn't help but notice she was still just as beautiful. I pulled her to me.

"Oh, honey. I'm sorry. Maybe it just wasn't meant to be."

"But I *am* a lady," she sniveled in my ear. "I thought men wanted a woman who was a lady in the boardroom and a rock star in the bedroom."

Well, I wanted to say that the Boo wasn't exactly the boardroom. And that the bathroom of the Boo wasn't exactly the bedroom. And I wasn't so sure about the rock star part. But I didn't want to make things worse, so I just held her and let her cry.

"Y'all were right," she said, pulling back from me and sounding ashamed. "I should have listened. I just thought he'd like it, you know?" She wiped at her nose and blinked back fresh tears.

Dallas's cell phone rang, and she fished in her purse frantically, then checked caller ID. Her face fell, and I knew it wasn't David on the other end.

"Where are you?" she asked. She listened for a while, wiping at her nose and making wide-eyed faces at me over whatever was being relayed on the other end. Finally she said, "I'm at Lucy's. Are you coming for Martini Saturday?" Once in a while we moved Martini Thursday to Saturday. It just depended on our mood. She looked at me and shook her head. "Okay. Well, call me tomorrow. We've *missed* you. And I have lots to tell you."

She hung up and dropped the pink phone back in her purse. "That was Cheyenne," she said, once again dabbing at her nose with the napkin. "She and Michael haven't gone on their trip yet. But she can't come over tonight. She's with Michael."

I cocked my head, confused. "She's been in town all this time? What's up?"

Dallas shrugged. "Apparently there were some *complications*." She used air quotation marks to emphasize the last word, and I sincerely hoped that wasn't code for *black and blue*.

Martini Saturday, and here I was all alone. In the beginning, the plan had been for each of us to take a turn hosting. But Mary Beth's house had all the warmth of a cell for the criminally insane. *Coincidence?* Cheyenne's boyfriend didn't want the four of us hanging out at his not-so-humble abode. And last week was Dallas's turn. So tonight it was my turn again.

But Dallas was in turmoil. Cheyenne was having *complications*. And Mary Beth was apparently busy sharpening her lock picks for the next assault on Cruella. That left me. Alone on my back deck. Drinking a martini by myself. How pathetic.

So when the doorbell rang, I was surprised. Even more surprised when I opened the door to Glacier Jones.

"What are you doing here?" I realized how rude that sounded after it was already out of my mouth.

"Martini Saturday." He smiled.

I smiled back. "Or Meditation Saturday."

"Exactly."

"Come on in."

He held up the same cloth bag he had used to tote our smoothies. "I brought my own."

I laughed and wondered what kind of martini might be in the bottom of his bag, then led him through the house and into the kitchen where a fire burned in the stone fireplace.

"Nice," he said, turning to soak up the warmth of the fire. It was the first comment he'd ever made about my house. Or anything else, as far as I could remember.

I peered into the cloth bag and smiled when I saw the bottle of pomegranate juice. Taking one of the funky martini glasses I'd set out for the girls, I poured the ruby red juice into the glass and added a couple of olives. We clinked glasses, his disappearing again in his big, square hand.

"To here and now," I said, very proud of myself.

Glacier nodded once and sipped his drink. "Perfect," he said.

⁂

We settled into chairs on the back deck, where we could watch the sun sink behind the mountains. Glacier ate the olives from his drink, and I wondered if the combination of flavors was perfectly awful. But he chewed slowly and seemed happy with the mix. And the company. And life in general.

"Well, I did it," I said, trying to get his attention. I sipped my drink and finally felt his eyes on me, though he didn't exactly look intrigued by my big lead-in. He just sat and waited for me to go on.

"I did the whole *get quiet and just be.*"

Again barely any reaction. No eyebrow raise or pat on the back. Just a little flicker of a smile as he watched my face.

"And at first it was horrible. I was wiggly. And itchy. And really uncomfortable. I felt sort of silly. And I kept thinking about all the things I needed to do. Errands and stuff. And about Dallas and Cheyenne and Mary Beth. And about my pathetic life. And I started to just get sad."

He nodded.

"But then I tried concentrating on my breath. Like I do when I run. And somehow, I got quiet. I stopped thinking about my grocery list and my crazy and needy friends and even my sad little life. And I think – I mean, this may sound crazy – but it was almost like a mental vacation. Like this sweet zone of blissful…." I shook my head, frustrated, searching for the right words. "Like the trampoline of my mind finally stopped and I felt a sense of…peace."

I felt sort of foolish, like maybe I'd said too much. Like I'd probably gotten it completely wrong. Maybe Glacier wanted me to sit and get quiet, just *be*, but not get carried away. Maybe just sit and think about the harmony of nature or global peace. Or how I should start using cloth bags and stop polluting the environment.

I worried he might laugh at me. Or think less of me. Or be disappointed in me. But he actually beamed at me. I hadn't imagined his smile could be any more brilliant until he turned the high beams on me, and I felt myself beaming back.

"Did I…do good?" I asked.

He nodded slowly, still smiling. "You did good."

"The *get quiet and just be* thing? I did it right?" The question dripped with my need for approval. It was pitiful. I waited for his praise, the proverbial gold star for my hard work.

"There's no right or wrong," he said. "It is what it is."

I felt my shoulders sag a little. No high five. No star, gold or otherwise.

"But it's about feeling clearer, right? Feeling more peaceful?"

Glacier nodded. "That's a good first step. It's about looking inside and seeing what's there."

He'd told me that a thousand times, but this time it made me stop and think. Did that mean there was peace and clarity inside of me? It didn't seem like a place where peace and clarity would really want to be. What with the martinis. And the occasional cigarette. And the…

Before I could stop myself, I opened my mouth and blurted out the words, "I steal things."

It was the most reaction I'd ever evoked from him – other than irritation. One eyebrow rose just slightly. But still, he didn't say, "*You're kidding me,*" or "*You what!*" or even the slightly curious "*What kind of things?*"

I decided to come clean.

"From my ex-husband. I still have a key and the code to the alarm, so sometimes I go over there and take stuff. You know, small stuff. Things he and his little pixie will never miss. Nothing big." I took a sip of my drink. "Is that so wrong?"

Glacier just looked at me. "What does your heart tell you?" he finally asked.

Oh hell. What kind of question was that? It was a trick. If I said my heart didn't like it, then I'd have to admit that it really was wrong and then I'd have to stop doing it. And if I said my heart didn't have the slightest problem with it, I'd look like a psychopath, like Mary Beth, and that couldn't be good. So I didn't answer. I gave him back a little of his own silent contemplation. Except I wasn't contemplating so much as scheming. Trying to figure a way out of this entire conversation and wishing I'd never said anything.

"It's funny," he said, but he wasn't laughing. "Every day is jammed full of choices. All day long. We don't usually even realize it."

He wasn't looking at me. He was looking off toward the mountains, and I had no idea what he was getting at. Finally he turned to me.

"Lucy, it's really important to witness all the choices you make." His voice was soft in the fading light. "Every choice you make affects the rest of your life."

"Well, I don't always get to make the choices. Sometimes they're made for me. What about being dumped? That was a choice I didn't make. How am I supposed to *witness my choices* when I'm not even consulted before they're made?"

"You won't find real peace until you accept circumstances and people the way they are."

Oh, what a bunch of hogwash! Even hearing it in his deep, gentle voice, beneath pale lavender clouds over the mountains, I wanted to gag.

"Are you kidding me? Really? I'm supposed to accept being alone after giving the best years of my life to Thomas? I'm supposed to accept being left behind? To accept that pixie driving *my* car, living in *my* house, sleeping with *my* husband?" The last word ended on a bit of a shriek, and I sat back in my chair and drained my drink.

"I get that you're hurt. And I'm sorry. I've been there. I really do know what it feels like. And that's why I'm telling you - not just your actions but every one of your thoughts has an effect. Thoughts are alive. They have power. Each one affects your life and the lives of others."

I crossed my arms over my chest. "The lives of *others*? You're saying my negative thoughts are causing trouble for the world? Now I'm responsible for the entire planet? Bloody hell," I said, feeling a little like a bratty twelve-year-old while he seemed to only get more calm.

We sat in silence while shadows settled around us in the growing dusk. The beauty of the evening was completely lost on me. I'd had just about all I could take of Glacier's new wave, all natural, Utopian, rah-rah baloney.

"Keep looking, Lucy." He stood and walked over to me, placing one warm hand on my shoulder. I felt a jolt of electricity where he touched me. "Just keep looking inside."

I looked up at him. "If I do that, will you tell me how you got your name?"

"Yes."

Chapter Sixteen

Thursday night we had a hootenanny at Dallas's house. Maybe not a full-blown hootenanny, but there was folksy music on the sound system, cocktail napkins that looked like little bandanas, and Dallas wearing Daisy Duke cutoffs and cowboy boots. Which I have to say, somehow worked on her.

The evening started off on a tender note but went drastically downhill from there.

I walked into the living room with Mary Beth, where sweet Baby Bentley was dancing to the banjo music coming from hidden speakers. Her nanny stood nearby clapping her hands, encouraging Bentley to shake it.

I was enjoying this moment of innocent abandon when Mary Beth did something that showed her true colors. Setting her martini on the closest table, she walked over to Baby Bentley and lifted her gently in her arms. And Bentley – who loves all humans and all creatures – laughed and put her arms around Mary Beth's neck and buried her chubby hands in MB's mane of dark hair. And Mary Beth melted. That's the only way I can describe the physical change in her. She had her back to me, but as I watched, her shoulders relaxed, her back curved around Bentley, and she started to sway to the corny music.

I stood there staring while Mary Beth cooed to Bentley and they danced around the living room. When Bentley finally got restless and wriggled to get down, Mary Beth seemed reluctant to let her go. But she set her down and watched as Bentley squealed and ran toward the nanny, who picked her up and took her outside to play.

Then Mary Beth picked up her martini as if nothing outrageous had just happened. As if she hadn't just morphed into a woman so different from the one she usually pretended to be. And I ached for her, for the part of her that missed her own little daughter. And for the little girl inside herself who had never been picked up and danced around the room. It was another layer of her secret, something she showed to almost no one. Mary Beth was a complete sucker for little kids.

I sat down next to her, almost close enough that our shoulders touched. I wanted to say something, to tell her I loved her. And then to throw her in my Jeep and drive the thousand miles to Alissa's boarding school and bust her out.

But before I could say a word, she put her hand on my arm and leaned in close. "Time for attack number two on the evil one. I'll pick you up Monday afternoon at two."

I pulled back and gave her a disapproving look, wondering at this person who could cuddle a baby one moment and plan an assault on a rival the next. But before she could call me a disparaging name or criticize my lack of mettle, Cheyenne and Dallas came in from the kitchen and sat down facing us.

"Y'all, Baby Daddy made news on the sports channel yesterday," said Dallas, crossing her long legs. "He had a motorcycle wreck last week and broke both of his legs."

"You're kidding," I said, although I knew she wasn't. Why do people say that? "Won't that sort of put a damper on his basketball playing next season?"

Dallas sipped her drink and nodded. "I sure think so. Although he hardly played last year."

"Poor guy," said Shy. "They'll still pay him though, right?"

Dallas's face tensed, and she shrugged. I changed the subject.

"Cheyenne, why didn't you tell us you were here all along?" I asked. "We thought you were long gone to St. Bart's."

Cheyenne wore multi-colored wedge thongs, and like the gathering itself, the shoes seemed to have a little bit too much going on to be comfortable. Especially paired with a wildly patterned blouse that laced up the back and funky silk cargo pants rolled up to the calf. And, of course, leopard sunglasses. She set her drink on the red and black bandana napkin and leaned in.

"This week has been totally off the hook, you guys. For some crazy reason Michael wanted people to think we were gone, so we sort of pretended we were hiding out in his house." She made a face like it was an exciting game of cloak and daggers.

"Sounds fun," said Dallas. "Did you ever leave the bedroom?"

Cheyenne's cartoon face seemed to fall a bit. "Michael was super busy most of the time. He had all these lawyers here from New York, and they had marathon meetings day and night."

"What's with all the lawyers?" I asked.

"I dunno exactly. He's talking about selling the house here and buying one in Florida. His lawyers want his main, you know, house, residence, whatever, to be in Florida."

I felt a warning bell go off in my head, and Mary Beth must have felt the same because she leaned across me as if reaching for the bowl of cashews – which she never ate – and used the opportunity to give me a look.

"I love Florida!" said Dallas. "Maybe he'll buy a house like Mar-A-Lago!"

Cheyenne giggled. "And remember last time when I showed you this beauty?" She held out her hand with the giant bauble she'd gotten as a reward for taking a punch to the face.

"Well, Michael's on a big jewelry buying jag! Get this, he bought me a diamond necklace, earrings, and I think a bracelet!"

"What do you mean *you think*?" asked Mary Beth.

"Well, I haven't actually seen any of it yet. It's locked up tight in a safe deposit box. But Michael gave me a key and told me to keep it somewhere safe. Isn't that the coolest thing?" She made a happy growl deep in her throat.

"Maybe," said Mary Beth. "But I don't like the way it's adding up. Michael's a miscreant. This could just be one of his schemes to take advantage of you as well as his stockholders."

"What?" Cheyenne looked from Mary Beth, to me, back to Mary Beth, and finally to Dallas.

Dallas shrugged. "Mary Beth, what are you talking about?"

"She's just saying—"

"No," said Mary Beth, interrupting me. "I won't let you water it down this time. This is too important." She looked at Cheyenne. "Shy, I'm really sorry, but it sounds to me like Michael is beginning to hide his assets. You need to protect yourself. Don't let him involve you."

Cheyenne bristled. "Why would you say that? He wouldn't do that! Why would he hide his assets? And what does that have to do with him buying me jewelry?"

I wanted to stop this before it got ugly, but we were too far in now. Mary Beth was concerned, Cheyenne was angry and probably a little scared, and Dallas was trying to follow the whole thing like a spectator watching a ping-pong tournament. Mary Beth clasped her hands together in front of her and looked as if she were begging Cheyenne to listen to her.

"Florida law allows homeowners facing legal judgments to fully protect their principal residence. Taking up residence in Florida has become the thing to do for people wanting to hold on to money that most likely belongs to someone else."

No one said anything. We were all staring at Mary Beth, so she continued.

"The diamonds seem like an amazing gift, but they're more likely part of a Byzantine plan to leave the country and have access to valuables that can be liquidated into cash."

Still no one said anything. There just wasn't anything to say.

"I'm sorry," said Mary Beth, picking up her drink and leaning back. "I hope I'm wrong."

Cheyenne was stunned. Dallas was confused. And I was just so sad for Cheyenne. Because I agreed with everything Mary Beth said. Although I'd never used Byzantine in a sentence.

Dallas's cell phone chirped from the table in front of her. She picked it up and checked caller ID. "Sorry, y'all. It's Baby Daddy. I better take it."

She walked into the kitchen to take her call while the rest of us sat there without saying a word. I walked over to Shy, put my arm around her shoulders and gave her a squeeze. I was trying to figure out something to say to make her feel better when we heard Dallas let out a wail from the kitchen. We all made bug eyes at each other. Dallas rarely raised her voice.

"This cannot be happening!" she said and started to cry.

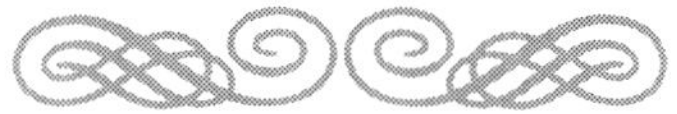

Chapter Seventeen

When Dallas was still on the phone to Baby Daddy half an hour later, we decided she needed privacy and left her crying in her kitchen. There seemed to always be drama where Baby Daddy was concerned, so I assumed this was just another one of their messy fights. The night was a bust, and I was asleep long before my usual bedtime.

So early Friday morning I was back on Smuggler, heading for my quiet place. With Glacier's encouragement, I'd made it a point to *get quiet and just be* every morning. And I have to say, I was really into it though I couldn't share those feelings with anyone but Glacier. Just the thought of Mary Beth berating me with a string of big words was enough to make me keep my mouth shut. But then, who knew? Maybe Mary Beth had been meditating all her life. Anything is possible, right?

I've heard that if you do something for twenty-eight days, it becomes a habit, so my goal was to try this *get quiet and just be* idea for twenty-eight days to see what happened.

Day seven. I found my little pine-needle-covered indentation and plopped down. It was another beautiful late June morning, still a little cool, which was nice since I was hot from my run. A little scratching, a little wiggling, a tiny adjustment here and there. And then I was still and breathing and relaxing. And it felt so good. Sort of like a vacation for my brain, for my whole body even. Like when you're exhausted at the end of a long day and you slide into a hot bubble bath and feel all your muscles start to unwind. Like that, but more internal. I felt everything slowing down – mind, heart, breathing. Something deep inside and long buried beneath thirty-five years of stress let out a giant *ahhhhhhh.*

But about halfway in, when I got good and quiet and looked deep inside, when I usually felt a warm cloud of relief around me like a cashmere blanket, something went wrong.

I tried to clear my mind, tried to push away the strange thoughts. But there it was. Something I didn't want to think about. Something I didn't want coming in and messing up my *get quiet and just be* time. Something that wouldn't go away. No matter how many times I started over, tried counting my breaths, tried pushing aside the thoughts, this one wouldn't budge.

Give it back. All of it. Give it back and let it go.

I opened my eyes and looked out over the mountains. Brushed the hair out of my face. Scratched my knee. Stretched my legs out in front of me and then crossed them again. Shut my eyes and gave up. I couldn't get away from the thought no matter how hard I tried. Something was telling me to give back all the things I'd taken from Thomas. And to just let that go.

I sighed and looked again at the incredible view. Give it back? And end my only source of fun these days? And whose idea was this exactly? Was it Something Bigger talking? Was it me? I shook my head. Things had been much easier before I started looking within. Before I cared what Glacier thought. Or what the universe wanted. Before I sprouted a conscience.

I got up and brushed myself off. And instead of finishing my run, I headed back down Smuggler and toward home. Fine. If that's what it took to get some peace, I would do it. I would give it all back. There was always Mary Beth and her shiny lock picks if I felt the need for a life of crime in the future.

Before heading home, I stopped at Main Street Bakery. I needed a pep talk. Or a high five. Some words of encouragement for coming up with such a noble plan. And if all else failed, I could at least get a really fattening muffin and a caffeine buzz. I stepped over a big brown dog tied up out front, and into a world of delicious smells and happy diners.

And there he was. Same signature jeans and T-shirt. Same small table by the front windows. Same patch of sun enveloping him like a spotlight. Same battered book of answers. And I wondered, how did he stay in such good shape if he spent all his time in a bakery? Where did the muscles come from?

He looked up and smiled when I pulled out a chair across from him and sat down with my mug of coffee.

"Well, I hope you're happy," I said.

He nodded once, "I'm pretty happy."

He smiled at me, and I laughed. I couldn't help myself. Anyone else on earth would have said, *What do you mean?* or *Happy about what?* But not Glacier.

"I just came from the beautiful place where I get quiet and just be."

"Good," he said, that ever-so-engaging half smile on his handsome face.

"Not so good," I said, taking a sip of rich coffee. "This morning I got a message. Sort of like a little thunk in the head."

He closed the Big Book of Answers and rested it on the table, then folded his hands in his lap. For Glacier, that was a huge show of interest in what I had to say.

I took another sip of my coffee, hoping to torment him. Trying to bide my time and build the anticipation of my big reveal, but the longer I waited the calmer he seemed. I decided to just get it over with.

"Something..." I rubbed my head, trying to figure out what had just happened. "Something told me to give all the stuff back to Thomas."

I lowered my voice and leaned in. "You know, I told you I took a few things from my ex and his pixie?"

Glacier nodded.

"So I guess I'll give it all back."

Glacier's eyes crinkled at the sides when he smiled. I felt very proud of myself. Very noble.

"Anyway, I'll call Thomas and see where he is. Find out if he's still out of town. If he is, I'll sneak back in one last time and put everything away." I laughed. "One last heist. It'll be kind of fun. Want to come?"

Glacier's happy smile seemed to slip just a bit. Oh hell. Now what.

"Maybe you should think it through a little more," he said.

"You think I shouldn't give the stuff back? Then what was the voice all about? The message on the mountain, so to speak."

"No, I think giving everything back is good, but there might be a better way to go about it."

"Like how?"

"This is more than just giving Thomas back his stuff. This could be a chance for you to heal. To grow stronger."

"I already do feel stronger. I feel good about giving the stuff back. Isn't that enough?"

He leaned his arms on the table and tucked his legs beneath his chair. "Lucy, this is a chance for you to sit down with Thomas and talk things over."

I looked at him the way Mary Beth looked at me when I said something she thought was stupid. "Are you kidding me? You mean, give him his stuff back in *person*?"

He nodded.

"No thanks," I said, dismissing his idea completely. "I don't see how that could possibly come to any good."

"It might give you a chance to come clean. To let go of the attachment you have to your life with Thomas. To your feelings of resentment and hurt."

"You mean, if I sit down with Thomas and tell him what an ass I think he is for leaving me that I'll feel better?"

He shook his head. "No. You don't need to try to give your point of view. Just make peace with things. With Thomas."

I looked at him and frowned, waiting for him to say something that made sense.

"When you can accept people and situations as they are, then you'll have real peace."

I huffed out a laugh. "That's not gonna happen. I'll never accept the fact that Thomas traded me in for a pixie."

"Then that hurts only you."

I shrugged. "I don't care. I'm the innocent party here. You don't know how it feels," I said, feeling sick inside. "You don't how much it hurts to be dumped and left behind."

I felt tears begin to tickle my throat and decided to leave before I embarrassed myself. Besides, Glacier was totally off today. I drove away with a heavy heart. No high five. No gold star. I sighed and wiped my nose on my sleeve. I didn't even get my stupid muffin.

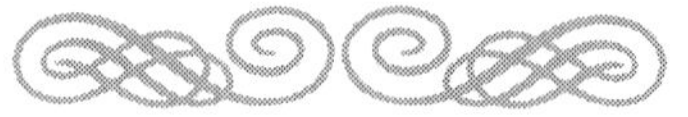

Chapter Eighteen

Monday afternoon at two o'clock. That was the time I'd picked for returning everything. A sort of tandem act of crime with Mary Beth. While she played out her second assault on the evil lady lawyer, I would sneak into Thomas's house one last time. I'd called him on Sunday and made up a big story about needing him to sign a paper on our home in Houston. He left a message saying he wouldn't be back in Aspen until the end of the week. Perfect.

Around noon on Monday while sucking down a Red Bull, I started the tedious task of gathering all the things I'd taken in the past few months. I found a plastic storage tub in a closet and emptied the odd wrapping paper and tissue out of it. From a hiding place in my linen closet, I loaded up the custom-made shirts, handmade shoes, Baccarat rooster, Montblanc pen, a small amber Versace vase, and a Faberge cradle egg. I knew there was more but I just couldn't remember what it was or where I'd put it.

I never stole anything I wanted. It wasn't like I decorated my house with the stuff. I always just crammed it in a drawer. Or a closet. Or some obscure place in my house. I should have kept a list. And a map.

After nearly tearing the house apart, I hit pay dirt in my closet. In a drawer, in the back, mixed in with an odd assortment of gifts from friends and family. At least, I hoped these were all things I'd taken from Thomas. I laughed at the thought of returning something that never belonged to him in the first place – like the faux-jeweled picture frame from my mother. Or the expensive but hideous Moroccan lantern from a friend in Houston. Wouldn't it be funny if I left the random ugly castoffs from my drawer all around Thomas's house?

I looked down into my tub of loot. It wasn't like I'd taken anything personal. I could have robbed them blind, but that wasn't the point. And as I carried the tub to the garage and loaded it into the back of my Jeep, I actually had trouble remembering exactly what the point had been. Something about showing Thomas I was a force to be reckoned with. That I couldn't be cast aside so easily. Or something like that.

But now the whole thing seemed sort of foolish, and I was relieved to be ending this little show of defiance. Or psychosis. Whatever it was, it was time for it to be over. Maybe Glacier was right: I should have called and asked to meet Thomas somewhere and given everything back in person. But I was just too embarrassed. This was better. This way, he would never know, and I could keep the upper hand as the innocent party in this marriage that was no more.

I parked near the front walkway of Thomas's house and rested my head on the steering wheel. I missed the house so much. Missed everything about it. But of course, that's silly. It wasn't the house. It wasn't the circle drive or the stone ledges or the chandelier in the window tugging on my heart. I missed Thomas. I missed our life together. I didn't need a big house. In fact, of all the houses we'd lived in, my favorite was the tiny, rickety, fixer-upper we bought right after we got married. It was in one of those neighborhoods where people bought just to raze the house and rebuild on the lot. But not us. We could barely afford what we had.

I smiled to myself, remembering the day Thomas went for a run and came back to our house pushing a wheelbarrow. And in the wheelbarrow was a pitiful little orange tree, donated by a friendly neighbor who found himself with too many trees to plant and who took pity on the poor young couple down the street who could barely keep their tiny house from falling down around them.

We planted the one little tree in our front yard. And as I stood admiring our work, Thomas threw me over his shoulder and laid me in the wheelbarrow. Then he pushed me all around the neighborhood, making me laugh so hard I almost wet my pants. That's the house I wish I still lived in. That's the life I wish I still lived.

My reverse heist had now lost all its appeal. I just wanted to get it over with. At the massive double doors, I set down the tub and slid my key into the lock. As usual, the shriek of the alarm assaulted me when I opened the door. But I set the tub in the house, closed the door, and walked over to the keypad hidden behind the little mahogany panel. One last time, I entered the five-digit code to silence the alarm. But nothing happened. The alarm continued to shriek, getting even louder it seemed. I hit *Cancel* and entered the code again, this time being more careful. And once again, nothing happened. I told myself to calm down. Maybe the alarm was on the blink. No worries. I would just call the alarm company and give them the password, which was surely the same. I mean, who would change the password and the code but not change the locks on the doors?

I was fumbling in my purse for my cell phone when a hand came from behind me. I whirled around and came face to face with Thomas.

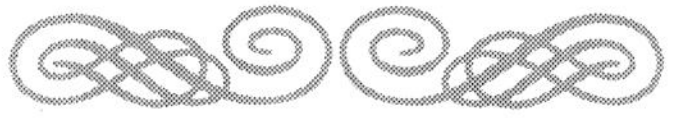

Chapter Nineteen

Thomas punched numbers into the keypad, and the alarm went silent. The quiet was a welcome relief, but now the sound filling the foyer was the hammering of my heart.

"Thomas! My God! You almost gave me a heart attack!" I held my hand to my chest.

Thomas crossed his arms and cocked his head. "What've you got there, Lucy?"

I felt dumber than dumb. Caught with my hand in the proverbial cookie jar. I stepped backwards toward the door, not knowing what to say. The only way this scene could have been any worse was for the pixie to have come around the corner - which I expected any minute.

"Did you really expect to get away with this?" Thomas's voice was angry, incredulous.

I wasn't comfortable with my feelings of shame and contrition, so I summoned my own anger. It wasn't very hard.

"Well, yeah, I did." I put my hands on my hips and threw my shoulders back. "You're so busy with your new life, I didn't think you'd notice."

"Did you really think I didn't know what was going on in my own house?"

"It used to be *our* house, Thomas. And yes. I did think you were oblivious to what went on when you were away with your new wife. If you were so worried about it, why didn't you change the locks?"

Thomas shifted his weight and leaned toward me, angry lines forming between his eyebrows. "I didn't think I needed to change the locks, Lucy. I didn't think you'd have the gall to sneak in and *steal* things!"

"How did you know I was even here? You'd never miss these things." I touched the toe of my sandal to the plastic tub.

"I had cameras installed throughout the property," said Thomas, his voice losing some of its wrath. "I've been watching you."

Now my cheeks flushed. My hands slid from my hips and hung at my sides. I wanted to be anywhere but here. Anywhere but standing in the sunny foyer that once was mine, facing the angry husband who once was mine, caught red-handed with a plastic tub of loot that should have been mine. It was too much. I turned for the door.

"I'm sorry," I said but in a tone that indicated anything but sorrow. More like bitterness mixed with embarrassment. I reached for the door handle.

"Not so fast." Thomas reached for my arm, but I jerked back at his touch. When I looked up into his face, I was surprised to see, not anger, but almost the opposite. Compassion. Which made me feel even worse.

"How could you *steal* from me?" He looked hurt, and that destroyed me. I had to look away.

"Don't you know," he said, his voice soft, "that I would give you anything. If I have anything you want, you can have it. You don't have to steal from me."

I dropped my head as tears came to my eyes. I couldn't look at him. I had never felt so sad. So ashamed. "I don't want your stuff, Thomas."

I stood there, trying to get my emotions in check. Trying to find the words to justify my actions. But there were none. And somewhere out of the depths of my misery, the truth came tumbling out of my mouth. "I just want you," I said in a strangled voice. "I just want you back."

He reached for me again, and this time I let him take me by the hand. "Come here," he said, his tone gentle. "Come with me."

He led me by the hand into the large living room and over to my favorite Christian Liagre couch. He sat beside me, his knee touching mine. I looked through the big windows and out over the mountains and wished I could disappear.

"Lucy?"

I looked into his deep gray eyes. It had been almost a year since I'd seen him, and that was across a table in the conference room of the attorney's office. At the time, I wouldn't even meet his eyes. I was crushed. Angry. So many emotions I couldn't even trust myself to speak.

But now I took a minute to really look at this man I had loved for as long as I could remember. This almost-movie-star-handsome man who still could make my stomach squish. The kindness in his face was so unexpected. So not what I would have imagined had I played this scene in my head. I shook my head and shrugged.

"I guess I just wanted to get back at you some way."

Thomas looked surprised. "Get back at me for what?"

I looked at him to see if he was being facetious, but he looked completely sincere. Was he seriously going to make me say it? I felt more tears welling up in the back of my throat – big, messy tears – and looked down at my hands, pretending to inspect my manicure.

"You left me behind," I said before I could stop myself. "After all our years together. You left me behind like a worn-out sweater." Tears spilled down my cheeks, and I tried to choke them back. "You didn't even give us a chance." My voice was raw. "How could you just leave me like that? I *loved* you."

Thomas moved closer and took me in his arms. I fell against his chest and let him hold me, remembering in an instant his familiar smell, the starched cotton of his shirt against my face, the warm reassuring strength of his arms. Being in his arms felt like coming home. A home destroyed by fire, or ravaged by storms, but still home.

He laid his head gently on top of mine. "Well, you had kind of a funny way of showing it," he said, his voice sad.

I pulled away and looked at him, wiping at my face. "What do you mean?"

He gently wiped at a tear on my cheek. "You were never there for me, Lucy. You were never around. I honestly didn't think you'd care whether we divorced or not."

I stared at him, dumbfounded. "How can you say that? You were *everything* to me!"

Thomas shook his head slightly, and his face turned sad. "Do you remember when I went to Paris on business and tried to get you to come with me?"

I tried to remember which business trip he was talking about. There had been so many.

"I pleaded with you, but you wouldn't budge. You were busy with some charity ball or something. I had to cancel a lot of plans when you wouldn't go. That trip was supposed to be our second honeymoon. A chance for us to renew our marriage and get back what we'd lost."

I felt my heart squeeze in my chest as sadness swallowed me whole. "Why didn't you tell me? Why didn't you give me another chance?"

"I wanted you to want to go," said Thomas. "I wanted you to want to be with me."

I looked to the mountains as far away as I could look. As far away from the sadness as I could get.

"You were never home, Luce. You were always shopping. Or running. Or playing tennis. Two summers ago we spent almost three months apart because you wanted to be at Martha's Vineyard, and I couldn't be there. I wanted you with me."

His voice became softer. "When I sat you down and told you I was leaving, you didn't even cry. You didn't even seem to care."

"But I was devastated," I said. "You had to know that."

"You never showed it. You have this thing about never letting anyone see your vulnerability. You never let anyone Band-Aid your wounds. You always have to come across as so strong."

"What's wrong with being strong?" I asked, feeling defensive.

"Nothing," he said, "if it's balanced with showing your true feelings." His eyes filled with sadness. "If you had just fought for us, Luce," he said. "When I told you I was leaving, if you had just tried to stop me. If you'd only shown me then what you're showing me now, I would never have left."

The breath died in my lungs. It was the most devastating thing anyone had ever said to me. It was as if the person you love most in the world has died, but you realize you could have saved them. You let them die because of your pride. I couldn't breathe. I couldn't take it all in. All I could do was shake my head sadly and cry for what could have been.

"I didn't know," my voice was a whisper through my tears. "You have no idea how much I miss you."

He reached for my hand, and my fingers curled around his. "Actually, I think I do. That's how much I missed you. When we were married."

I stopped trying to hold back the tears. I leaned into Thomas's strong arms once again – for what would surely be the last time ever – and cried as if my heart would break in two. All those times, all those days apart, I had always believed Thomas would be there when I got home from wherever I was, doing whatever I wanted to do. It never occurred to me that he would grow tired of coming in second or third to all my activities and comings and goings. I never imagined that he missed me. That he would feel lonely and eventually look for someone to fill the void I'd left in his life. Or that I could have changed the course of my entire life if I'd only shown him how hurt I was. If I'd only let him Band-Aid my wound.

And now I knew. Thomas wasn't the one who left me behind after all. I had somehow walked away from the only man I'd ever loved.

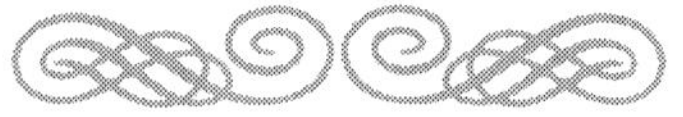

Chapter Twenty

I drove away from Thomas's house, exhausted and emotionally drained. It was very definitely Thomas's house now. No longer my house or our house. I didn't have a key or the code or an excuse to return. And even though I don't think I'd ever felt so sad in my entire life, I also felt something like a sense of…I don't know… reconciliation I guess. A tiny little bubble of feeling better in an ocean of sadness. Thomas and I had finally slit our hearts wide open and let all the mess inside tumble out. We'd told each other things we should have said a long time ago. And somewhere in the middle of that giant pile of heartbreak and sadness was the slightest glimmer of hope. That tomorrow would be better. Maybe. If I could just get through today.

I dug in my purse for sunglasses to hide my swollen eyes, then checked my cell phone – which I'd heard ringing from my purse in the foyer while Thomas and I were talking on the couch. Two calls, both from Dallas. I was relieved she was finally calling me back. Since leaving her crying on Thursday, I'd called her every day and missed her each time.

"Dallas, finally! I've been so worried about you since your call from Baby Daddy. Is everything okay?"

"Oh, Lucy..." I could barely understand Dallas through her tears.

"Dallas? What's wrong?"

Dallas sniffed and fumbled the phone, and I could imagine her holding a tissue to her nose, because her voice came back in a nasally whine. "Lucy, can you come over? Please?"

Well, how could I not. I mean, there was nothing I wanted more than to go home, pour myself a huge martini, and soak in the hot tub on my back deck. I needed to decompress and restore my battered heart. I looked like something the cat dragged in and I felt even worse. But Dallas hardly ever asked for anything.

"I'll be right there, sweetie. Don't worry. Everything'll be okay."

I don't know why I said that. I didn't even know what was wrong, so how did I know everything would be fine? Why do people say things like that?

I hung up and dialed MB, who should have been home from her attack on Cruella by now. No answer. I left a message and dialed Cheyenne as two cop cars whizzed past me going the opposite direction – hopefully not on their way to Cruella's house.

Cheyenne wasn't answering either, so I was on my own. Hopefully Dallas's crisis was something as simple as a giant pimple on her nose or her first wrinkle or a bad haircut. Whatever someone as beautiful and blessed as Dallas could possibly cry over. Surely a walk in the park compared to what I'd just been through.

Dallas opened the door and fell into my arms, crying into my shoulder. It was definitely a day of tears. I followed her into the living room and took a seat beside her as she crumpled into the corner of her couch.

"Oh, Lucy. What am I gonna do?" Her face was red and blotchy, and she wore torn jeans and a baggy rugby shirt – a look I'd never seen on her before. It kind of scared me.

"Aw, sweetie, what's so bad?" I asked, rubbing her shoulder and wanting desperately to make it better, no matter what it was.

Dallas sniffed and wiped at her red nose. "I thought I was so smart, you know? I thought I was doing the right thing for Bentley. And I wasn't being greedy. I mean, she *deserves* to be supported. Right?"

I nodded. "Honey, Baby Bentley deserves nothing but the best. Now, what's this all about?"

Dallas's beautiful face screwed up into a look of total despair. She held a balled up tissue to her mouth, and I had to listen hard to understand her words.

"Baby Daddy got cut from the team. His career is over!"

"What? He got cut? Why?"

"Something about his contract. He wasn't supposed to be riding a motorcycle. And now, with two broken legs..." She started to cry harder and buried her face in her hands. I took her in my arms. What a day.

"Oh, honey. I'm sorry. But he'll have to work eventually, right? He'll have to make money for himself. And when he does, you and Bentley will still be entitled to part of it, right?"

Dallas shook her head and reached for a clean tissue from the coffee table. She wiped at her face and sat back against the couch.

"He doesn't plan to work anymore. He said he invested his money, and he has enough to live on. He said I should have done the same thing instead of living so high on the hog, whatever that means."

Oh boy. It means, I thought, that Baby Daddy just found a way out of supporting his daughter. What a dog.

"I thought I was being so smart, Lucy. I thought taking a percentage of his earnings for eighteen years was way better than a lump sum. I'm so stupid! If I'd just taken the lump sum. If I'd just gone along with the offer, I'd be set for life. Now what will I do?"

"What about the back payments he owes you? He has to pay that, right?"

Dallas shook her head. "I'd have to get a lawyer, and that would eat up most of what he owes me."

"Have you put money aside?" I asked gently, trying not to cause more tears.

"A little," said Dallas, pulling her legs to her chest and looking pitiful. "But not enough to live on for very long."

"Well, let's see," I said. "You have your house in Dallas, right? And it's paid for?"

Dallas shook her head. "Not paid for. I could sell it, but it won't be enough to live on for very long." And that started the tears again.

"Oh, don't cry. I hate to see you so sad. Let's think about this. Maybe it's not as bad as you think."

Dallas looked at me like I was on drugs. And I have to admit, I was a little low on words of encouragement. She was right. She should have taken the lump sum and invested it, and maybe not have bought a house in Aspen. But at least I knew enough not to say that.

Honestly, I had no idea what she was going to do. I wanted to say, "What would Scooby Do?" Which was a joke from our early days and usually made her laugh. But I was pretty sure it wouldn't help now. And neither would jazz hands or funny faces or any of the things that helped when we were younger and our problems were smaller.

She was still beautiful. She could maybe get a job with her looks. But at thirty-five, she wasn't likely to get the primo jobs she'd gotten ten years ago. Really, I was out of ideas. Totally dry. Zilch. I didn't know how to help her except to hold her and let her cry. And I wondered what kind of friend I was if I couldn't offer even the tiniest hint of good advice.

I tried to think what I would do if I were in her shoes. If I lost all my money. Which didn't sound all that bad, honestly, because when I didn't have money, at least I had Thomas. Life was so simple back then. But I knew that admission wouldn't help Dallas. And I didn't have a three-year-old daughter to support, so it was hard to put myself in Dallas's shoes. Beautiful, sky-high designer shoes normally. But today she wore fuzzy pale pink socks and looked about twelve years old. I had to figure out a way to help her.

I would give her my last dime, of course. I would give her anything. But I knew she wouldn't want that. She needed a new life plan, not charity.

And then I got it. I knew exactly what I would do if I were in her fuzzy pink socks.

"Come on," I said, tugging at her hand. "Come with me. I know someone who can help us." Dallas didn't budge.

"Lucy, I'm not going anywhere. Look at me! I'm a mess."

She was right. But we didn't have a choice. "Me, too. I'm a mess too. But I know someone who can help us."

"Well, can't you just call them? Who is it, anyway?"

"Okay, you stay here. I'll be right back."

I drove into town and felt exhaustion filling every pore, worried I wouldn't be able to find him. But somehow, whenever I needed Glacier, he was just there. And sure enough as I came through the S-curves and started through town, I saw him. It was the oddest thing.

He walked across the street and over to his battered blue pickup. I pulled up alongside him, blocking one lane of traffic and getting honked at in the process. Aspen traffic probably wasn't the best place for a woman with nerves as frayed as the seats in Glacier's truck. I rolled down my window.

"I need your help," I said without any preamble.

"Okay," he said, leaning into the car.

"Follow me." I made a U-turn in the middle of Main and waited until he could do the same. Then I hurried back to Dallas's house. And all the while I marveled that someone I'd known such a short period of time would agree to follow me to who-knows-where with absolutely no explanation. But Glacier was one of a kind.

When we got to the house and parked in the wide drive, I hurried over to him.

"Dallas needs us," I said. "She just lost financial support from her daughter's daddy, and she doesn't know what to do. Will you try to help her?"

He looked at me, searching my face, then nodded. "Sure, I'll try." But as I turned to walk up to the door, he reached out and took hold of my arm.

"Are you okay?" he asked.

And then I remembered. Even hiding behind my sunglasses, my face was swollen and blotchy. I was paler than usual, my hair was scary, and my cat burglar suit was wrinkled from clinging to Thomas. The fact that Glacier cared, that he would even ask about me, made me want to cry all over again. So I just nodded and hurried up the flagstone walk.

Dallas answered the door and stood back in the shadows. I knew it would be hard for her to let a man see her this way. We walked inside, and I stopped and stared in disbelief. In the fifteen or twenty short minutes it took me to find Glacier, Dallas had completely transformed herself. She now wore a short sundress that showed off her long legs, and tan and gold gladiator sandals. Her hair was tied back in a sleek ponytail, and her face was composed and completely made up. Wow. The girl was fast.

"Come in," she said, smiling at Glacier. "Thank you for coming to my rescue." She reached to give him a hug.

In the sunny living room, Glacier sat beside Dallas, and I sat across from them. Dallas crossed her legs and sat with her back straight. No tissue. No squishing into the corner of the couch in a miserable ball. No crying into her hands.

"Can I get you anything?" she asked Glacier. She didn't ask me. I would have loved a Grey Goose straight up.

"No thank you," said Glacier, sitting comfortably with his hands in his lap.

"So, I guess Lucy told you about my, um, predicament."

"Not the whole story," he said. "Why don't you tell me."

"Well, the gist of it is, I thought I would have support for my daughter – and for me – for another fifteen years or so. But the baby's father has informed me he's no longer working. So there's no longer any support." Dallas's voice cracked, and she cleared her throat.

Glacier nodded, and Dallas continued. "And I don't know what to do. I have to come up with a new plan, and I'm freaking out. I have enough to last us maybe a year, but then I don't know what to do." Now the panic filled her voice, and she looked like she might start crying.

"What do you like to do?" he asked.

"What?" That came from me. Not Dallas.

"What do you mean?" she asked.

"What do you like to do? What do you enjoy spending your time doing?"

She looked confused, and so was I. We needed a plan for making money here, not a list of Dallas's favorite pastimes.

"Well, I like talking to people. You know, socializing. I don't think there's much money in that." She tried to smile.

"What are you good at?" he asked.

"Well, let's see, I used to work at car shows. I was pretty good at getting wealthy guys to buy expensive cars." Now she did smile.

"Sounds like you're good at sales," Glacier said, smiling at her.

Dallas shrugged. "I guess maybe I am."

"Do you have a computer?"

Dallas giggled and nodded, "Everyone has a computer."

Which made me wonder if Glacier owned a computer. Or if he relied only on the Big Book of Answers.

"You might see about taking online courses in sales. Think about what type of sales you'd like to be in. Concentrate on that. If you focus your attention on that, it'll grow. If you have a sincere, clear intention and work toward it, you can make it happen."

I never would have thought of that. Any of that.

"Wow," said Dallas, giving her first real sunny smile of the day. "I love this idea. You're so smart!" She threw herself into his arms and hugged him again.

"I'll do it!" she said. "I'll start tonight. How did you get so smart?" she asked him. "How did you know just what to say?"

Glacier shook his head. "I didn't. The answer was inside of you. Problems are really just opportunities for change. A chance for something good. Something you never would have had otherwise."

I sighed deeply and wished for a martini. And a hot tub. And a cigarette.

What a day. What a gut-wrenching, heart-breaking, emotionally exhausting day.

My cell phone rang and I glanced at caller ID, expecting the call to be from Mary Beth, or Cheyenne. But the screen on my phone read *Pitkin County Jail.*

Oh boy.

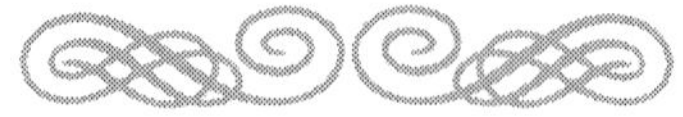

Chapter Twenty-One

I dug in the bottom of my purse for a much needed cigarette and tried not to panic while Dallas locked up her house and Glacier informed us that visiting hours for the jail were from six-thirty to seven-thirty each weekday evening. How he knew that, I have no idea. Maybe it was in the Big Book of Answers. But if we hurried, we could be there just after six-thirty. Dallas and I drove in my car with Glacier following us in his pickup. I tried to keep my mind on the road because it was tourist season, and the traffic was horrible. But as I cut in and out of long lines of vacationers and commuters, my mind was on Mary Beth sitting somewhere in the Pitkin County Jail. How could this be happening?

I thought I'd been to nearly every building in Aspen, but our trip to the jail was a first for me. Right behind the courthouse, just off Main, the jail looked more like a library or a post office, something innocuous, with its red brick and lush landscaping. But inside it seemed more like a jail. Glacier led us to a teller window where he spoke through a phone to an older woman with curly gray hair and a friendly smile. I'd expected the jail to be filled with angry burly men with shaved heads, toting machine guns and roughing us up if we got out of line.

The grandmotherly woman asked us for photo IDs, handed us forms requesting enough personal information for our autobiographies, then locked our purses, jackets, and the contents of Glacier's pockets in small storage lockers.

The lobby was sunny and comfortable with old-fashioned ski posters on the walls and cushiony benches. The three of us must have made a strange sight because the other visitors waiting in the lobby kept staring at us. Maybe it was because Dallas sat with her knees clenched together and a look of terror on her face. Or maybe just because Dallas looked like a European supermodel.

Once we were finally led to the visitation room, I stared through the small, blue-framed window at someone I didn't recognize. She wore orange pants and a hideous orange and white striped top. So I was wrong. No white linen. Her normally gorgeous long hair was pulled back in a rubber band, her face was pale and drawn, and her hands were naked of her usual tasteful yet oh-so-expensive jewelry.

I lifted the plastic phone to my ear, trying to smile. Mary Beth lifted the phone on her side of the glass window.

"What's he doing here?" she said. Not, *thank-God-you've-all-dropped-what-you-were-doing-and-rushed-to-my-rescue.*

"What happened to your hair?" I decided if MB was dispensing with pleasantries, I may as well too. When in jail, do as the jailed psychopathic narcissists do.

"Complimentary updo as part of my luxury accommodations," she said, running a shaky hand over her messy ponytail. The feel of the coarse rubber band seemed to remind her she was not in a position to be her usual controlling, critical self. Her face went slack, and she looked down into her lap. It was a Mary Beth I had never seen before and hoped I would never see again.

"Mary Beth," my voice was soft, "what happened?"

She looked up at me and the dejection I saw in her face made me want to reach for her. "I got caught up in what I was doing…miscalculated the time. The police response was…fast." Her voice was flat, hollow. The thick glass between us made her seem far away.

"They caught you in Cruella's house?"

Mary Beth nodded.

"I almost hate to ask," I said, "but what were you doing?"

Mary Beth swallowed. "Nothing so horrible. Nothing destructive really." She looked at Dallas and Glacier. "We'll talk about it later."

"What did she say?" asked Dallas, who could hear only my end of this insane conversation.

"What happens now?" I asked. "What can we do? Can we pay them and take you home? I mean, bail? Or bond? Or whatever?" It was my first time trying to spring a jailbird, and I had no idea what I was doing.

Mary Beth, who was usually very swift to correct me, just shook her head slowly. "I've been invited to stay the night," she said. Her lip quivered, and I could see she was scared.

"Okay," I tried to sound reassuring, "so you'll stay, and we'll be back here in the morning to get you out. You can leave in the morning, right?"

Mary Beth couldn't hold back her tears. She dabbed at her face with her free hand. "I'll meet with a judge in the morning. That's when I'll find out about bail."

I looked to Glacier for help. "She has to meet with the judge in the morning, and he'll set bail. Then can we come and get her out of here?" My voice rose on the last few words.

Glacier nodded. "Tell her once bail is set, she can call you, and we'll be back to post her bond and have her released."

I relayed the message to Mary Beth. She nodded, hung up the phone and stood to leave, never looking at me again. She turned and walked through the small sitting room and into an attached cell. I sat in the plastic chair, unable to move, still holding the dead phone in my hand. All I could think of was Mary Beth wearing a jail-issue pantsuit and shower shoes, being watched over by a woman who wore a badge and a gun.

Glacier gently took the phone from my hand and hung it up. He helped me out of the chair and moved Dallas and me toward the door. I stopped and grabbed his arm.

"Isn't there some way we can get her out tonight? I'll pay any price. I'll do whatever it takes. We can't leave her here!" A few people turned to look, but I didn't care.

Glacier's voice was calm. "Lucy, she'll be fine. More than likely she'll have a cell by herself. She'll spend a sleepless night, then see the judge in the morning. We can come back then and take her home. There's nothing more you can do for her tonight."

I looked back through the window to the empty chair where Mary Beth had been and started to cry.

Chapter Twenty-Two

Glacier drove off in his beater pickup on some mysterious mission, so Dallas and I went to my house. There was really nothing for us to do at this point, but drink. And so we did.

As the sun slipped behind the mountains and the air turned cool on the deck, I couldn't stop thinking of Mary Beth, all alone in jail. With her penchant for breaking and entering and her unquenchable thirst for vengeance, I guess we should have considered the possibility, but I never really thought she'd get caught. Or that she'd lose herself in the crime and stop being careful. And for what?

Dallas's cell phone chirped and brought me back to the present. Which, I reminded myself, was where I was supposed to be anyway. Here and now.

"A text from Cheyenne," said Dallas, reading the screen on her pink phone.

"What's it say?" I drained the last sip of my martini.

Dallas shook her head and put the phone down. "That Shy. She's horrible at texting. She says her fake fingernails get in the way. This text doesn't make sense."

"Let's call and make sure she's okay. And tell her about Mary Beth."

Dallas dialed while I went inside for more of the magic sauce that helped us forget our troubles. Glacier wouldn't approve of my use of alcohol as a relaxant, stress-buster, memory blocker, and all around best friend. I made the second round of martinis extra strong.

"Did you get her?" I asked, pouring a big dollop into each glass.

Dallas shook her head. "No answer. But I told her we had big news and to call us. She won't be able to stand the suspense. You know how Shy loves a good story."

I smiled tiredly, thinking of Cheyenne. She was wide-open, full throttle, all the time. Fun, perky, loved everyone. And yes, Dallas was right, Cheyenne did love a good story. And I loved that crazy perky girl. I prayed she was okay. Well, not exactly prayed. Wished was more like it. Hoped with all my heart.

By the time Glacier got back to my house, Dallas and I were feeling slightly past relaxed. He declined a martini. I offered coffee, but he declined that too, and I wondered if he was still trying to give up all vices. I poured apple juice into a martini glass for him.

"What's the big mystery?" I asked. We were in the living room now, the deck a little too chilly for Dallas in her sundress and me in a tank top.

He sipped his martini glass of apple juice - which would have been comical if things hadn't been so serious. He put down the glass, folded his hands in his lap, and took his time answering.

"The homeowner might be persuaded to drop the charges," he finally said.

I frowned. "Who? Oh, the *homeowner*. Cruella. Wait a minute. How did you get involved? What, you know the chief of police or something?" I was being facetious.

He nodded. "Yes."

That's what I get for kidding around. "So you and the chief cooked up a plan to have the homeowner drop the charges?"

"No. I just asked her if she would."

I was quiet for a minute, imagining her opening her door and finding Glacier. Who then, in his deep husky voice and with his calm, serene manner, encouraged her to drop the charges and probably made it seem like her own idea.

"There's a small catch," he said.

"There almost always is," said Dallas in a soft voice.

Glacier gave her a smile that seemed to acknowledge her present situation. "Mary Beth has to drop the lawsuit. Once that's done, the charges against her will be dropped."

"What a relief!" said Dallas. "That's an easy fix."

I slowly shook my head. "You know how Mary Beth is once she gets on to something."

"I know," said Dallas, "but this is a get-out-of-jail-free card. There's no other way."

I shrugged, not so sure what Mary Beth would do when push came to shove. I turned to Glacier. "Mary Beth believes the homeowner – let's call her Cruella – is siphoning money out of her fiancé's estate. He died just four days before he was set to marry Mary Beth, and the money was supposed to go to build a children's hospital."

Dallas gaped at me. "Really?"

I nodded. "Really."

Glacier hadn't asked, but I thought he deserved to know the particulars since he was working so hard to get Mary Beth freed.

"Her lawyers are working to find proof of the mishandling of the money, but so far they haven't come up with anything. That's why Mary Beth took matters into her own hands."

Glacier nodded and seemed to be thinking the whole thing through.

"Wow," said Dallas softly, snuggling back in the couch. "Every time I think I know Mary Beth, she pulls a fast one."

I wanted to laugh - it was such a major understatement. Mary Beth had more layers than my grandma's baklava.

It was late, so Dallas called her nanny to make sure Baby Bentley was fast asleep, then agreed to spend the night in my guest room.

I grabbed a nightshirt and robe from my bedroom, then met Dallas in her room.

"Wild day," I said, slumping on the bed beside Dallas. I draped an arm around her shoulders. "You okay? I mean, the whole Baby Daddy thing?"

She leaned into me and I got a whiff of her Joy perfume – rose and jasmine and summer sunshine. Perfect for her. "Thanks for helping me," she said. "I feel so much better. Somehow, just being around Glacier makes everything seem better."

I nodded. "I know. It's weird."

"What about you?" she asked, turning to look at me.

I dropped my arm and pulled back. "What about me?"

"Well," she said, reaching down to unbuckle her gladiator heels. "I didn't want to say anything before, but I could tell you'd been crying. Did something happen?"

I sighed, concentrating on Dallas's perfect pink toes and trying not to think about the past twelve hours. "Yeah," I said finally. "Something happened. But I don't think I can talk about it right now." My throat closed up.

She nodded. "I know. You don't like to talk about stuff that hurts. But if you ever do need to, I'm here. Always."

She looked at me and gave me a little smile. I hugged her and held her close for a minute. More emotion. More accusations of my inability to show my feelings. Sheesh. Would this day ever end?

I stood to leave, turning when I got to the door. "No word from Cheyenne?" I asked.

"Not yet," said Dallas, taking off her sundress to reveal a perfect body with no tan lines. "Do you think we should worry?"

I was already worried, but didn't know exactly what we could do about it. "Well, since she sent you a text, I'm guessing she's fine. Probably just on a hot date with the butthead, right?"

"Probably," said Dallas, pulling the nightshirt over her head. "I'll call her again in the morning."

"Sweet dreams." I said and shut the door behind me.

On my way back down the hall to the living room, I wondered if this might finally be the night I would have my way with Glacier. And by *my way*, I just meant a kiss, a hug, a little hand holding. Hot monkey love was too much for me to even think about after the day I'd just lived through. And besides, Glacier didn't seem like the crazy-casual-sex kind of guy. But every time his lips curved into a smile, I wondered what it would be like to kiss him. Everything about him made me think of sex. Those sleepy bedroom eyes. His hunky build and those rough hands that surely knew their way around a woman's body.

Maybe it was because it had been such a long dry spell since Thomas. Or maybe it was because Glacier was so perfectly put together, so ruggedly disarming. I needed to be touched by a man. Especially on this night, after finally saying goodbye to Thomas and closing that chapter of my life. I needed to be held. I needed to feel desired.

But when I got to the living room, Glacier was standing, waiting for me.

"I'll go," he said. "You've had a long day."

I smiled at him. "Not so long that I don't have the energy to entertain a handsome man."

His eyes crinkled and I actually felt butterflies in my stomach. Like when you're in high school and the cutest guy in the senior class walks by your locker and smiles at you. Like that. Except this wasn't high school. Because if it was, I would probably have a much easier time getting laid.

He reached for my hand, and I loved the very touch of him. His skin was warm, his hand rough and strong. He walked to the door, me following behind still holding his hand.

And at the door, just as I'd dreamed of so many times, he took me in his arms. Well, not quite like I'd dreamed. Because there was no swishy tongue kiss. No groping of body parts or heavy breathing. But he held me to him, and I put my tired head on his shoulder. And it was about the best feeling I'd had in a long, long time. Better than trying on a pair of perfectly fitting half-priced pumps. Better than the first sharp, cold sip of the best martini in the world. Better even than – I can't believe I'm saying this – sex. Because it was exactly what I needed.

I felt his steady heartbeat. Felt the warmth of his arms across my back. Smelled the clean, masculine scent of him. And wanted to stay in his arms forever. But as I shifted to get closer to him, to feel more of him, he pulled back.

"Goodnight, Lucy." He smiled at me and kissed me on my forehead. And then he was gone.

Chapter Twenty-Three

I tossed in my bed most of the night, worried sick about Mary Beth, and finally rose with the sun. Or in Mary Beth's case, the dawn of a new *error*. Dallas wasn't far behind me, anxious to get home to Baby Bentley. The doorbell rang and I couldn't imagine who else might be up at this hour, then felt silly when I peeked through the door because I should have known. Glacier.

"You're up early," I said.

He held up his ecologically-friendly bag. "I thought you might want breakfast before picking up Mary Beth."

I smiled at him. How nice.

On the back deck, I laid out sunny yellow napkins, silverware, and plates. Glacier passed around his original cure-what-ails-you smoothies and big, healthy-looking muffins. Dallas joined us, looking fresh as a daisy in yesterday's clothes.

"Yummy," she said, taking a seat and going for a muffin,

"Careful," I said. "Those are probably really, *really* good for you."

Glacier smiled.

Dallas popped a bite in her mouth. "Mmm, delish."

"What time do you think we should expect a call from Mary Beth?" I asked, never imagining he wouldn't know the answer. He was like one of those websites you can ask anything and it shoots out the answer. Like our very own magic 8-Ball.

Glacier sipped his smoothie. "Depends on how many others are seeing the judge this morning. It could be any time, really."

Hah. So he wasn't psychic or clairvoyant or magic.

"Are you going with me?" I asked him.

Glacier shook his head. "I think it's better if you go without me. Mary Beth's in a fragile state right now. She needs to be surrounded by friends and family, people who love her."

"She needs to be surrounded by orange caution cones and yellow police tape," I said.

The Mary Beth who walked out of the Pitkin County Jail was way different from the Mary Beth who had gone in...was it only yesterday? The newly freed Mary Beth was subdued. Maybe even contrite.

I guess I'd seen way too many cop shows because posting Mary Beth's bond was a total disappointment. A measly five thousand dollars, and they let her walk. I was expecting to fork over a huge sum of money to free this dangerous psychopath and lawyer terrorizer. I'd imagined myself going into the bank and walking out with a briefcase stuffed with hundred-dollar bills. As it turns out, five thousand is a fairly small stack of cash. And after a significant amount of red tape, I sprang my little jailbird, and we were on our way home.

Mary Beth was quiet. Her clothes were wrinkled, her makeup was smudged, her hair hung wild around her face, and she looked exhausted, slumped into the passenger seat of my Jeep.

"I think you should come to my house," I said, expecting her to put up a fight. "I'll fix you something to eat. You can take a nice soak in the hot tub and I'll give you some clean clothes. We can sit out back and have a mimosa."

"Fine," she said.

Since I was on a roll, I decided to keep on going. "Glacier spoke to the homeowner for you."

She turned to me. "Who?"

"Cruella. The evil one."

She looked out the window.

"She agreed to drop all charges against you."

Mary Beth didn't move a muscle.

"You'd have to drop the lawsuit."

I waited for her to rant and rave and remind me of the facts, as she perceived them to be. But she didn't.

"Fine," she said again, her voice sounding tired. "Consider it done."

Wow, I thought to myself. I'm really getting good at this.

We sat on my deck with mimosas, Mary Beth having bathed and dressed and groomed herself within an inch of her life. She wore my favorite Juicy track suit – which actually fit her better than it did me – and definitely did not look like a woman who had spent the night in jail. I was pretty sure she had slept even less than I had, but somehow she was able to cover up her dark circles better. And after two mimosas and a few bites of bagel, the beaten, contrite, agreeable Mary Beth faded away, and the confident, self-exalted egomaniac came screaming back to life.

"Why did your friend Glacier get involved in my private business?" she asked, dabbing at her mouth with an ivory napkin.

Oh boy. "Because he's a nice person and wanted to help you out of this giant jam you're in."

"And why do you take everything he says as gospel?" she asked. "He's a stranger. Every word from his mouth might as well be chiseled onto a stone tablet, the way you eat it up."

I stared at her, stunned. "Are you kidding me? He tried to help you! He went completely out of his way, expecting nothing in return. Doesn't that mean anything to you?"

Mary Beth looked slightly less full of herself for about fifteen seconds. "It does, actually. Mean something. But I never asked for his help. And I'm not dropping the lawsuit."

I couldn't believe my ears. I didn't even try to hide my incredulity.

"Mary Beth, are you nuts?" And actually, I probably shouldn't have asked that, because I was pretty sure she was. "This is the real deal. You just spent a night in jail. Where they put people who do *really bad things*. You've been arrested! For second degree burglary, which is a felony! This is your one chance to make this whole thing go away. How could you possibly even think of not taking this deal?"

Mary Beth leaned in. "I won't let her win, Lucy. This is too important. I'll go to jail for the rest of my life before I'll let that bitch take Rolf's money."

"I get that," I said, softening my voice. "I understand *why* you're doing this. And by the way, you never told me. *What* exactly were you doing when the cops found you?"

Mary Beth reached out and grabbed my hand, startling me. "I finally have proof! Exactly what I need to put Cruella away."

"What do you mean?"

She let go of my hand, and I wrapped both of mine around my mimosa, afraid she might try to grab me again. She had a crazy look in her eyes.

"I found a file on her computer, all the documents proving she's been taking money out of the estate and moving it to a Swiss account."

I made bug eyes at her. "You were on Cruella's computer when the cops came?"

Mary Beth nodded. "Thank God, I'd just emailed the file to myself. It made the cuffs hurt a little less." Mary Beth sat back as the story got stranger and stranger. "Now I just have to figure out how to use the proof. I can't very well turn the documents over since they're stolen. But you can bet your ass I'll figure something out."

"And if Cruella looks in her *Sent* file on her email and sees she sent something to you?"

"Wiped clean," said Mary Beth, finishing off her mimosa.

Now we were getting somewhere. Forget stinky cheese in an underwear drawer. This was more like what I had in mind for Mary Beth's life of crime. Espionage was much more her style.

Chapter Twenty-Four

I carefully wrote out the check, stuffed it in an envelope, and wrote Glacier's name on the front. I drove to town, expecting him to appear out of nowhere as he always did when I needed him. Except I didn't really need him this time, I wanted to thank him. For taking the time to help my friends out of their peculiar predicaments of late. Make that, my thankless friends. Take Dallas, for example. I drove her home before I picked up Mary Beth from jail, and the conversation went something like this:

"I can't wait to see my little sweetie pie," she said, smiling. "I hate being away from Bentley overnight."

I nodded. "You and Baby Bentley have big plans today?"

"Well, yes, but not together. Bentley has ice skating camp."

"She's only three years old."

"I know. Isn't it cute? So while she's at camp, I'll hit the computer."

"Good for you," I said. "Glacier's idea of taking online classes is brilliant. I wish I'd thought of it myself."

"I changed my mind on that," said Dallas, pulling down the visor on the passenger side of my car and checking her makeup. "Seriously. How can I support myself and Bentley and two houses and a nanny on a sales job?"

"But you said you were going home to hit the computer," I said, almost whining.

Dallas smoothed on lip gloss, then snapped the visor back into place. "I decided to get on those millionaire matchmaking sites. It's perfect! And I owe it all to Glacier. I never would have thought of using the computer!"

Oh boy.

I couldn't bear the idea of Glacier's generous efforts to help Dallas and Mary Beth going to waste. So I was on my way to thank Glacier the only way I knew how. Well, actually, I could think of a more personal way to thank him, but so far Glacier hadn't seemed too receptive to that.

I felt a happy buzz, playing the scene out in my mind, handing him the envelope, watching him peek inside, maybe even seeing his eyebrows rise in surprise. Which they rarely did. But surely seeing all those zeroes would trigger at least an eyebrow raise. Because now he could replace his old pickup or pay off debt, and maybe even buy a new pair of boots. And since this was Aspen, he could probably find a pair of boots with the same price tag as a truck.

It was the most exciting thing to happen to me in a while, this act of helping him out. I smiled big to myself, imaging how I was about to make Glacier's day. Maybe his whole year.

But as I made the familiar drive into town, I couldn't get Mary Beth's accusations out of my mind. The way she insisted I was letting Glacier run my life. That I took everything he said as gospel. What a bunch of baloney.

Most of the time I did believe what he said. Because most of what he said made sense. And if it didn't make sense at the time, it usually did later.

Besides, he never gave me advice unless I asked for it. And even then, he wasn't all that forthcoming. And it wasn't like he charged for his gentle admonishments and subtle suggestions. Not like one of MB's lawyers. Or my mother's psychiatrist. Or the psychic hotline.

I pushed Mary Beth out of my mind as I drove down Main Street, looking for the battered blue truck and imagining what he might drive if he had the cash. But my quick spin through town netted me nothing but the frustration of driving in Aspen traffic. No beat up blue pickup. No Glacier.

I parked as close to Main Street Bakery as possible, which wasn't very close at all since this was June. Inside the cool bakery, the smell of something wonderful and hot out of the oven hit my nose and made my stomach growl. But I didn't have time for anything as inconsequential as food right now. I was on a mission.

The small table by the front window was empty. Weird. I'd always been able to find him before now. Maybe if I waited. Maybe he was on his way.

To fill the time, I searched out the source of the incredible aroma and ended up practically inhaling a freshly baked scone. It was all Glacier's fault, and I would tell him so when he walked in and frowned at the incriminating evidence of butter and honey on my face.

But when the last of the scone was gone, and I'd started eyeing the brownies in the display case, I knew I had to get out of there. While I finished my coffee, I studied the workers behind the counter, trying to figure out who was in charge. There was one guy telling the others what to do, so I figured he must be the boss. I walked up to the counter.

"How can I help you?" he asked, seeming friendly and approachable enough.

"Are you the owner?" I asked.

"Owner, manager, all of the above."

I took the envelope out of my purse. "Would it be possible for me to leave this check for Glacier Jones?"

"Oh, you buy a piece of his art?"

"No..." I drew the word out, tilting my head. "I didn't know he was an artist."

"Really? He's pretty well known."

Now I was really confused. "No, I just thought he could use, you know, a little help."

The owner laughed. Hard. Really hard. "Are you kidding me? This is a joke, right?"

He continued to laugh while I stood there holding a sizeable check with Glacier's name on it in one hand, and my foolish pride in the other.

"Lady, I don't know you. I don't know how much money you have. But I'd be willing to bet Glacier Jones has more than you." He shook his head as if to say *women!*

I could hardly find the words. "You can't be serious! He looks so... needy."

That seemed to calm the owner down. He leaned his beefy arms on the counter, and his face became more thoughtful and less mocking.

"Glacier is probably less in need than anyone I know. And I don't just mean monetarily. He doesn't need more clothes. Doesn't need a fancy house. Doesn't need fame or fortune or attention or recognition. Makes more money on one sculpture than I make in a year."

"Really." I was stunned.

The owner nodded. "Yep. Gives most of it away though."

I looked past the owner, trying to understand.

"You still wanna leave your check?"

I stuffed the envelope back in my bag and walked out, shaking my head and thinking the day could not get any weirder. But before I could get to my car, Dallas called with the latest crisis.

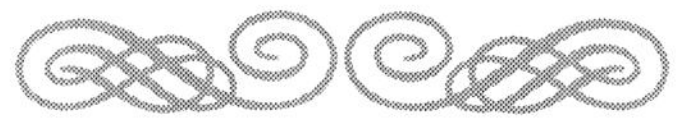

Chapter Twenty-Five

"Lucy, I'm pretty sure Shy's in trouble," said Dallas when I answered my phone. "We have to go check on her."

"I can be there in ten minutes. What happened?"

Silence on the other end.

"Dallas?"

"Well, don't get mad. It's just sort of a feeling I have."

Oh boy.

"What do you mean, a *feeling*?"

"Not just a feeling," she said. "More like, things just don't add up. Shy hasn't called. She hasn't texted. I've left, like, a million messages, and she won't answer her phone."

I pulled into traffic and tried to think. "Maybe her phone died," I said, slamming on the brakes as pedestrians walked out in front of my car.

"Maybe," said Dallas, sounding skeptical, "but we have to know for sure."

I pulled up to Dallas's house, and she hopped in my car, looking not so much worried as just plain gorgeous. Blond hair falling in soft waves, navy tank dress hugging her curves and showing lots of soft, smooth skin. She turned to wave at the front door, where the nanny held Baby Bentley, still in her ice skating togs.

"What's that on her arm?" I asked, waving at the funny three-year-old.

"A sticker from ice skating camp. They get a sticker if they do well. I took her to get ice cream when I picked her up, and there was this guy in front of us with tattoos all up and down his arms, and she yelled out, 'Mama, look! He did *real* good today!'"

I laughed. What a stress buster that kid was.

I wasn't convinced we were in an emergency situation with Cheyenne. For all we knew, she and the butthead were in St. Bart's. Or Florida. Or anywhere in between.

"How long since her last text?" I asked.

Dallas dug into her elegant, sunny beige handbag and came up with her pink phone.

"The last text was last night when we were on your deck. It just says *SLS*."

I looked at Dallas and screwed up my face. "SLS? What's that supposed to mean?"

Dallas shrugged. "It doesn't mean anything to me. But that's the thing. Shy's texts are usually like that. Then I'll ask her what she meant, and she'll tell me, and I never would have figured it out in a million years. She hits the wrong letters all the time."

I wound through the busy midday traffic while trying to mentally insert other letters into the puzzle, like on Wheel of Fortune. I wanted to buy a vowel. I wanted a giant martini and a nap. I wanted world peace. I wanted just one day without my friends going sewer-rat-crazy on me.

And that made me think of Glacier because he was my go-to guy whenever I had a problem. And that reminded me of my trip to the bakery. "Dallas, what do you know about art in Aspen?"

"What?" She looked up from doing something with her phone. The look on her face said, "What the hell does that have to do with Cheyenne?"

"Never mind," I said. I knew I should be thinking of Cheyenne and not Glacier. But I just couldn't shake the shocker of his true identity. Why had he never said anything? Why had I never asked? It had never occurred to me to ask about his occupation or his balance sheet. I just assumed he was out of work and low on cash. Shame on me.

"Do you think it's crazy the way we take Glacier's advice on things?" I asked. "Do you think we should question what he tells us more than we do?"

"Hmm?"

Dallas was ignoring me. Still fiddling with her phone.

I wondered where he lived. And why he continued to drive a truck that coughed and wheezed, and had a squeaky door and an Indian blanket for a seat cover. Why he wore the same worn, dusty boots and never strayed from his uniform of white T-shirt and faded jeans.

I felt dumb all over again, going to the bakery with my little thank-you check only to be told Glacier has more money than I do and doesn't need my charity.

But since he doesn't need money, and I spend most of my nights fantasizing about him, maybe it was time to consider thanking him the old fashioned way...

"Ohmygosh, Lucy!"

I glanced at the stricken look on Dallas's face. She held her phone up.

"Maybe it's supposed to be *O*," she said.

"What?" I was in my happy place, dreaming of a long, deep, slow kiss. Dallas clunked me back to earth.

"Maybe it's not an *L*. Maybe it's an *O*. *SOS?*"

Oh boy.

❧

I sped up the long drive to Michael's stupidly huge home. It seemed so peaceful on the outside. The horses moseyed in the deep green pasture. The aspen trees shimmered in the sun, and the bubbling fountain sounded like a tranquil mountain brook. I just hoped this elegant, sun-drenched setting wasn't a façade for something more sinister behind the closed door.

As we drew nearer, I hoped against hope we'd find Cheyenne lazing by the pool, which she loved to do and had the deep tan to prove it. But the pool was quiet. No one seemed to be around. Which was odd. The few times I'd been here there was usually a precision team of gardeners, pool guys, landscapers, and assorted minions keeping the palace fit for its king.

"Seems quiet," said Dallas.

"I was thinking the same thing."

I parked near the stone steps and turned off the car, a creepy feeling crawling up my spine. We moved slowly, hesitantly, our shoulders glued to each other's, walking side by side up the grand steps and looking around. I don't know what we expected to see. Or what we expected to find inside. We'd probably just watched too many episodes of *Dexter*.

"I'm sort of spooked," said Dallas as we came to the imposing double front doors.

"I'm sure everything's fine," I said, ringing the doorbell, and wishing I believed that.

Dallas turned and looked behind us. "Where is everyone?"

I shrugged. "Who knows? Maybe it's the Sabbath in this Kingdom of Crazy."

I turned back to the door and tried knocking, which just seemed silly. I mean, it was a twenty-thousand-square-foot house. Unless Butler Pennyworth was standing in the foyer, no one would ever hear it.

"What if no one answers?" asked Dallas.

"You mean like now?"

She nodded.

I looked around. "I guess we go to Plan B."

"What's Plan B?"

I shook my head. "I have no idea."

"Let's go to my house and figure something out," I said. The twenty-minute drive was quiet, both of us lost in our own thoughts, trying to believe everything was fine.

On the surface, it didn't seem like much. Just a misspelled text and a few unreturned phone calls. But I knew Dallas and Shy talked to each other at least once a day. Shy never went this long without returning a call to Dallas. Something really wasn't quite right.

We settled into our favorite chairs on my deck with iced tea and macadamia nuts. It was just after four o'clock, so we pretended it was too early for cocktails, knowing that on the dot of five I'd be back inside mixing a pitcher of martinis.

I held up my glass for a toast. "If we are what we eat..."

"We're cheap, fast, and easy," said Dallas. We clinked. But it wasn't as much fun as it usually was. We were too worried about Cheyenne.

"Let's call Mary Beth," I said. "Maybe she'll come over and help us make a plan."

I dialed and she picked up on the third ring.

"Hey," I said. "Come over. We need your Ivy League brain power."

There was a pause. "Who is *we*?" asked Mary Beth.

"Dallas. And me."

Another pause. "Sorry. I don't have time to help you two with the latest quiz in Cosmo."

She was probably just kidding around, but the whole thing hit me wrong. I was worried sick about Cheyenne, and I'd had enough of Mary Beth and her superior attitude. Especially after spending the past two days worrying about her and bailing her out of jail.

"Mary Beth, if you'd like to pull your head out of your ass and come over, we could really use your help!"

Dallas gaped at me. I held up my free hand in a gesture of frustration.

"Well, when you put it like that, I don't see how I could refuse. Except I'm on my way to meet with my attorneys."

"Make it quick then, and meet us here when you're through. You're dropping the suit, right?"

No answer.

"Mary Beth? You're dropping the suit against Cruella, right? I really do understand why this is so important to you, but this is your Get-Out-Of-Jail-Free card, remember? The one Glacier worked so hard to negotiate for you?"

"I didn't ask him to do that," said Mary Beth. "Maybe your friend Glacier should learn to mind his own business."

Even for Mary Beth, this was too much.

"Mary Beth, you self-righteous narcissist!"

Dallas hissed my name and looked at me like I was a rabid dog, but I was over the top now, and picking up steam.

"I think those words are redundant," said Mary Beth.

I shook my head. "I thought a trip to jail might help you realize you're not above the rest of the world. You think only your opinions matter. You think your needs are more important than everyone else's. Do you realize you *always* have to sit in the front seat, every time any of us are in a car together?"

"What possible difference could that make?" asked Mary Beth, seeming to think I was amusing. "And if I am a narcissist as you've so kindly pointed out, what's the harm in that? Maybe I value my own opinions because they're valid. Maybe I believe in myself because no one else ever did."

A little of the punch seemed to leave her, and now I felt kind of bad.

"Mary Beth, other people and their feelings do matter. And as long as we're laying the cards on the table, not all of your ideas are good ideas. What about breaking into Cruella's house? That didn't turn out so well, did it? Just let it go, Mary Beth. Drop the lawsuit and let someone else fight this battle. There's no way Cruella can get away with this in the long run."

No answer this time. No witty comebacks.

"MB," my voice softened and I leaned back in my chair. "You live a life of not connecting with anyone. Most of the time you treat everyone – including Dallas and Cheyenne and me – like servants. I know this probably all boils down to not feeling loved by your own parents. And I have to say, there's no excuse for their dismal parenting skills. But you're grown now. You have to get over that. I'm afraid if you don't realize how you're alienating everyone around you, you'll end up spending the rest of your life alone."

Mary Beth hung up on me. I was only surprised she hadn't done it sooner.

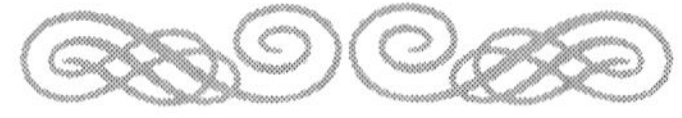

Chapter Twenty-Six

"Now what?" I asked, staring at my phone, wondering what I'd just done.

Dallas just looked at me with wide eyes and shrugged.

I rubbed my head where a headache was beginning to dance against my temples. "God, I can't believe I said all that. I can't believe I let Mary Beth get to me like that."

I shook my head and leaned back in my chair. I thought of Glacier, the day he blew up. How he'd rubbed a hand over his face, blew out a few breaths, and somehow restored his tranquility. I thought about trying it, but I was about a hundred-percent sure it wouldn't work for me.

"Now that I've completely alienated Mary Beth, what do we do about Cheyenne?"

Dallas set her glass of iced tea on the stone table between us and looked at me, seeming reluctant to answer. I raised my eyebrows at her.

"This may sound like a crazy idea," she said, "but I don't know what else to do."

I lifted my hands palms up as if to say, "What? Spit it out!"

Dallas chewed her lush bottom lip. I had a mental image of squeezing her elegant neck with my bare hands until the words popped out. I know that sounds really mean, and I'm not proud of it, but how much more I could take? The past twenty-four hours had been fairly action packed, and the telephone smackdown with Mary Beth was the last straw – before cocktails, no less. I was a little short on patience. More than a little short.

I think Dallas knew I was about to blow. "Maybe you should drive me home," she said. "I need to check on Bentley. I'll tell you my idea on the way."

Once we were on the highway and headed toward Maroon Creek, Dallas finally coughed up her idea. "I think we should call Shy's ex."

"What good will that do?" I asked. "We don't even know if she's in trouble. What will we say to him?"

Dallas turned to look at me, and I realized my tone was a little snarky. "Sorry," I said. "Go ahead."

"He's a cop. And he knows Shy really well. She hurt him bad, but I know he still loves her. If we tell him she's in trouble, he'll come and help."

I forced myself to stay calm. Took three breaths and counted to ten. Took another minute to make sure my voice wasn't snarky. "But what will we tell him?" I asked in the calmly modulated voice of a hostage negotiator. "We don't know for sure she's in trouble."

"Right, but we think she is. And that's good enough for me. I think we should do whatever we can. Even if it turns out she's fine. So what if we involve her ex for nothing and the whole thing is incredibly embarrassing. Isn't that better than not doing anything and wishing we had?"

She made a very good point. I smiled at her. Sort of. Maybe it was more of a grimace. But it was all I could muster. "Sure," I said. "You're right. Let's do it."

When we got to Dallas's house, Bentley was asleep, so Dallas and I settled into her decidedly feminine home office and tried to figure out how to reach Cheyenne's ex-husband. Luckily he had a quirky name, and there was only one in all of Denver.

"Dallas, are you sure it's Will and not William?"

Dallas nodded as she clicked the computer keys to bring up the phone number. "Yep. I asked Shy. I remember she thought it was cute."

I always knew Cheyenne's last name was Power. I just didn't know her ex-husband's name was Will. That's right. Will Power. Honestly. What were his parents thinking?

At this point I didn't really care because it made it easy for us to track him down. There was no answer at home, so Dallas tried the Denver Police Department and was directed to Sergeant Will Power's voicemail. But when the electronic voice encouraged her to leave a message at the beep, the usually confident Dallas seemed to falter.

"Yes, Mr. Power, I mean, Sergeant. Will. My name is Dallas, and I'm a very good friend of Cheyenne's. That is, your ex-wife, Cheyenne. Anyway, we're worried about her and thought you should know that she's, sort of…missing. I think I could explain this better in person. I mean, on the phone. Could you please call my cell?"

Dallas rattled off her cell number and hung up, clearly flustered. "I totally botched that."

I patted her on the shoulder. "You did fine. He'll get the idea."

Dallas typed something into the computer, her long nails making sharp clicking sounds. "Do you want to see my profile?" she asked.

"What profile?"

"My profile for the millionaire dating website."

Well, how could I say no?

⁂

An hour later I was still reading through the profiles of millionaire men all over the country. It was sort of like porn. I didn't really want to see it, but I couldn't stop looking.

"Listen to this guy. 'Like fast cars and mansions? Email me!' And this guy talks about his Miami Vice style boat and his 90210 beach house. Sheesh, he needs to move into this century."

"I know," said Dallas, leaning back in a comfy chair and filing her nails. "Some of them are really lame. Keep going. Get it out of your system. Then I'll show you the guys I like."

I flipped through a few more profiles. "Married and looking for a discreet relationship? Come on!"

"There's a lot of that on this site," said Dallas. "I always skip right over those."

"Well, I would hope so," I said, distracted by the next profile. "The caption on this one says 'South of France', but it looks like he's standing in his bathroom. This guy wants someone kinky and submissive. This one's face is scratched out in all the photos, so I'm guessing he's married. Oh, and get this, this one wants a woman who can speak intelligently about current issues but will shut up when he tells her to!" I turned around and looked at Dallas. "Honey, I don't think you should be on this site. These guys are giving me the creeps."

Dallas uncurled herself and came over to the computer. "You're just picking out all the freaks," she said. "Let me show you the guys I've been talking to."

I let her sit at the computer. "You've already been talking to some of these guys?"

"Oh sure. As soon as I put my profile up, I got quite a few hits."

No surprise there. Any man in his right mind – and plenty who weren't – would want a chance to be with Dallas. But I had a bad feeling about the whole thing.

"How about forgetting this and maybe meeting guys the old fashioned way?" I suggested.

"Which is?"

I shrugged. "I don't know. Through friends? So you know something about the guy and he doesn't turn out to be some perverted maniac."

"Okay," she said, "you're my friend. Who've you got in mind?"

She had me there. "Well, no one right at the moment."

"Look," she said, turning the computer screen so I could see. "He enjoys yachting, skiing, and the company of beautiful women."

"Cute," I said. "Except it looks like he's holding in his stomach. And his username is RealBig. Ewwww."

"Here's the guy I like the best," she said.

"Wow." I leaned forward to take a better look. "He's hot. At least his body. It's sort of hard to see his face. What's the catch?"

"No catch," said Dallas. "He lives in Denver. Successful businessman. Travels all over the world and wants someone to share all that life has to offer."

"There's got to be a catch. Is he a perv? Is his username HotRod?"

Dallas laughed. "No. His username is Delta9, he has his own jet, he likes intelligent, classy women, and he wants to take me to New York this weekend."

"No way!" I said. "You can't just hop on a plane with a guy you've never met before. Tell him to fly in and spend the weekend in Aspen. Then you two can get to know each other here."

"He can't. He has a business meeting in New York."

"On the weekend? Who has business meetings on the weekend?"

Dallas shrugged. "Important men who have their own jets, I guess."

She looked very pleased with herself.

I stood and crossed my arms over my chest, looking down at her as if she were a naughty child. "You're not thinking this through, Dallas! It's just not safe to go off with someone you don't even know."

"But I *do* know him. I know he loves to ski, and his favorite food is scallops with black truffles. I know he lived in France for two years and loves to cook. His parents live in Florida, he graduated from Yale, and his dog's name is Nasdaq. That's more than I normally know about a guy before I go out with him."

"Seriously?"

"Yes, seriously. I usually don't know half that much."

"No, I mean, seriously his dog's name is Nasdaq?"

Dallas laughed and turned back to the computer. "Look at these other pictures. Here's his jet. Isn't it beautiful?"

It really was a nice jet.

"Look," I said, trying to lose the Mom voice and go for more of a concerned best friend. "If you're dead set on this, at least let me meet the guy before you go."

"Well," she glanced at me, "I guess that's not a bad idea. He's coming in on Friday, sometime late in the afternoon. I told him I would meet him at the airport when he calls."

"Okay, new plan. I'll drive you out to the airport, and that way I can meet him, and it will all be very casual. No big deal."

"I don't know, " Dallas picked at a cuticle. "You promise not to act like a dorm mother? You promise not to ask a million questions or do anything to embarrass me?"

"I promise. Now let's look in your closet and figure out what you should wear."

She squealed. I knew that would get her.

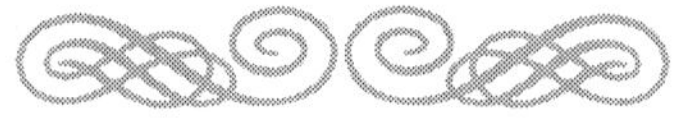

Chapter Twenty-Seven

The next two days were a total letdown because no one called us back. Not the Power Ranger. Not Cheyenne. Not even Mary Beth. By Thursday, I was much in need of Martini Thursday. But Dallas was the only member not missing in action at this point, and she was home packing. I half expected to see Glacier appear at my door with a cloth bag filled with some mystical concoction, but that didn't happen either.

I missed him. Being close to him was like a drug for me, like a glass of fancy cognac – exciting and comforting at the same time. I could really use one of his smiles about now - because they were full and sincere and warmed me from the inside out. They said *everything about this moment is good.* They spilled over with compassion and kindness, and made me believe everything he said.

I missed Cheyenne and even Mary Beth. My life was completely pathetic. So I dressed in jeans and my favorite black crisscross vamp sandals. And gave myself a pep talk, convincing myself that, like the shoes, I was smokin' hot. Uh huh, sure. Then I took myself to Jimmy's for some dinner and hopefully some company more interesting than my own.

Jimmy's was busy on this Thursday night in late June, but I found a place at the bar in between two just-handsome-enough men and ordered a margarita. I was feeling a little lonely. A little lost. And still just a little broken. So when the guy on my right turned and started chatting me up, I have to say I was relieved.

He looked like a local – cargo shorts, golf shirt, really nice haircut, expensive watch, and hiking sandals. His name was Charlie, his dog was tied up outside the restaurant – and his wife was in Tuscany. Oh well.

I was about to turn and check out the guy to my left, but then Charlie said something that would change the course of history. Well, my immediate future, anyway.

"Yeah, she loves spending time at our house there. I'll join her in a week or two. But I was hoping to lease our house here while we're gone. You know anyone who handles that kind of thing?"

"You mean, a realtor?" I asked. I sipped my Smokey Margarita – a Jimmy's specialty made with mescal and a splash of cranberry.

"No, no. I mean someone who can handle the whole thing. You know, find the client, get the house ready, take care of things while we're gone. I know a guy in LA who leases his house and has a woman who handles it all. Gets a chef for the lessees if they want it, nannies, transportation, housekeeping. All the guy has to do is tell her when the house is available, and she handles the rest."

My new friend Charlie turned as the bartender asked if he wanted to order, and that gave the little gears in my head time to work overtime. "Actually," I said, "this is your lucky day. That's exactly what I do."

He looked at me and a grin started on his face. "You're kidding me."

I shook my head and smiled. "Nope. No kidding. Where's your house?"

"Starwood," he said.

"Another coincidence. So is mine. We've probably driven right past each other coming and going." He didn't have to know mine was only a rental.

"Well, that's great! Do you have a card?"

"Sure," I said, making a show of searching through my black bag and thinking fast. I couldn't hand him my regular name and address card. I needed a real business card with a real business name. Something professional.

"Shoot. I was in a hurry when I changed bags tonight. I guess I forgot to put my cards in. But if you give me your card, I can fax you something in the morning."

"This is so great," said Charlie, reaching for his wallet. "It really is a small world, isn't it?"

"It really is," I said, smiling big.

❦

Well, how hard could it be? I mean, come on. I knew the area, knew the contacts, and had worked enough charity events to know exactly how to handle rich, pampered people. My life was empty and boring, and desperately in need of something new. I could use the money after giving up so much in the divorce. And I needed the challenge. The rush. This was just the thing to help me make a name for myself.

I pulled my first all-nighter since sophomore year in college. It took me that long to put together all my contacts for local services, search the internet for luxury Aspen homes on the market for lease, put together a dossier for the company, and come up with a kickass name. Just as the sun came up over the mountains, I finished typing up the sheet I would fax to Charlie:

Aspen Domain

A domain is sometimes defined as a sphere of influence. And that's exactly what you'll find with Aspen Domain – a firm of dedicated and professional Aspenites who have the influence and experience to provide a memorable and luxurious Aspen stay.

Spend your next vacation in Aspen, and let us make it the trip of a lifetime. We provide elegant homes and make all the arrangements from the moment you arrive.

We can pick you up in a limousine, provide a private chef for your dining needs, enlist the services of highly qualified nannies, and reserve a table for you at any of Aspen's elegant restaurants.

We provide full concierge service, including but not limited to the following:

Event Planning and Decorating
Private Chefs, Nannies, Caretakers, and Housekeeping Services
Private Jet, Limousine, and Rental Car Service
Daily Excursions for Skiing, Shopping, Rafting, Hiking
Personal Shopping
Listing of Recommended Restaurants and Clubs
Admission to the Exclusive Caribou Club
Come to Aspen, where the beautiful people play…

Then I put together a separate sheet that would go out to prospective homeowners – beginning with Charlie – listing the services we could provide for them. It was mostly fiction. Saying we handle only the most elegant homes and market to our growing list of elite clientele. Hah! That we prepare the home prior to the guests' arrival, including housekeeping, gift basket, stocking the kitchen with guest requests, and contracting with nannies and car services. We then return the home to pristine condition while charging a mere eighteen-percent for our trouble.

I stole most of this from the websites of similar companies. But the truth was, I really did have a lot of connections – on both sides of the equation. As soon as I faxed the information to Charlie, I got on the phone with an old friend in New York.

Stella was a friend from high school who now worked in the fashion industry. I was a bit fuzzy on exactly what she did, but it was something about providing personal assistants to top models in the industry. I wasn't so much concerned with what she did as who she knew.

"Stella!" I bellowed the name like Marlon Brando in *A Streetcar Named Desire*. Not original, I know, but it was our old gag from way back when.

"Luce! What a surprise! How are things in sunny Houston?"

"I'm actually in sunny Aspen. How are things with you?"

"Crazy busy," said my petite friend. "Like herding cats! It's making me old before my time."

"Maybe you need to come to Aspen and hang out for a while."

"I'd love to. Can I keep that in mind? The next month is insane. But after that?"

"Let's plan on it," I said. "And in the meantime, I have something that might help you out." Nice angle.

"Really? Spill it."

"I just started a new business here, leasing the best homes in the area as vacation homes to the rich and famous. A new one just came on the market, and it's fabulous. And I thought of you. Thought maybe some of your models might need a break. You could send them out, and I'll take care of the rest. I can set them up with a chef, reservations in the best restaurants, day trips for shopping or white water rafting. Even get them in to the Caribou Club. What do you think?"

"Wow, what brought this on? Last time we talked you were working on your tennis game and thinking of getting a pool boy!"

I bristled. "I've got to run," I said. "I'm meeting a celebrity client in ten minutes. Great talking to you..."

"Wait a minute! Hold on for just a sec. I've got my own celebrity client who desperately needs a nice vay-kay in Aspen. Talk about stressed out! She's been getting bad press lately for her little white powder habit. I need to get her out of town for a while. Let me check with her and I'll call you back. And you'll handle everything?"

I smiled to myself. Got her. "Of course. We'll pick her up at the airport, provide limo or car service, food, housekeeping, the works."

"Is it expensive?" asked Stella.

"Oh, yes, my friend. It's very expensive."

"Great. In that case, she'll love it. I'll call you back before noon."

I would later realize that I'd forgotten to explore a few tiny details while building my new empire. Like insurance. And taxes. And legal contracts. And the outrageous and abominable behavior of rich and pampered people. I was much too busy patting myself on the back for pulling together a thriving new business in the course of twelve hours. I leaned back in my chair and fell asleep.

Chapter Twenty-Eight

Friday started out as innocently as a Janet Jackson Super Bowl performance, with no hint of trouble ahead. I stood in Dallas's sunny bedroom and helped her decide on clothes for her trip to New York. Normally a peaceful, soothing place with buttery walls and spectacular views of the mountains, today it looked like a messy sorority house times ten. Except there were no pizza boxes on the floor. No hot fraternity guys hanging around. But every square inch of space was covered with clothes, and shoes, and accessories. And did I say shoes? I picked up a pair of hot pink starlet slides with bow accents on top and petted them.

I put the shoes on my hands and walked them over to Dallas, trying to make her laugh. But I should have saved myself the trouble. The millionaire from Denver would land at the airport around two that afternoon. Dallas was in full first-date, girly-girl panic mode.

"I don't want to pack too much," she said, standing beside her graceful four-poster bed. The soft yellow matelassé and mountain of lacy pillows were invisible beneath several layers of luscious clothes. "But I have to be prepared for anything. Oh! I need swimsuits!"

She hurried over to her bureau and opened a drawer bulging with bright bikinis. I shook my head to myself as she carefully culled through the strips of fabric and came up with three favorites. I hoped the millionaire was prepared. Dallas in a bikini was quite a sight.

"What if we go somewhere black tie? Maybe I should bring a long gown. But then I'd have to take the bigger suitcase. What if it's cold? New York sometimes gets chilly in the evenings. Will a cashmere wrap be enough?" Dallas turned toward her closet, all but wringing her hands.

I walked over and grabbed her gently by the shoulders, startling her.

"Honey, breathe!" I gave her a little shake. "It's one weekend. Not a year-long sabbatical. And I'll bet they even have stores in New York."

That seemed to perk her up. I helped Dallas whittle her choices down to a mere fraction of what she thought she might need. And even then, the amount of clothing would have served me well for a two-week vacation.

It took a ton of tissue paper and nearly an hour and a half, but we somehow loaded a large wheeled suitcase with everything Dallas thought she would need for the next two days. We were just picking up the mess and talking about going for an early lunch when her phone rang.

She squealed and hopped over a pile of shoes to lunge for her phone. "I bet it's him!" she said. "Maybe he's here! Ohmygosh! I'm not ready!" She picked up the phone, and her eyes got big.

"Cheyenne!" she almost shouted into the phone. "Where are you?"

I nearly broke my neck climbing over the pile of rejected clothes and jumping over Dallas's open suitcase. "Where is she?" I hissed.

Dallas shrugged and looked worried. "Are you okay? We've been trying to call you all week! And your last text was weird. What's going on?"

Dallas listened and shook her head at me. "What do you mean by a long time? How long?" I leaned my head close to Dallas, and she held the phone so I could hear.

"I don't know exactly," said Cheyenne, her voice lacking its usual cheerleader pep and high energy sparkle.

"Well, are you okay? Are you happy?" asked Dallas.

"Um, I guess you could say…it's…like an aberration," said Cheyenne, sounding stiff.

"Huh?" That was me.

Dallas and I looked at each other. Then we heard Michael in the background asking Cheyenne what she was talking about. No, not asking. More like demanding. His voice was harsh, his tone more like a drill sergeant than a boyfriend.

It sounded like Cheyenne moved the phone away from her mouth, but we could still hear her. "We're just talking about Mary Beth," she said, sounding like a pouting child. Then back to us. "I gotta go. I'll call you when I can." She hung up.

Dallas just stared at her phone and looked worried. "She sounds weird."

"What's she talking about?" I asked. "What's she mean by an aberration? She never uses words like that."

Dallas thought for a minute and then her eyes got big, and she grabbed me by the arm, her nails digging into my flesh.

"Aberration! Remember? Martini Thursday a few weeks ago, y'all were talking about Mary Beth's lawsuit. She said something about an aberration. And Shy asked what the word meant. And the only way I'd ever heard of it was a movie. A scary movie!"

I nodded my head and frowned, vaguely remembering the conversation. "Right. So?"

Dallas shook my arm, trying to get me to understand, and digging her nails in deeper. "I told Shy it was a scary movie! It's about this girl, and her boyfriend is like some kind of Russian mobster or something. But towards the end, he comes after her."

I still didn't quite get it. I tried prying her fingernails out of my arm, expecting to see blood any minute. "Did you tell Cheyenne what the movie was about?"

Dallas shook her head, frustrated with me. "No! Don't you remember? I told her it was a scary movie about a girl and her evil boyfriend! Lucy, Shy's in trouble!"

Chapter Twenty-Nine

This time Dallas drove, and I called the Power Ranger. No answer. So I dialed the main number and found my way to his secretary. After explaining there was a family emergency involving his ex-wife, she gave me his cell phone number. He answered on the second ring.

"Will Power," he said into the phone. And I was too worried to even think it was funny.

"This is Lucy Moore, calling from Aspen. Sergeant Power, Cheyenne is in trouble and we really need your help."

"Thank God! I've been waiting for your call! Where's Cheyenne?"

"What do you mean? Did you get our message?"

"I got a message from someone named Dallas late Tuesday, but her phone cut out, and I couldn't hear the number. I had no way of contacting her, so I left Wednesday and came here to the valley to try to help Cheyenne. Tell me what's going on."

His voice was kind, but stern.

"I guess you know Cheyenne is involved with a man here in Aspen. We think he's mistreating her. We're on our way there now, but we really need your help."

"What makes you think there's trouble?"

I explained the whole thing about Cheyenne's black eye, and her not answering her phone, and finally about the code word, which we'd interpreted to mean trouble with her evil boyfriend. And somehow, that jumbled mess of a story made sense to Will Power because he jumped into gear.

"Don't go over there alone!" he said. "Give me directions and I'll meet you there."

Finally the planets lined up on our side. I let out a sigh of relief and gave detailed directions on how to get to Michael's estate. Will told us to wait for him down the road, and we agreed on a meeting place. I described Dallas's white hybrid, and he told us he would pull in behind us in his Jeep Wrangler.

It was hard not to go storming over to Michael's, knowing Cheyenne was probably in danger. But we did as we were told and waited in the shade of towering aspen trees just outside Owl Creek, down the road from Michael's place. Owl Creek is one of the prettiest places on the planet, but it was lost on us today.

"Did he sound worried?" asked Dallas, putting the SUV in park and turning to face me.

I thought about that, and nodded. "Mmm hmm, worried, but also, in charge, you know? Like, he's used to emergency situations, gets the facts, and then moves into action."

"Thank God he's coming. I knew he would."

My mind wandered to Thomas and what he might do if someone called to tell him I was in trouble. Tears sprang to my eyes and I turned away from Dallas, remembering how Thomas had taken me in his arms and told me he would give me anything. I had a feeling he would come if he thought I was in trouble.

I sniffed and got my emotions under control, but Dallas wasn't paying any attention to me. She was looking at her watch.

"Oh honey, I'm sorry. I almost forgot about your big date."

"I don't care about that," said Dallas, looking into the rear view mirror. "I'm just so worried about Shy I can hardly sit here. I really think she was trying to give us a clue, using that crazy word of Mary Beth's. There's definitely something bad going down in that house."

"What do we really know about Michael?" I asked.

"Not much," said Dallas. "We know he doesn't like us hanging around his house and isn't too crazy about Cheyenne hanging around us."

"So he's controlling," I said.

Dallas nodded. "Shy's constantly calling to check in with him. I think he makes her do that."

"And the whole thing with him moving his assets and changing his residence to Florida," I said. "What was Cheyenne saying to you before I listened in? Something about 'a long time?'"

"She said she and Michael were finally going on their trip, leaving Monday. And that they would probably be gone a really long time."

"Oh boy. That sounds ominous."

Dallas glanced in her rear view mirror again. "Dark green Jeep, right?"

I nodded. "Jeep Wrangler. The little Army looking kind."

"I think I see it winding its way up the road, and it's coming fast!"

Dallas turned in her seat and prepared to take off. Within minutes the Jeep pulled in behind her, and Dallas put the car in gear and peeled out, spraying dirt behind the car.

Dallas drove like my high school boyfriend – over the speed limit and a little out of control – and Will stayed right on our tail. In minutes, we were turning in to the long drive up to Michael's mansion. Dallas slowed, and we both looked around.

Nothing seemed out of place. Nothing seemed any more unusual than usual. But just like three days ago when Dallas and I had come to check on Cheyenne, there didn't seem to be anyone around. No pool guys. No yard guys. No cars in the big circular drive. Not a sound, save for the splash of water from the Vegas fountain out front.

We parked in the circle drive with Will right behind us. Dallas and I got out, closing our doors quietly, and met the now famous Will Power as he climbed out of his Jeep.

And I have to say, he did look sort of like a hero, wearing jeans and hiking boots and a tight olive green T-shirt stretched across his chest. Where Michael was long and lanky and not the least bit muscular, Will was built like a rock. Stocky. Slightly less than six feet tall. Short dark hair, chiseled cheek bones and chin. And a couple days growth of beard on his tan face.

We made hasty introductions. "We think Cheyenne is inside with Michael Bennett," I said quietly. "Normally, there are all kinds of people working this property. Something doesn't feel right."

Will nodded. "Let's just go to the door and see what happens. If Cheyenne answers, she might not be too happy to see me, but we'll be able to see if she's all right."

He took the lead, with Dallas and me right behind him. I thought about what a strange spectacle we made - Will looking like a hiker who'd spent two days in the mountains before coming down sleep deprived and irritable. Dallas in white linen looking like she just stepped off the catwalk. And me in a state of desperation with dark rings under my eyes from no sleep.

Will rang the doorbell, and we waited in front of the massive double doors. I wondered if Will was packing heat...make that carrying a gun. If so, I didn't see how he could possibly have it on him. I tried to stop looking at his tight butt and thought instead of Cheyenne. My mind raced as I flipped through all the possible scenarios on the other side of those impressive doors.

Will rang the bell again, and I worried we were once again engaged in an act of futility. If Cheyenne was here, and if she was in trouble, wouldn't she come to the door? And if she wasn't in trouble, and saw Will standing there, would she be mad? Probably. But as Dallas had pointed out, it was better than not doing anything.

My heart skipped a beat when the big door was yanked open. Standing there looking a bit disheveled, but smiling pleasantly, was none other than Michael.

"How can I help you?" he asked, looking at Will. Dallas and I had met Michael once, briefly. If he recognized us, he didn't show it.

"Hello. We'd like to see Cheyenne, please."

Michael's smile was frozen in place. "And you are?"

"Friends of hers," said Will in a calm voice. Good answer.

"Well, you just missed her. She went into town a few minutes ago."

"She drove?" I asked.

"Yeah," said Michael, his smile beginning to slip. "Can I leave a message for her?"

"When do you expect her back?" asked Will.

Michael shifted his weight, seemingly tired of our questions. "Probably not for a while. She had a long list of things to do."

"She's not answering her phone," I said, looking Michael in the eye.

He smiled again, but it was cold, never reaching his eyes. "Maybe she forgot to charge it. She's always forgetting things. I'll let her know you stopped by."

As the door swung closed, I had a mental image of Will sticking his strong arm out, throwing the door open, rushing into the house, and saving Cheyenne.

But that didn't happen. The door closed in our faces, and Will turned.

"He's lying!" I said.

"Yeah!" said Dallas.

Will took each of us by the arm and propelled us toward the car. "Quiet," he said, softly.

When we got to Dallas's car, Will made a show of opening my door for me, slowly, gentlemanly, while Dallas climbed in on the driver's side.

"Why do you think he's lying?" he asked through his teeth.

"Because we've been sitting down the road from this house for fifteen minutes. If Cheyenne had driven to town, we'd have seen her. That yellow Volkswagen is hard to miss."

"Maybe she was driving a car you wouldn't recognize," said Will, acting like he was helping me with my seatbelt.

"Cheyenne *never* drives Michael's cars," said Dallas. "He doesn't allow it."

"We don't have any choice right now but to leave," he said. "We're on private property. We'll go back down to the spot where we met and regroup."

He slammed my door and walked back to his Jeep.

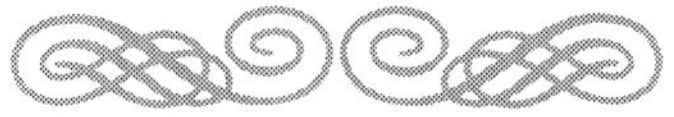

Chapter Thirty

"Michael gives me the creeps," said Dallas.

"Me too. I don't like this," I said, as Dallas started the car. "I don't like leaving."

"I don't either," she said, taking her time putting on her sunglasses and slowly buckling her seat belt. "If Cheyenne had really gone to town, the first thing she would have done is call us."

"And what was that crack about Cheyenne forgetting things?" I asked. "What was he trying to say?"

"I don't know. But he seems smarmy to me. Too smooth, you know?"

She looked in her rear view mirror. "Will's giving me the signal to move," she said, putting the car in drive.

We pulled back onto the long private road through the property, moving slowly. I had a feeling of dread in my stomach. There had to be more we could do. But what? We'd brought the police with us this time. What else was there?

"I'm worried he'll hurt her again," said Dallas, sounding close to tears.

I rubbed a hand on her arm. "I know. Me too."

"Will knows about Michael hitting Cheyenne before, so why isn't he trying to do more?"

"Like what?" I asked.

"Like pulling out his gun and shooting the smug smile off Michael's face!"

I smiled and would have laughed if things hadn't been so serious. "I think he probably wanted to. It's hard to tell what Will's thinking."

"I just feel like she needs us and we're driving away and I can't stand it," said Dallas. "Why didn't Will push his way into the house? He's a cop! Can't he do something?"

I sighed, feeling the same frustrations. "I think he knows the law and knows we can't do much until we have proof."

"Well that just sucks," said Dallas sadly, using the closest thing to a swear word I'd heard her use since Baby Bentley was born.

She continued slowly down the road. I looked back to see if Will was still behind us. And that's when I saw it: a flash of yellow deep in all the green of the trees. I did a double take, but there was nothing there.

"What?" asked Dallas. "What are you looking at?"

I shook my head, still looking out the window behind Dallas. "I thought I saw something."

I was probably imagining things, hallucinating, seeing what I wanted to see. I scanned the trees, but all I saw were leaves shimmering in the noon breeze. Sunlight filtering through the trees. The glistening white bark of the aspens.

"Wait! Stop the car!"

Dallas slammed on the brakes and I felt a little bump when Will ran into the back of us.

"What! What is it?" asked Dallas.

I opened my door and tumbled out, running around the front of the car and almost running into Dallas as she hopped out of the driver's side.

"Cheyenne!" I screamed the name.

Will was out of his Jeep and running up to us. "Where?" he asked.

I pointed through the trees, yelling her name again.

And then we heard it. The sound of her cries. The sound of her stumbling through the brush.

"Oh my God! Cheyenne!" Dallas cried out and we ran toward the trees.

Cheyenne broke through the trees in a dead run. Wearing a dirty yellow T-shirt and cut-off shorts. Her hair was wild around her head, and she was making wailing cries with each step.

Everything seemed to happen in slow motion at that point. I watched Cheyenne running toward us, my heart in my throat. I was so overwhelmed emotionally that I couldn't even cry out. We kept running toward Cheyenne, our arms outstretched, Dallas crying and calling Cheyenne's name.

Finally we closed the gap, but Cheyenne ran past us, right into Will's arms.

It was a sight to see. Will wrapping his muscular arms around her, Cheyenne crying as if her heart would break. Crying and saying over and over, "I'm sorry, I'm sorry." Will just held her and whispered gently to her. Cheyenne sobbed into his shirt. And then the big man, the cop who'd surely seen it all, the Power Ranger, started to cry.

We walked over to them and Dallas rubbed Cheyenne's back, but Cheyenne didn't move. She was wrapped around Will, and she was not letting go.

Her legs were scratched, her feet were bare and scraped, and her cries were the saddest thing I'd ever heard, turning into long, breathless sobs. I couldn't stand it. I turned around and cried. Dallas wrapped her arms around me, and we held each other.

Finally Cheyenne looked up and I saw that her lip was split open, and her eyes were wild and scared. Anger flashed through me like a wildfire at the very thought of Michael hurting her. There was no sign of the fun-loving Cheyenne in this beaten, traumatized woman. We couldn't let him get away with it.

"What do we do now?" I asked Will. "He has to pay for this!"

Cheyenne clung to Will. "Take me home. Please just take me home."

Will gently took her head in his hands and looked into her sad face. He used one hand to tenderly push her tangled hair back and wipe the tears from her face. "We have to go to the police," he said.

She shook her head violently. "No! I can't do it. Please! I just want it to be over." The plea was so pitiful. She started to cry again. Will held her and looked at Dallas and me.

"Why don't you go on. Give us a little time to figure this out."

I nodded. "Wait a second," I said. I hurried to the car and got my purse, reaching inside for my keys. I walked back to Will and Cheyenne, handing a key to Will.

"Here. It's a key to my house. Cheyenne knows the way. You guys go there, make yourselves at home, talk things over." I tried to smile at Will, but couldn't seem to make my face comply. I reached back in my purse for one of my personal cards and handed it to Will.

"Call us when you can, okay? Let us know how she's doing?"

Will took the card and nodded. The tears on his face just about undid me.

Dallas and I left Will and Cheyenne clinging to each other on the tree-lined road that Cheyenne once believed led to her future. Turns out, it was an aberration. A scary movie. Her very own road to perdition.

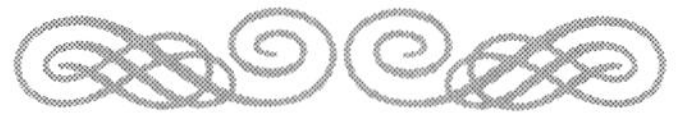

Chapter Thirty-One

"That," I said, slumping in the passenger seat and feeling about a hundred and twelve years old, "was just too much."

Dallas wiped at her eyes and pulled onto the highway. She shook her head. "Poor Shy." Dallas's voice broke. "Do you think she'll be okay?"

I thought about it for a minute, then nodded. "Yeah. I really do. She's right where she needs to be now. With Will. He'll help her figure out what to do from here. It may take a little time, but she'll be okay. She has to be."

Dallas nodded. "She has to be," she repeated.

"Wow," I said, massaging my temples and trying to get my emotions under control. I glanced at my watch. "I have no idea how we switch gears at this point," I said, "but we need to go get your suitcase and get you to the airport."

Dallas looked at me and her eyes were about as big as Bentley's the first time she went down a water slide. "I completely forgot! My millionaire!"

And finally, I started to laugh. Because her face was just so funny. And her tone was so much like a child's. And the day had been so unbelievably gut-wrenching. I couldn't help it - I laughed until my stomach hurt. And Dallas laughed with me. Then she squealed, and I knew everything was going to be all right.

❦

An hour later we were hurtling toward the tiny Aspen-Pitkin County Airport, also known as Sardy Field. But mostly just known as *the airport*.

And I have to say, after our day of drama, meeting the Denver millionaire was like a breath of fresh air. And being a witness to the moment when he and Dallas laid eyes on each other was priceless. Because he was almost as charming as she was beautiful. Their eyes locked, and I swear, the air around us seemed charged with something. Energy. Sexual tension. Carnal magnetism. Call it whatever you want. These two were made for each other.

But not so fast.

I held out my hand. "Hello, my name is Lucy. I'm Dallas's chaperone."

The handsome millionaire took my hand and looked a little confused.

"Lucy!" Dallas gave me the look.

I laughed and met the man's dark eyes. "Don't worry. I won't be getting on the plane. But you're a virtual stranger." I almost laughed at my own play on words. The day had been just too dramatic, so my lighter side was clamoring to come out. "I need to know Dallas will be safe," I said, trying to look serious.

He seemed to relax a little. "Of course. I promise you she'll be in good hands."

"I'm sure she will. Do you have a card?"

Dallas crossed her arms over her chest and gave me the hairy eyeball. But I ignored her.

The millionaire presented his business card. On first inspection, it looked legitimate. He pulled a gold pen from the breast pocket of what looked to be an Armani jacket.

"I'll write the name of the hotel for you."

"Great," I said. "Could you also write the ID number for the jet?"

He looked at me. "Of course."

I knew I came across as annoying and overprotective, and I also knew Dallas was ready to wring my neck. But I was kind of enjoying myself. I felt sort of like the hillbilly dad, sitting on the porch with a shotgun, interrogating the daughter's first date. Mostly, though, I needed to be able to drive away and not worry that something horrible would happen to my friend.

"Thanks," I said when he handed the card back to me. "Now you kids go have fun."

Dallas made a face at me, tucked her hand in the millionaire's arm, and walked off to board his private jet.

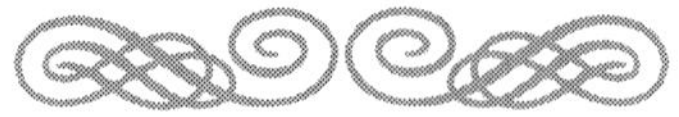

Chapter Thirty-Two

The drowsiness came over me like an evil prankster, sneaking up slowly, slowly, and then attacking me full force. Driving from the airport to my house became an exercise in determination and self-discipline as my eyes got heavy and my body started to wind down. And then I remembered I'd been up all night hammering out the details of my ingenious new concierge business. Which I'd totally forgotten about in all the excitement of the day.

There were five messages on my phone. I yawned like a hibernating bear and listened to the first one. Charlie – the homeowner – telling me he was turning the leasing of his home over to me, and what a fortuitous thing it had been that we'd met at Jimmy's last night. My brain did a double take. *Last night?* It seemed like weeks ago.

Message number two was my housekeeper, needing time off. Number three was a call from a friend in Houston. And four was Stella in New York. I called her back. Skipping my Marlon Brando routine, I got straight to the point. "Hey, it's Lucy. What's up?"

"Well," said Stella, drawing the word out like a harbinger of bad news with two L's. My heart sank.

I knew I could put Charlie's house online and find someone to rent it eventually, but I'd already told him I had clients and sources and a thriving concierge business. To call him today and tell him the deal was set would give me credibility. Sure, it was totally undeserved credibility, but still. I just needed Stella to send me a supermodel or two.

"I have to tell you," she said, still sounding cagey, "your call was really a surprise."

I cleared my throat and tried to think fast. "I know, Stella. I should have called much sooner. It's been too long since we had a good girl chat. And really, you should come out here and visit as soon as you can. Before the summer is over."

"I'll try," she said. "But in the meantime, you've saved my life."

"How's that?"

"I'm a hero around here for suggesting a little R&R for a certain girl who desperately needs to get out of town and wind down."

"So, you're sending one of your models?"

"I sure am."

It couldn't have gone any better. Not only was she sending me one of the most famous supermodels in the business, but she came complete with a matching high-profile musician boyfriend. I had myself a business! It was only weeks later, after the dust cleared, that I would remember that old adage – *if it seems too good to be true, you're screwed.*

Call number five was Power Ranger Will, letting me know he was taking Cheyenne home to Denver. Which was good news, in a way, because Cheyenne would be safe and cared for. But bad news in a way, because it must have meant she'd decided not to press charges against Michael. I couldn't stand for him to get away with what he'd done to her.

When I got home I called Charlie to tell him the good news. He was thrilled of course, and we made an appointment to meet the next day at his house. My last act before falling asleep in my chair was to give myself a big pat on the back. I'd pulled together a business in a matter of hours and leased a multi-million dollar property to an international supermodel. It couldn't have been any easier. God, I was good at this!

❧

I woke late Saturday and spent the day designing my business cards, registering my DBA online, and scoping out all the comparable homes for lease in Aspen to come up with a good price for Charlie's. With this research in mind, I met Charlie and toured his five-bedroom Starwood estate. It was gorgeous with all the amenities of the standard Aspen luxury home: granite, hardwood, home spas with hydro-massage tubs in the bathrooms, hot tub on the upper deck, gourmet kitchen, elegant furnishings, and views for miles and miles.

I stood on the deck and smiled as I figured the commission in my head and prepared to launch my new business. "I think we can lease this for thirty-five hundred per night. Or, if we get a longer contract, I'd say sixty thousand for the month."

Charlie's eyebrows rose like two highly groomed caterpillars "Really? Sixty grand?"

I nodded, feeling successful already.

"Does the supermodel want it for a month?"

"I'll find out today," I said, flipping open my black notebook. "So you agree to thirty-five hundred per night, sixty for the month?"

"I do. When do they arrive, the supermodel and the rock star?"

"I'll find that out today too. And you can go off to Tuscany and not worry about a thing. I've got everything under control."

Funny. I really believed that.

❧

Saturday nights had always been fun in Aspen and usually included Dallas, Mary Beth, sometimes Cheyenne, and an abundance of top shelf martinis. But Dallas was off on a private jet with her current multi-millionaire. Cheyenne was cradled in the arms of her ex-husband somewhere in Denver. And Mary Beth was...who the hell knew where. I only hoped she wasn't breaking the conditions of her bond. And wasn't that something you should never have to worry about when it came to your friends? I mean, honestly. Their safety, yes. Their sudden weight gain, sure. Even the occasional illicit affair, maybe. But you should not have to worry that one of your best friends might compromise the conditions of her bond and be tossed back into the slammer.

Anyway, my crazy friends were all otherwise occupied at the moment, so that just left me. Alone. Slumping into a comfy chair on my deck and wondering why I didn't have a handsome man to squire me about. Or even a semi-handsome man who was well traveled and thought I was fabulous. Or at the very least, an average guy with great game.

Miles Davis played from the hidden speakers, the cool, sensual notes dripping with romance. Making me feel even more pathetic. And then finally, my doorbell rang. I rushed through the house and swung the heavy door wide.

"You're late," I said.

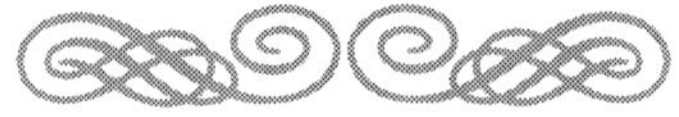

Chapter Thirty-Three

Glacier just smiled and walked into my house. Silently. Fluidly. Surprising me when he stopped to wrap me in a warm hug.

And that's all it took to jumpstart my libido. He smelled good. He felt good. He looked as good as always in his standard-issue Glacier suit. And all those middle-of-the-night yearnings came back to me in a flash. I needed him. It had been too long since a man had held me. I wanted a man to crave me the way I sometimes crave those fudge-dipped Ritz crackers you can only get during the holidays. I needed to feel desired. I needed strong arms and deep, slow kisses. I wanted to make love all night long in front of a crackling fire. And in the morning, I wanted him to look at me the way I look at those fudge-covered crackers. Like I was the treasure he'd been searching for all his life. His very own *Here and Now*.

Basically, I wanted to be adored. Is that so wrong?

But I tried to rein all that in while I refreshed my martini and poured juice for him. And out on the deck, I was encouraged when he looked at me instead of the breathtaking view. Being Glacier, he didn't try to strike up a conversation about trivial things or say the normal stuff, like *So, how've you been*. Or, *How was your week*. Or even, *Wow, you look great*.

"I came into town looking for you last week," I said, sipping my martini and feeling a little bit naughty, him with his apple juice.

He smiled and cocked his head just slightly. "Did you find me?"

I laughed. "You were nowhere to be found. But I found something else."

He didn't ask what I'd found. Didn't seem to need to know. Didn't seem to need anything.

"I found out about your secret life as a sculptor."

His eyes crinkled.

"I'm surprised you never told me," I said, realizing how very little we knew about each other. And yet, I felt such a connection to him.

"I guess it never came up." He sounded sincere, as if it had really never occurred to him to bring sculpting into one of our conversations. It wasn't the usual flip comment from a guy who didn't want to talk about the subject. Glacier was different from every other guy on planet earth as far as I could tell. It was like he was living *on* earth, but wasn't really *of* it.

"So tell me about it now," I said. "Unless it's a secret."

"No secret," he said, holding his hands up, sort of like a magician after a trick.

"How long have you been doing it? What kinds of things do you sculpt?"

Glacier crossed one boot over his knee and relaxed back into his chair. "Most of my life, really. I started when I was young."

"Really? How does a young boy go about sculpting?"

"I've always seen forms in the rocks," he said.

"You sculpt from stone? Not forming things from clay?"

He nodded. "There's a form inside every stone. I just help to free the form. I allow the stone to express itself."

Okay. Kind of mystical. Abstruse. But in keeping with his persona. At least now I knew how he kept the body of a gym rat and probably where he got the black thumbnail.

"So, what do your stones usually want to express?"

He smiled again. He knew I was teasing, but by now I knew it would be hard for anyone to really offend Glacier. He seemed beyond it.

"Their true essence," he said simply. "The glory given to them by nature."

I suddenly felt very insignificant. Very shallow. I'd actually considered sharing the news of my new concierge business with Glacier. But how could I? Let's see, pamper and spoil the already pampered, spoiled vacationers of the world *or* restore a stone to its nature-given glory.

"I want to see your work," I said, suddenly feeling the need to see his glorious stones. You know what I mean. "Is it in galleries?"

"Mostly in homes. A few in parks and office buildings. I do mostly commission work."

I frowned. "If you're freeing the stone to be what it wants to be, then how does the person who commissions your work know what they're getting?"

He smiled. I know I messed up the description of his work, but he didn't seem to mind.

"They don't."

"So, people commission your work and agree to pay thousands and thousands of dollars for a sculpture without knowing exactly what they're getting?"

He nodded.

"Are they ever unsatisfied with the end result?"

"If they are, they've never said so," he said, picking up his glass of juice. "No one's ever returned a piece to me."

"Well, I'm sure you don't offer a money-back guarantee." I sipped my martini.

He nodded. "I do."

Impressive. "So where can I go to see your work? Can I at least see your portfolio? You must have photographs of all your work."

He sipped his juice. "No photographs. I like letting the pieces go. No attachments."

Sheesh. There he went with his thing about attachments again. I didn't really understand. But I admired him just the same. He seemed to have a handle on things. On his emotions. His wants and needs. His desires.

Which brought me back to mine. My wants, needs, desires, and emotions. Which at the moment were all rolled up into one gleaming, throbbing package of lust. I wanted him. I wanted to touch him and pet him. I wanted to feel his skin against my skin. And since he'd shared his passion for releasing a stone to its true essence, I thought it might be time for me to share something with him about *my* essence.

"Are you making progress?" he asked, out of the blue and startling me.

I must have given him a strange look because he smiled. "With your path," he said.

"You mean my meditation?"

He nodded.

"I haven't exactly been able to get my morning runs in this week. It's been insane. If I told you everything going on with Mary Beth, Cheyenne, and Dallas, it would take all night. And besides, that wouldn't be *here and now*, would it?"

He smiled.

But I wanted to make progress. It was high time I made progress. But not with my meditation. I took a giant leap forward. "There's something I've wanted to talk over with you."

He gave me his patented, open, non-judgmental look. The one that said, "go ahead, you're safe here." I kicked off my little black ankle boots and tucked my legs up under me. I wanted to be like the boots – fun and flirty. Maybe even hot. Fingers crossed.

"So here's the thing," I said, choosing my words carefully so as not to scare him off. I took a sip of my martini for inspiration. "There's this guy I'm really drawn to, you know? And I think he might like me too, if he'd just give it a chance."

He smiled. "I'm sure he would."

That was promising.

"I think about him a lot. What it would be like to kiss him, make love to him."

No response, but rapt attention.

"He seems so in control most of the time. I don't know if he ever just lets his heart lead the way, lets himself fall. But if he did, I would catch him. I would hold him close, so he knew he was loved. But not so close he missed his freedom."

He nodded and smiled, and I thought I almost had him. Because honestly, what man wouldn't want that? Even Glacier, always so calm, so reserved, so composed. He would surely want a woman to love him if she didn't try to control him.

For a minute I wondered if I could really do that. Love him and not ever try to control him. He could use a good haircut. And new boots. And what was this thing about not drinking alcohol? That would have to change. But not right away.

I stood up and walked over to him, standing in front of him and reaching for his hand. The one with the blackened thumb nail. I rubbed my own thumb gently over the nail.

"Dance with me," I said, looking down at him.

And by the startled, wide-eyed look that came over his face – a look I had never seen on him before – I knew he finally understood. He didn't move for a minute. I worried he would turn me down and leave me standing there, feeling stupid. But I tugged gently on his hand and he stood. I pulled him toward me, then leaned slowly into him.

There was nothing he could do but move closer to me and wrap his arms around my back as my arms went around his neck. Rather than look into his eyes – which looked way more frightened than turned on – I rested my head against his jaw and moved slowly to Miles, feeling like I was at my first junior high dance, and I was with the cutest boy in the class, who seemed full of himself on the football field but was afraid of girls.

We moved slowly, in sync, but not smoothly. Not the way he moved most of the time – confident, easy, carefree. This was stiff. Unsure. Honestly, it was a side of Glacier I wasn't prepared for.

But determination was on my side. I tried not to do anything to scare him. Didn't push my B-cup breasts into his chest or pull his hips to mine or stick my tongue in his ear. I just gently, slowly moved to the sensuous, languid trumpet tones. We turned and his thighs bumped mine, causing him to move back a bit. But I didn't let him. I moved dreamily, lazily, closer to him, feeling the muscles of his shoulders and neck beneath my hands. He was warm, and I could feel his heart beating against my chest as I moved even closer.

I let the music be my guide in this strange foray into erotica with a man who suddenly seemed terrified of a close encounter. I waited until the song swelled to a dramatic crescendo. And then tipping my head back and catching a glint of the quarter moon, I put my lips over his and kissed him.

It didn't go quite like I'd dreamed it would. He didn't moan with pleasure or wrap himself around me. He gasped. And moved slightly back from me, stiffening up.

I persevered, keeping the kiss gentle, rubbing his neck softly. Sort of like holding a piece of bologna out to a scared puppy hiding underneath a car, knowing that if I was careful, the puppy would come out from under the car, gobble up the bologna, and be mine forever.

And ironically, as the song changed and Miles began to play "It Never Entered My Mind," Glacier moved in close and kissed me back. And I was pretty sure it never had entered his mind, and maybe that was what made it so good. Because I have to say, it was about the most romantic thing that had ever happened to me. And I felt like such a girl when my heart bumped and my stomach did a somersault. If I were Dallas, I would have squealed.

We kissed and moved to the music, and he finally, mercifully, pulled me hard against him. His arms tightened around me, and I was the one who let out a little moan as I felt every inch of his warm, toned body against mine. The kiss became almost urgent, Glacier's mouth hard against mine. We were no longer awkward teenagers at the junior high dance, but two people who had finally come together after growing close over conversation and friendship. And it was the first time I realized how truly intimate a kiss can be. Because we had most definitely moved light years beyond friendship, as both of us breathed hard and clutched at the other, trying to get even closer when there was nothing but an atom or two between us as it was.

And as I melted into him and we kissed, hungrily going for each other like two Jenny Craig graduates over a box of Godiva, I should have been thinking that I finally felt desired, maybe even adored. That after all this time without any male companionship, kissing Glacier felt like heaven on earth. And that it was so erotic being held by a man who was muscular and strong, yet whose hands on my back were almost tender. But instead, my mind left *here and now* in the dust and surged forward on a little tour of the future. It went something like this:

I wonder if I should move us closer to the door, then take him up to my bedroom. My sheets are clean, I shaved my legs. He'll love the view from the bed. And tomorrow we can go into town for breakfast, and maybe we'll run into Thomas. Wouldn't that be great! Or maybe he'll take me to his house. I wonder where his house is…

And just as I was planning what to wear to Glacier's house – my favorite tight jeans and distressed boots – the music stopped. And Glacier reacted to the sudden silence as if he'd just heard the riotous clang of a thousand cymbals.

He pulled back abruptly, almost causing me to lose my balance. I opened my eyes, expecting him to be looking at me with crazy desire, ready to lift me in his arms and carry me to my bedroom. Which, as it turns out, is at the top of a really long and winding staircase, so probably not the best use of his energy. I tried to curl into him when the cool air chilled the parts of me that had been cuddled so tightly into the warmth of his body. But he held me at arm's length. And his face was filled not so much with desire as horror. He looked as if he'd awakened from a dream to find himself doing something horribly depraved and completely immoral.

I was confused. I reached my hand toward his face, but he tipped his head back, still holding me away from him. "What?" I asked, thinking maybe he was just surprised that we had moved so easily from friendship to...this.

He shook his head, softly at first and then more forcefully. "No," he said in a strangled voice that didn't even sound like his own. "Lucy, I can't do this."

I looked into his deep blue eyes and came crashing back down to earth. Because the man I knew as completely unflappable, perpetually serene and composed, looked now as if he might cry. He moved his hands gently down my arms and took my hands in his.

I wanted to pull him to me, to hold him the way you would a child and tell him it was okay. Whatever it was that had him so spooked, so upset, was okay. We could work through it. Another woman? A wife? Please God, not a wife.

"I'm sorry," he said, and in all my life I had never heard anyone sound so utterly so.

Then he walked away. Not even through the house. He jumped easily off the rock ledge of the deck and disappeared. I heard the beater pickup cough to life and drive away.

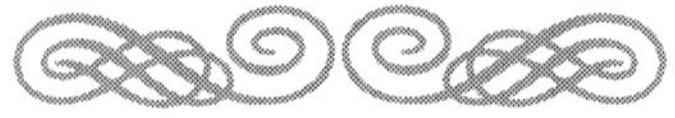

Chapter Thirty-Four

If life was a beach, then mine was surely Prince William Sound just after the Exxon Valdez oil spill. Dark. Messy. Devastating.

I sat on my deck wrapped in a camel cashmere throw and drank myself silly. I was mad and hurt and confused, and starting to wonder how my life had gone so horribly wrong. Like the Exxon Valdez, I had somehow run aground, and all my best stuff was spilling out all over everywhere.

A wife. Glacier Jones had a wife. Or a girlfriend. Or some kind of intimacy phobia or commitment issues. Or maybe a brain tumor or some rare syndrome that caused him to react inappropriately when a woman put her tongue in his mouth.

I freshened my martini from the pitcher on the table beside me and huddled back under the throw, leaving only my drinking hand exposed to the chilly night breeze.

How could Glacier do this to me? He, of all people, knew how broken and defeated I felt after being dumped by Thomas. How could he pull away from me like that? With a look that said he'd just witnessed a fatal ten-car pileup in Glenwood Canyon? Honestly, what was so horrible about me?

I sniffed and wiped my nose on the soft blanket. If Glacier had a wife, what was he doing coming around here with his silly cloth bag of smoothies and his wise-man-on-the-mountain routine? Why wasn't he home with her? His wife - who, I could almost guarantee, had long, braided, naturally blond hair, no makeup, and clothes made of hemp and unbleached muslin.

And why didn't he wear a ring? Married men should wear rings. Although, Thomas had worn a ring and look where that got us. Oh I was just so mad! If it was a wife, I would never forgive him. After all our talks about Thomas's cheating and leaving me for another woman.

I sipped my martini and tried to come up with another reason for his stricken look and mad dash off the deck. Something that wouldn't make me feel so rejected, a feeling that was becoming all too familiar. Like my favorite running shoes, or my little lavender robe, rejection was beginning to feel like something I just put on each morning when I woke up, part of my daily look.

Maybe Glacier really was just too weird for me. I mean, seriously. If he had some odd intimacy phobia, then I could write him off as too much trouble. If he were twenty, I might give him a pass and help him work through it. But a grown man with an old beater pickup, dusty boots, *and* an intimacy phobia was just too much.

It was late, and I'd had at least one too many martinis, so it wasn't the best time to be making decisions. But I didn't care. I was through with Glacier. I didn't really even care anymore what his problem was. It was his problem – not mine – and he would just have to deal with it. Because he had somehow managed to stomp on my heart, which still wore the bloody bandages of the complete ass-whooping it had so recently endured at the hands of Thomas.

The man who I'd thought was my safe place, a sanctuary for my bruised ego and my battered soul, was more like a haunted house with unknown danger lurking in every room. The last thing I needed at this point in my life was unknown danger. Goodbye, Glacier Jones.

Groggy and sleep deprived, confused and depressed, I started the day with a run up Smuggler. But it wasn't easy. I had to beg my legs to move, had to force air into my lungs. And I didn't stop to meditate. In fact, when my breathing finally fell into a rhythm, I purposely filled my head with details I needed to tend to later that day. I was so mad at Glacier, I didn't want to do anything he might approve of.

Silly, I know. Childish. But I couldn't help it. Thinking about the night before made me angry all over again, and I made the loop in my fastest time ever.

While I spent Sunday in an angry huff, Monday was all business, with Glacier pushed to the nether regions of my mind. Every time his face appeared in my brain, each time the memory of his body pressed against mine flitted across my synapses, I buried it under a pile of details and to-dos. And eventually, the thought of him stayed where it was destined to remain – in the past.

I spent the early morning compiling and editing my contacts and phone numbers so I'd be prepared for anything the supermodel and her boyfriend might throw at me. I made preliminary calls to line up a private car and driver, two chefs, housekeeping, and a nanny – just in case. Maybe the boyfriend had kids. Then I worked on planning a few fun day trips – shopping, kayaking, white water rafting, hiking, and spa treatments.

I made lists of my favorite restaurants and even mentioned some of my favorite entrees. Next came names and addresses of the best shopping in Aspen – Prada, Gucci, Bvlgari, Fendi, Burberry, Chanel, Louis Vuitton. The list went on and on. The shopping in Aspen would surely be fun even for an international supermodel. I decided she probably wouldn't care about two-for-one Tuesdays at the liquor store or the great bargains on day-old bread at City Market.

Then it was time to call Stella to finalize plans. "It's me, your saving grace," I said, trying to fill my voice with a perkiness I didn't really feel.

"Perfect," she said. "I have exactly five minutes before I need to be in a meeting."

"Okay, I'll make it short and sweet. When and for how long?"

"Sunday," she fired back. "For one week."

"Great. I have a beautiful luxury home in Starwood available for that time period."

"Starwood? Like in the John Denver song?"

"Exactly. One of the most exclusive areas in Aspen. Gated, private, views for miles."

"How much?"

"Thirty-five-hundred per night."

"Youch," said Stella. "What else have you got?"

"She'll love this one," I said, trying not to panic. "Five bedrooms, five baths, media room, gourmet kitchen, outdoor kitchen on the deck, and the best views in Aspen. I can arrange a private jet and limo service at my discount rate."

"Do it," she said, then held her hand over the phone and spoke to someone.

"Okay, I'll wrap this up," I said. "I know you're busy. Private chef and housekeeping?"

"Definitely."

"I'll fax you the particulars, along with the total amount. You sign, then wire the money into the account provided on the fax sheet. Got it?"

"Got it," she said.

"I'll fax the itinerary after I line up the jet. I can also plan day trips, shopping, rafting, that kind of thing."

"Awesome. Fax me the thing. I'll wire today. Gotta go."

My week was filled with finalizing details of the supermodel's stay ad nauseum. There was one bittersweet moment when I found a vase of wildflowers by my front door. No note, but the message was clear. Glacier had been there. I thought of throwing them out, but I just couldn't do it. Instead I did the girliest thing ever. I took them in the house, set them on the island in the kitchen, then wrapped my arms gently around them and inhaled their beauty. I didn't know the names of any of them, but their colors made me think of the Indian blanket in Glacier's truck. They melted my anger and even made me miss him a little, but I wasn't ready to forgive. So I put the flowers on the table by my bed and went about the rest of my week.

I ordered an enormous goodie basket for the supermodel, filled with caviar, champagne, gourmet delights, and a very expensive bottle of Château Mouton Rothschild Pauillac. Stella, true to her word, wired the money into my account. And I promptly wired money into Charlie's account, sealing the deal.

I hired a service to clean Charlie's home from top to bottom once he left the country. Then I walked through the house myself, inspecting every inch, moving a few accessories, adding some huge potted palms, and filling the fridge with Pellegrino, imported beer, and fresh fruit. By Thursday, I had everything in place and desperately needed a martini and a friend. Something to help me forget all about Glacier. It was time for Martini Thursday.

Dallas had returned on Sunday with her multi-millionaire – but only long enough to pack and meet him in Vail for the week. Cheyenne, as far as I knew, was still in Denver with her Power Ranger. And Mary Beth was, well, I still didn't know where Mary Beth was. But I was determined to find out.

I wanted to sit down with her over a nice dry martini and tell her I was sorry for all the things I'd said. Maybe even tell her what happened with Glacier. I know, I know, drinking went against the conditions of Mary Beth's bond, but it's not like we'd be out in public or anything. Besides, Mary Beth loves breaking the law. I dialed her cell phone and almost died of shock when she answered.

"Mary Beth? Is that really you?"

"Who else would be answering my phone?"

Yep. It was her. "So where are you? I've left a million messages on your phone. It's Martini Thursday. Please tell me you'll come for Martini Thursday."

There was a slight pause, and I wondered if we'd lost our connection, but then Mary Beth spoke up, and her tone was slightly less snotty.

"Okay," she said. "I have something to show you."

"Great," I said. "I have something to tell you. We'll have show and tell."

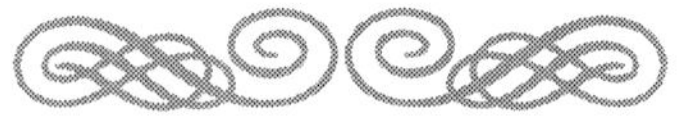

Chapter Thirty-Five

To my complete astonishment, the whole crew agreed to come for Martini Thursday. Cheyenne said she and Will were looking for an excuse to come back to the valley – whatever that meant. And Dallas was just back from six straight days with her cyber-millionaire.

I opened my front door to shrieks of laughter. Dallas and Cheyenne stood with their arms linked like two six-year-olds on a play date. I couldn't help but laugh with them.

"It's about time you two came home," I said, hugging them both. "Long time, no martini!"

"Tell me!" said Cheyenne, looking happier than I'd ever seen her look, and without her oversized leopard print sunglasses.

I rubbed her shoulder as I shut the door. "You look great," I said. "You look happy."

Dallas nodded. "I told her the same thing."

I walked them into the living room where martinis were waiting, and we all took our usual spots on the sofas. Cheyenne beamed and couldn't sit still, and Dallas wore the afterglow of six days of sun and sex. It was a little hard to take after Glacier's vault over the side of my deck. But I concentrated on being happy for them, hoping a little of their bliss would rub off on me.

"So," I said, filling Cheyenne's glass, "how is your Power Ranger?"

She giggled. "Ohmygawd, things are so good. He's so totally sweet, I can't even tell you. I don't even know where my head was when I left him."

I moved to fill Dallas's glass. "Y'all belong together," she said. "I could tell that the minute you ran into his arms."

I wanted to ask Cheyenne about that butthead Michael and what she'd been through, but it didn't feel like the right time for that. She would tell us when she was ready. Instead, I filled my own martini glass and sat across from Dallas and Cheyenne.

"Shy, Martini Thursday just wouldn't be the same without you," I said. "It's only a three hour drive from Denver. And you can stay the night here. Bring Will, if you want."

"Great idea!" said Dallas, her face lighting up. "We have to keep Martini Thursday going."

"Here's a way better idea," said Cheyenne, kicking off her discount-store flip-flops and squishing back in the couch. "Will's sick of me dogging him about how much I love it here and ragging about the traffic in Denver. So we spent the day in Glenwood Springs, and we found a house."

Dallas's eyes got big. "You're moving back to the valley?"

Cheyenne nodded, and Dallas made one of her girl sounds. A really happy girl sound.

"Eventually," said Cheyenne, laughing at Dallas. "The house is totally a fixer-upper. That's all we can afford. But Will's really good at that stuff."

"What about his job?" I asked. "His cop job?"

"He's ready to retire from the force. He's been ready for a while, but he just couldn't pull the trigger, so to speak. He's jazzed to work on the house and then maybe get on with a security company around here or something like that."

"Retire?" I asked. "How can he retire? He's too young."

"He has twenty years with the force. He started when he was super young, barely twenty-two," said Cheyenne, her voice becoming tender. "He's doing it for me. We totally need a new start. I think this'll be perfect."

"Will you marry each other again?" asked Dallas.

Cheyenne smiled and nodded. "I know it's sorta crazy – divorced and remarried all in the same year. Too bad you can't have a divorce annulled."

"Sounds like something Mary Beth would try to get her attorneys to do," I said. "If they weren't so darn busy keeping her out of jail. So when and where for the wedding?"

"Soon," said Cheyenne. "Maybe up at Maroon Bells. At the amphitheater."

"Ohhhh," said Dallas, nearly drooling at the idea. "I would *love* to do that!"

"So, you and the new guy can come," said Cheyenne. "Maybe he'll get the idea."

"Speaking of the new guy," I said, "tell us everything. How was New York? How was Vail? How do you like your new daddy?"

Dallas blushed. "New York was amazing. Vail was even better. He's pretty wonderful."

"My plan was to order a background check," I said. "But I got busy this week and totally forgot."

"You can skip that," said Dallas. "Your Dirty Harry routine worked. He's been nothing but a perfect gentleman. I think he's a little bit afraid of you."

"Good," I said, dusting off my hands. "My work is done."

The doorbell chimed, and we all looked at each other. "Mary Beth!" I said.

I jumped up, so happy to finally have all my girls together again. Dallas and Cheyenne were right behind me as I swung wide the big front door, ready to hail Mary Beth with a barrage of questions and maybe even chastise her for disappearing without a word. You can bet she'd have let me have it if I'd done the same to her. The days of letting Mary Beth slide on everything – just because she had the more prickly personality – were over. I was feeling a little prickly myself these days.

But when I saw Mary Beth, I stopped dead. Cheyenne bumped into the back of me, and Dallas slid to a stop beside me. We all seemed to be trying to reconcile the image of Mary Beth in our minds with the reality standing before us.

The hair looked pretty much the way I remembered Mary Beth's hair looking. Full and shiny and pushed back over her shoulders. And the shoes. I knew the shoes well. They were definitely Mary Beth's shoes. Black stilettos with sleek silver heels. I loved those shoes. But not much else between the hair and the shoes looked like my friend. I heard Dallas suck in a breath beside me. It was clear to all of us what Mary Beth had brought for show and tell.

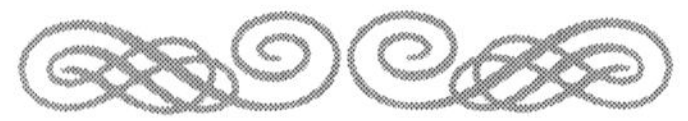

Chapter Thirty-Six

"You could maybe let us in," said Mary Beth. "Or you could just stand there gawking like you've spotted a Yeti in Snowmass Canyon."

Okay. It was definitely Mary Beth. No doubt about that. But she wasn't alone. Wrapped around Mary Beth's leg and looking very unsure of the whole situation was a little girl. Dallas squatted down so she was eye level with her.

"And who is this beauty?" she asked. "My name's Dallas. What's yours?"

The poor child clutched a small stuffed horse for dear life and shrank back behind Mary Beth's leg. And I almost fainted on the spot when Mary Beth gently pulled the girl around in front of her and spoke in a soft, loving tone.

"It's okay, baby. These are Mommy's friends. Can you say hello?" She looked up at us. "This is Alissa. My daughter."

I was astounded. Not only by the presence of Mary Beth's long lost daughter. But because the look on Mary Beth's face was much like the look on Cheyenne's face earlier. And on Dallas's face. A look of deep happiness. Of everything being right with the world. How had all my dysfunctional friends suddenly found their bliss, while I floundered around in a sea of disappointment and devastation?

"Come in!" I finally found my tongue. We stepped back and let them in. And sure, the normal thing would be to hug a friend you hadn't seen in a while, but we all made a big to-do over Alissa instead.

In the kitchen, I poured some of Glacier's apple juice into a glass and found a notepad and some colored pens. Everyone settled in the living room where I gave the juice to Alissa, and put the pad and pens on the coffee table in front of her. Then I poured Mary Beth a martini.

"Okay, sister," I said, sitting on the sofa near Mary Beth. "Spill it."

Mary Beth sipped her martini and made a face that seemed to say the drink met with her approval. Alissa looked to her mother once for permission, then climbed off the couch and sat on the floor in front of the coffee table. Choosing a red marker and drawing on the note pad, she kept the fuzzy brown horse tucked in her lap.

"I think my story's self-explanatory," she said. She looked at Alissa, and her face seemed to soften until she was almost unrecognizable to me.

Dallas was smitten with the pretty little girl. "How old are you?" she asked, leaning forward and looking at Alissa. The child kept coloring on the note pad as if she hadn't heard.

"She's still a little shy," said Mary Beth. "She's six."

"Almost seven!" said Alissa, looking up at Mary Beth.

Mary Beth smiled. "Yes, babe. My mistake. You're almost seven."

"And is this a...vacation?" I was trying to choose my words carefully as it was clear Alissa heard each one whether she reacted or not.

"No," said Mary Beth. "It's permanent. Alissa's back home to stay."

"She missed me," said Alissa, not looking up from her coloring.

"Yes," said Mary Beth, taking a sip of her martini. "I missed you more than anything in the whole world."

Dallas got misty, and Cheyenne leaned forward. "Aw, Mary Beth, she's totally beautiful. She looks just like you."

"Thank you Cheyenne. I think she's beautiful, too. And by the way, you're looking pretty great yourself tonight."

Dallas shot me a look – the bug-eyed, mouth open, what-the-hell-is-this look. I gave just the slightest shrug of my shoulders, trying not to get caught by Mary Beth. But of course, she caught me.

"What?" she said, a tiny bit of the old iciness returning to her voice.

"Nothing," I said, going for innocent but coming across more as defensive. "I was just about to ask Dallas to tell you about her new man. The G-Rated version, of course." I made wiggly eyebrows toward Alissa and Dallas laughed.

"A new man?" asked Mary Beth. "And how did you manage that?"

"The *how* isn't really all that important," I said, not ready for Mary Beth to turn into her real self and start lecturing Dallas on the dangers of computer dating. "Tell her about the *howabunga*!"

"Howabunga!" said Alissa.

Mary Beth gave me a look. And even though it was her *your-vapidity-is-a-bore* look, it made me happy. Because she was back. I have to say, I'd really missed her. Everything about her. Even her razor-sharp tongue. I gave her a shrug and smiled.

"Well," said Dallas, "he's handsome. And kind. Has great manners."

"And his own jet and about a zillion dollars," I said.

"Of course," said Mary Beth.

"A zillion dollars?" said Alissa.

"Well, sure, he's successful," said Dallas. "But y'all, he's so much more than that. He's smart and funny, and he *loves* Bentley. He's so good with her."

"Does he have kids?" asked Cheyenne.

Dallas shook her head. "No, and maybe that's why he's so crazy about Bentley."

"Maybe he'd like to make some with you," I said, winking at her.

"Maybe," said Dallas, smiling big. "The thought has definitely crossed my mind."

"Well, good luck with that," said Mary Beth, surprising me once again. "Just be careful. I don't want him to break your heart."

Mary Beth sipped her martini, and Dallas looked at me, uncertainty written all over her beautiful face. We were all wondering who this imposter was, and what she'd done with Mary Beth, but I couldn't shrug or make a face because Mary Beth turned to me.

"You said you had something to tell me," she said.

My mind went blank for a second. "Oh!" I said, finally pulling myself together. "I have to tell all of you. I started a business."

They all looked moderately interested. "And I want you all to join me!"

"What kind of business?" asked Cheyenne.

"In Aspen or Houston?" asked Dallas.

"Does it involve breaking and entering?" asked Mary Beth, her face a wash of innocence.

"What's breaking and entering?" asked Alissa, still coloring, now in purple.

"Nothing that exciting. But it could be pretty fun. I met a guy at Jimmy's who wanted to lease his house here in Starwood while he's in Europe. He asked me if I knew anyone who could handle the details for him. And I told him I would."

Mary Beth just looked at me.

"He wants someone who can take care of everything, so all he has to do is hand over the keys. It's a concierge service. That's my new business." I said it in that "ta-da!" sort of way, expecting all kinds of excitement and maybe even a squeal from Dallas. But I got nothing. Except some doubtful faces looking back at me.

"Don't you see?" I asked, leaning forward. "We get wealthy people to let us lease their homes when they're not here – and everyone knows most of these beautiful houses get used for only a few weeks each year. Then we find other wealthy people to lease them, and we set them up with chefs, cars, shopping, housekeeping, the whole nine yards."

"And what do we get in return?" asked Dallas, starting to look slightly interested. After all, she was the one who needed to replace the income stream so abruptly halted by Baby Daddy.

"We get eighteen percent!" I said.

"And where do we find super-rich people looking to rent a high-dollar crib like that?" asked Cheyenne.

"Well, for starters, I have a friend in the fashion industry. She's sending me an international supermodel and her boyfriend, and they're getting here Sunday." I named the model and this time Dallas did squeal.

"So just say," said Cheyenne, tucking one bare foot up under her on the couch, "if we jumped on board and helped you. And you rented this house. How much would we make?"

"This house," I said, clasping my hands together, "is fabulous. It rents for thirty-five hundred a night."

"Yeesh!" said Dallas. "How many nights?"

"Seven," I said.

"If we all helped you, and split that commission four ways," said Mary Beth, not even using her toes and fingers, "that would be just over a thousand dollars each."

Dallas's face fell, and Cheyenne curled her lip like she'd just run over a skunk in her VW convertible.

"Yes," I said, trying to sound enthusiastic, "but that's just one house. Just one commission. If we all worked together, we would come up with a whole slew of houses to lease and a bunch of supermodels to lease them, or rock stars, or just plain old rich people. And—"

"Thanks, Lucy," said Dallas, "but I think I'll be too busy traveling with Burt to help out right now."

"Yeah, thanks, Lucy," said Cheyenne, "but I'll probably be too busy helping Will fix up our new house."

Mary Beth raised an eyebrow at Cheyenne. And I didn't even bother asking MB if she wanted in on my fabulous new endeavor. It was clear. No one was interested.

"Who is Will?" asked Mary Beth.

"Oh! That's right," said Dallas. "You've been gone. Cheyenne has lots to tell you."

So my idea was trumped by a story of an abusive billionaire. My extraordinary vision was left dying in the dust while Cheyenne told Mary Beth all about being rescued by her Power Ranger.

"I don't understand," said Mary Beth when Cheyenne finished her story. "How did that heinous man hold you against your will? And how'd you get away?"

"What's heinous?" asked Alissa. But she didn't seem to really want an answer to her questions, just to be part of the conversation. She sat back from the coffee table and worked at the buckle of her sandal. Designer sandals if I knew Mary Beth. But I didn't recognize the designer, which was unusual for me. And suddenly I felt a sharp pang, catching me by surprise. I get pangs over shoes all the time – pangs of longing for a beautiful shoe in the window of Barney's, pangs of horror when Cheyenne pairs classic pumps with her Vivienne Westwood over-the-top-crazy modern punk dress. But this was a pang of regret, because I didn't recognize Alissa's little black sandal. Because if I had, that would probably have meant I had kids.

"He took my cell phone," said Cheyenne, answering Mary Beth and ticking the words off on her fingers, "he wouldn't let me leave his sight unless I was in the bathroom. He cut me off from everyone, even the staff. He gave them two weeks vay-kay with pay. He didn't even tell them he was planning to blow the country. He was, like, totally jammed when Will rang the doorbell that last day. I thought he was gonna explode."

"Jammed?" asked Mary Beth.

"Furious," said Cheyenne. "I think he was afraid if he didn't answer the door, there'd be trouble. He pointed his finger at me like *don't move*, but while he was at the front door I went out the side door and ran my cojones off."

"What's cojones?" asked Alissa. Of course.

Mary Beth lifted her eyebrow at Cheyenne.

"Sorry," said Shy.

"So back up," I said. "How did you call us?"

"I told Michael I had to or you guys would get freaked and go to the police. Which, thank God, you did." She smiled.

"So he let you make that last call to us?" asked Dallas.

Cheyenne nodded.

"And that's when you decided to give us the code word?" I asked.

"Right," said Cheyenne. "I knew I had to sound legit to Michael when I told you everything was A-okay. But I had to make you guys realize I was in deep—"

She paused and seemed to search for a word that wouldn't get her a disapproving glance – or worse – from Mary Beth.

"Trouble?" I offered.

"What code word?" asked Mary Beth.

"Aberration," said Cheyenne. "I got that from you."

MB looked confused. "And how did that word let you know she was in trouble?" she asked, looking at me.

I looked to Cheyenne, wanting her to answer. And for the first time all evening, Cheyenne looked uncomfortable. She blushed and looked away, but then she seemed to come to a decision, and she looked at Mary Beth.

"Because," she said, "you use words like that a lot. And it always makes me feel stupid. So I've started trying to remember each one and to figure out what they mean. I don't want you to think I'm stupid."

I wanted to cry, and I think Dallas did cry a little. Then Alissa saved the day.

"You're not stupid," she said, looking up at Cheyenne. "I think you're smart. You got away from that heinous man and you used a secret word. Right, Momma?" She looked at Mary Beth, who, I swear to you, seemed to get a little bit misty eyed. I mean, maybe it was pollen season, or she was allergic to her expensive mascara. But her eyes got watery.

"Right, baby. You're right." She laid a hand on Alissa's head and smoothed her dark hair.

"And tell me," said Mary Beth, still looking at her daughter's soft hair. "What's become of this Michael creature?"

Cheyenne shrugged. "I don't know. And I don't care. Everyone told me to press charges. But trying to prove everything would've been a giant drag, and I just couldn't do it. I couldn't face him again. He's mean. And controlling. And abusive. And I think you were right all along, Mary Beth. Since he had me stuck to his side like glue, I listened in on his phone conversations. He's running some kind of scam, and his investors are starting to get wise. I think he was trying to blow the country with all their dough."

Mary Beth looked at Cheyenne, thinking. Then she reached for her handbag and found her cell phone. Without a word to us, she placed a call.

"Edward, hello, it's Mary Beth. How are you, darling? Say, is your brother still with the SEC? He is? Wonderful. I've got a lead on a case I think he'll be very interested in. I have a dear friend with valuable inside information on a possible scam. Yes, tomorrow is fine," she looked at Cheyenne, who nodded. "We'll plan for a conference call at one o'clock tomorrow afternoon. Thank you, Edward."

Mary Beth calmly slid the phone back into her handbag. I looked around my cozy living room, birthplace of Martini Thursday. And I couldn't help but smile. A big goofy grin. Everyone else in the room wore the same goofy grin. Even Alissa. On some level, she knew her mother had just helped bring down a bad guy.

Mary Beth even smiled. Tonight she wore the smile of a woman who was no longer fighting her way through a life that felt more like a battleground than a haven. No longer angry and bitter over never having been loved. Because as Alissa got up off the floor and curled up beside her mother on the couch, easing her little hand into Mary Beth's, it was clear to see that Mary Beth had found the love she needed.

It was such a beautiful moment. And I felt partly responsible for it. It was my living room, after all. My idea to start Martini Thursday with a few women I barely knew at the time. So it was my moment. My shining moment.

Glacier would have been proud of me, because I was most definitely *here and now.* I would have to tell him about it, if I ever spoke to him again. And then I realized, if I was considering his reaction, I had jumped into the future. Oh hell.

But what I would later learn about good moments, and bad moments, and everything in between, is that nothing is constant. Life is always changing. And so it wasn't so much my moment in the sun as my moment of standing completely unprotected while a burning asteroid from hell hurtled straight for me.

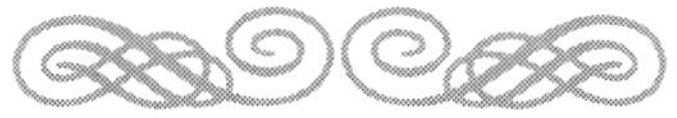

Chapter Thirty-Seven

Supermodels are much skinnier in person. That's what I kept thinking as I introduced myself, handed over my card, and told the undernourished woman with big eyes that I was ready to meet all of her needs, large or small. She basically ignored me, blowing a puff of cigarette smoke in my direction and turning to her musician boyfriend, who seemed to be wearing eyeliner. Not a good look on a man, if you ask me. But then, I'm not a supermodel.

We stood in Charlie's lush gourmet kitchen with warm afternoon sun bouncing off a row of Mauviel pots hanging over the island. The black granite countertops were now covered with cigarette cartons, a leather jacket, two guitar cases, and a dirty red nylon backpack. And my very first pampered, spoiled clients in my fabulous new business weren't even a little bit interested in anything I had to say. Charlie's gorgeous house was teeming with people – assistants or roadies or servants of some kind because the skinny supermodel and the eye-lined musician barked orders left and right to anyone within earshot. I might as well have been invisible.

It was weird, I thought, as I got in my car and drove back to my own house. Sort of strange to be on this side of the equation. In the past few years, I'd had my first taste of being on the other side. Being the pampered, spoiled client. Now suddenly I was the groveling, submissive, minion – being dismissed by a couple of twenty-somethings wearing dirty designer jeans.

I turned into my drive, suddenly unsure of this new enterprise, unsure of myself in general - which was a horrible way to feel. I wanted to feel confident and self assured. Or at least, marginally optimistic for my future. So I pulled into my garage and gave myself a mental slap across the face – not hard enough to leave a mark, but just bracing enough to snap me out of my self-pity and uncertainty. Then I gave myself my weekly pep talk.

This concierge business was my chance to shine on my own. My opportunity to prove to Thomas I no longer needed him. To show off to my friends my staggering ability to build an empire while they buried themselves in trivial matters like jetting around with billionaire boyfriends. And remarrying ex-husbands. And reuniting with lost daughters.

Okay. That was mean, and I take it back. Those aren't trivial things. Those are really important things, and I wanted all that and more for my crazy friends. I was just stinging a little from their total brush-off of my ingenious new endeavor.

I dropped my handbag on the kitchen counter. Not just any handbag. It was the mother of all handbags. Birkin. Pale taupe. The one thing I owned that would be really hard to explain to my Grandma. A calculated, totally on-purpose choice for today. Because it was beautiful and rare and meant to give the message to a spoiled skinny supermodel that I was nobody's minion. But now I felt stupidly transparent for using a purse as a prop just to impress a supermodel. I sighed, wishing I could finally feel good about myself without making someone else feel bad in the process.

Then for some strange reason, I felt the urge to make tea. Which I hardly ever do. Coffee, for sure. A ginormous pitcher of martinis, oh yeah. But hardly ever tea. It was too late in the day for coffee, and too early for martinis, and maybe I just wanted something comforting.

So I dug through the cupboards for the copper teakettle Thomas and I had brought back from England and filled it with water, then hunted through the pantry and found a box of herbal tea bags left over from my parents' visit early in the summer. While I stood in my kitchen waiting for the water to boil – and by the way, it's true, water takes way longer to boil when you do that – the doorbell rang. And even before I got to the door, I knew who was on the other side.

I stood at the door and considered not answering, but then I remembered Glacier had superpowers – like intuition and x-ray vision. He probably knew I was home. So I opened the door and stood with my hand on my hip, trying not to look like the girl who'd so recently been abandoned on her own deck after one of the most passionate kisses of her life. Glacier smiled at me in a way that told me he knew he had hurt my feelings. Not his easy, carefree smile. I felt all my defenses begin to fall away.

"What's in the bag?" I asked.

"Muffins," he said. His new smile loosened the knot in my stomach and made me smile back. And now I knew why the sudden itch to make tea.

He followed me into the kitchen where the teakettle whistled like a train. I moved the kettle off the stove, then took down two hand-painted pottery mugs.

"Tea," said Glacier. "Perfect."

And it made me laugh. I just couldn't help it. Because it was as if things always fell into place for him everywhere he went. As if the universe provided exactly what he needed, right when he needed it.

On the deck, in our usual chairs, we sipped chamomile tea and ate healthy muffins. And I worried my body would go into some kind of herbs-and-granola shock or that my liver and stomach would turn on me since they were all set to process Grey Goose and olives and not oats and wheat germ, and whatever else these ridiculously nutritious muffins were made of.

Glacier chewed slowly, savoring each bite. He didn't wolf the food down and reach for another bite. He gave each bite his full attention. I tried doing the same thing, and almost choked. I had to grab for my tea, taking a big swig and burning my tongue.

When he'd finally eaten the whole thing, at a snail's pace and in total silence, he took a sip of tea then set his cup on the table between us. He tucked his hands in his lap and looked across at me. "Lucy, I owe you an apology."

Not only was my tongue burned, but now it seemed broken. I couldn't think of a response. I pushed the uneaten half of my muffin away and sat quietly for a change, waiting for him to tell me about his wife.

"You've become one of my teachers."

I frowned. "How is that possible?"

"You helped me realize I still have a lot of work to do."

I just looked at him. Under the circumstances, I was pretty sure it wasn't a compliment.

"You should know," he said, looking into my eyes. "I have feelings for you."

And suddenly I couldn't breathe.

"I never meant for it to happen. But I've fallen in love with you."

My heart thudded against my ribs. I was speechless. Of all the things he might have said, I was least prepared for that.

"That first day when you walked up to me in the bakery," he said, leaning his arms on the table in front of him, "I thought you were so full of confidence. So self-assured. But then gradually, you let your guard down and showed me your true self. Not self-assured at all. Searching. Lost. And I fell in love with the hurt and broken woman, the one fighting so hard to show the world how tough she is."

The half-eaten muffin suddenly felt heavy in my stomach. I immediately remembered sitting beside Thomas and crying, having a similar conversation. Similar but completely opposite, when Thomas told me that had I shown my true feelings to him, he never would have left me. And now here I had finally shown a man my broken insides, and I was losing out once again.

I set my tea on the table and prepared for the worst. "This is the part where you tell me about your wife."

Glacier's face went from sober, to confused, to slightly amused. He shook his head. "No. I don't have a wife."

I looked at him and held up my hands. "What, then?" This was almost worse. As my vision of his blond and braided wife evaporated, I felt his rejection all over again. "Why did you look so upset after we kissed?"

Glacier linked his hands together and seemed to be choosing his words carefully. Which he always did, but today his words came out more slowly, as if weighted down. "One of the reasons I think I fell in love with you, is that you remind me of me. Broken and searching and trying so hard to find a way to the other side. I was there. I remember how much it hurts."

It was a sadly accurate description of me and my broken insides. I shook my head. "I can't imagine you like that."

Glacier looked down at his hands. "I made some bad decisions when I was younger. My parents wanted me to follow their lifestyle, a simple life. But I thought I knew better."

This was a surprise. "So you haven't always meditated? You haven't always been so perfect?"

He looked up but didn't smile. "I moved to Denver in my early twenties and lived a pretty crazy life. Drinking. Women. My ego was out of control."

I almost wanted to laugh, because this person he described was so unimaginable, so vastly different from the man sitting across from me. But the look on his face told me there would be nothing funny about this story.

"Did you work?" I asked, wondering why I chose that particular question in a sea of questions swimming in my mind.

He nodded. "I sculpted. But not like I do now. I went commercial. Sculpted anything anyone wanted. Made a lot of money. Spent a lot of money."

Unbelievable. This peaceful, ego-less monk-like man had once been a hard-boozing, womanizing party boy? I couldn't wrap my mind around it.

"I bet women were crazy about you," I said softly, imagining him in a whole new light.

Again, he looked down at his clasped hands. "This is the hardest part to talk about," he said softly. "There were a lot of women in my life back then. I didn't respect relationships. I didn't even respect myself. I hung around with a wild crowd almost every night at a bar in LoDo. One night, a girl I'd been with a few times came in. She said she needed to talk to me. She was crying and making a scene. So I took her to my car, and she told me she was pregnant."

Glacier looked up at me, and all I could do was raise my eyebrows.

"I didn't know what to do. I told her we needed to drive around and figure things out. But I'd been drinking – a lot – and the roads were icy. I slid through a red light. She was killed."

The abrupt end of his story caught me by surprise. I didn't know what to say.

He looked at me. The sadness in his eyes made my throat close up with tears. This man I'd believed had just been born with *here and now* tattoos and a peaceful, serene countenance had actually been through hell and back. Just like the rest of us.

"What happened?" I asked. "Were you arrested? Did you go to jail?"

He nodded. "But that wasn't the hard part. You can get out of jail, but you can't get away from yourself."

"So that's when you started meditating?"

He nodded again. "Eventually. I moved back here. Back to my parents' house. They helped me, got me to make some hard changes." His voice was rough. "They saved me."

A tear slid down my face and I brushed it away. I wasn't sure if I was crying for Glacier or for myself. I wished desperately someone would step in and save me.

"I stopped drinking and started sculpting – from a deeper perspective. And made a vow to myself that I wouldn't get involved romantically, sexually, until I was whole. Until I was healed. I know I'm not ready, not now, maybe not ever. But that doesn't mean I don't love you. Please believe me."

I frowned. "But that doesn't make any sense. None of us are whole. No one has it all together all the time. Why can't we figure it out together?" I reached across the table and took his hand. His fingers closed around mine.

He looked intently into my eyes. "Lucy, you're on the path. That's the reason we're here on earth," he said, his voice low and passionate. "The best thing I can do is help you any way possible. You became my teacher when you showed me that I blurred the lines between wanting what's best for you, and just... *wanting*. I thought my intentions were good, that I was caring for you. But then I fell in love with you, wanted you. Real love is when you care about the progress of the other person's soul."

I shook my head, totally confused. "I don't understand. Can't you love my soul, and the rest of me too?"

He smiled, but shook his head. "No. I don't think so."

I sighed and tried to understand. I rubbed my thumb over his rough knuckle, realizing how hard it must have been for him to tell me his darkest, blackest secrets. I felt closer to him than ever, which was ironic since he was telling me I could never have him.

"What about someday?" I said. "When you're healed and I'm not such a train wreck. What about then? Do you think you'll ever have a relationship?"

Glacier was quiet for a minute, just looking at me with those sleepy blue eyes. "I don't know," he finally said.

We were quiet as the crazy world went on around us and I tried to understand this unusual revelation. This idea that he couldn't be with me but could still help me on the path. But most of all, I was trying to come to terms with the fact that Glacier wasn't perfect. He was human after all. Damaged and flawed, just like the rest of us.

We went inside to make more tea, and I felt emotionally exhausted. From realizing that the person I thought I knew so well, I didn't know at all. From trying to understand his deep personal commitment to the path – to chastity and celibacy and loving another's soul. And even though I didn't really quite understand it all, I was humbled by it. To know he loved me so much that he wanted my highest good. Wanted to help me on the path. It was the most beautiful thing anyone had ever done for me. And I knew then that I would always remember this day, finding out that at least one person on this earth cared what happened to my soul.

But also, I had to wonder: if there was perfect harmony in nature, as Glacier was always saying, if all the laws of the universe came together just the way they were supposed to, why didn't the universe make the really holy men less attractive?

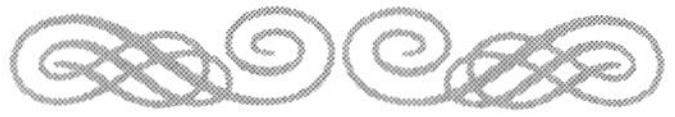

Chapter Thirty-Eight

Well, I wondered. Where do we go from here? We'd settled back on the deck with cups of fresh tea. There was a heaviness hanging over us, a seriousness, yet there didn't seem to be any more to say on the matter. He loved me but wouldn't let himself do anything about it. He was more concerned with my soul, with helping me on the path. Sheesh.

"I've been living in the moment," I said, trying to fill the awkward silence. "Or trying to. Most of the time."

Glacier smiled and nodded once. "How's your meditation going?"

"Not bad," I lied. He looked at me, and I was afraid he could read my mind. "Okay, I haven't exactly gotten back into it yet. But I will. Soon. I've just been so busy."

His face was serene, and I was relieved to see the shadows of sadness were gone from his eyes. He didn't give me a disapproving look. Didn't tell me I needed to get back to meditation, which somehow made it worse.

"I've been really buried," I said, breaking off a piece of my battered muffin and picking out the raisins. "I started a new business."

I ate the raisin-free bite while Glacier waited for me to go on. At least, I guessed he was waiting for me to go on. He didn't stop me.

"It's a concierge business," I said. "I lease out people's homes, and provide different services for the people who rent them." It was a bad description of my new enterprise, but I was still a little unhinged realizing Glacier wasn't unaffected by me after all. Knowing that maybe I wasn't the only one who'd been having outrageous carnal fantasies about the two of us. But that those fantasies would probably never come true now. It was a lot to take in.

"So it's a business designed to help people?"

I thought about that. "Not really. I mean, sort of. It does help people. It helps the homeowner because I find someone to lease their house. And it helps the lessee, because I get them a chef, and a limo, and housekeeping, and just generally bow and scrape."

He nodded slightly. "You make their stay more enjoyable," he said.

"I guess I do. Not that I care much if their stay is enjoyable. They're spoiled and out of touch with reality." I realized how bad that sounded once it was out of my mouth, but I was thinking of the supermodel and the musician, who'd completely ignored me and treated me like yesterday's garbage.

"And so, what *do* you care about?" he asked.

"I care that I get eighteen percent every time I lease a house. And I'll only lease expensive luxury homes, so that means big commissions."

"You're doing it for the money?"

"Well, partly. I have some money put away, but I need to start planning for the future."

"What would you say is the main reason for your new business?" he asked.

I took a sip of my tea and looked at him over the cup while I formed an answer. I thought of all the things I'd reminded myself of just before he showed up on my doorstep. Wanting to show my independence to Thomas. Wanting to show off for my friends. Wanting to prove something to Glacier. Realizing it all came down to rejection. All of those people had rejected me in some way, and I wanted to show them. But I couldn't say that.

"I guess I want to make a name for myself," I said, playing with the last bite of muffin. "I want to prove I have skills and intelligence. I just really want to show the world what I can do."

Glacier studied me. "So," he said, "it's about power?"

"Yes."

"Prestige?"

"Of course."

"Your reputation? Your dignity? Your expertise?"

"Exactly!" I said, happier with his description than with mine. "You hit it on the head. My reputation, which got run over when Thomas dumped me. My dignity, for the same reason. And my expertise, sure. I want to show my friends that I'm more than just a woman with a small divorce settlement and a mean martini shaker. I want to be respected."

He nodded. But he didn't look happy.

"What's wrong?" I said with a sigh. I did a quick mental recap of all Glacier had told me in the past and wondered which rule I'd just broken.

He leaned forward. "Lucy, what do all those reasons have in common?"

I tried to think of the right answer. "I don't know. They're all about trying to recover some of what I lost when Thomas kicked me to the curb. It's about trying to feel better about myself. What could possibly be wrong with that?"

"It's all ego," he said. His face was still serene, but he wasn't smiling. He was serious.

"So what's wrong with repairing my ego? It took a major hit in my divorce."

He sat back in his chair and was quiet. I sipped my tea and wished for a Bloody Mary. So far, it had been a hell of a day. Treated like dog food by the supermodel. Denied what had promised to be a very hot relationship because of my soul. And now being scolded for trying to repair my battered ego. When would I ever get things right?

He put his fingertips together and rested them under his chin. "Have you ever thought of doing something to help others?"

Well, that ticked me off. "Of course I have!" But I looked at his face, at the kindness there, and remembered he wasn't trying to badger me. He was trying to help me. So I dialed down a little on the indignation. "I've done a lot of charity work," I said, trying hard not to sound defensive.

He was quiet.

"But I want something that's mine," I said, sounding whiney and childish. I changed my approach. "I *need* this. Don't you get it? I need to prove to myself that I can do this."

Glacier finally smiled at me, a compassionate, loving smile. "I understand completely," he said. "You need your purpose in life."

"Exactly!" I said, smiling big. "You're exactly right! I need a purpose in life."

"No," he said, "not *a* purpose. *Your* purpose in life."

"What's the difference?"

He leaned forward again, which seemed to be his stance when he really wanted me to understand something. "You've been given a purpose for this lifetime. There's something important that only you can do. And you won't be happy until you find that purpose."

"Really. And how do I find my purpose?"

"Meditate," he said. "Ask your heart. Be still and ask what you can do to make this world a better place."

I made a face. I couldn't stop myself. "How am I supposed to do that?" My voice rose with disbelief. "You've seen my life. You know better than anyone what a mess I am. Shouldn't I make things better in my own life before I start trying to improve the whole world? Why is that suddenly my job?"

"Not just you," he said. "Everyone. We're all here to improve things."

"So now my little side business, my little enterprise, has to save the world." I slumped in my chair and put my chin in my hand.

Glacier laughed. "Maybe not the whole world. Start small. With one person. What can you do to help one person?"

I rolled my eyes. What a day. Why couldn't I have just one friend who understood me? Just one. Just one single friend who would applaud my new business and wish me the best as I built an empire to power, glory, and money. Was that so wrong?

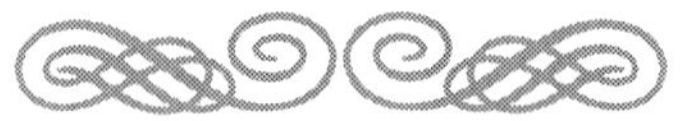

Chapter Thirty-Nine

I thought of having a sign made. Something stylish, tasteful, lightweight, so I could wear it around my neck: *ONE CRISIS AT A TIME, LINE FORMS TO THE LEFT.*

Wednesday started out with more tears from Dallas and went drastically downhill after that.

I gave her a tissue and a Bloody Mary and tucked her into her favorite couch in my living room. Although I noticed she was more interested in the Bloody Mary than the tissue. She wasn't crying so much as pouting.

"So start at the beginning and tell me what happened," I said. "Obviously Burt lied to you. Tell me about it."

She looked at me with her big brown eyes. "How do you know he lied?"

"Because you came in here screeching, 'Burt is a big fat liar.'"

"Oh. Yeah. Anyway, it's over and I hope he realizes all he's missing!"

"I thought everything was going great," I said, stirring my drink. "I thought he loved Baby Bentley and thought you were the answer to his prayers!"

"The girl of his dreams," she said, licking the celery stalk and placing it on her cocktail napkin. "He told me I was the girl of his dreams."

"Uh huh. And then what happened?"

"Well, we didn't get together this weekend because he said he had to work. And I was missing him like crazy. So we texted and emailed, but he said he couldn't really even talk on the phone because he was in meetings."

"Yeah, so? He's a gazillionaire. It stands to reason he has meetings and busy weekends."

"But I really missed him. So yesterday I got the idea to drive to Denver and surprise him."

"Uh oh."

"Right. Uh oh. I left after Bentley woke up and got to his office before noon. And I'm thinking what a great surprise this will be and how he'll be so happy to see me. That I'll whisk him away for a private lunch."

"And by lunch, you mean—"

"Just lunch, maybe some kissing. Don't worry, no sex in the bathroom this time. But somewhere nice, somewhere private."

"Good for you," I said, wondering if I believed her. Dallas almost always told the truth, but this time I thought she might be lying to both of us. Like I said before, she always does the right thing – except when it comes to men. "So, was he surprised?"

"Oh yes. He was surprised. And so was his wife!"

I made bug eyes at her.

"Yes. He has a wife." She sipped her drink. "And she was in his office too. Apparently there was a big board meeting, and she's on the board!"

"What did she look like?" I asked, before I could stop myself.

"Well," Dallas sniffed. "Sort of like an Ambassador to the United Nations. Only with maybe a Heidi Fleiss-like prostitution ring on the side."

"Huh?"

"Like all sophisticated wedge hair and a dark, understated suit, but low cut and showing lots of cleavage and nails as long as Cheyenne's. And dark red lipstick."

"I *knew* I should have had him investigated," I said. "Did it get ugly?"

Dallas shrugged and tossed her hair over her shoulder. "Not really. I walked in and he was standing in the reception area with a bunch of people. His eyes about popped out of his head. That was sorta funny, thinking back on it."

"Was his wife in the reception area too?"

"Yep. He introduced me as one of the shareholders. Told his wife I was there to pick up some paperwork. He actually went over to his secretary's desk and handed me an envelope."

I laughed. "I hope it was full of money."

"Empty," she said. "I gave him a seething look and walked away. I won't answer his texts or his calls."

"Good for you," I said. "You could have made a big scene and told his wife what he was up to. Or at least given her the name of your manicurist and asked her where she kept her hookers. But I think you did the right thing."

Dallas shrugged again and sighed.

"I have to say, you're taking this pretty well. You don't seem all that upset."

She smiled and sort of batted her eyes. "Well, there's a new guy..."

Of course.

"His name is Chaz. And he's looking for a yacht!"

"I see. So you're trading in a private jet for a yacht."

"Exactly!" she smiled. "I've always been a water girl. And besides, he's a lot younger than Burt. And hotter."

"Okay, this time I'm checking him out. As soon as you have his name and any information on him, *please* let me order a background check."

"Well, okay. But you'll have to hurry. We're having dinner to-night."

Crisis number two came in the form of a phone call. And required much more than a tissue and a Bloody Mary.

"Hello?" I answered my cell phone on my way up Smuggler for a much-needed run after Dallas left to find an outfit for her dinner date with Cyber-Boy.

"Ms. Moore?"

I frowned at the unfamiliar male voice and slowed my pace to a walk. "Yes, this is Lucinda Moore."

"This is Jason, the chef you hired for—"

"Oh, sure, sure." The chef for the supermodel and the musician. "How's everything going over there?"

"Well, that's what I'm calling about," he said. His voice sounded wary.

"Problems?" I asked, imagining the skin-and-bones woman and the raccoon-eyed guitarist were exhausting Jason with their orders and requests.

"Well, yeah. I think so. I'm at the house now. They wanted a light lunch and then I planned to start working on dinner."

"What's the problem?" I stepped off the trail and stretched my hamstring, dying to get back into my run.

"I think they're gone."

I rolled my eyes. Why was he calling me? "Jason, they're probably in town. I'm sure they'll be back. Just make lunch and leave it in the fridge. They'll find it."

"No, I mean I think they left for good."

I stopped stretching. "Why do you think that?"

"Well, all their stuff's gone. They were kinda messy, and there was stuff all over the house. Even here in the kitchen. It's all gone."

I mentally ticked off the days in my mind. Stella had sent me a wire prepaying for seven days. The couple had so far been in Charlie's house for only three.

"I'll make a call," I said. "I'll find out what's going on and get right back with you."

"Okay, but there's more..."

I sighed and put my hand on my hip. "Don't worry, Jason. You'll be paid for the full week regardless. A deal's a deal. Now go home and don't worry about a thing. I'll call you."

"That's not what I was worried about."

"Then what?" Jason was young and probably too inexperienced to realize that wealthy people had a tendency to do whatever they wanted, whenever they wanted.

"I think you might want to come over here."

I really needed a run, desperately needed meditation. I needed to work out the whole thing with Glacier. And wanted to be able to tell him my meditations were going really well. But before I could do that, at some point I would have to actually, you know, meditate.

"Jason, can't this wait? I'm really kind of in the middle of something right now."

"I guess so," he said. "But you probably need to get over here as soon as you can."

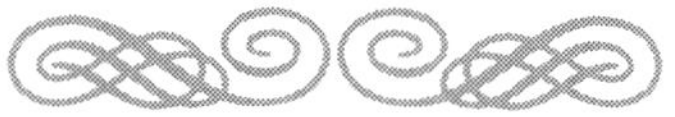

Chapter Forty

Destroyed. I walked through what had been one of the ritziest homes in Starwood. But now Charlie's elegant home was destroyed. Ruined.

Jason was there, trying to clean up the kitchen. Broken wine bottles on the floor. The remnants of what looked to be a food fight. Expensive Mauviel copper pots scattered around, looking as if they'd been used as a drum set. And a smell I couldn't quite put my finger on but might have been marijuana mixed with incense.

Or maybe scented candles. Marijuana mixed with scented candles. Because when I walked from the kitchen into the great room, there was a trail of red candle wax on the rich cream colored carpet. But it didn't stop there. Splatters covered nearly every surface of the house. The hardwood floors. The limestone floor in the master bath. The marble tile in the foyer. It looked like a slaughterhouse, or the scene of some horrible sacrifice.

And as I stood there stupidly trying to come to terms with the total annihilation of Charlie's house, I realized there truly had been a sacrifice. It was my reputation. My good name. My illustrious new career, ruined. Sacrificed. Wiped out by a skinny, blond, chain-smoking supermodel and her not even the least bit attractive rock star wannabe boyfriend.

And although it was the worst thing I could have imagined happening – and the damage was worse with each room – I wasn't even mad, except at myself. I should have seen this coming. Because every time Glacier tried to tell me something, every time he leaned forward and offered his wisdom, something like this happened.

I walked outside and sat on the deck. At least the damage was only to the inside of the house. The pasty musician was probably afraid of sunlight. Maybe he was a vampire. I slumped into a deck chair and let out a long, mournful sigh. Here I was, once again, drowning in a sea of are-you-freaking-kidding-me, all because I hadn't listened to Glacier. I hadn't stopped and regrouped when he'd told me to look inside and find my purpose in life. And really, how could I have done that? The house was already booked. The supermodel was already here. So I just charged forward with my brilliant idea. My fabulous new concierge business.

And why couldn't that have worked? I mean, until I had time to figure out my real purpose in life. Why couldn't I have made a go at leasing luxury homes and making a commission? What was so wrong with that?

Glacier said I was stroking my ego, but all I really wanted was to feel better about myself. And in a startling moment of oh-I-get-it-now that I really could have done without, I realized the two were the same.

I dug my phone out of my bag, feeling a little like a storm chaser trying to warn my friends about the deadly tornado heading their way. "Dallas, it's me. Whatever you do, don't go on your date tonight. Call that yacht guy and tell him you can't see him. Ever!"

"Lucy, what are you talking about? Did you have him investigated? Wait a minute," she said, "I never even told you his last name."

"It doesn't matter," I said. "I don't care what his name is. Just drop him! And then get on your computer and start looking into online classes."

I hung up on her and put my phone back in my bag. Then I sat looking out over the mountains – the best view in Aspen – and tried to summon the energy to put Charlie's house back together.

You know what they say…if you think things can't get any worse, you just don't have a very good imagination. God, I hoped this was the worst. Because I really couldn't imagine my life getting any bleaker.

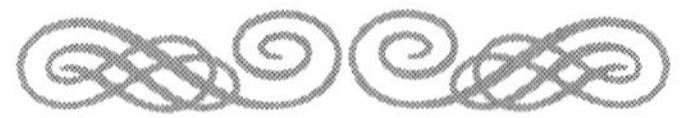

Chapter Forty-One

The next night we met for Martini Thursday at Dallas's house. I was late. By the time I got there, Baby Bentley, Alissa, and the nanny were outside playing in the life-size play house, and Dallas, Mary Beth, and Cheyenne were halfway through their first martini.

"Finally," said Dallas, leading me into her sunny living room. "We were starting to worry about you. You're never late for Martini Thursday."

"That's because it's usually at her house," said Cheyenne, laughing.

"You look a bit done in," said Mary Beth, which was fairly mild for one of her barbs. But she was right. Every bone in my body ached, and my brain felt like mush.

"Rough day?" asked Dallas, who looked as if she'd had a celebrity stylist fluff her hair, perfect her makeup, and dress her in a skinny white strapless dress with gold piping. Anyone would look a bit done in next to her.

I nodded and sipped my martini. "The roughest," I said, slumping back in the couch with my drink.

"Me too," said Cheyenne, kicking off her Uggs sandals. "I don't think Will and I should work together."

"Uh oh," said Dallas. "Too much togetherness?"

"For sure," said Cheyenne. "This morning he said he needed a little space. So I locked him outside."

I laughed, and even Mary Beth chuckled.

"But you're still glad you're back with him, right?" asked Dallas. "I mean, he's being good to you?"

Cheyenne nodded. "Oh, sure. He's the bomb most of the time. It's just, he asked me for a screwdriver, and I handed him the wrong one, and he gave me a look. And that's when I told him to bite me, and stomped out. The only screwdriver I'm on a first name basis with is made of orange juice and vodka and comes in a glass. He'll just have to deal."

I was slightly worried Cheyenne might have jumped out of the frying pan and into the line of fire with her Power Ranger. I guess Mary Beth was too. "You know," said Mary Beth, "if you need a place to stay while you and Will get things back on track, you can always stay with me."

"Thanks, Mary Beth," she said almost in a whisper. Cheyenne looked at MB like she'd just offered her one of her organs instead of an extra bedroom. "You're the best, but I think I'm good." She reached for her martini and I noticed her acrylic nails were gone. In their place were nice, short, natural nails – a big improvement.

"You know, with Michael, no matter how hard I tried, I was never good enough," she said, looking down into her drink. "He acted like I was some kind of possession, only not even a really good one. Not like one of his precious horses or even one of his dumb Ferraris, but more like some ugly sweater he got off the bargain table and never really wanted in the first place."

"What an ass," said Mary Beth.

"But with Will," she said, her face softening, "I can just be myself. He loves the real me. I don't have to worry about whether my shoes are designer or that I'll screw up and use the wrong word in a sentence. We're a team. I always felt like I was mooching off Michael."

"Have y'all started counseling yet?" asked Dallas. This was news.

"Counseling?" I asked.

Cheyenne nodded. "We started with a guy in Denver. You know, Will was still pretty cheesed that I left. Plus, we had old issues. Nothing horrible. I never would've left in the first place if things had been totally wicked good, you know? So we're talking it all out."

"And it's working?" asked Dallas.

"Most of the time. Will's not too crazy about the process. You should see him when we walk in the door for counseling. He looks like he'd rather take a bullet from a drug dealer than talk about his feelings for fifty minutes."

Dallas laughed. "That's a guy for ya. But good for y'all. I'm proud of you." She hugged Cheyenne.

"Now what about you?" asked Dallas, walking toward me with the martini pitcher. "What went wrong with your day?" She filled my glass, and I have to say, it was about the best thing that happened to me all day.

"I hardly know where to start," I said. "The day was a suckfest from beginning to end."

Dallas laughed and Mary Beth rolled her eyes at my choice of words.

"Start at the beginning," said Mary Beth.

"Yesterday I got a call from the chef I hired to cook for the supermodel. He told me I might want to come by the house and check things out."

"What happened?" asked Cheyenne, leaning in.

"Well, apparently staying in a gorgeous luxury home and having an army of people jump at your every whim is just too boring. The brats destroyed the house."

Dallas sucked in her breath.

"No way!" said Cheyenne.

"Every way," I said. "Red candle wax on every surface including the wool carpet. Cigarette burns on the furniture. Broken bottles, food everywhere. And the place reeked of pot."

"But you secured a deposit before you leased the house, right?" said Mary Beth.

I took a sip of my drink and wished for about the millionth time that I had. Secured a deposit. Like most normal people would have when leasing a multi-million dollar home to strangers. I steeled myself for Mary Beth's tirade. She would never let this pass. And I really didn't think I had it in me to listen to her tonight. I was running on empty.

"Well," she said, looking at me with compassion, "the devil is in the details, right?"

I looked at her. Gaped is probably more descriptive.

"Will the repairs take your whole commission?" she asked.

I nodded and rubbed my temple. "And then some. I know it sounds crazy, me not getting a deposit, but I went through one of my oldest friends to lease to the supermodel."

"If she's one of your oldest friends," said Mary Beth, "she'll do the responsible thing and share in the damages."

I nodded again, wishing we could talk about something else. Anything else. "She is. She's paying half. But things are strained between us now. I don't think she'll be sending me any more models."

I couldn't bear to discuss this depressing topic for another second, so I changed the subject. "Tell us about the new guy," I said to Dallas. "Yacht Boy."

Dallas looked at me. "How about you tell me why you called and told me to dump him?"

I shrugged and lifted the glass to my lips. I just didn't have the energy to explain to Dallas that Glacier was always right. That we should always do exactly what he told us, because life would be oh so much simpler and we could avoid learning things the hard way.

She looked so happy as she poured martinis all around and started to tell us about the young hot guy with the exotic gray eyes and athlete's body.

"His name is Chaz Hilton," she said, all but twinkling. "He's somehow related to the Hilton hotel people. And he's been shopping for a yacht!"

I sagged back into the couch with my drink and kept quiet about her cyber boy toy. I was wiped out. I didn't want to be the mom tonight. I just wanted to sit with my drink and let the world revolve without my input. I would regret this tiny act of laziness and complacency before the week was out.

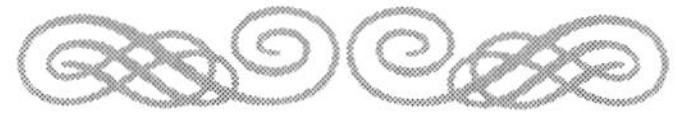

Chapter Forty-Two

Dallas was deep into her monologue on Chaz and his red corvette. Make that, red corvette with the vanity plate of something like HRDNFST, which I guess was supposed to mean hard and fast – ick – but to me looked more like infest, which made me think of creepy crawly things, which I would later discover described him very well.

Anyway, she was interrupted when Alissa came in from playing outside.

"Mommy," she said and put her hand on her mother's knee. MB put her drink down and covered Alissa's hand with hers.

"Yes, baby." MB smoothed the hair back from Alissa's forehead.

"Can we go home now? I think we should check on Stephanie."

I raised my eyebrows.

"Who's Stephanie?" asked Cheyenne.

Mary Beth smiled at Alissa. "Should we tell them about Stephanie?"

Alissa nodded and smiled.

"Why don't you tell them?" said Mary Beth.

Alissa turned to Cheyenne. "She's my friend," said Alissa. "She's at home."

"You left your friend at home?" asked Cheyenne.

MB cut her eyes at me, and I thought I understood. I put my drink on the table and stood up.

"I'm beat," I said. "Sorry to be a party pooper, but I think I'll head home too. I'll walk out with you," I said to Mary Beth.

"Party pooper," said Alissa, skipping toward the front door.

After Dallas and Cheyenne walked us out and shut the door, the nanny came around to the front yard with Bentley. Alissa ran over to them and I stood in Dallas's circle drive with Mary Beth, looking after the little girl who looked so much like MB.

"Stephanie;" I said. "Imaginary friend?"

"Yep," said Mary Beth. "I had one when I was at boarding school. I'm hoping now that Alissa's home, she won't need her anymore."

"I've been wondering, why boarding school?" I asked. "Your secret's out. I know you love being around kids. You hated being away from Alissa. So why did you send her to school?"

Mary Beth crossed her arms. "Her father wanted it. Insisted is more like it. Convinced me it would be the best thing for her. He didn't want her around another man, a stepfather. I was with Rolf at the time, and I thought it might be better for Alissa to be at school while Rolf and I settled into our new life. Better for her. Not for me."

"And after Rolf died?"

"I called Alissa. Asked her if she wanted to come home. But they were starting equestrian lessons. She said she wanted to stay. So I let her."

"So what made you do it?" I asked, watching as Alissa took Bentley's tiny hands and played ring around the rosy. "What made you decide to bring Alissa home?"

"You," said Mary Beth, also watching the girls. "All those things you said to me."

My stomach clutched, remembering the harsh words I'd hurled at Mary Beth on the phone. "But you never listen to me!" I said.

Mary Beth smiled. She kept watching the little girls, who were shrieking and falling onto the grass in a pile. "You were right," she said. "You told me I didn't integrate with anyone, and I realized that was true. You said my narcissistic tendencies were alienating everyone to the point of me ending up alone."

I swallowed. "I said all that?"

Mary Beth finally turned to look at me. "I couldn't bear for that to happen to Alissa."

"Well, I didn't mean—"

"Yes," she said. "You did. And you were right." She turned her attention back to the little girls. "I was repeating the pattern with Alissa. Screw the education. I'll spend the rest of my life making sure she knows she's loved."

Well, that got me. Already tired enough to drop on the spot and emotionally drained from cleaning up after a supermodel, I felt myself getting teary. "I worried about you when you were gone," I said. "We didn't know where you were. I was afraid you were breaking the conditions of your bond."

"Ah," said Mary Beth. "Not to worry. That's all been taken care of."

"What do you mean *taken care of?*" I asked. With Mary Beth, that could mean anything.

"I withdrew the lawsuit," she said. "All charges are dropped. My lawyer will eventually get the arrest sealed and my record expunged."

"And what about Cruella?"

"She resigned from the firm, and somehow, magically, all the money has been returned to the estate."

I looked at Mary Beth, and she was standing straight and tall, arms crossed over her chest, smiling a half smile. She looked like a superhero at the end of a movie. All she needed was a cape blowing softly behind her.

"Ohmygawd," I said. "You blackmailed her! You somehow blackmailed Cruella, didn't you?"

Mary Beth ignored me and called out to her daughter. "Come on, Alissa. Tell Bentley goodbye. We should go home. It's time for you and Stephanie to have your dinner."

"You feed the imaginary friend?"

"Of course." Mary Beth looked at me like I'd just said the dumbest thing. "We can't let the poor thing starve."

I woke up Friday morning no longer an entrepreneur. No longer catering to spoiled, baleful barbarians with the hubris to believe they could destroy a beautiful home and just leave town.

I woke up cranky. Irritable. And apparently channeling Mary Beth. The old Mary Beth. The one who used big words while shooting tongues of fire from her eyes.

The new Mary Beth was relaxed. Happy. It was so incredible. I wouldn't have believed it in a million years if I hadn't witnessed it with my own two droopy, bloodshot eyes. It was nice to know my good deeds were finally yielding results. Hah. Kidding. I knew Mary Beth's happiness was all due to Alissa. And maybe a tiny bit to blackmailing an evil lawyer.

All my crazy friends seemed happy these days – especially Dallas. But not so fast. Before heading to Smuggler for my run and a desperately-needed meditation I made a call to start the background check into Dallas's Yacht-Boy.

Over the years, Thomas and I had investigated the backgrounds of a few people. If we were thinking of investing with them. If we were considering hiring them. If we needed to be able to trust them in any way. So requesting a background check was old hat to me. We had a lawyer, and he had a guy, and the guy did all the dirty work. The guy's name was Guy. Seriously.

"Guy, it's Lucy Moore. It's been a while. How are you?" I gave him the information I had on Dallas's newest conquest, which wasn't much. Just his name, that he was currently living in Aspen, and his California license plate with the ridiculous testament to his enormous ego. But it was a start.

Here and now, I told myself, slowing my breathing, trying to stop twitching. My first meditation in weeks was not going all that well. I was out of the groove. Off the path. Much more *There and Then* than *Here and Now*. Totally engrossed in the outside world to the point that I could barely look within.

I thought about praying, but honestly, the last time I'd prayed I had braces and an algebra test the next day. So I just tried to breathe. My mind was stuffed with red candle wax and broken bottles. Thoughts of Dallas's cyber exploits and Cheyenne's attempt to rebuild her marriage. Mary Beth's new smile and Alissa's invisible friend. My grocery list, hair appointment, need for a facial, and overwhelming disappointment over my dismal failure at becoming a respected businesswoman.

I sighed in frustration and opened my eyes. The view was awesome, but I barely saw it. All I could see was a ridiculously long string of recent defeats and failures, beginning with the end of my marriage. I felt worn out from trying to fill my life with something. Anything. My new thing, my next thing. An ingenious new business. An exciting new man. Something to prove to myself that I was still me. That I was still interesting. That good things still happened to me. The effort of trying to be somebody was exhausting. I didn't know who I was anymore. I only knew that whoever it was, she was one unhappy, unfulfilled, beat-up, sex-starved woman.

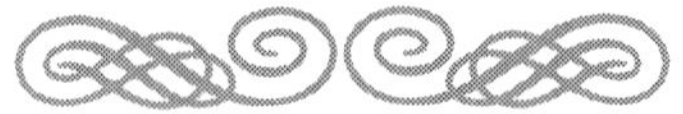

Chapter Forty-Three

I needed Glacier. I needed to feel as peaceful as he looked. I wanted off this crazy merry-go-round of reaching for my new life yet always coming up empty handed. And there he was. Right where he was supposed to be. Sitting at the sunny table by the front window of Main Street Bakery. With his Big Book of Answers and his worn out boots and clean white T-shirt.

I felt my body relax just knowing he was there, my one constant in an otherwise mad world. I could feel his peaceful vibe from the front door. He looked up and smiled when I walked over to him. And I just couldn't help thinking what a darn sexy holy man he was. Sigh.

"Lucy," he said, as if he'd been expecting me.

I pulled out the chair across from him and sat, not even bothering with coffee. "I need you," I said, putting my arms on the table and leaning forward.

"I'm here," he said in his deep, rich voice, and I almost laughed. I don't know why. It was just the matter of fact way he said it. Most people would say something like, *What's wrong?* or *How can I help?* or *Why do you have that freaked out, wild-eyed look of desperation?* But he just looked at me and waited for me to spill it. Just like he'd always done. Before he told me he loved me. Now I wanted everything to be back to normal between us.

"Mary Beth says I shouldn't take everything you say as gospel," I said. I sort of smiled at him, suddenly embarrassed for blurting that out.

I thought he might be a tiny bit peeved. But, of course, I was wrong.

"She's right," he said.

I cocked one eyebrow.

"You should test everything for yourself."

"How?" I asked.

"Through intuition. Through personal experience."

I wanted to laugh again. Because I had definitely tested everything he said through personal experience. Mostly by not taking his advice and meeting with a disaster from hell on the other end.

I leaned back in my chair. "I need what you have," I said, my voice tired and tense.

He didn't answer so I struggled on, feeling a sense of urgency. A sense of needing to get his attention. I leaned forward again. "I *have* to find my purpose. Remember? You said there was something only I could do? I need to know what that is! I need you to help me."

He marked his place in the Big Book of Answers and put it to the side. "You already know how to get what I have," he said, his voice quiet.

I looked into his ice blue eyes, pleading for him to help me. "Here and now?" I asked.

"Yes."

"Meditation?"

He nodded and looked pleased as if I'd just answered a complex, trick question. When I was in school, my dad gave me riddles at the dinner table. Like 'brothers and sisters I have none, but that man's father is my father's son'. That one took me all of one summer to figure out. I hate those things. They are the mental equivalent of a gym teacher busting in on Martini Thursday and shouting, "Everyone drop and give me fifty push-ups!"

"Are you meditating?" he asked.

"I'm trying," I said, sitting back in my chair and crossing my arms over my chest. "But it's not going all that well."

"Why do you think that is?"

I rolled my eyes. I couldn't help it. "Stop with the questions," I said, exasperation creeping into my voice. "If I had any answers, I wouldn't be here in the first place."

Glacier sat quietly for a few minutes, studying me. I finally looked away, around the room, out the window, at my lap. His scrutiny made me uncomfortable. Like he was peering into my brain trying to see why I was such a screw-up.

"Get a cup of coffee," he said.

I looked up at him. "I don't want a cup of coffee." Actually it didn't sound bad, but I didn't like being told what to do.

"Please get a cup of coffee," he said, not sounding irritated at all. Like I would be if someone was acting like I was. "I want to show you something."

Another eye roll, a loud screech of my chair as I shoved back, and then loud clicks as I all but stomped over to the coffee bar and poured myself a nice big mug of hot coffee. A little bit sloshed over the rim and splashed on my brand new sky blue half-priced pumps with the horse bit accents. I swore under my breath.

Back at the table, I took a tissue out of my purse and rubbed furiously at my adorable shoes, making a show of threading the tissue beneath the shiny horse bit and taking my time, checking for any errant drops of coffee.

Why the games? I wanted to ask. *Why the big mystery?* Why couldn't he just give me a simple answer? I was willing to do whatever he said at this point just to feel better. I wanted desperately to go to my happy place. I just didn't know where the hell that was.

If he had told me to travel to Tibet and sit on a mountainside while chanting a mantra and weaving a rug from the hair of an albino goat, I would have done it. If he had told me to feed the poor, adopt orphans, join the Peace Corps, stand on one foot and throw a chicken bone over my shoulder! Sure! Fine! Whatever! Just give it to me in black and white. No more games.

But I didn't say any of that. After spending an inordinate amount of time cleaning my shoes, I tossed the wadded up tissue onto the table and sat back. Most guys would have been ticked off by this point. But not Glacier. He looked as cool and calm as when I first walked in.

Maybe it was because there was a cup of coffee sitting in front of him today. Apparently someone had fallen off the wagon again.

"Okay," I said. "I have coffee. Now what?"

He was just as happy as if he were sitting with someone who wasn't trying to be an ass. Someone kind. Someone who successfully meditated every day and felt peaceful within. The complete opposite of me.

I held my palms up and raised my eyebrows at him. Essentially saying *What! Let's go! Let's move! I don't have all day to sit here and play games!*

He smiled. "What would happen if you asked me to pour my coffee into your cup?"

I frowned at him. "Why would I do that?"

"Because you want my coffee."

I let out a little exasperated breath. "Why would I want your coffee? I have my own, thanks to you. And a little on my shoes as a bonus. Besides, I thought you weren't drinking coffee these days."

"You want my coffee because you think my coffee is better than yours."

Now I was really getting mad. But he looked like he was having the time of his life. I shook my head. "I don't want your coffee. I don't even want my coffee now."

"But what if you did? What if you asked me to give you my coffee, and I did." He lifted his cup and started to pour. Immediately, coffee ran down the sides of my cup and onto the table.

"Stop!" I held up my hand. "Are you nuts? My cup is too full!"

He stopped. I reached for the wadded tissue and mopped up as much coffee as I could. He didn't even try to help. He just sat there, smiling. I wanted to punch him.

"What's wrong with you?" I asked, making angry, jerky motions as I cleaned up his mess. "I asked you a simple question. And you go off on some coffee tangent. Is this how you get your kicks?" I was furious.

"Lucy, stop. Look. Look at your cup."

Now I huffed out a breath. A full-blown pissy-fit sigh. I looked at him with my head cocked to the side, indicating without a doubt my feelings over this insane game.

"Just look," he said.

I looked at my cup. "Yeah, I see it. It's too full. Thanks a lot. I'm outta here." I reached for my handbag and got ready to leave.

But the look on his face stopped me. He still wasn't mad at me. Wasn't frustrated. And I could see now that he wasn't playing with me. He wasn't smiling anymore. His look was intense. Concentrated. Like maybe he had just taken the training wheels off my bike. And centered me carefully on the seat. And given me a gentle push. And it looked like I wasn't going to make it. I was going to crash. And I could see by his face that he wanted so badly for me to ride. To get on and pump the pedals and ride as if my life depended on it.

I put my purse down, took a deep breath, and tried to relax. I looked at the cup in front of me, full to the absolute top, ready to slosh over at the least movement. I shook my head and looked back at him. "I don't know," I said. "I don't get it. All I know is that my cup is too full."

His face burst into one of the most beautiful smiles I'd ever seen. It was breathtaking. Contagious. And heartbreaking. Because I had no idea why he was smiling.

"Yes," he said, nodding his head. "Yes! Your cup is too full."

I sighed again. Maybe he wasn't wise after all. Maybe he was a total nutcase. Maybe there's a fine line between the two, and what comes off as quiet and wise in the beginning is really stark raving cracker-brained crazy once you break the shell.

"Lucy," he leaned in. It was that stance again. The one he always took when he really wanted me to get something. I tried to listen, but I was just about done. Just about ready to give up on wisdom and purpose in life and go back to feeling better the way I used to. With my two best friends – Grey Goose and dry vermouth.

"Your cup is too full," he said, his voice so earnest and full of passion I wanted to cry. But I still didn't get it. He leaned farther in. "When you sit in meditation, you won't hear anything if you're too full of your own ideas and thoughts and beliefs. Your preconceived notions of what you should do and how things should be."

The anger left me in a whoosh. My shoulders released, and I locked my eyes on to his.

"You have to sit with an open heart. Let go of everything you know. Everything you believe to be true. You say you want guidance. You want me to teach you what I know. But nothing gets through to you because—"

"...my cup is too full," I said softly, finally getting it. Like a punch to the stomach. Like a thump over the head with a sledgehammer. I started to cry.

Chapter Forty-Four

Well sure. It was a big moment. One of those life-defining moments. But then Glacier explained that the whole coffee cup parable wasn't really his idea. It was his take on an ancient Zen story about tea. I was so relieved. For a few minutes back there in the bakery, I'd thought he was some kind of prophet. That I was unworthy to even be asking him questions.

But now I felt better, knowing he was just one of those really special people. Flawed and imperfect – thank goodness – but way down the path from the rest of us. And I knew he had my best interests at heart. He'd proven that when he traded in loving all of me for loving my soul. So when he started to tell me the changes I needed to make in my life, I mentally poured my cold, bitter, stagnant coffee down the proverbial drain and tried to listen to him with an empty cup. And I guess it worked, because even though some of the things he said seemed mean, they ended up making sense to me.

In a nutshell, it seems I have a few destructive patterns – drinking too much, looking for outside happiness, living in the past, negative inner dialogue, and ego-driven pursuits. It sounds like a lot, but when you really think about it, it could be worse. And wasn't that very thought a great start at overcoming my negative inner dialogue? I smiled to myself. I was really good at this!

An amazing thing happened when I tried to listen to Glacier with an empty cup. He actually talked. Not in riddles. Or in one-word sentences. He talked more to me than he ever had.

I asked him about my purpose. I told him I desperately wanted to find my purpose, but I didn't have a clue what it should be.

He looked at me in that *training wheels are off* kind of way. I leaned in.

"I don't know what your destiny will be, but one thing I do know: 'the only ones among us who will be really happy are those who have sought and found how to serve.'"

I looked at him, sort of confused by the *those among us* part, but pretty sure he was telling me my purpose had to do with helping other people.

"Albert Schweitzer said that," he said. "A long time ago. But he knew what he was talking about. Martin Luther King said, 'Everyone can be great, because everyone can serve.'"

"Okay," I said. "I get it. I need to serve. But how? My last attempt at serving was a fiasco."

"But your motives may have been misplaced."

I lifted one corner of my mouth. "Okay, I'll give you that one. But what can I do? I'm only one person. What can I do that will make a difference?"

"You should spend some time around a child," he said.

I gave him the look that said he had just lost me.

"A child believes he can be a ninja warrior, a dinosaur, a tree, the ruler of a kingdom. He isn't limited by his body, by his surroundings, or even by his abilities. He's fearless. He's unstoppable. He's a brilliant ball of potential. And so are we. But we put limits on ourselves. Not enough time, enough money, enough education, enough designer shoes." He smiled at me and I rolled my eyes. But this time I thought he was funny. "Not enough ability, enough self-confidence, enough beauty, enough stamina, enough willingness to take risk. We forget that our true nature is limitless."

Wow. He was really good at pep talks. I felt almost unlimited.

"Be like a child," he said, leaning forward. "Have enthusiasm. Be generous. Find the wonder in everything. Kids don't care if their hair is messed up. They don't worry if their shoes don't match their outfit. They don't care if you're black or white or red. They just live in the moment. The wonder of this moment."

I nodded, starting to get it. Sort of.

"Got it. You want me to be creative. Unlimited. Generous. You want me to stop wearing designer shoes and sit in a sandbox with my hair messed up."

I thought I was kind of funny. Glacier gripped my hand and leaned forward even more.

"I want you to be fearless," he said with intensity, looking into my eyes.

I just looked at him.

"I think some of your destructive patterns come from fear," he said softly. "Fear of being alone. Fear of what people think of you."

Well, that made me sit up. I'd never thought of myself as a fearful person. More the opposite, really. I hardly ever backed down from anyone. I met things head on. I...completely lost my train of thought as I watched Glacier use his empty water glass to gently capture a spider from the windowsill. Then I watched as he walked outside and released the spider. I wasn't the only one watching. The people at the table closest to us were watching too. And laughing. I felt my face turning red.

Glacier came back in and sat down, smiling happily.

"Why did you do that?" I asked, sort of like a ventriloquist, barely moving my mouth.

"Why not?" he asked.

"Okay, I get it, we're here to serve, yada yada. But what difference does it make if you save a spider?"

"It made a difference to the spider," he said, still smiling.

I sighed. "Well, fine. Meanwhile, the whole place thinks you're Looney Tunes."

Glacier looked around and gave a little wave to the people at the table near us.

"You're embarrassed," he said, seeming to find that funny.

"You got up in the middle of a conversation, in the middle of a room full of people, to save a spider."

Glacier was quiet for minute, just studying my face. Then he leaned forward for the final time. "Find a child," he said, peering into my eyes and using a tone someone else might use to say, *You need emergency open-heart surgery.*

"I really want you to spend some time around a child. Children haven't learned to be embarrassed or self-conscious. It's time to stop being self-conscious and be limitless."

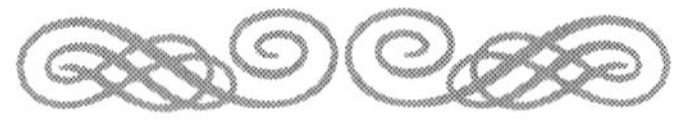

Chapter Forty-Five

On my way to Mary Beth's Monday afternoon, I had to remind myself why I was doing this again. Oh right - Glacier told me to find a child. Be around a child. And the only children I knew were Baby Bentley and Alissa. Dallas and Bentley were otherwise engaged, spending the afternoon with Hard and Fast. Besides, it felt like forever since Mary Beth and I had shared the afternoon doing something constructive. Something that didn't involve breaking and entering.

Mary Beth seemed surprised to hear from me, especially when I told her I wanted to come over and get to know Alissa better. It did sound a little weird coming from me. I only hoped Alissa wouldn't take one look at me and scream, "Stranger danger, stranger danger!"

I drove up to Mary Beth's house – otherwise known as the mausoleum because of its drab and cheerless presence. It had the look of an institution. Maybe it was all those years in boarding schools that drew her to the stern architecture and boxy style of this imposing six-bedroom house.

But when I pulled into the drive, I did a double-take.

In the side yard, where there used to be only a hedge trimmed with military precision, now stood a playhouse almost identical to the one in Dallas's yard and a giant jungle gym in bright, happy colors. Weird.

I couldn't stop smiling at the playhouse as I walked up to the front door. It was exactly the kind of playhouse I would have loved as a child. Sunny. Animated. With window boxes full of real flowers and a welcome mat that said 'Wipe Your Paws.'

I was still smiling when Mary Beth opened the door. "What?" she said.

"Nothing," I said, still standing outside.

"Why are you smiling?"

"No reason," I said. "It's my new look."

She eyed me and held the door open. I walked past her and immediately lost my bearings. Because this was not Mary Beth's house. This was Disneyland.

The main living area was scattered with dolls and books and a tiny fake kitchen complete with pretend food. There was a red plastic barn and a whole herd of little plastic horses on the marble coffee table. I looked at her, but she turned and walked to the stairs.

"Alissa, Aunt Lucy is here. Come down, babe."

"Aunt Lucy?" I raised one eyebrow.

"It's that or Evil Godmother. You choose."

I laughed. Who was this funny, relaxed woman with the messy house?

Alissa came galloping down the stairs. "Aunt Lucy!"

She ran right up to me, then stopped. Suddenly unsure. I knelt down to be at her level. "Hey Alissa! I'm so happy to see you!"

That was all it took. She threw her arms around my neck, almost knocking me over. Something shifted inside me. Something long forgotten. Something warm and happy. I looked at Mary Beth, who was smiling that new smile of hers. The sincere one. The genuine one. I felt like I was in a scary movie. The kind that starts out all nice and fun and happy. And then suddenly the music goes into a minor key and the clown turns deadly.

"Alissa has a surprise for you," said Mary Beth.

Alissa skipped into the living area and over to the little child-size kitchen.

"Aunt Lucy, you sit over there." She pointed to the sofa. "You too, Momma."

"Are you sure it's okay if we eat in the living room?" I asked.

Alissa laughed. And before you could say *parallel universe* or *alternate reality*, I found myself sitting on Mary Beth's expensive couch, eating a plastic roasted turkey, a bowl of dry Lucky Charms, and sipping on a tiny teacup of what tasted sort of like root beer.

Mary Beth looked happier than I'd ever seen her. Sitting with her legs crossed, sipping on her own cup of root beer. I wondered if hers was spiked. Maybe she got the *special* root beer. Maybe that was why her eyes were so bright and her coat was so shiny. But I didn't think so. I watched Mary Beth watching her daughter. And I had a feeling Mary Beth's happiness came from living in the moment. With Alissa.

Kids live in the moment - all the time. That was the first thing I learned from watching and playing with Alissa. They are absolutely spot on *here and now* - all the time.

I watched as Alissa concentrated on making our dessert – stacking plastic cookies on a plate beside a rubber glob of ice cream. Then she walked the plates, one by one, over to Mary Beth and me, one foot carefully in front of the other, her little pink tongue sticking out in concentration.

"This is my favorite!" said Mary Beth, with lots of enthusiasm and not one single big word.

We enjoyed our dessert while Alissa washed the dishes and left them in the drainer next to the sink.

"Couldn't afford a dishwasher?" I asked. MB ignored me.

"Alissa, shall we go outside and show Aunt Lucy your new playhouse?"

"Yea!" The dishes were forgotten as Alissa hopped up and down. I followed Mary Beth and Alissa into the kitchen. Alissa ran ahead and out the door, but Mary Beth stopped to fix us a tray. Sparkling water and French bread with soft Brie cheese and apple slices.

"In case you need something more substantial than latex," she said.

Outside Alissa was already well into her role as lady of the playhouse. Mary Beth led the way to a wrought iron table and cushioned chairs nearby. She placed the tray on the table, then sat and crossed her legs, leaning back and watching Alissa. She looked so normal. Like a normal mom watching her child play, a look of complete joy on her face. She was relaxed. Peaceful. Very much here and now.

Where was the woman who usually had to be coaxed to sit outside? The woman who always had a drink in her hand? Who loved nothing better than to tear you a new one over the tiniest infraction? Who wore designer clothes to the post office, looked right through waiters because they weren't real people, and never, ever smiled in such a sincere, free kind of way?

"Who are you," I asked, "and what have you done with my friend?"

"Hmm?" she turned to me and smiled. She hadn't heard me. Too involved in listening to Alissa sing some song about monkeys.

"How are things with you?" she asked, as if she'd just remembered I was there. And even that was weird. I didn't remember MB ever asking me how I was.

"Good," I said. "Pretty good. I've been working on some things."

She cocked one eyebrow. "A new business?"

"God, no," I said, sipping my sparkling water and wondering what Mary Beth had done with all her booze. "I'm still recovering from the last one."

We watched Alissa take a tiny broom and begin to sweep the floor of the playhouse, something I was pretty sure she'd never seen her mother do.

"No, I've been working on some things Glacier mentioned," I said, sort of hoping she wasn't listening.

"Such as?"

Darn. "Well, he thinks I have some behaviors that could use tweaking. Destructive behaviors."

"Oh, those," said Mary Beth, turning back to watch Alissa.

I frowned at her. "You think I have destructive behaviors?"

"Of course," she said. "You're human."

I relaxed a little. "Do you think I'm trying to replace the void in my life left by Thomas with things like drinking and hanging out with my friends?"

"Yes."

"Hmm. Do you think I have a negative inner dialogue and that I'm living in the past?"

"Definitely. You're like some warrior goddess. You never put down your sword."

I looked at her and frowned. "You're one to talk!"

"Right," she said, watching Alissa. "But I'm usually fighting other people. You're always fighting yourself."

Well. That shut me up. I'd never thought of it like that. I crossed my arms over my chest.

"Why didn't you ever say anything if you felt that way?" I was sort of angry. I don't know why. I'd already admitted Glacier was probably right. I guess I just wanted Mary Beth to argue the point. To stick up for me.

She turned to me. "I've been a little busy slaying my own demons," she said.

And I smiled. She was right. It was easy to forget everything MB had been through in the past month when you looked at the happiness in her face.

"Glacier's helping me find my purpose in life," I said, thinking she would probably laugh. Or say something snide.

But she turned and watched Alissa fill a plastic watering can with water from the hose and water the flowers in the flower box. Water spilled everywhere. Down the side of the playhouse. Down the front of Alissa's yellow sundress. Mary Beth smiled.

"You should definitely do that," she said. "Find your purpose. I've found mine."

The warm and fuzzy moment was ruined by my cell phone. It sat on the table beside my plate of cheese and bread. I was waiting on a call from the carpet cleaners to find out if Charlie's carpets would ever recover from their supermodel wax job. But this wasn't a call. It was a text. And it wasn't from the carpet cleaners. It was from the private detective doing the background check on Hard and Fast.

I have information. Call me!

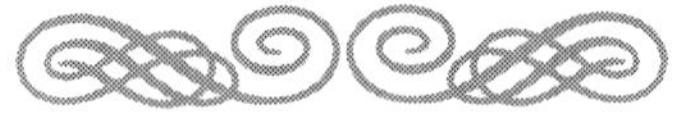

Chapter Forty-Six

I expected at any minute to be pulled over by a Pitkin County Sheriff's deputy and arrested for speeding. Possibly the same deputy who'd arrested Mary Beth. But I couldn't help it. I had to get to Dallas's house. I called her, dialing while whipping in and out of after-work traffic.

"Dallas, it's Lucy. Are you home?"

"Yep," she said. "But not by choice. Chaz is here. He's watching something on ESPN. As soon as it's over, we're going out."

"Wait for me!" I said, trying not to sound too crazy. "I'll be right there."

Dallas paused. "Okay. Sure. Come on over."

I pulled into Dallas's drive and parked next to the shiny red Corvette. Which just seemed kind of cheesy. I mean, come on! A red corvette? Puh-leeze! But my disgust was more likely due to my new information on Mr. Hard and Fast. I rang the bell, and Dallas came to the door wearing tight, low-slung jeans and a red halter – looking about as hot as a girl can look. I suddenly felt frumpy in my black cotton jersey dress and flat sandals. But I reminded myself that I was dressed for a day of fun with Alissa, not for a night of bathroom sex with a hot boy toy.

I could hear the TV in the background. "Where's Bentley?" I asked.

"At the library with the nanny."

"Where's what's-his-name?"

Dallas frowned. "Chaz? In the game room," she said.

I took her hand. "Let's go."

Dallas teetered behind me in her five-inch peep-toe pumps with python detail. Beautiful shoes. Such a waste. Dallas wasn't going anywhere with her boy toy tonight as long as I had breath in my body.

"Lucy, what are you doing?" she asked. "Why are you walking so fast?"

"To get this over with," I said, walking into Dallas's game room.

The boy toy sat sprawled on the leather couch, his feet up on the slate table, sucking on a beer. He looked a little surprised to see me.

"Hello," I said, still holding onto Dallas's hand.

He sort of sat up and looked at Dallas, then back at me. "Who're you?"

I smiled at him. But it was one of Mary Beth's trademark smiles. Before she got all happy and centered. It said, *don't screw with me.*

I led Dallas over to the facing couch and sat beside her, finally letting go of her hand.

"Could you please turn that down?" I asked. "Better yet," I reached over and grabbed the remote, turning the TV off. The silence in the room was loud and obvious.

"What the hell—"

"Lucy!" said Dallas, looking at me like I was a naughty child. "Chaz was watching that. What's going on?"

"Yeah," he said. "Who the hell are you?"

"I'm Lucy," I said. "And I'm your worst nightmare."

Dallas jabbed me with her elbow. "What's gotten into you?"

"Well, for starters, his name isn't Chaz," I said.

"What?" said Dallas.

"It's Chad. Right, Chad?" I looked at the handsome, built guy with the bedroom eyes and torn jeans. He put his beer on the table and eyed me.

"And his last name isn't Hilton." I wanted to say it was Marriott because that would be kind of funny. Or better yet, Motel Six.

"It's Milsap. And he's not the least bit related to anyone named Hilton." I turned to Dallas, and my voice softened when I saw the panic on her face. "I think you told us he was somehow related to the Hilton hotel people? So maybe he meant he used to be a bellhop."

Now he was mad. The boy toy. The loser who looked so at home in Dallas's house, drinking her beer, watching her TV.

"Look lady, I don't know who you think you are—"

"It doesn't matter," I said, leaning forward, "because I know plenty about you."

I turned to Dallas. "Has he asked you for money yet?"

Dallas turned pink, looked at the guy and back to me. She didn't want to answer. She didn't have to.

"I thought so," I said.

"He needs it for a down payment on his yacht!" she said, grabbing my arm. "It's not what you think. All his money is tied up in investments!"

"Did you give it to him?" I asked, panic rising in my voice.

Dallas shook her head. "Not yet. My broker has to sell some stocks."

I looked at him, Chad Milsap, doing that thing liars do, his eyes shifting back and forth. He looked like he wanted to find a secret door and escape. But I wasn't finished with him.

"Too bad you're not a bellhop," I said, looking at him. "I would respect that. But I guess it doesn't pay as much as preying on women."

"Lucy!"

I took her hand again. "Honey, he's a gigolo."

She sucked in a breath, and Chad stood up, putting his hands on his hips. "Don't listen to her, baby. She's crazy!"

"What are you talking about?" Dallas looked like she wanted to cry.

"He's a gigolo. From San Diego. He hooks up with wealthy women – usually much older than he is. But in this case he obviously found a wealthy *young* woman."

"But I thought—"

"I know," I said, softening my voice. "You thought he was rich. And successful. And crazy in love with you."

Dallas's bottom lip trembled.

"I *do* love you, baby! Don't listen to this garbage!" He turned on me and his eyes were cold and mean. "Get the hell outta here!" he yelled, pointing to the door. I wanted to laugh. "Whoever you are, just get the hell outta here before I call the cops!"

Well, then I did laugh. I had to. "Oh, that's rich," I said. "I somehow doubt you'll call the cops since there's a warrant out for your arrest."

Dallas's hand tightened in mine. "Really?" she asked, her voice barely a whisper. "He's wanted?"

I nodded. "For bilking some poor woman in California out of millions."

"Get out!" he screamed, looking like he'd really like to kick my ass.

"No!" Dallas stood up. She looked down at me. "Lucy, are you a hundred percent sure about this?"

I nodded, wishing I didn't have to ruin her day this way.

"You get out!" she said to Chad. "Now! Get out of here before *we* call the police!"

Chad looked at her with the same hateful look he'd given me. No more honey-baby-darlin' routine.

"Go ahead," he said, his voice low. "Go ahead and call. And I'll stay and talk to the police. I'll tell them how you like to take men into the john and have sex! You'll be arrested for prostitution! Maybe we can share a cell!"

I stood up beside Dallas, who was shaking. I leaned closer to her, but my focus was on Chad.

"I'm not kidding you," I said, my voice hard, not a trace of humor in my face. "You leave right now and stay away from Dallas. Because the private investigator who gave me this information? Is going to call the police in..." I looked at my watch, "exactly seven minutes if I don't call him back. So here's your choice. Go now. Get a head start. Get in your silly little Corvette and drive to another state. Or stand there making threats and accusations until the police arrive."

Chapter Forty-Seven

For the third time in as many weeks, I had Dallas crying in my arms. But this time, she wasn't crying over a man. She was crying over her rotten inability to choose a good one. "I can't believe he said that," she sniffed. "That I'm a prostitute. I've never taken *money* when I had sex in the bathroom!"

I patted her back. "I know, honey, but I thought you were giving that up. What happened?"

She sat back and wiped her tears with her fingertips, careful not to smudge her makeup.

"I was! I mean, I meant to. It wasn't my idea this time. Chaz wanted to. I told him no at first. But he kept begging and I really thought he might be the one and now I just feel so stupid," she said sadly. "I thought he really cared about me."

"Oh, sweetie. Don't feel stupid. He's one of those guys who'll never be able to care about anyone except Chaz Hilton. And that's not even a real person." I smiled, but Dallas didn't.

"But I believed him," she said, wrapping her arms around herself as if she were cold. "He said he wanted to get a yacht and take Bentley and me around the world before she started school. I thought that was so sweet."

"He really told you he needed money for a down payment on a yacht?"

"I know it sounds crazy now," she said, sighing deeply. "But it didn't at the time. We were having dinner at Cache Cache, and drinking wine, and he made it all sound so romantic. How we would sail around, and stop when we wanted to. And there would be a chef to fix our meals. It went on and on."

"But his funds were tied up, and he didn't have money for the down payment? That was his story?"

Dallas nodded.

"I thought you only had enough put away to last a year or so," I said. "You were willing to give most of that to him?"

"I thought of it as investing, you know? Like investing in the future." She shook her head. "It sounds dumb, especially with everything we know about him now."

"And without the wine and candlelight." I smiled at her.

She finally smiled a little. "You know when you said the private investigator was going to call the police? Was that true?"

I shook my head. "No. I lied."

Dallas looked worried. "But shouldn't we—"

"He already called. I had him call right after we got off the phone. Probably a half hour ago."

Now she did smile. "So he won't get away with this?"

"I'm guessing they're on their way to the slammer with Hard and Fast as we speak."

"And if he tells the police about having sex in the bathroom with me?" She looked mostly tired but a little bit scared. "What then?"

I laughed. "The police would probably tell him he's a lucky bastard, but that's about it."

"I can't get in trouble?"

"Honey," I put a hand on her knee, "having sex is not against the law. Having sex in a public bathroom might be some kind of misdemeanor, but they'd have to have proof."

She looked out the window at the view, lost in her thoughts.

"Maybe," I said, taking my hand away and sitting back on the couch, "this is a good time to think about letting go of that little hobby – for good this time." My voice was gentle. I didn't want to sound like I was judging her. She felt bad enough already.

She looked at me, her face so serious. "Yeah," she said softly. "For sure."

She hugged a pillow to her chest, looking miserable. "Lucy, I feel like I'm on the wrong road. I don't know what to do. This thing I have about wanting a rich guy to support me," she said. "I'm setting a bad example for Bentley. I want her to be something wonderful. On her own. She can be anything she wants to be! I want her to know that."

I nodded, brushing the hair back over her shoulder.

"I've spent all this time and energy trying not to end up like my mother, and now I'm afraid Bentley might do the same thing. That someday she'll try not to be like me. I want her to be proud of me," she said. Her chin trembled and then the real tears started.

It felt like a turning point to me. For Dallas. For Baby Bentley. I took her in my arms, rocking her the way my mother used to rock me. "It's time you realized, "I said. "You're so much more than beautiful. You can be anything you want to be too, you know."

She didn't seem to hear. I held her tight and whispered into her ear.

"I'll tell you what, honey. I'm working on finding my purpose in life. And just as soon as I find mine, I'll help you find yours."

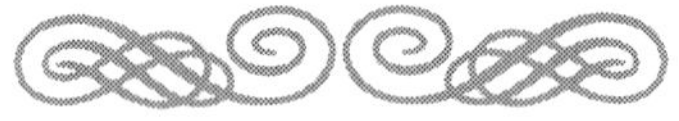

Chapter Forty-Eight

I wiggled my toes. Scratched my neck. Swatted at a bug near my ear. Rubbed my bottom where pine needles poked through my cute running shorts. Which looked really good with the matching black short-sleeved jacket with lots of pockets for my iPod, phone, keys. And even better, the hot purple running top with magic fabric to whisk away moisture.

Oh hell. This wasn't Project Runway. I was supposed to be meditating.

I sighed and shut my eyes, concentrating on my breathing. I was determined to get it this time. Stick with my meditation. Stay in the here and now. Listen to Glacier. And empty my cup. So I mentally poured my cup out and let all my thoughts, worries, and preconceived ideas dribble down the mountainside. *Sit with an open heart*, he had said. And so I tried to do that.

And I guess it really worked. Because I sat for almost forty minutes without ever wiggling again. Or scratching. Or thinking about my hot new running suit. I felt restored. I still didn't know what I was supposed to do with my life, but it was a start. When I stood up, I felt a little lighter than when I'd sat down. Like maybe I was on my way. To where, I had no idea.

Steady, even paces, getting back into my run, stretching my long legs out, feeling the air in my lungs. Smiling. Because I no longer felt like I was running away from something. No longer trying to get away from myself. I was living in the moment, and loving it. A mental image flashed through my mind – of me, with *Here* and *Now* tattoos, just like Glacier's. Hah!

By the end of the week, after making meditation a priority each day and trying very hard to stay in the moment, I finally felt ready to call Charlie and let him know about his house. And he took it rather well. Maybe it was because I stayed calm and told him everything had been restored, and that if he found anything not to his liking when he got home, I would take care of it.

Once that was out of the way, I felt lighter, as if a heavy rock had been lifted off my back. I'd been dreading that, dreading the part where I told Charlie I'd failed him. But it wasn't so bad. And it was history. I made a point of letting all that go when I hung up.

I thought of Alissa on Monday, getting in trouble for forcing the new kitten to ride on the swing. When Mary Beth talked to her, she'd stuck out her bottom lip, said she was sorry - then went right back to playing with a smile on her face. On to the next thing. Staying in the moment.

We skipped Martini Thursday because everyone was busy. Dallas let the nanny have a night off and took Bentley to the new Disney movie. Cheyenne and Will were in Denver, packing up their house and planning their move to the valley. Mary Beth and Alissa had a going away party for Stephanie, the imaginary friend. She was going back to boarding school, where she was needed by one of the little girls whose mother had not had the same epiphany as Mary Beth.

And me, well, I was no longer drinking martinis. At least not every day. There's nothing wrong with a martini once in a while. But

Glacier explained to me that alcohol takes us below thought. And with meditation, we're trying to get above thought. And God knows, I needed all the help I could get. So I was learning to love a bargain martini glass of apple juice while I watched the sun sink over the mountains each evening. Okay, not really loving the apple juice. Looking forward to the next Martini Thursday.

By Saturday, I was getting a little tired of my own company, so I took Mary Beth and Alissa into town. I remembered earlier that summer, running into Glacier as he watched the kids playing in the dancing water on Hyman Avenue Mall. I thought it might be something Alissa would enjoy, but I worried Mary Beth would turn her nose up at something so plebeian. And the old Mary Beth most definitely would have. But the kinder, gentler version asked Alissa if she'd like to do that, and the ear-splitting shriek that followed seemed to say yes.

Driving over to Mary Beth's, I wondered about all I'd missed out on by not having children. Once in a while someone would ask me if I regretted not having kids. I sometimes told them I imagined it was sort of like being born blind, you don't really know what you're missing. But I knew. Deep down. I could look at my friends' faces when they looked at their children and know I was missing the greatest love in life.

When we were building the company and working eighteen hours a day, Thomas constantly worried we would get pregnant. I was on the pill, but he still worried - especially since I sometimes forgot to take the magic little white tablet. There was no time for children. No money. And no inclination on Thomas's part to procreate. So he had a vasectomy. I went along with him, believing at the time he was right, that the company was our baby. But then we sold the baby. And now there's nothing left of our family.

Now I'm left with my regrets. I wonder sometimes if it would have made a difference. Would it have been more difficult for Thomas to walk away if there had been kids involved? And if not, would I at least have been less lonely? Would my kids have filled the hole in my heart left by Thomas? Or would they have been devastated by the divorce and made me even more sad? Or maybe both.

Mary Beth and I sat in the shade where we could watch Alissa jump and squeal and play in the bubbling water. In less than ten minutes she was fast friends with two little girls who looked like sisters – all holding hands and trying to time the water as it came shooting up in streams from the ground.

"I'm learning some things from Alissa," I said, licking my double-fudge waffle cone and wishing I'd gotten sprinkles on mine like Alissa had.

"So am I," said Mary Beth, putting a spoonful of vanilla ice cream in her mouth.

I looked at her. "Like what?"

She watched Alissa and thought. "Share things. Say you're sorry when you hurt someone's feelings. Don't take things that aren't yours." She looked at me rather pointedly, and I looked away.

"I'm over that," I said. "My cat burglar days are over."

She looked at her daughter, holding tight to her new friends, sopping wet, and shrieking with laughter. She smiled. "I learned two things that always make you feel better, no matter what kind of day you're having."

"I used to think that was martinis and designer shoes at half price. But I think I was wrong."

"Warm cookies," she said. "And holding hands."

"Aw," I smiled and bumped my shoulder into Mary Beth's. In my wildest dreams, I couldn't have imagined this Mary Beth. The one who sat beside me in the shade, eating ice cream out of a paper bowl, who'd given up a summer sale at Gucci to watch little girls play in the water, and who could get all warm and fuzzy over cookies and holding hands.

I'd heard of jail changing people, but this had to be some kind of Guinness record book change.

"Did we know all that when we were her age?" I asked.

"Probably," said Mary Beth, wiping her mouth with the paper napkin and tossing her ice cream bowl in a trashcan. "But we forgot it all. I'm worried that'll happen to Alissa. That on her eighteenth birthday, or maybe her thirteenth, she'll forget all the wisdom of the young. She'll forget friendship, and sharing, and the joy of running through the water. Instead she'll have the stress of fitting in, of overachieving."

I nodded, suddenly wistful. "You're right. Growing up changes everything."

"And you?" she said. "What did you learn from Alissa?"

"I love the cookies and hand-holding thing. But I was thinking more along the lines of living in the moment. You know how kids are always so engrossed in what they're doing?"

Mary Beth nodded. "If Alissa's playing, and I ask her to do something, she doesn't even hear me."

"But that's good," I said. "We should be more like that. We're always trying to multitask to the point we don't give our attention totally to anything."

We watched the girls in silence. At least, silence between the two of us. The girls were making enough noise to wake the dead.

"I'm also learning to stop limiting myself," I said when the girls settled down. The three of them lay down on the sidewalk in the sun with their arms outstretched.

"Mommy!" yelled Alissa. "We're angels!"

Mary Beth yelled back that they were the most beautiful angels she'd ever seen.

"What do you mean about limits?" she asked.

"Well, like now. They're angels. When I was at your house the other day, Alissa was a horse, a mailman, a mother, and an airplane. All in one afternoon. No limits. Be anything you dream you can be."

Mary Beth looked at me. "And what would you be, if you could dream your way there?"

I shrugged. "I don't know yet."

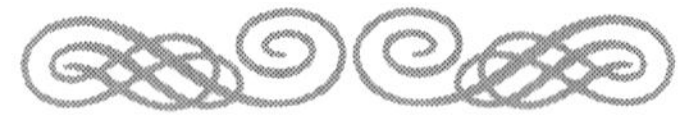

Chapter Forty-Nine

It was very strange, the way things began to line up. The more I tried to empty my cup, the more things just seemed to come together. It started with my housekeeper, Maria, who is not only really good at what she does, but sweet and loving and almost like having an extra mother. I would do nearly anything for her. If she wanted a mini-zamboni for doing the floors, I'd find a way to get her one. If she wanted a flat screen TV mounted on the vacuum...done. Whatever she wants, I make sure she has. But her needs are few, her requests so humble that I always give her something extra. When she asks for a can of scrubbing bubbles, I add a bag of Dove chocolates. When she tells me we're out of glass cleaner, I get her cinnamon rolls from Paradise Bakery. And when she does come to me with a real need, it's usually for someone else.

"Miss Lucy, do you have anything you want to get rid of? Anything that could go in a garage sale?"

I jumped. I was on my deck sitting cross-legged on a fuzzy bathmat I'd dragged from one of the downstairs bathrooms. Facing the mountains. Trying to meditate.

"Oh! Miss Lucy! Are you doing yoga?"

"Something like that," I said, turning around to face her.

I couldn't always make time for my run up Smuggler and my *get-quiet* time on the mountain. But I was determined to meditate every day. To test the *28-days-to-habit* theory. To finally start taking Glacier's advice.

I made a mental note to meditate earlier, as the sun climbed up over the mountains. To try to be finished before Maria arrived in the morning. And to find a more fitting mat to sit on. Maybe a nice Indian blanket. My morning sunrise service deserved better than a fluffy white bathmat.

"Garage sale, huh?" I said, unfolding my legs and stretching them out in front of me. "Raising money for the church?"

Maria was always helping her church. Gathering things for people in need. Or for Bible School. Or to help out the pastor and his family. I always tried to help her out by giving her things I didn't need anymore: bedding, clothing, household items, and even food from time to time.

"No." She looked sad, which was unusual. Maria's nature was to breeze through her days with a big smile on her face. "For my sister. Her husband has cancer, and they can't afford the treatments."

I frowned. "What about insurance?"

Maria shrugged. "I just know she needs five hundred dollars or he can't get his treatment."

That didn't make any sense to me. I wanted to ask more about it, but she didn't seem to have the whole story. Instead, I went through my house and gave her everything I could think of.

But the thought stayed with me the next morning when I ran up the mountain to meditate. The thought of so many people in need. And how Glacier told me that happiness could be found through serving others. Which was a concept I'd never considered before. A year ago, I thought happiness could be found in a top shelf martini, a five-star hotel on a white sandy beach, a half-price shoe sale. Happy hour at Jimmy's. Spa treatments. Two-for-one margaritas.

But those things never really did make me happy. Now I had a burning desire to find my purpose in life. And in that process, to help Dallas find her purpose too. Lofty goals, for sure.

But that day on the mountain, it all came together.

I sat down in my usual spot, a warm little patch of pine needles with a view to die for. And as I wiggled and tried to get quiet and empty my cup, I was thinking of helping people and how I could make a difference. I didn't want to just keep chairing benefits, helping to raise big dollars for a single group. There were people out there like Maria's family, who needed help but didn't have a charity to represent them.

By the time I got up to finish my run, I had an idea. It was kind of vague, fuzzy around the edges, but it was a start. The more I ran, the clearer the idea became. I stopped off in town to run a couple of errands. On my way out of town I was driving down Main, watching for Glacier's old beater truck, when I saw it. Not the truck. The house.

There were colored flags and a big sign – *Open House.* Otherwise, I might have missed it – this jewel of a house, straight out of the Victorian mining era. Shingle style, with a gable and dormer and wide front porch.

I slammed on the brakes, ignored a couple of angry glances and a honk, and pulled into a small parking lot beside a white Mercedes convertible. I walked up the steps to the porch, and my heart actually started pounding in my chest. The perky real estate agent was more concerned with making a phone call than showing me around, so I showed myself around. The architecture was old and classic, but inside was modern and updated. Already made into an office, with a handful of sunny rooms for private offices and a large conference room with slate on the floors and pendant style lighting.

I knew immediately it was perfect. I just wasn't completely certain what it was perfect for. But I knew I had to have it. Ideal location in the downtown core of Aspen, with onsite parking – a miracle in this town. Beautiful muted colors. Weathered, dark hardwood floors. And even an updated kitchen complete with stainless steel refrigerator and stone and glass dining table.

I walked into one of the large private offices and held my breath. I closed my eyes and envisioned a desk with rich patterned chairs in front of it, and gorgeous palms, maybe an orchid for color. And behind the desk…me. Wearing a cool black business suit and a wide smile.

"Can I help you?"

I jumped. Busted. The tiny woman stood in the door.

"Yes," I said, recovering nicely I thought. "I'm assuming this property is zoned commercial?"

"The zoning is mixed use," she said with a bright smile. "But most recently used as an office."

I nodded. Thinking. My head spinning.

I walked back through the entire house, slowly, trying to breathe, reminding myself of my Grandma's warning against impulse shopping. The kind where I might walk into Barney's and lust after the half-priced handbag with the bamboo clasp and braided handles. But this was not a handbag, I reminded myself. This couldn't be stashed in my closet, then handed over to my housekeeper a year later for her latest garage sale.

The sales agent was right behind me. All the way. Chattering on about all the great storage space. And the location. And how it had just come on the market and wouldn't last long.

"It's practically a steal," she said, "at a thousand dollars per square foot."

I looked at her. "And that would make the total price?"

"A little over four million," she said. As if she'd just offered me tacos, two for a dollar. Like it was nothing. Like I had that kind of change sitting on my dresser at home after I emptied my pockets.

Four million dollars. My heart sank. I tallied the cost of everything else I would need: furniture, computers, phones, stationery… employees.

My years of experience bargaining with salespeople had never come in more handy. I worked that poor woman for almost an hour. She made calls back and forth to the owner and clicked her nails on her calculator keys. When it was all over, I'd knocked the price down to nine hundred per square foot. And it still took nearly every penny I had and some from the bank. I would have to mortgage my house in Houston. But this was one purchase I would be proud to explain to my grandma.

❧

Walking back to my car, exhausted and excited, I dug my cell phone out of my purse and dialed my friend. "Dallas, I found my purpose in life. And while I was at it, I found yours too!"

"What? What are you talking about? What's our purpose?"

"I'll explain tonight. My house. Martini Thursday."

"It's only Tuesday."

"Details," I said. "Martini Tuesday then. Be there."

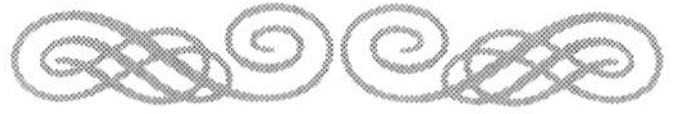

Chapter Fifty

I lined up my cute Target martini glasses and told myself it was a darn good thing I loved penny pinching and bargain hunting. Because unless Dallas had a coupon in her purse for Aspen real estate, I was about to be poor again.

Rather than trickling in one by one as was the norm, the Martini crew arrived at my house en masse. I'd secretly hoped Dallas would show up ahead of the others like she usually does. I wanted to talk over my new idea with her. Alone.

Mary Beth was completely committed to making up for lost time with Alissa, and Cheyenne was busy putting her marriage back together. I didn't think either one would be the slightest bit interested in my newest venture. My purpose in life. Something so important to me I even dreaded bringing it up to Dallas, who was by far the kindest of all of us and would never say a disparaging word on purpose.

But this idea was special.

Unlike the slapped-together concept of my now defunct concierge business, this new idea was not born of the union of a Jimmy's margarita buzz and the need to restore my battered ego.

It had surfaced from many hours of meditation – some on the mountain and some on my bathmat – and from the determination to find a way to serve others. Because if there was one thing I'd finally learned in life, it was that Glacier really knew his stuff. And if he said that to be truly happy I needed to serve others, then serve I would.

"So how is it you all arrived in one big happy bunch tonight?" I asked as we settled onto two gold couches scattered with dark red accent pillows. The two-story windows let in the fading light while the sun made its way behind the Elk Range. "And where's Alissa?" I asked.

"At my house," said Dallas, tossing her long silky hair and looking cool and hot at the same time in a white mini-dress with spaghetti straps and shocking pink peep-toe pumps. "Bentley loves to play with Alissa, so Mary Beth brought her over. Nanny said she'd feed them macaroni and cheese and let them eat in the playhouse."

"Sounds pretty good. What about you?" I asked, pouring a martini for Cheyenne.

"I showed up to give Dallas a ride," she said. "Mary Beth was already there, so we just rode together in my car." This was new, I thought, pouring a martini for Mary Beth. MB gave me a mischievous look as she took the martini.

"For your information," she said, "I sat in the back seat. All the way to your house."

I raised my eyebrows at her. "Did it hurt?"

"Hardly at all," she said, and I laughed. I would have given big money to see Mary Beth squished in the back seat of Cheyenne's little yellow Volkswagen convertible.

Cheyenne and Dallas were busy attacking the cheese platter. I poured Dallas a martini and then one for me, settling on the couch near Mary Beth.

"How's your new yacht guy?" Cheyenne asked Dallas, clearly not in the loop.

Dallas froze for a second with a sesame cracker in one hand and her martini in the other. "Gone," she said, shooting me a look that begged me to keep quiet about the details of her most recent mistake. Dallas normally shared everything with Cheyenne, so I knew she must really be ashamed of the whole Chad thing and probably just wanted it to go away.

"I don't want to talk about him," she said. "I'm off men."

"You're off men?" I said with as much incredulity as if she'd said she was getting a sex change or becoming a barrel racer.

"Seriously?" asked Cheyenne, also skeptical.

Dallas nodded and loaded her cracker with herbed goat cheese. "Men are too much trouble. I'm just concentrating on Bentley for now. And trying to figure out a way to support us."

Commendable for sure, but I would believe it when I saw it.

"So Lucy," she said, licking cheese off her thumb, "what's my purpose in life?"

I looked back at her blankly.

"You said you found your purpose in life and mine too. I've been dying to hear about it."

I waved her off. "I'll tell you later," I said, trying to sound bored when in fact I was so excited I could hardly sit still. "I don't want to bore everyone with it tonight."

"Come on," said Cheyenne. "No secrets!"

"It's not a secret—"

"I'd like to hear this myself," said Mary Beth.

"Out with it," said Dallas.

"Okay, okay," I said, setting my martini on the table and scooching forward on the couch. "I'll tell you. But you'll probably think I'm crazy."

"Maybe," said Mary Beth.

"So what?" said Cheyenne. "I've had lots of crazy ideas."

They were not exactly what you could call cheerleaders.

"You're one of the smartest women I know," said Dallas. "So what's the new idea?"

Okay. One cheerleader.

"Well, I've been trying to figure out something good to do with my life. Something that might make a difference. Glacier says the best thing we can do in life is serve others."

Mary Beth sort of rolled her eyes, but at least she didn't let loose a string of big words.

"And I'm pretty good at organizing and getting things done," I said. "Like my charity work in the past. I'm pretty good at making things come together and helping people work as a team."

"You really are," said Dallas. "You started Martini Thursday."

Cheyenne cheered and she and Dallas clinked glasses.

"Well, I'm hoping for something a little more significant than a weekly happy hour."

"Like what, exactly," asked Mary Beth.

"I wasn't sure at first," I said. "I was worried about saving the world, but Glacier said to start with one person. And then Maria, my housekeeper, told me she was collecting things to have a garage sale for her brother-in-law who needs cancer treatment."

"That's horrible," said Dallas. "How sad."

"So I was thinking it would be good to find a way to help people like that. People who need something as important as medical treatment and can't afford it."

Cheyenne nodded and told us about a friend of hers whose mother couldn't afford her medications.

And while she talked, I had one of those *eureka* moments. One of those moments when you finally get something, and you want to smack yourself on the head like in those vegetable juice commercials.

The spider. I finally got the thing with the spider. Glacier saved one spider and I made fun of him. But he said it made a difference to the spider. I thought he was just being his funky child-of-the-earth, peace-and-love self at the time. But it's all about helping. Serving. Reaching out and giving a hand when you can. One spider – or person – at a time.

"So you want to do something to help people who can't afford medical treatment?" asked Mary Beth.

"No," I said. "I mean, yes. But not just them. I could start a charity to help some cause, but that's too specific. I don't want any limitations. I want to start a fund that's available to help all people – no matter what their cause. I mean, each single person. You know?"

Cheyenne looked unsure, but Dallas and Mary Beth were nodding their heads.

"I love it," said Dallas.

"Quite an undertaking," said Mary Beth.

"So how would it work?" asked Cheyenne.

"I'm thinking we could put together a fund by talking to people we know who normally give money to charities. After all the charities I've worked on in the past, I have long lists of contributors in my computer. We do all the paperwork to form a non-profit and do everything by the book. We'll definitely need lawyers to set it all up." A fleeting thought of my concierge business made me wince.

"I know some attorneys with time on their hands," said Mary Beth.

I shot her a knowing smile.

"And how would you know who needs help?" asked Cheyenne.

"And how much to give them?" asked Dallas.

"Well, all of that has to be figured out. I was thinking there might even be a board of directors, or governors."

"Governors," said Cheyenne. "That sounds important."

"Okay," I said, starting to believe this might actually work. "Governors."

"So," said Mary Beth, and I braced for some snide comment. Some quip or jab or obscurely worded remark that would completely take the wind out of my sails and defeat me before I'd even gotten started. I looked at her and felt myself sigh in resignation.

"You want to form a fund to help people. But not the people who are already being helped by other organized charities. A fund to help people in need who might otherwise fall through the cracks."

The knot in my stomach untied itself, and I wanted to kiss her right on the lips. "Yes!" I said. "Exactly. A fund to help one person at a time."

Dallas looked like she might cry. "I love it, Lucy. Really I do. I'd love to be involved in something like that."

"That's why I said it was your purpose in life too," I said. "You'd be great at talking to people and convincing them to give away their money."

"I really wish I could do something that makes a difference, but I need a job with a real salary. I can't afford to donate my time right now."

"But that's the thing," I said. "You won't have to donate your time. The fund will pay you a salary." My voice was pleading at this point because Dallas was part of the dream. I could imagine her dressed to the nines and wheedling large amounts of cash out of wealthy men. And maybe even a few women.

"And you?" asked Mary Beth. "You'll be earning a salary as well?"

"I'd have to, yes. I just spent my last red cent on an office building."

"And what about me?" asked Cheyenne, looking hurt. "I want to be part of this."

"But I didn't think you'd—"

"Why? I have skills. I've worked."

"Well, I know, but—"

"I have tons of connections. I could handle all the food and drinks for the events."

"That would be great!" said Dallas. "Can't Cheyenne be part of this too?"

"Of course," I said, getting flustered. "I was just going to say that I thought she would be too busy with Will."

Cheyenne made a face. "Oh, puh-leeeease! If I don't get away from him for a few hours, we'll kill each other. I definitely can't help him remodel houses. It just won't work."

"What am I?" asked Mary Beth. "Chopped liver?"

And I laughed out loud. It was not a Mary Beth kind of thing to say.

"I think of you more as foie gras."

"Very funny," she said.

"I didn't think you'd be interested. I thought you were too busy with Alissa."

"She's crazy for horses," said MB. "She just started equestrian lessons, so I actually have some time on my hands. I could handle all the accounting, banking, finance. That kind of thing."

I stared at her. Seriously. Who was this compliant, pleasant, helpful woman?

"Yeah," said Cheyenne, "you need all of us. We're a team. Together, we can make this happen."

"I definitely wouldn't need a salary," said Mary Beth.

"I definitely would," said Cheyenne.

And so it was settled. This most unlikely group of friends who met once a week to drink martinis would join together to try to make a difference. To stop thinking about ourselves for a while and start thinking of others.

"You know," said Cheyenne, "when you think about it, we're all connected. All people. So when we do something nice for someone, it's sort of like doing something nice for ourselves. Maybe that's why it makes you feel so amped."

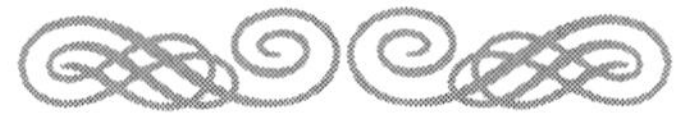

Chapter Fifty-One

Mary Beth's lawyers were working behind the scenes, building the framework for our fund and keeping us out of trouble. Cheyenne was busy culling through her contacts and touching base with suppliers for our food and drink needs. Dallas was actually taking those online classes Glacier had recommended – getting ready to put the hurt on the pocketbooks of the wealthy. And Mary Beth was buying and installing software, brushing up on accounting for non-profits, and making lists of some of the equipment and supplies we would need. We were on a roll.

And me? What was I doing? I was on top of my mountain. Working out an entirely different problem. And it didn't have anything to do with our venture.

It was Thomas. I was working on Thomas.

With Glacier's help and a little nudge from Mary Beth, I realized now that I had been trying to replace Thomas. With things. Or other people. Or exciting new ventures. But that had to end. Because Thomas could never be replaced.

I still loved him. Still missed him every day. Still couldn't believe I would be spending the rest of my life without him. But I was learning to accept it. Learning to love him in a healthy way. To wish the best for him. And hardest of all, to wish the best for his pixie.

It wasn't happening overnight. It was a process.

Glacier helped me see that my need to come off as fearless was an attempt to cover up the fact that I was very afraid. Of losing. Of being left. Of no longer being sure of my road in life. It may sound strange, but it felt really good, knowing that it was okay to be afraid. Being able to let go of the fearless act. And realizing in a blinding moment of clarity that there was nothing to be afraid of after all. Another one of those *here and now* lessons.

The biggest realization of all came last week, during my mountaintop musings. When I was ticking off all the things I missed about Thomas and letting them go. Sort of like emptying my cup. Listing all his best stuff, putting it in the cup, and then pouring the contents down the mountain. Things like the way he held my hand when we watched a movie - even if we were at home. His manners. His hair. The way he always smelled good even after a long day at his office. His smile. The gray at his temples. The way he kissed me to wake me up in the mornings. The way our bodies fit together so perfectly. The funny nicknames he had for me. Like *Woman*. Or *Slick*. Or *Slugger* when I blacked an eye after boxes fell on me in the warehouse.

One of the hardest memories to let go of was the way Thomas used to love to run my bath. There was no shower in the tiny fixer-upper house we lived in when we were first married. So Thomas would fill the old tub with hot water and bubbles, sometimes flower petals, always candles. Then he'd sit back and watch while I stepped into the tub and leaned back into the foamy water. He looked at me with such adoration. Such wonder, and yearning. And even after we sold the company, when we had six bathrooms – all with marble showers – Thomas still loved to run my bath.

I thought there would be years and years of lying back in the bath while Thomas took a sponge and trickled water down my back or talked to me about his day or just sat and looked at me in the candlelight.

I would have given anything, gladly given anything I owned. Just for one more bath.

Well, sure. First I cried. But then, when the cup was about to spill over with good stuff, I very carefully, slowly, poured it down the mountain. Emptying my cup. Letting go of the memories.

Losing someone you love – especially when it's your own fault – is gut wrenching. It rips your heart out, stomps it flat, then impales it on a stake for everyone to see what a loser you are. Getting over Thomas would be a process. Probably a long process. But emptying my cup of memories felt like a good start.

Somehow that left room to think about Glacier. And when I really thought about him, seriously considered all of his good stuff, I realized with cloudless certainty that we were not meant to be lovers. Because when you're in love with someone, you spend a lot of time together. And I had a feeling I would eventually grow tired of his hippy-dippy ways, his old squeaky truck, his calm countenance, and the way he always knew exactly the right thing to say. All good things in a teacher, no doubt. But probably not in a lover.

So I would just have to settle for him loving my soul. And let's be honest, it's not very often in this life when you find someone willing to love your soul. Someone who always has your back and your best interests at heart. He was my teacher. My spiritual guide on this path to true happiness. And for that, I would forever be grateful. Just as there would never be another Thomas in my life, there would never be another Glacier. They were my once-in-a-lifetime boys.

I found my cherished holy man sitting at his table in the bakery and joined him for a cup of coffee. Although he was drinking herbal tea. Which made me want to laugh. I wondered how long he would stay on the wagon this time. Today he was writing in the Big Book of Answers, instead of reading. That was a first. He put the book away and smiled as I took a seat across from him.

"I'm just curious," I said. "Why a bakery? Why do you always hang out here?"

Glacier smiled. "Why not?"

Why not, indeed. What could be better than a bakery. It was warm. Sunny. Smelled like hot muffins and brownies. And had the best coffee in town. Even the workers looked happy.

"I came for my gold star," I said, leaning back in my chair.

He tipped his head, allowing me to talk.

"I did what you said. I've been working on loving Thomas in a healthy way. It's taken a while. Lots of hours on the mountaintop. But today, I think I really did it. I still love him. I always will. But I accept that things are different now. And I want him to be happy."

This was huge. This was bigger than big. Harder than anything I'd ever done in my life. Seriously, who does that? A man cheats on you and leaves you for another woman, and you not only forgive him and love him, but wish the best for him? I know. It sounds crazy. And without Glacier's help, the process would have required lots of shrinkology on a psychiatrist's couch and probably medication.

"And how does it feel?" he asked.

I wasn't disappointed by his lack of emotion. I was used to it. And although I would have really liked to have had some kind of recognition – maybe a trophy or a parade in my honor or at least a round of applause – I had learned that the results themselves were my reward.

"Great," I said, smiling. "It feels really great."

He gave me his crinkly-eye smile.

"There's more," I said.

He waited.

"I think I found my purpose in life."

This time his eyebrows went up. Just slightly. It was turning out to be a big day.

"And the best thing is, Dallas and Cheyenne and even Mary Beth are on board with me. You told me to find a way to serve, and I think I have."

I took a sip of my coffee in case he wanted to say something. You know, jump in and say, *Wow, that's great.* Or, *I can't wait to hear this*. But that was one thing about Glacier - he didn't waste words. When he spoke, he had a purpose.

So over a cup of bakery coffee, I told him everything. From the orchid in the office to how all my crazy friends wanted to be part of this dream to help others. And when I finally ran out of words, I sat back and took another sip of my coffee.

"You've done really well, Lucy. You've come a long way in a short while."

I choked. I made a little slurpy sound and then coughed to get the coffee out of my windpipe, where I sucked it when I took in my breath of surprise. I used my napkin to cover my mouth and looked at Glacier with wide eyes. "Thanks," I said, more of a croak than a word. "I needed that."

He shook his head. "No you don't. You don't need me to tell you how well you're doing. You know it instinctively. By the lightness you feel. The joy."

Well, true. I did feel light. Happy.

"Work for the pure joy of knowing you're doing a good job, and don't be bothered by criticism. If you know you're doing the right thing, just stay true to your cause."

Good advice. Hard to follow, I was pretty sure. But sound advice. I would give it a try. "We just have one problem at this point," I said. "The lawyers are bugging us for a name. And we can't agree on anything."

Glacier was quiet for a moment. "When you told me about it, you called it *the fund*. Why not stick with that?"

I looked at him like he was on crack. "Call our fund *The Fund*?"

"Why not?"

"Okay, you are so not in charge of PR. Maybe we can find a nice spot for you on the board. But as far as publicity, I'm thinking no."

He smiled.

Chapter Fifty-Two

Well, the girls loved the name. And so did the attorneys. The girls loved it because it was simple. The attorneys would have loved *anything* at this point. We could have called ourselves Boozers Without Boarders, and they probably wouldn't have even blinked. They just needed a name for the documents. And in the spirit of here and now and not always having my own way, I acquiesced.

Our first week in our new office was insane. I had an MBA from CSU, but what I really needed was ESP and CPR.

ESP might have helped me avoid the drama between Cheyenne and Mary Beth, who both wanted the same office and fought like wildcats over the parking space with the most shade. In the end, Mary Beth got the office, and Cheyenne got the parking place.

Cheyenne looked better than ever these days. No longer worried about trying to impress an abusive billionaire, she dressed for herself. Today she wore tight faded jeans, a black T-shirt, and a belt whose buckle was in the shape of two lovers embracing. And it made me realize, nothing looks better on us than being true to ourselves.

"Hey, Lucy," she said, barging into my office and startling me. I had my head buried in the computer, working on notes for our kickoff party.

"Geez, you nearly gave me a heart attack," I said, turning back to the computer. "What's up?"

"Come outside for a minute," she said. "There's something you gotta see."

I sighed. "Cheyenne, if Mary Beth is in your parking place again, you're just going to have to take it up with her. I can't be the referee today."

"Come on," she said, walking over and taking me by the arm, pulling me up out of my chair. "This'll give you a *real* heart attack."

I rolled my eyes and let her drag me out of my office, down the hall and out the front door, expecting to see Mary Beth's car parked in the primo parking space, but having been vandalized by an angry Cheyenne. I imagined rotten eggs, shaving cream, slashed tires, a burning corpse of Mary Beth's white Maybach.

But this wasn't about the car. And Cheyenne was right. Now I needed CPR. Because there in front of our new office, shining in the late August Aspen sunshine, was our newly installed sign – *The Fund* – carved freeform out of a huge piece of limestone. And standing beside it, Glacier Jones, wearing dusty jeans and an old denim jacket and a smile as big as the lump in my throat.

It was perfect. I stood for a moment, unable to move, just taking it in. The block of limestone. The sun hitting Glacier in the face and making his eyes crinkle at the sides. The perfect moment. The culmination of so many things. I walked slowly up to Glacier and wrapped my arms around him, holding him close. Only this time, there was no burning desire. No ulterior motive. He was my teacher. My friend. The lover of my soul.

"Thank you," I whispered. And I think he realized my gratitude was for far more than just the limestone sign.

Maybe I do have ESP after all. Maybe the vision of Mary Beth's burning white Maybach was a portent of things to come.

"Are you busy tonight?"

Startled again, I looked up from my computer to see Mary Beth standing in my door.

I shook my head, distracted. "No. Why?"

"Alissa has a sleepover with a girl she met at her equestrian lessons. Would it be possible for you to build a fire in your outdoor fire pit?"

Now she had my full attention. "Um...sure. Any particular reason?"

"Yes," she said. "I'll be there at eight."

I didn't get home until almost seven, which didn't leave a lot of time to change my clothes, flip through the mail, throw together bread and cheese and wine, and of course, build a fire.

I have to admit, I was a little nervous, stacking pieces of pinion together and lighting them. Mary Beth had never requested a fire before. And although she had become a different person around Alissa, some of the old Mary Beth still peeked through when she was around grownups. She was still feisty, still irascible with a razor sharp wit. I wouldn't have it any other way.

The door chimes pealed as I uncorked the wine. I opened the door and what I saw made me even more apprehensive. Mary Beth was dressed in black, which wasn't all that unusual, but her hair was pulled back, which was very unusual. And she carried a large Louis Vuitton bag.

"Don't worry," she said, when I eyed the bag. "I'm not moving in."

I shrugged and led the way to the back deck where the flames were crackling and glowing in the fire pit.

"Perfect," said Mary Beth.

"Don't do anything crazy," I said, pointing my finger at her. "I'll be right back."

Against my better judgment, I left MB alone on my deck, with a blazing fire and a bag of who knew what.

When I returned with a tray of wine and bread and cheese, Mary Beth had pulled two chairs and a small table up to the fire pit. She sat calmly in one of the chairs, the bag of secrets resting beside her on the deck. I set the tray on the table and poured wine.

"So, I'm guessing the fire is not so much about keeping warm, but more about whatever's in the bag."

"Correct," she said, taking the glass of wine.

"Is this the part where you tell me you're into witchcraft?"

"Don't be absurd."

We clinked glasses, and I settled in the chair beside her. "Are you a pyromaniac?" I asked.

"Hardly."

"Flaming batons," I said. "That's it. You said you wanted some kind of entertainment for Alissa's birthday slumber party. You're going to twirl!"

Mary Beth didn't even grace that with an answer.

I sipped my wine. Mary Beth sat quietly with her legs crossed, gently swinging one Lanvin sandal – black with a puffy orange band across the toes. Perfect shoes for a fire ceremony if ever there was a pair.

I had to admit, the fire felt pretty good. Fall was fast approaching the valley. Soon the trees would turn, snow would fly, and the four of us would leave the valley for warmer climates. The thought made me sad.

"I hope it's marshmallows," I said, taking a piece of bread and some cheese. "I love toasted marshmallows."

"God!" said Mary Beth, clearly perturbed. She put her wine on the table with a loud clink. "I thought maybe we could just enjoy our wine. Relax for a while after our busy day." She turned to the bag. "Let's get on with it."

"Goody!" I said, leaning forward in my chair, satisfied that I could still push MB's buttons.

She stood and dropped the bag in her chair. "I could have done this alone," she said. "In the privacy of my own home. I'm beginning to wonder why I didn't."

"Oh, come on," I said. "I'm just goofing with you. What's in the bag?"

MB gave me a look as if trying to decide if I was worthy of the secret.

"Pieces of my life," she said, with not a trace of humor. "My old life."

I kept quiet. Clearly the joking around was over.

"A life I want to shield from Alissa. Things I'd rather she not ever know about."

Yikes. I nodded. "Okay."

Mary Beth reached into the bag and pulled out a small leather pouch. It looked vaguely familiar.

"Your lock picks?" She nodded.

"But I thought the police kept those."

"They did. This is an old set." She threw it into the fire. "No more breaking and entering," she said. "No more crime."

The pouch smothered part of the fire, then burst into a fiery blaze.

"I used to need adventure in my life. Risk. To make me feel alive."

I nodded, knowing the feeling. "And now you have Alissa for all of that," I said.

Mary Beth smiled. "Exactly."

She reached again into the bag, pulling out a sheaf of papers.

"Your memoirs?" I asked, temporarily forgetting my vow to be serious.

"My lawsuit against Cruella," she said, reaching into the bag for another stack of papers.

"Um, Mary Beth, I love the symbolism and all. I applaud the idea. But if you put all those papers in the fire pit, it's entirely possible you'll burn down my house."

She rolled her eyes.

"How about this," I said. "How about you burn the initial lawsuit now, and later we'll go inside and shred everything else. Deal?"

She didn't say anything. Just tucked the bulk of the papers on the deck beside her chair, then threw the top page of the remaining document on the fire. We watched as the edges curled and burned until nothing was left of the page. She threw the remaining pages in, one page at a time and I was glad she did it that way. Partly because I was still a little worried about starting a blaze that would require firemen and a safety net. But mostly because it took longer and gave Mary Beth a chance to really think about where she had been and where she was going.

"Nice," I said, when the last page succumbed to the flames.

Next she reached in the bag and pulled out what looked to be photos, some black and white.

"What are those?"

"My childhood," she said. "The most unhappy time of my life." She threw the photos on the fire without hesitation, then watched, mesmerized, as they were destroyed. "I'll never let that happen to Alissa."

Her voice was soft, almost as if she were speaking to herself. I thought of just how close Alissa had come to a life like Mary Beth's and was relieved to know the cycle of pain had ended.

Next were mementos from Mary Beth's time with Rolf – a birthday card, a playbill from Broadway, another legal document. "The prenup?" I asked.

Mary Beth nodded and threw the papers in the fire.

We watched as the flames surged, then eventually settled.

"Did you love him?" I asked, knowing it was none of my business. I half expected MB to rationalize. To sidestep the question. Or to completely ignore me.

"No," she said, watching until no trace of the prenup remained. "But I liked him. He made me laugh. And he wanted to help kids. We would have worked well together, building the hospital."

When she turned back to the luxurious Louis Vuitton, I sat spellbound, anticipating the next fascinating and intriguing expression of a life gone wrong. The bag was so large, my imagination ran wild.

A shrunken head. A bloody hammer. Colonel Mustard in the library with the candlestick. This was getting good. But to my great disappointment, Mary Beth pulled out a single sheet of paper, then dropped the bag on the deck, indicating the show was almost over.

"What's that?" I asked. "The map of where the bodies are hidden? The combination to the secret locker at the bus station? A hit list?"

I thought I was kind of funny. But Mary Beth ignored me. She read over the paper.

"It's a list," she said finally. "Of all the things about myself I'd like to change. All the bad qualities I could think of. Maybe burning them will help me leave them behind."

I never would have thought of that. "Like what?" I asked. I was dying to read the entire list. A really long list, I was betting. Probably a fairly significant list of things like *snotty* and *using big words to make others feel small* and *feeling superior to all other earthlings*.

"I can't be a good mother and still be a narcissist," she said.

Well. Now I felt kind of bad. "Mary Beth, I'm sorry about shooting my mouth off like that. I should never have said those things to you."

"Yes," she said, turning to face me, "you should have. I spent a night in jail. My daughter was thousands of miles away in boarding school. My own family was nonexistent. You told me if I didn't change, I would end up alone."

Well, when you put it like that.

"You were my last tether to the world," she said, looking away. "I thought I was losing even you at that point. It scared me. That's when I knew I had to change."

She wadded up the paper and tossed it into the flames. I wanted to go to her, hug her. Tell her how proud I was of her for doing the hard thing – changing. Realizing her mistakes. But even with all the wonderful new changes in Mary Beth, I knew she would not want me hugging her.

She stood and watched the fire, seemingly locked in her memories. And I let her be. Even I was feeling the emotional weight of this very symbolic ceremony. This moment of leaving one life behind and moving boldly into another. Of cleansing the dark, the ugly, the destructive...and making room for the young, the innocent, the child almost lost to a pattern initiated long ago.

Finally Mary Beth sat in her chair, leaning back, looking totally drained.

"Thank you," she said sincerely. "I feel free."

Chapter Fifty-Three

The cute phone guy was back in our office on Monday, tweaking our new hi-tech phone system. I wanted to stay and flirt with him, but I promised myself a run and an extra long meditation. I left him in Dallas's capable hands. She was a much better flirter anyway.

The morning was almost chilly, and the breeze felt good as I broke free of the hardcore hikers, meandering women on cell phones, and vast menagerie of dogs. I needed aloneness, and solitude. I desperately needed to get quiet and just be.

My meditations usually started while I ran, so that by the time I found the perfect spot to sit, my mind was already quiet. I craved this time alone. This part of the day when I left everything and everyone behind and just got still.

But today would be different. Today would be a turning point in a summer of major turning points. Because today I had company.

I saw him before I ever sat. Or her. Hard to tell from here. Massive wingspan. Graceful beyond words. Circling high in the air but coming closer, closer, until I could see the light colored underbelly, the dark band on the wings. A hawk. A magnificent creature who seemed to be showing off for me today.

I sat, slowly, quietly, wondering if I was disrupting the nest of this bird who flew so close I could almost hear the sound of its wings. But even I – who know almost nothing about birds or nature in general – knew it was surely too late in the season for a nest of baby birds. They would never survive the coming cold weather.

So beautiful to watch, the hawk made it hard for me to close my eyes. To shut out my senses and the outside world and to go within. With an empty cup.

But I did. Because I now knew from experience that, when I did, when I made the effort, the rewards of peace and serenity were great.

Thirty or forty minutes later, when I opened my eyes, my friend was still with me. Circling. Gliding. Putting on a show. And my heart surged in my chest. Because I felt a strange connection to this exquisite bird. Something I couldn't really name, but a feeling of such release, such freedom.

Sure. I know what you're thinking. There was probably road kill somewhere nearby. Or a nice juicy ground squirrel. Not everything is a sign from the universe. Sometimes a hawk is just a hawk. But this hawk brought out feelings in me. Deep, emotional feelings. I thought of Mary Beth and her fire ceremony. How she seemed to be saying goodbye to her old life. And how she said she was free. That's exactly what this felt like for me. A swelling sense of freedom - from old, bad behaviors. Destructive habits. Negative thinking. Painful memories.

I felt new. Lighter than before and somehow liberated. With an optimism for my future I hadn't expected to have at this point. I felt as if things were finally falling into place for me. There was only one thing to do. I had to tell Glacier.

I walked into Main Street Bakery, and my soaring heart took a disappointed dip. Glacier was not at his usual table in the sunny front window. How could this be? I could nearly always find him when I needed him. And I really did need him. To tell me I was crazy. Or not. To let me know whether I'd witnessed a life-changing event or maybe just watched a hawk in flight. And did it really matter? If it felt like a big moment to me, wasn't that all that truly mattered?

"Lucy."

I turned at the sound of my name. And there he was, standing behind the counter. Having a laugh with the same guy I talked to the day I brought my check, my laughable and misjudged donation meant to save Glacier from the deep trenches of poverty. Just the sight of him made me smile and caused the tension in my shoulders to relax. I helped myself to coffee, then settled in a chair at Glacier's table. Before I could take my first sip, he sat down across from me.

"Thank goodness," I said. "For a minute I was worried you weren't here."

"But I am," he said.

I laughed. "Yes, I see that. I need your help." I sipped my coffee, thinking this would give him a chance to respond. He didn't.

"I just came from the mountaintop," I said, lowering my voice so only he could hear. "And something happened up there. I need you to tell me if what I think happened, happened, or if I'm making too much out of it."

He nodded once for me to go on.

"It was a hawk," I said. "Which I know is not an unusual thing to see around here. But this was different. It hovered right near me. The whole time I was up there. And I felt this connection." I put my hands over my heart. "I know it sounds weird. I can't really explain it. But I really felt somehow connected to that bird."

Well, here was the part where he could die laughing. Most people would. But not Glacier.

"If it felt that way to you," he said, "do you need anyone else to validate your feelings?"

"This is all so new to me. I don't want to become some crazy lady who sees signs in the coffee grounds, and symbolism in the oil stain on my garage floor. But this was different - I had this huge sense of being right where I'm supposed to be, you know? Of going in the right direction."

He smiled. All of his smiles were contagious. But this was one of his best. The kind that made me feel good all over.

"So, do you think it was a sign?" I asked.

"Do you?" he asked.

I sighed. We were back to the land of no straight answers. But I nodded. "That's the way it feels. Do you know anything about hawks? What they symbolize?"

He nodded. "A little. The Celts had an interesting take. For them, a rabbit sometimes symbolized greed or materialism. Celtic art often showed a hawk clutching a rabbit in its talons. You said you felt a sense of freedom. The hawk could represent freedom from those behaviors."

I nodded. "Maybe so. I don't know that I'm all that greedy, maybe a little materialistic. But I'm definitely trying to move away from bad behaviors."

Glacier nodded.

"But this felt like more than that," I said. "More spiritual, if that's the right way to put it. I felt more in line with who I'm supposed to be. Does that make sense?"

Glacier looked pleased. I mean, he never looked particularly displeased. But he beamed at me. "The hawk is a bird of the heavens. It symbolizes our yearning for clarity. Our spiritual awareness."

I sighed deeply, happily. That was what I needed to hear. "So I'm on the right path?"

Glacier smiled. "There's only one path. And yes, you're on it."

We sat in silence for a while, me basking in the glow of his approval, which I knew he would not want me to do. He wanted me to stand on my own. To not need praise. To not worry about criticism. But it's a process, I reminded myself. The fact that I'm even on the path is enough for today.

"You're pretty smart," I said, smiling at him. "Or maybe you're just good at making stuff up."

He laughed.

"I could look it up, you know. All that symbolism. I'll be able to check your work."

"You should," he said. And I knew he meant it.

And then I had a flash. "That reminds me. You've still never told me about your name. You said you would tell me when I'm ready and I think I'm ready!"

He nodded. "I think maybe you are."

"So what's the deal? Are you sure it isn't about your icy blue eyes?"

"I'm sure."

"What then?"

He paused, as if thinking things through, but I knew he rarely needed to do that. Maybe he was just giving me time to be quiet. To sit still. To stop fidgeting and listen.

"What do you think the work of a glacier is?" he asked.

Of course he couldn't just tell me. That would be too easy. I drummed my fingers on the table, then remembered I had a secret weapon. I took out my iPhone and looked it up. "Glaciers alter the earth by erosion and transportation. The earth resists," I said, skimming the article, "but the gentle, constant work of the glacier eventually succeeds in wearing away the surface..." My voice trailed off as the words began to make sense.

"Do you remember how you reacted when we first started talking about things?" asked Glacier. "About staying in the moment. About meditation. Attachment. Forgiveness?"

I felt the blood crawl up my neck and into my face. "I wasn't exactly an easy sell, was I?"

"And look at you now," he said.

My eyes widened. "You gently and constantly wore me down! You wore away my surface."

He smiled.

"It says erosion and transportation," I said. "What's the transportation part?"

Glacier just smiled at me, and I realized this man of no ego was having a hard time answering without tooting his own horn. So I went back to my secret weapon.

"The dictionary says transportation is to carry from one place to another. Especially over long distances," I said. And all at once, I got it. Boy, did I get it. It was one of those huge moments you'll always remember, like when you finally understand algebra or electricity or why boys pull your hair when you're in second grade. "You wore me down. You slowly eroded my crusty exterior."

He smiled.

"And then you transported me. Over a long distance. From my previous shallow, miserable, painful existence. To here," I said, my eyes filling with tears. "I still have a long way to go. But at least I'm finally on the path."

And a very long distance it was, I thought. From the way I felt at the first of the summer when I met Glacier. Hurt. Lost. Finding solace in social activities and dry martinis.

"I have a ways to go too," he said. "You taught me that."

I looked at him, remembering the pain in his eyes when he told me about his old life, his wild days. It was still hard for me to imagine him like that.

"So when did you figure out the meaning behind your name?" I asked, dabbing at the corners of my eyes with my fingertips.

"A long time ago," he said. "But just like you, I resisted. I had to be transported too, from my previous shallow, miserable, painful existence." He smiled.

"Your dad?" I asked. "He was your glacier?"

He nodded. "Both of my parents. They're still my guides. And thanks to you, now I know anyone can be a teacher if we really listen."

"So how many people have you eroded and transported before me?"

Glacier was quiet, more serious. "Only a few. You're the first woman."

For some reason that touched my heart. I smiled at him, but not in a flirty way. Just in a grateful, loving, what-would-I-do-without-you way.

"Well, I'm glad I was your first. You always remember your first."

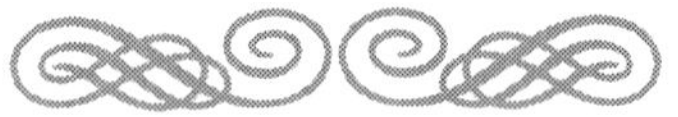

Chapter Fifty-Four

It was a slumber party like no other I had ever been to. Alissa's seventh birthday party looked more like Cinderella's welcome home bash at the magic kingdom. The house was decorated inside and out with lots of pink, and bows, and sparkly things. Little girls ran wild through every room. And the food! You'd have thought Mary Beth was feeding the entire elementary school, not just eight little girls. Most amazing of all, Mary Beth had no outside help for this shindig. Unless you counted Cheyenne, Dallas, and me.

I was beginning to think that was why she invited us. I thought at first it was a fun idea, a chance for the big girls to hang out while the little girls played. But so far I had cooked hot dogs on the grill, cleaned up a spilled milkshake from the kitchen floor, loaded the CD player with Justin Bieber and the Jonas Brothers, and put a Band-Aid on a howling little girl who'd fallen during a raucous game of hide and seek. We finally herded them all into the media room, where Mary Beth put a Miley Cyrus movie on the enormous screen, and the girls went instantly still. It was like magic.

The big girls took advantage of the situation to load our plates with leftover food and park ourselves outside on Mary Beth's deck – where she could see the girls through the floor to ceiling windows. No alcohol tonight. Mary Beth didn't want us drinking in front of the girls, and we all agreed. Instead, we enjoyed root beer floats with our hot dogs, French fries, and pizza. A far cry from a healthy muffin and all natural smoothie, which I would probably need tomorrow to purge all the sugar and saturated fats out of my body.

"This is delish!" said Dallas, taking a tiny bite of pizza.

"I'm famished," said Cheyenne, dunking French fries in ketchup. "Will and I were looking at property all day. I missed lunch."

"What kind of property?" I asked. "Another house to fix up?"

Cheyenne's face lit up. "I'm so stoked I can hardly stand myself! We found a place just outside Carbondale where we can have horses!" She pumped a fist in the air and I smiled. She was just so...Cheyenne.

"Really?" asked Dallas. "You're finally getting your horses?"

Cheyenne nodded. "Will's being so awesome. He totally gets how much I want horses. I rode all the time when I was a kid. There's just something so ace about horses."

"I thought there were horses at Michael's," said Mary Beth, who wasn't in on Cheyenne's passionate connection to horses. "Did you ever ride when you lived with him?"

Cheyenne made a face. "Get real. He said they were too expensive and didn't want me anywhere near the poor things. They were just for splash."

"Not to put too fine a point on it," said MB, "but how can you afford another property?"

Cheyenne didn't seem offended by this nosy question. "We just flipped the fixer-upper," she said. "Plus, when I left Michael's that day, I had this in the pocket of my cutoffs." She reached into the front pocket of her jeans and came out with the giant bauble Michael had given her after he punched her in the face. "I felt like I deserved it, you know? I mean, he gave it to me. It's not like I took something that wasn't mine."

Mary Beth nodded her approval. "How many horses do you think you'll have?" Which I thought was a strange question, but then, it was Mary Beth.

Cheyenne shrugged. "I don't know yet. Hopefully a bunch. I'm jazzed because the barn we found has room for six. Why?"

"Alissa's clamoring for a horse, but we can't exactly put one in the front yard. I've been trying to find a place where she can ride. She loves her equestrian classes, but she needs a place where she can just go and ride for fun."

"Oh, this would be the place for fun," said Cheyenne. "You should totally bring her. I've already talked to a guy I know who has a ranch outside Durango. His horses are like, as gentle as lambs." Cheyenne looked at Mary Beth. "You could ride too, you know."

Mary Beth raised one perfectly arched eyebrow.

"Seriously," said Cheyenne, biting into her hotdog. "It's a total rush."

Somehow, I just couldn't picture it. Mary Beth in her designer jeans and stilettos, taking a gallop around the property. But then, a few months ago I wouldn't have pictured her here on the deck, eating a hotdog, while eight little girls destroyed her media room.

"Why don't we get the kickoff party behind us," said Mary Beth. "Then we'll talk."

"That reminds me," I said, looking over at Dallas. "Did the invitations come back from the calligrapher yet?"

Dallas didn't seem to hear me. She was entranced in stirring the ice cream around in her root beer. "Dallas? You okay?"

She jumped. "Oh. Sorry. What did y'all say?"

"I was just talking about the invitations. Is everything okay? You seem sort of quiet."

And now that I took a minute to really look at her, I could see that some of Dallas's usual spark was missing. She shrugged.

"Something kind of crazy happened today," she said. "I can't quite get it off my mind."

"What?" we all asked in unison.

Dallas sort of smiled then, looking at the three of us, our curiosity getting the best of us.

"I got a letter from Baby Daddy," she said.

"No way!" I said.

"The slime dog!" said Cheyenne.

"What did it say?" asked Mary Beth, the only voice of reason.

Dallas put her plate on the table beside her and pulled her long legs up under her in the chair. "He got a new job. A color commentator or something like that, for televised games."

"Score!" said Cheyenne. "Now he can get back to paying what he owes you."

"He said he would," said Dallas, but her voice was soft, and she didn't seem the least bit excited.

"So what's the problem?" I asked, reaching over and laying my hand on her arm. "I thought that was what you wanted."

Dallas looked at me with her soft brown eyes. "He wants visitation with Bentley. He wants her two weeks every month. I'm not doing that. I'm not putting a three-year-old on a plane for unsupervised visits with a man who's never shown the least bit of interest in her."

My eyes went wide. "He really wants visitation?"

"Could be a trick," said Cheyenne.

"Does your legal agreement grant him visitation?" asked Mary Beth.

Dallas shook her head. "He didn't want anything to do with Bentley at the time we made that agreement. He was married and didn't want his wife or anyone else finding out about her – that was the whole reason for the payoff. Bentley's barely even mentioned in the agreement. Just that he'll support her until she's eighteen."

I was confused. "So how can he have visitation now without his wife finding out about Bentley?" I asked.

"He said he's getting divorced," said Dallas. "I guess it doesn't matter now if his wife knows."

"Well, then, good enough!" said Cheyenne. "Take the money and run. You don't have to give him Bentley, but he does have to give you the dough. You could take him to court."

Dallas sighed and shook her head again. "No, ya'll, I don't want his money. He might try to get legal visitation with Bentley. I just can't put her on a plane and send her halfway across the country. She's too little. And she doesn't even know him. I won't do it."

I nodded. "I don't blame you."

"Besides," she said. "I like the idea of supporting myself for a change. Between my savings and my new salary, I think I can make it on my own. So I told him he could come here and see Bentley, with my supervision. But no deal on the two weeks every month. And I told him to keep his money."

"Excellent," said Mary Beth. "You did the right thing."

"Coolness, Dallas," said Cheyenne. "You're my hero."

I squeezed her arm. "Why so quiet then? Are you worried you made the wrong decision?"

"No, I'm completely happy with my decision, but I'm worried he might try something. I just can't bear to see Bentley hurt by him."

"But why the sudden interest in being a father?" asked Mary Beth.

Dallas shrugged. "Who knows? I read that his wife dumped him when he got cut from the team. Maybe he's just feeling lonely."

"Too bad," I said. "He should have thought of that when Bentley was born."

"Monday," said Mary Beth. "You and I'll meet with my attorneys. You'll tell them everything, and we'll find out how you can protect Bentley."

Dallas's eyes spilled over with tears she'd been trying to hold back. "Thank you," she whispered.

"Which reminds me," said Mary Beth, turning to Cheyenne. "I had a call today. The SEC opened a formal investigation into your abusive former boyfriend. From what I understand, the SEC, Department of Justice, and FBI raided Michael's home and office, and took possession of all documents and data, including his computers. Assuming there's enough evidence to support probable cause, he'll be arrested."

"That's almost too good for him," I said.

"What if he already bailed?" Cheyenne asked, sounding a little afraid. "What if they can't find him?"

"Don't worry," said Mary Beth. "I'm told they took his passport early on. He won't be going anywhere."

Cheyenne seemed to relax. "Thanks, Mary Beth. For making the call. I owe you."

Mary Beth shrugged. "Well, it definitely wasn't as satisfying as beating the hell out of him with my bare hands. But I'm trying to avoid another night in jail if possible."

Chapter Fifty-Five

Eight little girls can sound like a lot more than that when they're all screaming. They converged on the deck like a flock of adorable banshees, and I could only guess that Miley had sung her last note and the movie was, sadly, over. But an odd thing happened as I watched from the safety of my chair, across from Mary Beth and slightly out of the line of fire. The more shrill, the more earsplitting the little girls' voices became, the calmer Mary Beth seemed to be.

The sound crawled right up my spine and made me wish for earplugs and a martini. But Mary Beth seemed to almost enjoy this riotous, rowdy scene. One little girl with auburn braids and a cupid mouth went up to Mary Beth and whispered something in her ear. Mary Beth took the tiny hands in hers and talked to the little girl, who nodded and then skipped away looking carefree and mollified. She ran to catch up with the crew of terrorizers, who were running in the direction of the playhouse.

"Who was that little cutie?" I asked.

"That's Courtney," said Mary Beth, looking after her and smiling. "She's staying with us for a few weeks."

"A few *weeks*?" I said. "Are you running a hotel now?"

"Her parents are in Europe," said Mary Beth. "She was meant to stay at home with the nanny, but Alissa didn't like that idea. She was worried about her and asked if she could stay here. I couldn't think of a reason why not."

Mary Beth taking in strays. I never saw that one coming either.

"She made a special request for popcorn in the little paper sleeves like at the movie theater. This may take a group effort."

We followed Mary Beth into the huge kitchen and pitched in to make enough popcorn for a platoon of marines. I poured cherry Coke into plastic glasses and Dallas added colorful straws while Cheyenne counted out candles and placed them on top of the pink birthday cake.

"Lucy," said Dallas, "something came up in my meeting with some possible contributors to The Fund today."

"Yeah? What's that?"

"Well, the Prices want to give money, but they want to have a fund within The Fund. They want it earmarked to help the homeless."

I stopped pouring Coke and looked at her, thinking. "I guess we could do that. I'm assuming that money would need to be in a separate account?"

Dallas nodded. "I think so. And when they said that, the Schmidts suddenly wanted the same thing. They want it in their name for the benefit of military veterans and their families."

"I hadn't really planned on earmarking individual donations, but now that it's come up, it might be exactly what we need to get some people to donate."

"I was thinking," said Dallas, almost shyly, "about maybe selling my house in Dallas. I'd have to pay it off, so it wouldn't be a lot of money. But it might be enough to start a little fund in my mom's name. To help single mothers."

Well. When you put it like that, how could we not? The more I thought about it, the more I liked it. "Sure. Let's do it. I can see right now I need to line up a slew of investment experts to handle all this. Maybe I'll call Thomas. He'll know some good investment firms we could use."

"You're on speaking terms with Thomas?" asked Mary Beth.

"Sure, why not? I trust his judgment. Besides, I miss talking to him. It'll give me an excuse to see how he's doing. I just want him to be happy."

"Hey, is everyone bringing dates to the kickoff party?" asked Cheyenne. "Should I bring Will?"

"No date for me," I said, almost laughing at the very idea. "But definitely bring Will."

"Mary Beth?" asked Cheyenne.

"Please," she said, sounding a little like the old Mary Beth.

"What about you, Dallas?"

Dallas flipped her hair over her shoulder and suddenly became very interested in counting out birthday napkins. She sort of shrugged, sort of mumbled. And before we could pin her down, the kitchen was overrun with chattering, laughing little girls.

Dallas put the glasses of Coke on a tray and headed for the back deck. I picked up the napkins and silverware and followed, hoping she wasn't involved with another online millionaire with his face scratched out or a gigolo with a vanity plate.

Chapter Fifty-Six

It's funny the way things happen sometimes. Before I could call and ask Thomas for advice on investment firms, he called me. It was Monday morning, and it was wild. Three days until our big kickoff party for The Fund. We decided to have it on Martini Thursday, feeling like it was a good omen. Between now and then we had a lot to do.

"Lucy, line one," said our cute little receptionist. "His name is Thomas. He said you would know who it is."

I smiled to myself and reached for the phone. "Hey, I was just going to call you."

"You were? Is something wrong?"

I laughed. "Does something have to be wrong for me to call you?"

"No, of course not. How are you, Luce?"

"I'm great, actually. I have a lot to tell you. Something really exciting."

"Not a new man," he said, sounding almost alarmed. Which I thought was very strange.

"Nothing like that. It's a new sort of venture."

"Oh, that's great news," he said. "I can't wait to hear all about it."

"And what about you? How are you and Missy?" I stopped myself from saying *the pixie* – or worse – and felt very proud of myself.

"That's why I'm calling. I wanted you to hear it from me before you heard it through the grapevine."

Oh boy. Now what. I kept my silence and let Thomas talk. Something I learned from a certain peaceful sculptor.

"Missy's pregnant," he said, his voice all hard edges.

I sat completely still. I don't think I could have been more shocked if he'd said she was an ex-con. Or really a man. Or Secretary of State. "You reversed your vasectomy?"

"Um. No."

Yikes. "Well, maybe, it's just one of those unusual instances. You know the doctor warned us...vasectomies are not a hundred-percent foolproof."

"She tried to convince me it was a fluke," he said, sounding sarcastic. "That the vasectomy just didn't take. But after a tip-off from the housekeeper – you remember Delma – I walked in on Missy and the landscape designer in the guesthouse."

I didn't know what to say. My mind reeled with visuals I'd really rather not have bouncing around in my head.

"I've filed for divorce," he said. "I just wanted you to know."

You'd think this turn of events would bring me pleasure. Some tiny sliver of satisfaction. But I didn't feel any of that. Just overwhelming sadness.

"Oh, Thomas. I'm so sorry. I don't know what to say."

"I feel like such a fool," he said, sounding tired and defeated.

"No," I said, shaking my head to myself. "Don't say that. You're not a fool. She is. For losing you."

Thomas was quiet for a moment. When he spoke again, his voice was hoarse with emotion. "Luce, I miss you. Things never felt right with Missy. I never stopped loving you."

Oh boy. I definitely hadn't seen that coming. My stomach clutched, and my mouth went dry.

"Have lunch with me," he said. "Please?"

"Um. Sure...we can do that. Sometime. Soon." This was all a little bit hard to take in. An hour ago it was just the crazy Monday before the big party that would officially introduce The Fund to Aspen. But now it felt like much more than that. Now it was the crazy Monday when my former husband divorced his current wife because she was having a baby that wasn't his. The day he said he missed me. And loved me. And asked me out on our first date.

The Caribou Club pulled out all the stops for our big launch party. Handsome waiters breezed through crowds of Aspen's upper echelon, carrying trays of drinks to those who preferred a glass of Macallan 18 over the array of champagnes being poured by beautiful model wannabes in every corner of the room. Most of the women milling around the food tables filling china plates with chevre tarts and Petrossian caviar wore short cocktail dresses, mainly black. But there were splashes of color here and there – fuchsia, yellow, red. The invitation specified black tie, so every man in attendance wore a black tuxedo. I was in heaven.

Six months ago, I could never have imagined any of it. That I would be here, in the beautiful dining room of the Caribou Club, with my three best friends. Surrounded by wealthy benefactors ready to give us millions of dollars. Officially kicking off our venture designed to serve the world, one person at a time. Or that standing to my left would be a man who, over the past few months, taught me compassion, acceptance, living in the moment. A man who showed me that happiness couldn't be found outside. You had to go within to find it.

Or that standing to my right, would be Thomas. Looking about as good as a guy can possibly look. Wearing his custom Armani tuxedo and a smile. I'd invited him to the party, so he could see what we had built. To show him that I wasn't sitting around at the club drinking martinis or playing tennis or planning my next shopping trip. I was trying to make a difference.

I wasn't the same woman he'd walked out on. Or the woman who, in her anger and pain, had sneaked into his house and stolen his worldly possessions. I was new. Changed. But he was changed as well. A little less cocky. More attentive. Hanging on my every word.

Oh sure. I knew that would never last. He was on his best behavior, no doubt. But all the things I loved about him were still there. The familiar smell of his cologne. His quick wit. His boyish smile. Feeling him standing beside me, the heat coming off him and warming my bare arm, took me back to another time. When we were young and falling in love, and the world held such promise. No pitfalls. No dark corners or dangerous switchbacks. Just a golden road of promise before us.

We couldn't have known then that the road would take a hard left and leave us split and broken. And I wasn't delusional enough to believe that another golden road of promise lay before us now. I had no idea what would happen. Tonight was the first time I'd seen Thomas since the day I'd broken into his house and returned a plastic tub of loot.

There was much to talk about. Much to be repaired. And maybe we would just be friends. But even that felt good to me after imagining a life without him. I loved him. I couldn't help it. I loved him, and I knew I always would.

Glacier stepped around me, and I have to say, Glacier in a tux was a sight to see. It was the first time I'd ever seen him without his standard-issue jeans and T-shirt. And I wasn't the only one noticing. Most of the women in the room stole glances our way, some at Glacier and some at Thomas. My two beautiful boys.

Glacier held his hand out to Thomas. "Glacier Jones."

"I'm sorry," I said. "I was lost in another world there for a minute. Glacier, this is Thomas Moore."

They shook hands, and I had a brief flashback to a time weeks ago when I fantasized about their meeting. Of having Glacier as my arm candy and running into Thomas. Of rubbing my new boy toy in

Thomas's face. Of making him regret the day he ever walked out on me. What a long way we had all come since then. Most of all, me.

Thomas smiled and shook Glacier's hand. "I'm Lucy's husband," he said.

I looked at him. "Ex-husband."

"Yes," he said, flushing. "Of course. Ex-husband."

"Glacier is a sculptor," I said. "And my—" I couldn't quite put into words all that Glacier was to me. To call him my teacher was too vague. To tell the truth and say he saved me from a life of misery and self-destruction was too personal.

"He's my friend," I said, softly. Glacier smiled at me.

Mary Beth and Cheyenne walked up with their dates – Alissa and Will. Barely seven years old, Alissa wore what I'm guessing was her first little black dress, and Will looked like a million after taxes in his rented tux. What a good-looking group. Mary Beth arched her eyebrows and leaned to whisper in my ear. "Take a look behind you. Looks like Dallas has a new man."

I spun around toward the door to the dining room. And sure enough, there was Dallas.

I felt my jaw drop and tried to hide my surprise. But it didn't matter. Dallas wasn't looking at me. She was looking into the eyes of the man by her side. He was gorgeous – no surprise there. But as long as I'd known Dallas she'd had an insanely wealthy man at her side. With the exception of the gigolo, who'd only pretended to be wealthy.

It was Dallas's prominent prerequisite. Her most crucial qualifier. A definite deal breaker. The man had to be wealthy or she wouldn't give him a second glance.

It came from growing up poor and wanting more for her daughter. I got that. It was a choice born of fear. The fear of not being able to support herself and the most important person in her life – Baby Bentley.

And so when she told us weeks ago that she was off men, I didn't take her seriously. Because even if Dallas sincerely tried to stay away from men, they would never stay away from her. It would be like the ocean staying away from the shore. Like protons staying away from neutrons. It wasn't possible. So I wasn't surprised to see her with a man. I wasn't even surprised to see her looking so enraptured.

I was a little bit surprised to see the way she was dressed. Beautifully – no surprise there – in a black dress and sky high platform sandals. But showing very little skin. No plunging neckline. No slits up to here or cut-outs or micro-mini hemlines.

But I was more than surprised – call it shocked – by the date she'd chosen for this very important occasion. And by the looks they were giving each other and the pure joy on their faces, I was guessing this wasn't their first date.

"Hey," said Cheyenne, looking to see what we were so interested in. "Isn't that the cute phone guy?"

Yes. It was. The man Dallas clung to like napkin lint to black wool pants was very definitely the cute phone guy. A man who drove a service truck, not a Mercedes. Who wore a shirt with his name on it to work, not a cashmere jacket. A man who always had a smile on his face and something nice to say to everyone.

It was perfect. I don't know why I hadn't thought of it myself. Not only were they the most beautiful couple in the room, but they were equally good. Gentle spirits. The cute phone guy could very well be the only man I knew worthy of Dallas.

Chapter Fifty-Seven

The night before I left Aspen for my trip to Houston was bittersweet. I was excited about the future but sad to say goodbye to summer. A summer of change to put it mildly. Had I known, that day in early summer when my eyes locked on to Glacier's, all the changes he would bring about in my life, I might have been scared.

But that was one of the best changes of all. No more fear. Nothing to be afraid of.

The doorbell rang and I hurried to answer it in my fuzzy slippers, almost tripping over the luggage by the front door.

Glacier. Smiling. Holding his ever-present cloth bag of goodies.

"You're packed," he said, looking at the mess of bags.

I nodded. "I am. It feels weird. Come on in."

He looked down at my feet. "Nice," he said, smiling at my slippers.

He followed me to the kitchen - which I knew to be his favorite room in my house. There was a fire in the stone fireplace and freshly baked muffins on a plate. They were horrible. Awful. My first stab at all-natural hippy-dippy muffins. Glacier reached into his bag and brought out two smoothies. I almost cried. One last smoothie for the road.

We settled at the breakfast table, and Glacier tried one of the muffins. I started laughing when he washed the bite down with a gulp of smoothie. No thoughtful chewing tonight. "I'll work on it," I said. "The recipe called for stuff I didn't have so I made a few substitutions."

It was the first time I'd seen him since the kickoff party two weeks past. He looked good. Same serene face. Same Glacier uniform. But missing was my longing to jump his bones. It felt good, this sense of just being able to sit with him and not need anything more.

"Back to Houston tomorrow, right?"

I nodded. "I'm torn. I know I need to be there for a while to round up more contributors for The Fund. That's where most of my contacts are, and I'm already planning a big shindig in a few weeks."

"But you'll miss being here."

"I really will. I'm the only one of us leaving. I'll still be working through faxes and emails, but it feels strange to leave the team for a while. I made a deal with the landlord on this house. He came down on the rent so I'll keep it, and come back and forth."

"What about the rest of the crew?" Glacier leaned back and sipped his smoothie.

"Dallas has a new man, and it looks like this may be the real deal. She's staying. Cheyenne and Will have property in Carbondale and just bought a stable of horses, so they're staying. And Mary Beth. Ah, Mary Beth. I have so much to tell you. She wants stability for Alissa, so she's staying."

Glacier nodded. "She's made some good changes since her arrest."

I barked out a laugh. "You could say that! Sometimes I can't even believe she's the same person. Until she opens her mouth and says something snotty. Then it all comes back in a wave of relief. Turns out she doesn't despise all people. Mostly just grown-up people."

"She's good with children."

"She is," I said. "She's still feisty around adults, but she's patient and nurturing and *nice* around the kids. It's amazing."

"She's learning to see the world through her daughter's eyes," he said.

"Exactly. When she's with Alissa, she seems to truly live in the moment." Glacier nodded.

"Oh, and get this," I said. "At the kickoff party, I thought I would faint. Cruella – the one who was stealing from Rolf's estate? Well, she came – probably to save face – and made a huge contribution. So I told Mary Beth she should go over and speak to her. But she wouldn't at first. I told her to take the high road. Let go. Pour her cup out, right?"

Glacier nodded and smiled. "Did she listen to you?"

"I don't know. But something got through to her. Because when Cruella was leaving, Mary Beth grabbed one of the goody bags and walked over to her. It was amazing. MB won't tell me what was said, but before it was all over, Cruella was clutching the goody bag and crying, and she hugged Mary Beth! That's when I almost died. No one hugs Mary Beth."

"Maybe they should," said Glacier.

Maybe he was right. Maybe all this time, I was wrong. Maybe Mary Beth was the huggy type after all. I didn't tell him that Mary Beth's final comment on the matter was to always forgive your enemy...because it totally screws with their head.

We sat in comfortable silence for a while, both gazing into the fire, lost in our thoughts. I would miss this. My time with Glacier. His presence brought a serenity and clarity that I couldn't find anywhere else, except on my mountaintop.

"I like Thomas," he said, surprising me.

I smiled. "So do I."

After a while I turned to Glacier. "I'm not sure what will happen there," I said. "But I'm not afraid. There's no more fear. I'm not afraid of losing him. We'll always have a bond. Always love each other."

He nodded.

"Do you think I'm crazy to date my ex-husband?"

He smiled and shook his head. "I don't think you're crazy."

"I'm trying to be open to him," I said. "With my feelings. Trying not to protect my heart, you know?"

"Love has to be shared in order to grow," said Glacier. "If you hoard it, the flow stops."

I looked at him and really listened.

"Imagine a stream of mountain water," he said. "If you build a dam and stop the flow, the water becomes stagnant."

"You're saying if I don't love Thomas, my heart will become stagnant? I guess that makes sense."

Glacier smiled. "Love everyone."

I laughed. "Even Mary Beth?"

"Especially Mary Beth."

I walked Glacier to the door and prepared to say goodbye. But how do you say goodbye to someone who has given you back your life? Someone who loves your soul. How else could I ever have learned all that I'd learned in the past few months, if not from him? To live a life of harmlessness, truthfulness, simplicity. To look inside for my happiness. And to be more like a child. In the past weeks I learned lightness, openness, to be fearless, unstoppable, to empty my cup, and be a brilliant ball of light. Or at the very least, to stop being afraid and open up to all possibilities. I was just about to try to put all this into words when I heard my cell phone ringing from the kitchen. I left Glacier standing among my mountain of luggage.

"Sorry!" I said, running toward the kitchen. "I'll be right back. This might be Thomas."

And it was. I made the call as quick as possible, without rushing Thomas. He was calling to wish me a safe flight, and to let me know he would see me in four days. We had a date.

When I returned to Glacier, my throat closed up, and words escaped me.

"Thank you," I said, standing in front of him. "Thank you for eroding and transporting me."

I held my friend tight that night, not wanting to let him go. Not knowing when I would see him again. But knowing a part of him would be with me forever.

The hum of the air conditioner seemed unnatural, out of place after a summer of fresh mountain air. The second week in September, and the high later in Houston would be over a hundred degrees. It would take some getting used to.

With my unpacking almost finished, I reached for my carry-on bag. Filled with books and magazines, I hadn't even bothered to open it on the flight home. Too consumed with my thoughts. Wondering about my friends. Thinking of my mountaintop, where the trees were turning gold and red. And trying to imagine how I would ever survive without being able to drive to Main Street Bakery and find Glacier when I needed him.

I tossed the bag on the silk bench at the end of my bed and reached inside. But instead of the legal pad with my to-do list that I knew I'd left on top, my hand closed around something soft, thick, heavy. It was wrapped in a piece of burlap, and tied with a leather cord. My heart squeezed in my chest. It had to be from Glacier.

The exact size and shape of his Big Book of Answers. My eyes filled with tears and my knees buckled. I sat heavily on the bench beside my bag and held the gift to my chest. It felt alive in my arms, filled with light. But at the same time heavy with significance, substance. Weighted with the secrets of the universe. I couldn't move. Couldn't see through the tears. Gulped for air when I realized I was holding my breath. Not here, I thought. Not on this bench at the end of my bed. I needed a special place for this moment, and longed for my mountaintop.

I stood and walked on wooden legs through my house and outside onto the back patio, where the summer heat hit me in the face like a blast from hell. But I kept walking and came to the cool garden around the pool and the little rock waterfall.

I fell into a chair, and my hands shook as I worked to untie the leather cord. I smiled through my tears at the Glacier-like gift wrap and wondered how many times the cord and burlap had been used for other things.

Finally the cord fell free and I sat back in the chair, filling my lungs with deep breaths. Trying to slow my racing heart. I pictured Glacier, the night before - taking the Big Book of Answers out of his cloth bag while I ran to answer the phone. Checking out the bags in the entryway. Choosing the bag that was left unzipped and held nothing important, just books, and notes, and lists.

Would it change me, I wondered. Would the wisdom in this book fill in all the holes, teach me all the lessons, answer all the questions I had on this path? Did Glacier know I would still need him, still yearn for his serenity, his guidance?

Probably so. But as powerful as the book was, it could never replace him. Never replace the feeling of tranquility and peace that washed over me every time I sat across from him at his sunny table in the front of Main Street Bakery.

I knew Glacier probably wouldn't approve of my sissy tears. He'd tell me to avoid attachment. To remember that nothing is permanent. That everything changes. To live in the moment and not grieve for the past. But I missed him. Away from him for only a day, and I missed him. I would work on attachment tomorrow.

I reverently unfolded the burlap, my fingers shaking and feeling not part of my body. Rich brown leather. Pages edged in gold. And the dark blue silk ribbon peeking out at the bottom. I rubbed my hands over the leather, feeling its warmth, its velvety texture.

And if I hadn't been so overwhelmed, so drowning in emotions, I might have noticed that the leather wasn't battered. Not scarred. Not blemished in any way. I held my breath and opened the book to the first page, the smell of new leather finally filling my senses and giving me the first hint. The first whisper that what I held was not what I'd thought.

This was not Glacier's Big Book of Answers. This was my own. Full of blank and thirsty pages. Waiting for me to fill it with the secrets of the universe.

And just inside, on the creamy first page, a note from my forever teacher:

For Lucy,
A brave heart, an eternal spirit. Cherish the here and now,
Glacier

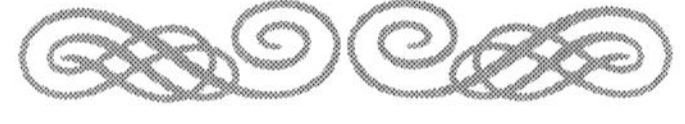

Epilogue

Liberator, Renovator, Procreator, Chief. I looked around the living room of my rented house in Aspen and smiled at the secret nicknames I'd given my crazy, loveable friends. The names weren't perfect. But they would do for tonight. I had all summer to come up with better names. I sighed with sheer happiness at being back with my tribe.

It was our first Martini Thursday of the summer. And a lot had changed in the past year. I looked down at my beloved fuzzy slippers. They were fast becoming my new look. Mary Beth gave me the hairy eyeball when she first saw them, clearly not approving. But I loved them. They were way more comfortable than anything I'd worn in a while. And at least they were cheetah print. That counts as stylish, right?

The early June breeze drifted through the open windows, and Mary Beth handed out sweaters and hoodies to the three little girls chattering by the back door – Alissa, Bentley, and a little girl who liked to ride horses with Cheyenne. There was a tea party set up for them on the deck, and no, I hadn't baked the muffins. I would never do that to innocent kids.

I laughed as Dallas leaned over and tried to reach her glass of juice. Wearing a cute pale pink T-shirt and gathered shorts, she looked as fresh and sunny as the first day of summer. But so unlike the peep-toe pump days of her past, she could no longer move easily from day into evening. In fact, she could no longer move easily at all. For Dallas was great with child. She was now Mrs. Cute Phone Guy, and they wanted a house full of children. Dallas was no longer Beggar Woman. Dallas was Procreator.

Cheyenne helped Mary Beth settle the three girls at the table on the deck. I shook my head.

"I still can't believe Mary Beth and Cheyenne are such good friends," I said.

"I know," said Dallas. "It's crazy. But don't worry, they still fight over stupid stuff."

I laughed. "That's a relief."

"You should see them out at the horse arena," she said. "Even Mary Beth rides now. And Alissa is in heaven. She brings her friends out all the time and it's amazing how they just seem to bloom and open up. You wouldn't believe how much the little girl out back has changed, being around Mary Beth and Cheyenne. She used to be afraid of her own shadow, and too shy to even look you in the eye. Mary Beth's really good with kids, but once in a while she and Shy still nearly come to blows over whose turn it is to feed the horses or who left the halter on the wrong hook or whatever. They're looking for a bigger place so they can have more horses."

No longer Grave Robber, Mary Beth was Liberator. The short-tempered, fiery tenacity that had kept her alive as a child in a loveless home helped fuel her newfound passion for saving children, which started when she saved her own child. In the past year, she had gradually won back the parts of herself she thought were lost forever – love, family, happiness.

Cheyenne was Renovator, because she used the same love and wild energy to heal kids as she did putting the finishing touches on the houses she and Will dismantled and put back together. Restoring. Rehabilitating. One broken child at a time. She left her gold-digging ways behind when she remarried Will. No longer fighting her feelings of being an outsider looking in, Cheyenne had found a place to belong. With Will. And the horses. And all the kids she and Mary Beth were putting back together.

In the past nine months, these women who had become sisters of my heart worked together to help make The Fund a raging success. The first official act of The Fund was to pay for Maria's brother-in-law's cancer treatments, and I was happy to report he was doing really well. The doctors were optimistic, and Maria was ecstatic. Through the generous donations of countless contributors, we'd also been able to help an endless list of people who needed a hand – from veterans and single mothers to the elderly and those down on their luck. If there was a need, The Fund was ready to fulfill it. We had found our purpose, this unlikely band of martini drinkers. And for once, it didn't involve shoes.

You've probably guessed by now that I'm Chief. But I didn't give the name to myself. It's a nickname from Thomas, who thinks he's funny. Just yesterday he said, "Chief, I think someone's off their meditation." His little play on words. His way of telling me I'm cranky.

He was flying in tomorrow, and I couldn't wait to see him. It had been a wild year for him as well, a year of changes. Selling the big house on Red Mountain. Divorcing the pixie and giving her part of his fortune. Losing an important lawsuit and forking over restitution. And losing another large chunk in a risky investment. One that would have paid off in a huge way if it had worked out. But there you go. Greed will sometimes bite you back.

I was falling in love all over again with the new Thomas. This slightly less cocky version, more like the man I first married. We'd both been knocked down a few pegs at this point, both come through our own trials. And somehow, all of that was helping us get back to who we really were.

We were happiest when we were working together to make our dreams come true, so now we have a new dream. Thomas agreed to come on board with The Fund, and with his help, we might just take it worldwide. According to the United Nations, almost two billion people in undeveloped regions live below poverty level. So with Thomas's international business experience, maybe The Fund can start helping people around the world. We've always been big dreamers, Thomas and I. Might as well shoot for the moon.

Mary Beth and Cheyenne came in from the back deck, arguing.

"No I didn't," said Cheyenne. "You were for sure the last one using the hose. If the front of the barn flooded, it's your bad, not mine."

Mary Beth's nostrils flared and I buckled in for a firestorm. I wasn't disappointed.

"If you recall," she said, hands on her hips, "you've demonstrated a proclivity for leaving water running from every conceivable spigot!"

"Don't impugn my word," said Cheyenne, throwing her shoulders back and leaning toward Mary Beth. "And stop acting like I'm some vacuous dimwit! You're the doofus who left the water on!"

There was utter silence...and then we all burst out laughing. Even Mary Beth. Actually – *especially* Mary Beth. It was great to see Cheyenne giving as good as she got. Within minutes the two were sitting side by side on my couch, looking about as happy as two peas on a log, as Cheyenne might say.

"Is Glacier coming?" asked Dallas. "I want him to help us name the baby. Anyone with a name like Glacier is bound to have some original ideas."

"He's gone," I said.

"What do you mean *gone*?" asked Cheyenne.

"I went to the bakery this morning, and he wasn't sitting at his table. I talked to the owner. He said Glacier moved to New Mexico. Said there was something he had to do."

To say I was disappointed didn't even come close. I was crushed. And had no way of contacting him. No cell phone, no home phone, no email, no forwarding address.

I wanted to show him how much progress I'd made over the winter. But part of that progress was that I no longer needed his approval. Or anyone else's.

I realized I'd had Glacier when I needed him most. And now there was probably someone else who needed him more. Maybe he was, at that moment, eroding some poor unsuspecting soul's crusty exterior and preparing to transport him - or her - over a long distance. As he had me. And I know this is small of me, but I secretly hoped it was a man.

The doorbell rang as I was about to pour drinks. Rufus II jumped up from his nap on the cool tile by the door and began barking madly. A rescue dog I adopted from the shelter, he was still learning a few manners. But this rescue dog didn't need to worry about rescuing me back. He could just be my dog. I shushed him and rubbed his head, then opened the front door to a beefy, sweaty man in a blue uniform.

"You Lucy Moore?"

"I am."

"I have a delivery. Please sign." He handed me a clipboard and a pen.

"What kind of delivery?"

"I don't know," he said. "But it weighs a ton."

I sighed. Probably the new mini-fridge the landlord promised for the bar. Horrible timing. I didn't feel like messing with it right now. But I scrawled my name beside the X and handed the clipboard back.

"Which way to your deck?" he asked.

I frowned. "Why?"

"I have instructions to deliver this to your back deck."

Maybe something from Thomas, I thought, and shrugged. "Fine. That way." I pointed around the corner. "I'll meet you back there."

I walked back into the living room. "Does anyone here know anything about a delivery to the back deck?"

They all looked at me with blank faces. None of them were any good at lying or keeping a secret. I could tell they didn't know anything about it. It took a few minutes to hoist Dallas up off the couch. Then another few minutes while we helped her fill a plate with hors d'oeuvres. She was eating for two now.

By the time we got out to the deck, the poor delivery guy was surrounded by three excited little girls and one frisky dog, all jumping around while he uncrated the mystery monstrosity - almost four feet high and just as wide. Finally the wooden crate was removed, and whatever was inside sat on my deck, wrapped in burlap. An electric jolt hit my heart.

The muscular man started to use a box cutter to slice through the burlap, but I stopped him.

"That's okay!" I held up my hand. "You can leave it like that. If you'll just take the crate, that'll be good. Let me go inside and get you a tip."

I came back outside and handed the guy a hundred-dollar-bill. I was feeling generous.

He smiled for the first time, and gave me a look that said *crazy lady*. But I didn't care.

"Open it, open it!" said Alissa, jumping up and down.

"Yeah, open it!" said Cheyenne, almost jumping up and down. Rufus II gave a high pitched bark.

I walked slowly over and ran my hands along the burlap until I found the opening, not wanting to cut it. I worked it gently, finally freeing the burlap from the bottom and feeling the cloth give way all around.

And there it was. My breath caught in my throat. There were no words. Even if I had been Mary Beth. Even if I had known the big words she knew. There would still be no words big enough. No expression deep enough. Nothing I could ever do or say that was worthy of the sculpture.

Carved from a solid piece of white marble, and flying up and out of the rock, a hawk. So pure in detail. So graceful in form. A stone chosen by Glacier and allowed to freely express the glory given to it by nature. Symbolizing my freedom from bad behaviors. My spiritual awareness. A hug from the man who taught me to look inside for happiness – where it had been all along.

The End

Acknowledgements

So many people to thank, so little space. First, two women I would love to hang out with if only I were cool enough: my tireless agent, Marly Rusoff – one of the kindest and most brilliant people on the planet – and my editor, Adrienne Brodeur, whose passionate, insightful work on the book was priceless.

To Michael Radulescu and Julie Mosow for your generous and diligent work to make this book the best it can be. You are both amazing, and I appreciate you more than I can say.

To the law enforcement officials who helped explain the ins and outs of characters in trouble: Sergeant Mike Harris, Ector County Sheriff's Office, and dear to my heart. Also Captain David Bright, Ector County Sheriff's Office; Keith Ikeda, former Chief of Police, Basalt, Colorado; and Don Bird, CJM, Jail Administrator, Pitkin County Jail, Aspen, Colorado. You were all so patient and forthcoming; I couldn't have gotten the facts right without you.

To the lawyer who explained how to bring down a Ponzi scheme – George E. Greer, Partner, Orrick, Herrington & Sutcliffe LLP. Thank you for taking my crazy call out of the blue and for being so generous with your expertise.

A few other very special people: Ruth Booker – always my first reader, head cheerleader, and dearest, most precious friend. Didi Dieterich, also a precious friend, who answers all my architecture and interior design questions and provides lots of ideas for character hijinx from our crazy times together.

Other first readers – dear and much loved people who were willing to read and give invaluable advice: Carol Pitts, Kim McElroy, Karen Wells, Cassandra Hoehle, Martha Cochran, Melissa Sumera, Junanne Mosley, and Toby Thurman.

Thank you all from the bottom of my grateful heart. This book was most definitely a group effort; I couldn't have done it without you.

†††

Coming next from Andi Bryce:

***Crazy, Party of Three*, a novel**

As young girls growing up in Texas, three fun-loving friends, Cat, Tommie Beth, and Lexie form an exclusive club and dub themselves the WOLOs. Now in their early 30's, the girls believe nothing could ever tear them apart. When a misunderstanding over a man threatens to destroy the group, eighty-five year old widow Amelia Blakemore, whose husband's former mansion becomes the site of the three friends' posh new boutique, comes to their rescue when she reveals secrets from her past and shares with them her hard-earned wisdom. The elderly Amelia is embraced by the three wholeheartedly, thereby earning herself an exalted membership as the fourth and likely final member of the WOLOs.

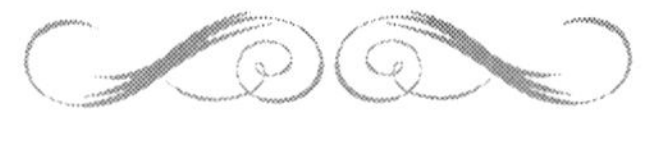

Chapter One

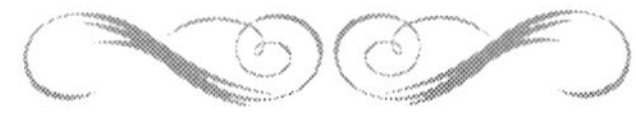

The day we poisoned my cheating husband, I wish I'd known Amelia Blakemore lived just down the road and probably would have helped us. Believe me, we really could have used the help.

"He's dead!" said Tommie Beth, but I was pretty sure she was kidding. Tommie Beth has a fairly wicked sense of humor. We couldn't have given him that much, could we? Sure – I gave him that little extra squirt at the end. And I didn't have the slightest idea how much it would take to kill a man. And our measurements had been random at best. But still.

"Quit kidding around, Tommie Beth, and help me move him over." Lexie shoved her auburn bangs out of her eyes while I stared down at my naked, unconscious husband.

"Y'all, seriously," said Tommie Beth, her wide mouth set in a straight line. "There's no pulse."

All of a sudden I began to question our ingenious plot for revenge. Terry Max Murdock had been the love of my life from the time I was in eighth grade, and he was a sophomore in high school. I used to ride my bike past his house and watch him wash his Mustang, his blond hair hanging in his eyes and his bare chest gleaming in the Texas sun.

His friends started calling him Frog after he proved he could belch and sound just like one. Unfortunately, the name stuck. And so did I. Right by his side. Through the rest of high school, straight through college at the University of Texas – Terry Max was on the six-year-plan – and up until this very night. There was just one problem. Seems a few other women had been sticking to him at the same time. A whole crowd, actually. It wasn't until last night, when Lexie, Tommie Beth, and I were watching *Texas Chainsaw Massacre* at Lexie's and drinking Speedy Chihuahuas, that the truth squeaked out.

Lexie hadn't had a date in over a month since breaking up with her boyfriend, J.D. As dry spells go, it was the longest one I'd ever known her to have. Born with the sex appeal of Brigitte Bardot, and long, wavy auburn hair and pouty lips, Lexie attracted men the way a picnic attracts ants. Sultry voice, high cheekbones, self-assured but not cocky like Tommie Beth. She was comfortable in her skin, confident around men. Probably from looking like a bombshell all her life.

So on this night of tequila, blood, and guts, Lexie was complaining about not having had sex for over a month. Tommie Beth was trying to cheer her up by telling her the world was now her oyster, and she could have sex with anyone she wanted. Tommie Beth's only 5'2", but that doesn't stop her from throwing her weight around and acting like she knows everything about everything. Athletic and tan, all muscle and mouth. And not just mouthy as in talking all the time, which she does, but a wide, full mouth. Messy blonde ponytail and one of those packed-tight little bodies. Divorced for just over six months, Tommie Beth's a little down on the institution of marriage. She tried one of her skewed analogies on Lexie.

"Okay, Lex. Think of it this way." She loaded a tortilla chip with guacamole and took a swig of her girly pink drink. "My kids get sick of the same old thing, so I buy cereal in those multi-packs with the individual cups. Same thing with sex. I used to get corn flakes every day, but now I can have the variety pack – and so can you."

I rolled my eyes because even though Tommie Beth talked a big game, I knew for a fact she wasn't having sex with anyone. Not corn flakes. And definitely not multi-packs.

"Every day? You got corn flakes *every day*? No wonder you're so grouchy about being divorced."

Tommie Beth reached across the plate of real fresh fruit for a watermelon Oreo. "I'm not saying I got corn flakes every day." She unscrewed the cookie and licked the pink and green icing in the middle. "I'm saying that's all I ever got. Sure, I had a nearly endless supply of corn flakes, but they were still just plain ol' boring been-in-the-cupboard-for-weeks corn flakes."

I couldn't weigh in on this deeply intellectual discussion because I'd only had sex with Terry Max in the eight years since we'd married. And in all the years we'd dated before that, if you didn't count one little time on spring break at South Padre during my college sophomore year when Terry Max and I broke up for two weeks.

Lexie cracked a sunflower seed with her front teeth. "Not every box of cereal comes with a prize. You probably think we'll get Tony the Tiger or one of those totally buff guys on the Wheaties box, but what if it's that tiny leprechaun or the kook on Cocoa Puffs?"

"You still get variety. Kooks need love too."

Oh brother. I shook my head at Tommie Beth's dating wisdom and reached for a handful of chips.

"Yeah, well, my cereal cupboard is empty at the moment," said Lexie. "You used to just open your cupboard and there it was! Ready to jump into your bowl."

"Believe me," said Tommie Beth, moving to Lexie's kitchen to make herself another drink. "Most of the time I wished my cupboard wasn't quite so full of itself."

Lexie and I followed her into the kitchen, giggling as Tommie Beth went on about not caring two hoots in hell about her cupboard or its dusty old corn flakes. We slumped into chairs at the long oak table and watched Tommie Beth pour lime juice, grapefruit juice, orange liqueur, and a healthy glug of tequila into Lexie's funky purple pottery pitcher.

Sitting beside Lexie in the bright light of her kitchen, I suddenly felt a little plain. I'd always felt slightly ordinary beside my two, above-average-looking, nutty girlfriends. It wasn't like I was horrible or anything, but Lexie was a sexpot and Tommie was a natural athlete. Brown hair and brown eyes in contrast to their slightly more exotic coloring. And I was tall and gangly, so I always felt like I stood out. Or up. Not exactly the willowy, graceful kind of tall most of the time either. More like clumsy enough to trip over a cordless phone. With a tendency to talk with my hands. And really, really fast, apparently, because people were always making fun of me. Tommie Beth says I talk like a radio announcer doing a car commercial after a six-pack of Red Bull.

If forced to choose, I guess I'd have to say my eyes were my best feature. Even so, they weren't the smoky eyes Lexie seemed to wake up with every morning. Give me half an hour in front of a makeup mirror with a "How To" instruction card from Maybelline and an eye shadow three-pack, and my eyes still wouldn't smoke like Lexie's.

Tommie poured a fresh Chihuahua into her glass, and Lexie and I slid our glasses forward on the table so she'd top us off. She added a splash of soda and a lime slice to each glass.

"Seriously, after a month of no sex, I'd even go for the stinky old been-in-the-cupboard-for-weeks corn flakes," said Lexie, continuing the madness. "Believe me y'all, after a while you get really hungry."

"Lordy, Lex," I said. "You're starting to make me feel guilty about breakfast!"

"Easy for you to laugh," said Lexie. "You probably get corn flakes every day from Terry Max."

I put my arm around Lexie's shoulders and squeezed. "Lex, you know I love you, and I'd give you the Jimmy Choo floweredy pumps right off my feet, but I'm not sharing my cereal with you."

Tommie Beth let out a noisy mournful sigh and shook her head. "Gawd, Cat. I really hate like hell to tell you this, but since you brought it up."

"Brought what up?"

I knew I was in bad trouble when Tommie couldn't seem to look me in the eye.

"Tom? Brought what up?"

Tommie Beth shook her head and finally raised her eyes to mine. "I think maybe your precious Terry Max has been sharing his cereal with about anyone who's the least bit hungry."

Surely I heard that wrong. I squinted at her, like maybe that would help me hear. "What did you say?"

Tommie Beth looked over at Lexie, and I saw Lexie shake her head out of my corner eye.

"Come on, Tommie," I said. "You have to tell. We spit in each other's hands in fourth grade and promised never to lie to each other."

The memory and the tequila made Tommy Beth's eyes fill with tears. Or maybe it had less to do with childhood memories and Speedy Chihuahuas and more to do with knowing she was about to end my life as I knew it. Tommie Beth dabbed her stubby fingers at the tears in her eyes, and Lexie stopped cracking sunflower seeds. Both very bad signs.

Tommie Beth sniffed and reached for a cocktail napkin that said something about wine counting as a serving of fruit. "Damn his worthless hide, Cat, Terry Max has been sleeping around."

This time the words slammed into my stomach like a sucker punch. The air backed up into my lungs, and I felt like I might lose my Speedy Chihuahua right there on Lexie's scarred oak kitchen table.

"Who?!" I demanded, leaning across the table toward Tommie. "*When*? When would he even have time? He's always either with me or at his dad's drilling company working."

Tommie Beth just stood there, hands wrapped around her drink, looking like she wished with all her heart it wasn't true. Finally she dropped her voice to a near whisper – something she almost never did. "Tell her, Lex."

I turned to my other best friend in the whole wide world – the world now crumbling beneath my perfectly pedicured feet. The very feet I'd taken just that day to the salon for a sea salt soak and a lemongrass scrub so they'd be soft and smooth when I curled up beside Terry Max in bed.

Lexie slowly nodded her head and broke my heart. "Cat, darlin'," she reached for my hand. "We just couldn't for the life of us figure out how to tell you."

I sat there with one hand in Lexie's, the other balled into a fist in my lap, and actually saw my world lose its glorious colors and turn a muddy shade of gray.

Chapter Two

We hopped out of Lexie's old blue Mercury Cougar convertible and walked up to the cluttered home of her two great aunts, Grace and Glory. Dried herbs hung in bundles from the porch, fat pots spilled over with flowers so bright they almost hurt your eyes, and exotic, secret aromas drifted from inside the house.

Grace held open the door, wearing cropped jeans and a bright pink Life Is Good T-shirt. Glory stood behind her, wearing a tie-dyed caftan and holding an orange striped cat. Apparently the two had been pretty hip, pretty happening thirty-somethings back in the psychedelic sixties. My grandmother was about their age and kept a once-a-week beauty shop appointment for a curly wet-set. Not these two. Grace had long, straight silver hair pulled back in a braid and tied with a leather cord. Glory had wavy, ash-blonde hair, pulled up on top of her head. They shared Lexie's love of jewelry, wearing chunky rings with colored stones and lots of bangles. Glory wore a large, pale crystal on a velvet rope that hung between her ample breasts. Seems Lexie came by her curvy breasts naturally.

"Girls, come in this house and let me hug your necks. We're so excited, aren't we, Gracie?"

Grace smiled a secret kind of smile. "We've been brewing a special tea all morning." Normally this would have thrilled me, but knowing what I knew now, it pretty much scared the hell out of me.

After staying up half the night listening to Lexie and Tommie Beth tick off all the women Terry Max had shared his cereal with, I'd had enough. According to Teensy Ledbetter – who worked for Terry Max as his executive assistant – the list was long and colorful, and included her.

During the telling of this painful tale, my respect and adoration for the only man I'd ever loved slowly drained right out of me, replaced mostly by tequila – eventually in the form of shooters.

"I want revenge," I said. My two tipsy friends looked at me like they hadn't heard me. We were sitting on the floor around the big colorful trunk Lexie used as a coffee table, aromatherepy candles blazing away in Lexie's attempt to get my chi back in order. I had news for her. My chi was too far gone.

"What'd you say?" asked Tommie Beth, trying to focus on my face.

"I want revenge on the sonofabitch, and I want it now!"

A gleam came into Lexie's eyes, and she leaned in toward me. "If you really want revenge, I know how you can get it. But you have to be sure."

This was a different side of Lexie, who was usually all about peace. Zen. Spreading harmlessness throughout the world and beyond. But girlfriend loyalty superseded all that.

I studied the deep green eyes of my friend, almost black in the low light of the room. Inside of me, a little ball of anger with a core of devastating sadness burst into flames and roared through my body. "I've never been so sure."

"Okay then. Are you in?" Lexie asked Tommie Beth.

"I'm in like Flynn," said Tommie Beth, and we all did a very serious finger-clutching, secret handshake thing we wouldn't have been caught dead doing in a sober moment. That's when Lexie told us about

Grace and Glory's potions. It seemed herbal tea was not the only thing they concocted in the big sunny kitchen on Mockingbird Street. The aunts collected old books with recipes for tonics and potions and actually went so far as to grow some of the strange ingredients. Lexie swore by the love potion she used on Digger McCoy at senior prom. I didn't give a flying fig about love potions or dumb Digger McCoy. I wanted Terry Max Murdock to squeal like the cheating pig he was.

Now, being handed a dainty china cup of fragrant tea by one of Lexie's aunts, I only hoped it would cure my wretched hangover, or if not, just kill me quick.

"Aunts," said Lexie, "we need your help."

"Yes!" said Grace, pumping a fist in the air. "That's what we were hoping, isn't it Glore?"

Glory leaned in. "What's the story?"

"Cat's husband, Terry Max, has been doing the horizontal bop with every girl on the dance floor. And Cat wants a little revenge. Have you got any ideas?"

Oh my. Did they ever. Those two sweet ladies came up with schemes and suggestions that would have made a sailor blush, and I began to wonder about their history with men. We had to dial them down until they finally came up with something we thought we could handle. I didn't want to maim Terry Max, or do him grave bodily harm. Although I have to admit, there was a point when I considered a few of the ideas that would have made it impossible for him to *share his cereal* ever again. But I knew I wouldn't look good in a bright orange jumpsuit with numbers across the back.

"Okay, dolls, pay attention," said Glory. "Hand me that clump there, Gracie. Now you take these leaves and crush them until they're very fine. You can put them in a blender, about two tablespoons should do it, then add about one teaspoon from this bottle. You'll need frozen fruit punch and some ice. Add a little rum, a little limeade, sugar, just about anything else you want. But you need the fruit punch to cover up the dark purple color. Then twirl it all in the blender, and voila!" A dimple deepened in her cheek, and her smile was full of sweet innocence as if she'd just taught us how to make teacakes for ladies' bridge club rather than how to render a man unconscious.

We left with our treasures in a paper bag and stopped at the grocery store for frozen punch, limeade, lemonade, a large bag of ice, and some little paper umbrellas. Lexie was a stickler for presentation. Back at my house, we set out all the ingredients on my kitchen counter.

"We need a plan," said Tommie Beth, putting her hands on her hips and taking on the role of leader as usual. "What time will Frog be here?"

I chewed a fingernail and looked at the ominous clump of leaves. "I don't know. I'll call and tell him I'm fixing dinner. When he gets here y'all need to be hiding in the bedroom, so when he passes out we can get his clothes off and get him into his truck. Grace and Glory said we'd have about an hour or so before he wakes up."

"You go call Terry Max, and we'll start crushing leaves."

❧

"I smell chaos and confusion," I said, walking back into my own kitchen after calling Terry Max. My red blender was on the counter, Lexie was using my coffee grinder to pulverize herbs, and every drawer in the kitchen was open.

"Where are your measuring spoons?" asked Tommie Beth, using her hip to slam a drawer shut.

"I don't exactly have any. I usually just guess." I started looking through drawers while Tommie Beth leaned on the counter and watched me.

"Cat, how did you get this far along in life without being able to cook? Seeing you in the kitchen is like watching a fish on a bicycle."

I rifled through every conceivable thing a self-respecting Southern girl might stick in a kitchen drawer. No measuring spoons, but I did find a tube of weird navy blue mascara. I leaned over and used my reflection in the toaster to apply the mascara. "Tommie Beth, I believe that saying is something about a woman needing a man like a fish needs a bicycle. I don't cook, so I don't need measuring spoons. And I sure as hell don't need a man."

"Do you *ever* cook for Frog?"

I made the funny mascara face and worked on the other eye, then blinked a few times. "Nope, and he was a little suspicious. I told him I got a special recipe from Lexie's aunts."

Turned out Lexie was the only one who knew anything about cooking, having had her own catering business for the past several years. The butterflies in my stomach turned into giant pterodactyls while I watched Lexie and Tommie Beth concoct a revenge cocktail without the use of measuring spoons, all the while arguing over Grace and Glory's exact instructions. When Tommie Beth added the powdery fine herbs, shrugged, and added a little more, I hid my eyes.

"Now for the special sauce," said Lexie, and I assumed she was adding the goo from the little bottle. But honestly, the whole thing had started to look a little hit or miss, so I turned my back and wondered how many men the aunts had poisoned in their long careers as herbologists. Herbalists? Voo doo queens? God help us.

I heard Terry Max's big diesel truck pull in to the garage and shooed the girls back to my bedroom. Then I madly hid all the evidence in the tiny pantry, poured the slushy purple cocktail into a giant margarita glass, and added a bright green umbrella just as Terry Max came through the garage door and into the kitchen.

"Hey Sugar," he said, stepping toward me and taking me in his arms. "So you decided to fix dinner for your old man, huh? That's a first. What're we havin'?"

I could hardly stand the feel of his arms around me, knowing they'd been around half the women in three counties. I wriggled away.

"Here. I made you a special drink." I handed him the margarita glass. "Go on in to the den, and I'll be right there."

He looked at the drink and sort of sniffed it, and I felt my stomach flip over. "Where's yours? Aren't you gonna have one with me?"

"Um...sure." I pulled another glass down from the cupboard and poured a splash of the purpley poison, then added a yellow umbrella.

"Fancy," said Terry Max. I pulled him out of the kitchen and into the den and almost pushed him onto the couch. He thought I was playing and pulled me down beside him.

It was a flat out miracle we didn't spill two glasses of poison on my good couch.

"Bottoms up," I said and moved a little ways away from him.

"What is this stuff?" He took a sip and licked his lips, then tipped the glass up for a bigger drink. My stomach balled into a fist, and I stared at him, half expecting him to immediately fall over or foam at the mouth.

"It's called passion punch. Supposed to make you want to rip my clothes off." I tried giving him a sexy smile, but my lips were stiff, and I imagined I looked more like a vampire on True Blood who gets pushed just a little bit too far.

"Sugar, I don't need any encouragement in that department." He set his drink on the big slate coffee table and stood, turning toward the bedroom. "I gotta use the little boy's room."

"No!" I said, too loudly. He turned and looked at me like I was nuts. And really, sitting there watching my husband drink the poison I'd prepared for him complete with little green paper umbrella, I realized some might argue in his favor. Maybe I was nuts. But if I was, it was Terry Max who had driven me down the long road to Crazy. "Let me just go make sure the bathroom's picked up."

He rolled his eyes but stayed where he was while I walked past him and into our bedroom, shutting the door behind me.

"Y'all," I whispered in a panic, "get under the bed! Terry Max is on his way in here to use the bathroom." Lexie and Tommie Beth scrambled off the bed and squeezed underneath, shoving aside three shotguns and half a dozen boxes of shells. Two shells rolled out from under the bed, and I kicked them back under.

"Okay," I said, opening the bedroom door with a sweep of my arm. "All yours."

Terry Max shook his head and walked past me into the bedroom, muttering under his breath and shutting the bedroom door behind him. It seemed odd to me that he would shut the door, but I had other things to worry about just then. Like what if my friends were overcome with a giggling fit while they listened to Terry Max pee. I went back to the bedroom door and pressed my ear against it, trying to make sure my friends kept quiet. They did, but Terry Max didn't. He wasn't using the little boy's room. He was using the phone.

"Hi Sugarpuss," I heard him say in a low voice as a knife sliced through my heart. "I'm gonna be a little late. I know honey, but I can't help it. Okay, see you soon." Then he actually made a kissing sound ,and I thought I might get sick. My knees threatened to buckle on me, and my heart honestly hurt inside my chest. I could hardly believe this was happening, but I took a deep breath and told myself to suck it up. My two best friends were hiding under my bed, and I owed it to them to hold it together. There would be plenty of time for falling apart down the road.

When I heard Terry Max go into the bathroom, I rushed back to the kitchen, grabbed the mysterious dark bottle, and added an extra little squirt to Terry Max's drink, stirring it with the umbrella. Then I stashed the little bottle down between the couch cushions.

When Terry Max came out of the bedroom, I was sitting on the couch trying to look normal and hoping like hell whatever was in the bottle of goo would make his little man turn green and fall off. I handed him his drink, but I couldn't stand to sit beside him, so I walked over to the antique armoire that held our sound system and flipped blindly through CDs.

I wanted to melt into a puddle. I wanted to disappear and wake up in a world where a man would never do such a despicable thing to his wife. And then, when Terry Max started rambling about how we needed to get on with dinner because he had to get back to the office, I wanted to gather all of his belongings – especially his favorite shotgun and his lucky University of Texas sweatshirt and his stupid horrible beloved brown leather recliner – and pile them all up in the front yard and set fire to them.

I thought of myself dancing gleefully around the fire, just to keep from crying. But it wasn't working. All I could think of was our life together, all those years, all going to hell on a sled because my husband couldn't keep his 501s zipped. How could I have been so dumb? Did he tell them he loved them? All of them? Did they all know about me?

Tears stung the backs of my eyes and filled my throat. Not yet, I told myself, gulping for air. But I couldn't help it. He called another woman from our *bedroom*! Are you kidding me?

"How could you *do* that to me?!" I closed my eyes and stopped trying to hold back the tears, leaning against the armoire with my back to Terry Max. "I know all about your cheating and lying, you know." I wiped at my tears, imagining the fresh coat of blue mascara running down both cheeks, but I didn't care. "You're the most miserable, pathetic, rat bastard excuse for a man..." I turned around, ready to let him have it. All of it. All of the pent up frustration and gut-wrenching pain. But it was too late.

He sat with his head tipped back and his mouth open, out cold, while the last little dribble of purple poison cocktail dripped onto my new sage chenille couch.

I wiped at the tears on my face, then walked over and picked up the empty glass. I jabbed him hard twice in the ribs to make sure he was really out. Then I ran to the bedroom to get my friends.

(End of excerpt)

Made in the USA
San Bernardino, CA
12 May 2015